THE MARK OF CANE

by

Jonathan Barry

To Cristina and Roberto and family and friends.

CHAPTER 1

ENGLAND 1970

"And so I have decided to beat you".

Julian did not hear the words the first time. He was still stunned by the letter had in his pocket. It was from his father, written on the usual smooth, white vellum, a strangely classy writing paper he had always used. The letter was a shock.

"Bates, are you listening to me? I said that is why I have decided to beat you".

His housemaster was hoping for a different reaction. Indifference was not usual. Colour usually drained from their faces, a reaction he enjoyed. Julian focused on the face in front on him, sitting on a leather swivel chair. The room was small and looked out onto the large green quad. A gas heater spluttered behind his housemaster. Two horn-rimmed circles of glass looked up at him from a bald brown head. Julian heard his housemaster's exasperation and knew he had to say something.

"Mr Darke, Sir?"

"I said I was going to beat you".

"Why, what have I done?"

"It's your attitude. There have been complaints from other staff. Back chat, slovenly dressing, contempt. Your father has been informed and backs me on this one. Two o'clock. Here in my study. Today".

They stared at each other. Julian started to take in what was going to happen. He started imagining the pain, the humiliation. He had been there before as a younger kid. It was licensed torture. The last time at his previous school he had nearly fainted from the pain and was sick afterwards.

"Why? Who?" he stammered.

"General complaints, and we've had enough. Two o'clock. In my study. Now I have other things to attend to. That's all, you may go. Darke raised his voice: "Next".

Julian turned and went through the half-open door. Other boys were waiting for chits to be signed, papers to be dealt with. He lowered his eyes and walked past, out the door and up the stairs to the long barracks-like dormitory. There, pre-breakfast activity was almost a frenzy. Dressing, washing, shaving, making beds, fags doing chores for their masters, water everywhere in the bathroom, the smell of the toilets, the banging of doors. Nowhere private, no peace or calm. Julian went and sat on his bed.

He tried to ignore the noise and took out the letter again. He skimmed the words. So, it was a factory back home or a beating here. He could run away, but he knew of one boy who had done that, Mathew Best, and he just got caught and was sent back. They bullied him even more after that, and he was now in an asylum, although the family never admitted there was anything wrong with him, or that his school or their attitude had anything to do with his breakdown. A sensitive boy who got stomped by the animals. Every group likes a victim. So that was out for a start. And the idea of working in a factory for the rest of his life was terrifying. He had done a summer job in a food processing factory and lasted only a few weeks. Most of the staff seemed to be on the verge of physical or mental breakdowns. One woman stared into space with her hands shaking and somehow pressed the right buttons. All of them had a dead-in-the-eyes look of long term convicts. He was not going there. At sixteen.

So, it was a beating. Julian thought back to his closest friend Jamie, a kid he knew from way back. They saw each other in the holidays, their parents driving from one side of Sussex to another. Jamie was a lovely kid, blonde hair, bright blue eyes and a rosy complexion. Wonderfully funny and bright. He was in another house, and they got hold of him and whipped him into submission. He was about to become Head of House now, but the price for this dubious honour was all that was sacred in him had been destroyed, bullied, beaten out of him. Gone was the humour, the irreverence. Instead there was a God-fearing solid burgher-to-be, a good sort, a club man, a rugby hearty, who would marry a girl at University and have 2.2 sprogs and be the salt of the earth. It made Julian sick. Julian wanted to shout at him: where did you go? Where's the fun, great little kid I knew? The place was just licenced fucking torture, the shame, the humiliation. That did it. Well, they might beat him, but they would not reduce him to that. They could hurt him, but not destroy him.

It was time for breakfast. Julian had resorted to just eating the white bread and butter and marmalade. There was always something cooked, but either it was fried eggs swimming in oil, or scrambled eggs as if someone was suffering from a nasty gastric complaint, or, the worst, kidneys stinking of urine, a scum of yellow effluent covering the meat. His own mother cooked so well, and he had to eat this stuff. It was calories but not cuisine. So many bodies and so much food, some sort of algebra known only to army and school bursars: $a + x - b2$ equals the cheapest hamburgers known in Christendom made up of gristle and cows' udders. Eating was something one did because it was what a boy was programmed to do at that time in that school—but enjoyment was not on the menu.

Julian sat in his place on one of the long benches. His house was near one of the entrances. The noise of boys talking rose up into the high dome. The super privileged did not eat with the plebians but had their own so-called Parnassus, the Gods, up in another room above the main dining room. The food was the same, though, just a bit fancier. It all made Julian sick. Houses, special ties, privilege, beatings. Some houses let the older boys beat the younger ones, just for fun. We won a bloody war to do this to our kids, thought Julian. Some boys bought the whole deal, loved the climb to privilege, the power over others. They went on to command battalions, he supposed. After this, trench warfare was a doddle. Pass me some more rat, could you Peter? There's a good lad. Can't get enough of it these days, what with the war on! Damned fine cook we've got, can make a kedgeree of dead dog in a jiffy. Much better than what they gave us at school!

Breakfast over, Julian went to prepare for Chapel and then lessons. He had French and English that morning. Chapel was from 8.30 to 9 every day. Julian did not mind as the music was one of the few things he enjoyed. He loved the hymns, the harmony, the sound of the organ as the music swelled. The first music master was a lovely guy, from up North. Fabulously talented, he seemed to be able to play any instrument incredibly well, sang beautifully, composed, had a great family with lovely kids and a fun wife. And he wrote with the most beautiful flourish, a calligraphy which seemed a work of art in itself. He had a large florid face and receding red hair, and often appeared unshaven at breakfast to make sure the boys knew when their lessons with visiting teachers were to be. He was OK. He was more than OK. He was a breath of sanity in an otherwise madhouse run by perverts and weirdoes.

Julian filed up to the choir loft and took his place. He kept himself to himself. The hymn was 'Come down O love divine, and fill every trembling heart'. He wished it were true. His was certainly trembling. He looked to the music master for comfort, the hands and stubby fingers like white cigars flicking over the keys; then the glance down at the pedals, never a note wrong, all in place.

Where had he learnt to play like that?: the assurance, the deft touch, the innate musicality. The impression was of a modern day Bach, a face which could just as well sell you a pound of sausages or write a sonata. The jowls could be on a pork butcher, but the mind behind that face was pure gold.

Outside the Chapel a dense fog had descended. A sudden mist like this was common. It was joked that the weather came straight from the Ural mountains, and in fact there was nothing but the icy Baltic sea between the Russian steppes and the College. Cold was the normal temperature, with gradations of icy and brass-monkey. Even in the summer it never really warmed up. But today the fog suited Julian. Faces came towards him in a blur, and he did not have to acknowledge them or be polite to Masters or Prefects. He went to a room in the quad he shared with 8 other boys, and where he had a locker for his books. He took out the French books: Phèdre, and the English text: Othello. French first. The teaching block was an ugly brick and stone edifice at the entrance to the school, as if to say to prospective parents: this is what we do here, Jimmy! Pound some knowledge into these young brains, that's our job! The rooms were always cold (Julian's toes often went numb) and the dark wooden benches and inadequate lighting gave the whole scene a Dickensian air. Lesson after lesson, more and more pounding.

Lessons were finally over. Julian looked at his watch. Another three-quarters of an hour before he had to present himself at Darke's study. Well, it would be over quickly. 3 minutes of agony, then the welts and possibly blood. He would not cry. He had never cried before, and was not going to now. The cuts would take a few weeks to heal, and he would have to sit down with care. He remembered how his arse felt on fire for days after.

Julian gathered his books and made his way to the common room where he had his locker. The mist was still thick with shafts of sunlight trying to get through. In other circumstances he would have appreciated the effect. All he felt now was dread. He decided not to go to lunch but sit it out here.

Other boys were leaving, going to the hall. He pretended to be doing something with the books in his locker so as not to attract attention. When they had all left he sat down and watched the quad clock sweep round to 2pm. It chimed the 3/4. Then it was almost two. Well, other people had gone through worse ordeals. He thought of torture victims, of their nails being pulled out, of martyrs at the stake, of electric shocks. Others had survived.

Two o'clock. The quad clock struck out the hour. Julian got up and walked as convict must feel as he walks towards his death. It was up the steep climb in the quad. He got there in 30 seconds and knocked at the door. Darke was waiting for him impatiently, and Julian got the feeling he was strangely excited, a sort of frenzy of impatience.

"Ah, there you are. Good. Can't have these things delayed. Now, um, come through into the sitting room and we'll get on with it".

Julian noticed Darke's voice was all matter of a fact, as if he were talking of Maths prep or the rugby team. There were no noises of his family in the house. Perhaps he had sent them all away for the day. Perhaps he did this when he had to beat someone, thought Julian.

"Now, um, the thing to do is to assume the position, which

is to kneel in front of the armchair with your hands out on the sides. It, um, gives me a better view, um.........a better shot".

Julian did not say anything. A better shot. What was this? Bloody coconuts? Scores for bulls' eyes on all strokes. The gas fire was on still, and the room was quite warm.

"And take your jacket off, if you don't mind, so I can see what I am doing better".

He might have been a GP on a house call asked to give an injection. All detail, matter of fact, no emotion. Julian thought he must have been through this rigmarole many, many times, and got it down to an art. Julian took off his jacket, threadbare and dirty, and placed it on top of the armchair.

"That's right, it'll do fine there", said Darke.

Julian heard almost joy, exaltation in the man's voice. Darke was enjoying this. How could he be?

Julian then knelt down and put his arms on the sides of the armchair. He waited for the terrible, unexpected, immense pain he had known before. It was unlike anything you could imagine, so sudden, so intense. He braced himself for the first blow. It did not come. He waited more, then looked around to his left slightly to see what Darke was doing. The long mirror in the wardrobe had come ajar. Darke kept his canes there, and Julian, by chance of the angle, could see Darke in the reflection. He had his back turned to Julian and was rubbing himself in his trousers. Julian could not believe it and started to get up. He's bloody wanking himself!
    Darke suddenly turned, realising he had been caught out. He tried to regain control, to order Julian back.

"Get back down. Assume the position, Bates".

"But I saw you rubbing yourself!"

Julian could see the man was rattled, and uncertain.

"I'm not going to be beaten by a ......wanking pervert". Julian was amazed at his language, but it was all he could find.

"Assume the position, Bates", Darke repeated.

"No".

At this Darke raised the cane over his head as if it were a weapon.

"Get back down there, Bates".

"No, I won't".

Darke then, out of rage at being contradicted, brought the cane down on Julian's face. It cut him on the left side of his face. The pain brought tears to his eyes, and with the pain Julian lost control. No one should ever do that to another human being, he thought. Julian was much larger than his housemaster and he caught hold of Darke's jacket lapels and shouted into the man's face:

"You are a nasty pervert and you get a kick, don't you, out of beating boys? Don't you?"

Darke's face showed terror. He made one last attempt to gain control, and shouted:

"Get back, assume the position!" and tried to bring the cane down on Julian's face again.

Julian pushed Darke back towards the wall, but as he did so they lost their balance, tripping over the arm of the armchair. They both fell, Julian on top. In falling, Darke hit the back of his head on the brass knob at the side of the fireplace. Suddenly there was no struggle. After a few seconds Julian got up off the floor. He looked down at his tormentor. His eyes were staring upwards, unblinking, a strange deadness, a film already appearing over them. A trickle of blood came out of his mouth, which was horribly open. Julian could see the dark fillings and the yellow tobacco-stained teeth. Silence but for the ticking of the clock in the hall. No one was around. He walked closer and knelt beside his housemaster. He listened for breathing. Nothing. He took the man's hand and felt for a pulse. Nothing. He let the hand fall back on to the floor. More blood was coming out from behind his head and making a pool around the fire fender.

"Shit! I've killed the bastard", he said under his breath. He looked at the man who thirty seconds before had tried to hurt him so much.

"You shouldn't have done that, Mr Darke".

Julian could not think of any better words at that moment. As an epitaph it was not much.

⊨+⊩

The mist was still thick when Julian walked out the door. He had to stop himself running so as not to arouse suspicion. There were very few boys around as they were all off playing rugby or other sports. Julian was in a panic now. He had just two ideas in mind—leave the school and get to friends. It was cold, so he went to get his coat. It was an ex-army coat, with brass buttons and a high collar. In his desk he had 4 pounds and 12 shillings. It was enough to get him to London. He also put his passport in his pocket.

"Don't panic, don't panic", he kept on repeating to himself.

He had to get to the bus stop in the village about a mile away. He'd go up by the Sanitorium and the new teaching blocks. In the mist he'd hardly meet anyone. He put his collar up high and sank into the coat, trying to hide his face as much as possible. His heart was beating hard, as if he'd just been running a marathon. Up through the iron gates, up through past the Sanitarium. No one yet. Past the art block, into the asphalted street and he was out.

The bus stop was outside the pub. Julian had not taken the bus that often, but he knew it went straight to the station. He saw two old ladies waiting with their shopping baskets, so a bus was coming. He started thinking about disguise, and immediately took off his tie and put it in his pocket, then ruffled his hair so no parting showed. He was obviously one of the College boys to the women, but once out of the area he could be any 17-year-old. He joined the queue, trying to behave as normally as possible. His heart was still thumping so loudly he thought they might be able to hear it through his coat. He fingered the money in his trouser pocket. He couldn't afford to lose a penny now, and he had no idea where he was going to get any more. He couldn't go home, he couldn't ask his parents. His sister would help but he didn't want to involve her. It had to be Simon.

"Come on, come on!"

Still no bus. He quite expected to see a posse of policemen at any moment. He shifted from one foot to another, blew into his hands as if he were cold. The mist was still around but lifting, and the afternoon sun was winning though. The two ladies murmured something to each other. Then Julian saw the bus coming.

Thank God, he said under his breath. The fare was two shillings to the station. His hands were shaking visibly. He hoped the bus driver had not noticed: College boy, in army great coat, shaky hands, got off at the station. He could imagine his statement at the police station.

As the bus pulled away he thought of the normality of the life outside and the madness inside those walls. Here they were on a bus in the centre of England, two women going shopping with their bags, their children at a local school. Just simple, normal life. He wondered how they would treat him if they knew what he had done only a few minutes before. The bus passed the main gates. Would he miss anything? Like hell! Just the cricket and the music, perhaps. The rest could go fuck itself. The countryside was dull. Winter was over but the leaves hadn't started growing back yet. Take it all in, thought Julian, because you may not be seeing it for a long time, either in or out. He looked at the trees and hedgerows as if for the last time, as perhaps a dying man might look at them. The start of tears pricked his nose. Not now, he though. Tears are for later. Not now.

The station at Broxborne was simple, just a ticket office and a waiting room. Down to £4 pounds and 10 shillings already. That was another problem he had to solve. The train for Liverpool Street was on time, and Julian sat facing the engine. There was hardly anyone else in the carriage, and no ticket collector came to check tickets. So normal, thought Julian, and yet it could never be his again.

Liverpool Street was grimy and busy. It was Friday afternoon, the usual scramble of passengers trying to get out of the city was underway. There were no police visible. Either the police were not on his case, or the body had not yet been found, or it was not being treated as a murder enquiry yet. It allowed Julian to relax. Julian headed for the tube and Waterloo, and sat quite calm among the tourists and office workers. Two hours ago I killed a man, and you don't know this, he thought to himself. He felt as if his crime was written on his brow, and flashing lights announced his where-abouts. But no one paid him any attention at all.

He then took a train to Deptford where Simon was living in a small flat which was designated short-life housing. Getting out at the station, everything seemed short-life. Or abandoned. It was clear no one came to Deptford if they could help it. There seemed to be endless flimsy walls of corrugated iron hiding what must be bomb sites from the last war. The council had chosen to deal with it like this, but it gave scope for the graffiti artists. As Julian walked to the flat he noticed the psychedelic art, the figures hold-ing joints and praising weed. Other walls had cryptic phrases on them: *Love over Gold*, or: *Corrugated iron is the character armour of the council*. Witty, intelligent, Reichian weirdness here. Normality. Julian's heart lifted.

It was getting dark now, and he felt safer. Wind rattled the flimsy iron walls. Almost a shanty town. Walking to the flat in these streets dressed as he was, in the John Lennon coat, he could be anyone. He did not feel hunted yet. The flat was about half a mile from the station and he had no idea if Simon would be in. It took Julian a bit of time to be sure which block it was, and which floor. He had only been there twice, and that was a year ago and he had been half-pissed. But he finally was sure of the block and buzzed.

"Hello". A woman's voice.

"Hi. I'm a friend of Simon's. Is he in?"

"No, he's out in the swimming pool after his Akido lesson. But you can come up if you want".

"Thanks. I will".

The door buzzed open, and Julian walked up the concrete stairway and to the flat. He rang the bell and a young woman opened the door. She was so matter-of-fact. Curly red hair, waif-like body, big brown eyes.

"Hi, I'm Rosie. Simon's not here yet. I rent the place with him. I'm just going out now, so you were lucky you caught me in. You can stay till he comes back, if you like".

"Yes, I'd like that very much, actually".

"Well, there is milk in the fridge, so make yourself some tea". And she was off into her room to get her things.

Julian walked into the kitchen and sat down. My God! he was getting weary, but he was in a safe haven for the moment. He remembered reading a book called 'Rogue Male' and felt like the main character. Would he have to dig a hole in the ground like a fox and hide there for eternity? He took off his great coat. One of the brass buttons was missing.

CHAPTER 2

FRIENDS

Suddenly he heard a key turn in the lock and Simon was in the flat. Julian was so glad to see him. His spirits always rose when he saw this bearded, gangly, smiling figure walk in, with a nose like the prow of a boat and a beard like some latter-day prophet. He was in his Akido phase, about to leave for Japan where he was going to teach English and understand the mysteries of the Orient. He had just come from his weekly evening class with a visiting guru, and was full of the wondrous teachings of this Japanese expert. His wooden sword was strapped to his back like some sort of long machete.

"Hi".

"Hi".

"What's up? Why no College? You've run away at last? Killed the bursar's cat? Rogered your housemaster's daughter?"

Suddenly he whipped the Akido stick from out behind his back and began a series of quick sharp movements, bringing the sword down close to Julian's head, then back out and up, turning on himself, then down on the other side, all this accompanied by guttural Japanese shouts. Julian heard the swish of the sword through the air, many times brushing his hair, coming close to touching him but never quite. Then Simon stopped as suddenly as he had started, put the sword back into its cloth sheath and sat down.

"That was impressive", said Julian.

"It's nothing compared to the master I met this evening".

"Impressive to me". Simon shrugged.

"So, spill the beans".

"I've gone and done it now. Big time".

"How bad? Scale of one to ten. One being caught stealing the collection box in the chapel. Ten being found in a pub with half-a-pint of shandy".

Julian could not help but smile. Simon was a tonic. He stared off into the distance, trying to find some sort of words which might at once be the truth and not too dramatic.

"I killed my housemaster" Julian heard himself say. He imagined he would have to hear himself say it again in the future. It sounded so remote, so unlikely. One moment you were drinking tea with a friend, the next you were saying you had murdered a man. He stole a look at his friend. Simon was staring at him from under his brows, not sure if this was some kind of elaborate joke or what. It was not like Julian to joke in this way.

"And?" asked Simon.

"And what?"

"And ... you killed your housemaster. How, why, when, where?"

Julian looked at his watch.

"About four hours ago, in his home, because he was a pervert and he was trying to beat me. He hit me in the face and we fell together. He smashed his head against the metal fire-fender. And died".

Simon took in a big breath and then sighed.

"Well, on the scale of one to ten that is worse than drinking shandy, at least in some people's books".

Julian did not say anything and waited for Simon to speak. Simon's usually brown face went pale as if he were going through all the permutations before he spoke. When he did mathematical calculations he seemed to go off into another world where planets and black holes were part of his universe. Finally Julian interrupted.

"I can't think what to do. So I came here" he said.

"Quite right. Who knows you are here?"

"No one".

"Will they have found the body?"

"I expect so by now".

"And they'll know it's you".

"I imagine so. My housemaster dead, body with blood pouring out of his head, and me not around. It doesn't need a Sherlock Holmes".

"Although they may not make the connection straight away, and there is no proof. Is there? Is there" said Simon.

"No but....."

"No: no 'buts'. Did anyone see you?"

"No".

"Did anyone see you come here?"

"No". Again, the deep intake of breath.

"I think this calls for a joint" said Simon.

As Simon began taking out some tobacco and papers, he started going through the alternatives.

The worst-case scenario was getting caught, brought to trial and getting a life sentence with no early release for good behaviour. The best was not to get caught, and that would take a bit of doing.

Other permutations came: getting off altogether (unlikely); getting a light sentence (possible, but still a massive gamble, lawyer's fees etc); of living in Australia (at least they spoke the same language, but easy contact with the police); or South America (how to earn a living?); of having plastic surgery like the Japanese Mafia (expensive); of going to Casablanca and having a sex-change.

"That'd keep them off the scent for a bit, as it were", said Simon.

"Bit excessive, no? One moment I'm on the run, the next I have a fake fanny? I think I'd prefer South America, thanks".

The joint was ready and he lit it and took long drags, handing it over after a while. Julian refused at first, not wanting to have his head more muddled than it was. Besides, he wasn't a smoker. But he eventually took it and had a few puffs. It never really did much for him.

"So". Simon looked down his long, Semitic nose. "We need to go and see Hugo. I'll give him a ring now".

"Who is Hugo?"

"Hugo is French, sort of".

"And why?"

"Because one, they could trace you here, and I'd be harbouring a criminal".

"Hey! Watch your language. I thought you were on my side".

"Better get used to it. And two: because Hugo has got me out of a lot of scrapes. Besides, he has great dope and a beautiful girlfriend".

Simon went into another room and phoned Hugo. Julian heard a short explanation. He came back.

"So. He was in. Off we go. *Allons-y*. No luggage, I presume?"

CHAPTER 3

FRENCH LEAVE

The trip to Lewisham took only 20 minutes. Simon filled Julian in on Hugo's life details. These were subject to elaboration and alteration by Hugo and there was never a final version. At the moment Hugo lived in a flat over his sister who had three children of her own. Hugo was the last of a strange brood of kids. Of mixed French and Italian parentage, immigrants after the war, they had somehow survived and produced seven children, Hugo being the last. Hugo loved to recount how, by the time he arrived on the scene, his parents had no strength to try and impose any sort of discipline. He had run wild, and was still running wild as an adult. He had lost his virginity at 11, and had never looked back. His last count was over a thousand women. He smoked and drank anything that was going. Quite some friend.

Simon parked the 2CV close by in the dark, grimy streets and they walked to the red-brick house. They buzzed and were let in. To get to the flat they had to climb a flight of narrow stairs. Julian noticed the once burgundy-coloured carpet was very worn and littered with cigarette butts.

A door opened on the right, and they walked in. Hugo was on his own. He was not what Julian had expected at all: something French, a small moustache, dark, wiry, a sort of Tour de France cyclist.

Instead, a quite tall and rotund man stood before them. He had long, straight hair worn in a fashionable pop idol way, a pale face and dark, deep-set eyes. This was the Casanova? Julian found it hard to believe.

"Simon".

"Hugo".

They exchanged a sort of bear hug, the easy intimacy of those who have been on the road together and faced dangers.

"This is Julian, the guy I was telling you about".

"Hi". Julian offered a hand, which Hugo took. His grip was solid, firm, simple.

"Let's go into the kitchen. Have some tea".

Julian noticed now the French accent.

They went into the adjoining room. The kitchen was bare and untidy. Enamel surfaces, and empty mugs with tea bags here and there. A gas stove was on the right-hand side. Hugo obviously was not one for decoration. Some record sleeves were on the fridge with an ash-tray full of butts, and the air was stale.

"*Asseyez-vous*. Tell me all".

Hugo handed Simon a cigarette, and offered one to Julian.

"No, I don't".

Hugo shrugged. Everyone smoked. He turned to the stove and lit the ring and put the kettle on, then sat down again smoking with deep pulls on the cigarette.

"So, Simon tells me you have been in a spot of trouble".

"Yes, trouble. You could say that".

Julian looked to Simon for reassurance that he could speak openly. Simon intervened.

"Go ahead, you can say anything and everything here".

Julian hesitated, as if saying what he was about to say would start him on a lifetime's journey.

"I killed my housemaster today". The silence was deafening.

"You just didn't like him, or what?" Hugo asked.

"No, I didn't like him, but not enough to kill him. He was trying to beat me and I saw him touching himself and I turned and he hit me in the face, and then we fell, and he hit his head on the side of the fire and ....he's dead".

"*Mon dieu!*"

"It was not my fault. It was self-defence, I suppose". Julian's voice trailed off.

"Tell me again. What was going on?"

"He was going to beat me for something I did not do".

"Ah, these boarding schools. Like the Navy, *quoi*? Rum, sodomy and the lash!"

Hugo and Simon chuckled.

"So, he is going to beat you, and you kill him?" said Hugo.

"No, I was waiting, and I saw him rubbing himself".

"Pardon? You see him wank himself? That is what you say, no?" asked Hugo.

"Yes, I see.... saw him...... touching himself".

"And how did you see him doing this touching/wanking?"

"I saw him in the mirror".

"He has a mirror and you are watching him touch himself. Ooh, la la!. What do you get up to in these schools? I mean, what we call...*frottage*, and then you watching and the sado-masochism, and mirrors. I mean, it is amazing. *Vraiment incroyable*. And so...mature, one might say".

"No, no it was not that at all! It was not like that!" Julian's voice rose in anger.

"I told you, I just saw him in a mirror by chance".

"But did he know you were looking, perhaps? Ah-ha! better still, a voyeur with a mirror. *Fantastique!* I mean in France we pay for this, you know? There are some houses where these things are done, you simply ask and pay a nice, perhaps not so nice, lady, and she whip you, and.............. judges, politicians, *oui!* Even those. Especially those. They deserve it. "By the way, did he wear any rubber?" asked Hugo.

"Rubber?"

Julian was now exasperated.

"Yes", said Hugo. "Rubber underpants, something of that sort?"

"It was not like that, I told you. I just saw him in a mirror by chance".

Simon calmed him down.

"I think he's joking", Julian.

"Oh, sorry". He tried a faint smile, and looked at Hugo's grinning face.

"You see, I'm not quite up to jokes at the moment".

"*Bien.* So: you kill this little pervert".

Julian started a bit at the word.

"Yes, he hit me on the face with a cane"...Julian pointed to the weal on the side of his face..... "and I tried to stop him and"........ Julian sighed. "We fell over and he hit his head".

"Good".

"What do you mean, 'good?'"

"You did humanity a service", said Hugo.

"He has a wife and child. Children".

"You did them a service".

"You can't go around killing people and say you are doing humanity a service!"

Hugo smiled. "Julienne, it is you who did the killing, not me!"

"Yeah, well, I'm sorry I did it".

"Perhaps he needed to be taken from the planet; and you may have done his wife and kids—and others boys—a favour if he was as you say".

Hugo got up and made the tea. He placed mugs in front of them with the tea-bag floating inside. A bottle of milk and some sugar were on the table.

"We'll need a drink later. Something stronger. And you need a plan. For the moment you are safe here. No one knows me, although they might go after Simon".

"Mum's the word", said Simon.

"Yes, be very, very careful. We go for a drink now, but after, you, Simon, cannot talk to him on the phone for a long time. Perhaps not see each other for a long time. Believe me, when you deal with murder, *les flics* are very, how do you say?........... obstinate. They don't give up easily".

⇌ ⇋

Later that evening they went to the local pub. It was a typical South London barn of a place, with several rooms all filled with smoke. Hugo went to the bar to buy drinks while Simon and Julian found a table fairly close to the door. Simon began rolling a cigarette. Hugo came back with the drinks. After the first sip Julian found himself dizzy and almost drunk. He had not eaten since breakfast. He got up to get some peanuts, which was also a good excuse for the other two to plot and plan. When he came back some things had been decided.

"So", began Hugo, "it is like this. You have to leave the country if you don't want to sew mail-bags for the rest of your life. You are officially 'on the runs'".

"On the run", corrected Simon.

"Ah *oui*. 'On the run', and 'to have the runs'. *Merci*. Either way, unpleasant. Like this pub"

'How's that?" asked Simon.

"Because everyone here is running, the Jews to the synagogue, the blacks from the police, and the Irish to the pub".

"Hugo!"

"*Mais, c'est vrais*. I just tell the truth".

Simon outlined their plan.

"We think you have to change your image for a start. You look and sound private school, and that is exactly what they will be searching for. So, different clothes. Hugo will sort you out tomorrow. We like the idea of hippy guitar-player".

"I can't play the guitar".

"You can tomorrow. You have a week to practice" said Simon.

"Why a week?"

"You have to have time to change your hairstyle and grow a beard. And you have to learn French and Italian".

"Why?"

"Because you are about to become me", said Hugo.

"What?"

"You don't like me? I am not good looking enough perhaps?"

"No, it's not that. I just don't get the idea, that's all".

Both Simon and Hugo took a drink from their beer.

"Listen", said Simon, "you are probably in denial".

"The Nile? I have never been to Egypt".

Both Hugo and Simon cracked up.

"Not The Nile, 'denial'". Simon looked at Julian to see if he had understood.

"Look, it doesn't matter. Let's say: a state of shock. You either give yourself up, and we have decided that is not such a good idea, or you escape abroad".

"And so, you need a new passport, and that's why you become me", said Hugo.

"And you?" said Julian.

"I declare it lost in three months' time. If they have not picked you up by then, we are all happy. I get a new passport, and you get a new identity".

"And the languages bit?"

"You need to become me in everything. How much French do you know?" said Hugo.

"I can speak Alexandrine couplets from '*Phèdre*'".

"Very useful when you are ordering a meal".

"I can do more".

"I hope so. And the Italian will be essential. Just in case. And you'll need to know all about my family, bothers and sisters, date of birth, that sort of shit" said Hugo.

"And", added Simon, "you are going to Israel".

"Why Israel?"

"Because", said Hugo, "I know people there; because I can get you a job; because it is a place where no one asks too many questions; because it is a place where you can earn and send me back the money we are going to lend you; and it is a country at war and they need manpower".

And so it was decided. Israel it was within a week. They had another round of drinks. By this time Julian was quite drunk and so tired he could hardly keep awake. He kept nodding off what with the alcohol and the fug and the temporary feeling of security. He tried to imagine himself back in College, what the boys would be doing there at this time. Dormitory, prep, lights out. It all seemed so far away, and ridiculous. But at that very moment, the police and forensic experts were in Harold Darke's house, and the boys were whispering from bed to bed about the police cars and sirens and ambulances they had seen and heard that evening.

⇌ ⇋

Julian heard Hugo get up the next day, make coffee and place a mug near his head. He was sleeping on a mattress on the floor.

"I'll be back in the afternoon".

Julian dozed through the morning and early afternoon. He couldn't make himself get up, he had no energy. Instead, he drifted in and out of consciousness. He thought of the boys in the dormitory, the cold showers, the scramble for breakfast, chapel. What would Jack think high in his organ loft?

He looked at his watch. 9.00. History with Kemble. Then French. All that gone: the essays, the rugby games, all over. It already seemed long in the past.

He tried to imagine what they were saying about him—a nasty piece of work from the start. He knew many masters disliked him, although quite why he had never fathomed. Now they had good cause. He could hear their joy, crowing with self-righteousness. Finally that 'scum-of-the-earth' Bates had shown his true colours: a murderer, no less! They knew it all along.

But he was sorry for Darke's wife and kids. He hardly knew them, but they were good people he imagined. Now they would

27

hate him and want his capture and punishment. Could he ever tell them that the man he had accidentally killed was a pervert and sadist? They would never believe him. The police would never believe him. A jury would never believe him. He hoped the occasion would never arise.

Hugo came back when the light was fading.

"Get up. It stinks in here. Take a shower. Then we talk".

Julian was not used to be spoken to in this way, but he was a guest, and he probably did stink.

Better do as he was told. The bathroom was small and the bath had a green stain from the taps. He turned on the hot water and there was a whoosh as the gas faucets lit up. What was the Rupert Brook line: the benison of hot water? Something like that. But it was a great invention. Brooke could keep his honey in Grantchester, but hot water on demand, this was truly wonderful. Julian soaked for a bit, used some soap, then got out and dried himself on a small towel. It had the name of a hotel written on it. No doubt Hugo had liberated it from somewhere on his travels. Julian got back into his underpants and walked back into the living room. Hugo was smoking and staring out of the window. The curtains were nothing more than bits of cloth hung up with string. It was enough.

"So. Clean?"

"Clean".

"So now we work. Here is my passport".

Hugo pushed the little green embossed book towards Julian.

"This is now who you are. I'll test you tomorrow. Place, date of birth. Other details I'll tell you as they come to me. Have you started playing the guitar?"

"No".

"Well, start this evening".

Julian took the passport and was about to open it when Hugo gripped his wrist.

"Hey, that hurts! What is this for?" Julian tried to pull away, but Hugo held him fast in a strangely powerful grip.

"*Ecoutez*! This is not a game".

"I know".

"No, you don't know. Not yet. This is not a game of cricket, where if you lose they shake your hand and say 'better luck next time, old boy'. They are after you. They will come to Simon and try and get him to say things. They may come here. They will search for you everywhere and perhaps never give up. You are now like a wolf, do you understand? You will be hunted, and you will have to live on your wits. You are no longer Julian, you are me. *Compris?* If you want to live free, you have to become someone else. Do you understand now?"

Hugo released his grip on Julian's wrist. Julian pulled it free and rubbed it. There were clear signs where Hugo's fingers had been. Julian stared angrily into Hugo's eyes.

"Yes, even me. You will have to learn not to trust even me. If ever you are in difficulty, you can call me. I may be able to help you. But, trust no one if you want to survive. Eh, *maintenant, le* fashion show!" Hugo stubbed out his cigarette, got to his feet.

"Come into the bedroom". Julian followed.

Hugo opened the wardrobe. An amazing array of brightly-coloured clothes were suddenly on display: Kaftans, yellow bell-bottom trousers, bright-red shirts with sequins, dark-red leather jackets, pin-striped jackets, wide-brimmed hats, caps, leather boots, white winkle-pickers. Trinkets from a designer's treasure chest.

"My plumage. For the pick-ups. You have to be noticed".

Hugo looked Julian up and down, the disinterested gaze of a tailor.

"Well, we are sort of the same height. Now, what did we say? The hippy guitarist? *Bien*, try this".

Hugo pulled out the kaftan shirt. Then the blue bell-bottom trousers and a leather jacket and threw them on the bed.

"Or wait, perhaps......a transvestite". Hugo looked Julian up and down as if seriously considering the matter.

"No, too tall. Too much Adam's pear".

"Apple. Adam's apple" said Julian. Hugo shrugged.

"Whatever. And the beard. Don't shave at all for a week, and then we'll shape what you have got. You are off on Sunday".

"Why Sunday?" Julian was getting into the trousers.

"Because no one works on Sundays, not even *les flics*.. Who wants to get up and catch a schoolboy on the run at 6 am on a Sunday morning? Even for promotion. So, you leave from Dover. There will be police, maybe at the port, but they will search for drugs, illegal immigrants, and possibly a clean-shaven young man in a tie and coat. And now the jacket".

Julian put the jacket on.

"Look at yourself in the mirror".

Julian turned and looked at himself. Truly there was a transformation. Hugo went to get the guitar and placed in Julian's hands.

"What do you think?"

"I think I look pretty weird".

"Vrai. You look weird. A bit more beard, and a bit more hair, and you could fool them. Just now you look as if you have dressed up for a party. And you have to buy some blondes".

"Blondes?" Julian thought this was another of Hugo's elaborate sexual jokes, that somehow he would have to purchase the favours of a blonde escort lady to finish off the tableau.

"Blondes, oui! Les blondes. Cigarettes. None of that Gaulloise *merde".*

"Ah, fags! Of course. May I ask why?"

"Ask away, *mon brave".*

"Please tell me why I am going to buy some blonde cigarettes".

"Because you need a lift into France with a lorry driver. Because if you turn up like that, even with my passport, you will look suspicious. But if you are riding in a truck with a Frenchman stinking of garlic high up there, and you both have French passports, and the lorry driver is thinking of another twenty packets of blondes on the ferry and is your best friend, at least for the crossing, then, perhaps, perhaps, *mon brave*, you will get through".

Hugo turned to Julian and fixed him with his dark eyes.

"And, listen very carefully, if you get caught, you stole the passport, OK?"

"OK".

"Even if they whack you around a bit. You stole it from me on the tube".

Julian nodded his assent.

"*Bien*. Get out of those clothes. They look ridiculous. I look cool and sexy in that stuff. You.......you look.......*fou*. Concentrate on growing a beard. And playing the guitar".

CHAPTER 4

INVESTIGATION

The call came through to Watford Police station at ten past four. A distraught Mrs Darke from the College was saying a murder had been committed, that her husband was dead. Detective John Pendelbury and Sergeant Hatton were put on the case. An ambulance and forensics were on their way too.

John Pendelbury had been at Watford Police station since the end of the war. He was from the South originally, and still had a strong Sussex accent. He had met his wife during the war and they had married as soon as it was over. He moved up to her parents, and sought work in that area and the force was a good job for someone with a military background. He had come out of the war reasonably unscathed, although a minor injury to his feet had made it imperative to wear protective steel toes on his shoes. He had been in the gunners at El Alamein, and the risks were slight. He often told the story of Monty going to sleep when the barrage began: "Nothing more I can do, gentlemen. Goodnight". It gave his soldiers such a sense of security; no doubt in the general's mind that they were going to win. And they did.

He had never been to the College. There had never been any reason to, apart from the story of minor theft a few years' back. One of the boys had stolen several medals left to the College by Old Boys, and had tried to sell them in London. But the theft was reported, and the buyer alerted the police. The seller was easy to trace, and from being a College Prefect he found himself leaving in ignominy. The College did not press charges, as the medals were returned, but nothing was heard of him afterwards.

"Hatton here, Sir. I'm your driver".

"Thank you".

"We'll take the Jaguar, Sir. It's waiting outside".

Pendelbury and Hatton drove the fifteen miles through the flat, uninspiring Hertfordshire countryside. Bleak hedgerows and small, dull villages. But Pendelbury had come to like the area and like his job. He did it well, and felt a grim satisfaction when he caught his man. Behind the light blue eyes and the ruddy complexion was a man who was thorough in all he did. He was a good gardener, and all his crops were planted with care and precision, yielding what they promised they would. His wife, Maude, kept the house the same way and their two children were doing well at the local school. Yes, reason to be satisfied with himself.

"You ever been to the College, Sir?"

"No, never. No reason to. They tend to keep themselves to themselves".

"Murder, did they say it was?"

"Well, a death at least. We shouldn't jump to conclusions. People can get hysterical when they come across a body".

Hatton went silent for a bit. Pendelbury looked the wooden dashboard, and the leather fittings. He ran his hand over the wooden inlay.

"Did you see much action in the war, Sir?" asked Hatton.

"I saw enough. Enough to make me realise I didn't want to be there for long. But it was what we had to do".

Pendelbury was always reluctant to talk about what he had seen. Some blathered on about it, but most were reticent. Although the young'uns who missed the war seemed terribly keen to hear about it, those who had been there did not want to say much. Probably a defense mechanism, to be put in a box somewhere in the brain with the words: Do not open. He reached for his pipe and leather tobacco pouch. There would be enough time to fill it even if he couldn't smoke it.

"Another five minutes and we'll be there, Sir".

And soon they were outside the gates of the College with its long sweep up to the main teaching block. The Headmaster's Lodge was to the right of the gates.

"What do you say we proceed to the main building? I imagine they are expecting us".

As the Jaguar stopped outside the main gates a porter came out to meet them. He was dressed in very formal clothes, a black suit, tie, waistcoat and a bowler hat. Pendelbury wound down the window:

"Detective Pendelbury?" the Porter asked. "My name's Skinner, Detective. Glad to see you. I'm the College Porter".

"Can we leave the car here?" asked Pendelbury.

The porter looked around for a second.

"Of course. There is enough room if others need to get here".

So Pendelbury and Hatton parked, got out and followed the porter through the large mock Roman pillars and vaulting roofs into the quad.

"I'll take you straight to Mr and Mrs Darke's house. I think that'll be best, under the circumstances".

"Is someone with Mrs Darke at the moment?"

"Yes, the College nurse has been. She may still be there. And a friend, Mrs Miller, is with her now. The Headmaster is away at the moment on a conference. He has been informed, but won't be back till late tonight, if not tomorrow morning".

"Most unfortunate", remarked Pendelbury. "There are children?"

"Yes, they are staying with relatives for the moment".

"Yes, probably best under the circumstances".

"Here we are, Sir".

The front door was in the corner of the quad, with ivy all around. The porter knocked, and the door was opened by a middle-aged woman. Her face was pale and her hair was disordered.

"The Detective is here, Mrs Miller".

"Ah finally. Thank goodness" she said.

"I'll leave you to it if I may", said the porter, and he walked back down to the main lodge, seeming happy to be out of it.

"Please come through this way" said Mrs Miller. Dorothy is in the kitchen. Or would you like to see ..... Mr Darke first?"

"I'll have a word with Mrs Darke first, if that is alright? How is she?"

"Shocked, naturally. The children are with their aunt's" she said.

"I heard. Hatton, could you stay by the door for the moment? Don't let anyone in, that sort of thing, unless it is the ambulance crew. Forensics the same".

Mrs Miller led the inspector through to the kitchen area at the back of the house which led on to a small garden. Mrs Darke was seated at the white enamel kitchen table. He eyes were blotched and red, her face white with shock. Her hair was tied back in a bun, like a peg-doll. She held a handkerchief to her nose. In front of her were two mugs of tea.

"Dorothy?"

She raised her eyes to see who the visitor was.

"The Inspector", said Mrs Miller.

"No, don't get up, really". John Pendelbury offered his hand, and Mrs Darke got up to shake it. She then sat down. Tears came again. John Pendelbury muttered words of condolence.

"I'm so sorry. I'll be as quick as I can. If you are up to it, I'd like to ask a few questions after, if that is all right?" Mrs Darke nodded an assent.

"But right now, I need to see where the body is" Pendelbury said.

Mrs Darke indicated the front room.

"Perhaps Mrs Miller would show me?" suggested Pendelbury.

Again, the nodded assent and the tears.

"Poor dear". Mrs Miller put her arms around the grieving woman's shoulders.

"I'll take the Detective through, Dorothy. We'll be just here if you want anything".

Mrs Miller led the way to the front room where the body lay. There was a great deal of blood now, and much of it had seeped into the carpet. Mrs Miller looked with the Detective at the scene. Darke's mouth was wide open, his eyes staring into the ceiling. His head was at a strange angle, blood was at the side of his mouth, and a cane was lying by his right side, close to his hand.

"If you don't mind, I'll go next door". Mrs Miller's face had gone very pale.

"Of course. It isn't a pretty sight. I'll just be here for a few minutes, taking notes".

Pendelbury took out his notebook and followed his usual procedure. Date, time, place. His writing was a neat copper-plate. He walked closer to the body, noting the details, the angle of the head, the amount of blood, the cane. He then imagined the fall and the blow to the head.

The question immediately was: did he fall or was there a struggle? There were a lot of papers and souvenirs from holidays on the floor. Could there have been an intruder? Theft as a motive? A possibility. But the cane? Perhaps Mrs Darke might help him out there. He bent closer to the body. A strong smell of tobacco came off the mouth and clothes. He looked around, saw the pipe rack and pipes—a smoker like himself. The cause of death seemed to be fairly obvious, but as his eye went down the corpse he noticed a small stain in the groin area. It was duly noted. He would get back to that when the forensics team had finished. The furniture seemed to have been moved—he saw the imprints of the chair and settee on the carpet. He made a little drawing before anyone moved things back into their original places. Presumed hour of decease? He would say around 2.30 pm, a bit either way. He went to the door, taking in the scene for a last time, then returned to the kitchen.

Mrs Miller was there at the kitchen table, her right arm around her friend.

"There, there. You have the children to think about Dorothy. Don't do anything silly, there's a good girl".

"He was my whole life, she said through tears. My whole life. How could anyone do this?"

Pendelbury cleared his throat.

"I'm sorry to bother you. Are you up to answering a few questions?"

Mrs Darke nodded. Then tried to speak. A whisper came out: "I am, yes".

Just then there was a knock at the front door and he heard Hatton open the door and talk to gruff voices. He heard 'forensics' and 'ambulance'. Pendelbury turned and called out:

"Let them in, Hatton, I've seen what I needed to."

There was the sound of heavy steps and men carrying equipment. Pendelbury closed the adjoining door.

"I'm sorry to bother you, but I would like to get as much information as possible".

Mrs Darke cried into her handkerchief, but nodded an assent.

"Now, were you here at the time of the death?"

"No" Her voice was a whisper..

"Where were you?"

"With the children out shopping".

"And when did you come back?"

"At about four I think. I phoned the police straight away".

Pendelbury was making notes.

"And did you find the body?"

"Yes". More tears. More comfort from Mrs Miller.

"Did your husband say anything to you before you left?"

"He said .... he had to deal with someone that afternoon".

"Deal with?" A nodded assent.

"That meant he had to......... punish someone?"

"Those were his words he used when he had to ....the words he used when he had to discipline someone".

Another nodded assent.

"Just a few more questions if you don't mind" said Pendelbury." "Did he mention any names?"

"He said Bates was giving him problems and he had written to his father".

"Bates, I might have known it", said Mrs Miller. "That nasty piece of work! Just like his father".

Pendelbury was surprised by the venom.

"Well, we don't want to jump to conclusions, do we? But why did you say 'just like his father?' His father was here at the school too?"

"Yes, my father was a teacher here. Bates's father played the organ for the school sometimes. But he could never keep himself in line, I was told".

"So, just to get something straight. Your father was a teacher here?"

"Yes".

"And you married? asked Pendelbury".

"Andrew Miller. He teaches the sixth-form English".

"I see. So one way or another you know a lot about the history of the College, then?"

"As much as anyone, I suppose.

"Anything which might help us here? You mentioned Bates's father".

"Well, the whole family is mad, of course". Mrs Miller took a long drag on her cigarette, gold tipped, expensive.

"I mean, they're Irish, aren't they?......... which explains a lot. Poor Irish, if you know what I mean, not the rich horsy types at all". Coughing interrupted the narration.

"Yes, his father was here in the twenties, a runt of a thing. Underfed, undernourished. He looked as if he had never had a mother. No care for him, his clothes. Played on the wing for rugby. But musical, yes, very musical. Seemed to live for that alone, sometimes. Did classics with Jowett for the University, if I remember. What they all did then when they were destined for the church. Went to one of the good colleges in Oxford or Cambridge".

She lit another cigarette. Another dry cough.

"He had a pretty tough time, of course here", she continued.

"In what way?"

"Oh, there was a story of a beating.

"I'm sorry?" Pendelbury was writing fast in his notebook.

"Yes, in public too. In front of the whole school. It was the way they did the things in those days".

Pendelbury decided not to interrupt, although his disbelief was evident.

"Yes, they did things like that in the old days".

Here, Mrs Miller stubbed out her cigarette. A lot of red lipstick was left on the butt.

"Well, it was the times, wasn't it?"

"What had he done wrong?"

"Well, it was the music which did it. From what I heard he played a voluntary based on a popular tune. The Head took offence, I mean, it was chapel and all that. So, he came a cropper. They beat him in front of the whole school"

She ended up the short narrative coughing hard. Pendelbury waited until she had regained her composure.

"In front of the whole school. For a voluntary?" Pendelbury could hardly believe his ears.

"Well, it was how they behaved in those days, wasn't it?. They always said: if you see a head about the parapet, hammer it, hammer it hard. Andrew said it didn't do him any harm. I mean, it was a tough school, my God it was tough! It is a pretty tough school now. But it gave them backbone. I mean, if you could survive this, you could survive anything, they said. A lot went into the army and had careers. And there was India still, of course. That sort of thing".

Pendelbury remained silent, but wrote some notes slowly. His face betrayed no emotion.

"You'll be seeing Brian Sawbridge later on I expect?" she asked.

"Why is that?"

"Because he's the second master, and the Headmaster is away at the moment. Couldn't have picked a worse time, could he? I mean, nothing happens, and then this? And poor Dorothy and the children. I mean. It is just wicked! And I knew there was something odd about that Bates boy. Too nice, if you know what I mean".

"Too nice?"

"Yes, I'm sure he was into drugs or something. Kept himself to himself all the time. But a rebel. Always undermining authority. But I must get back to Dorothy. You'll be needing to see Brian, I'm sure. I'd take you there myself but I feel I'm needed here. Just ask the porter, he'll show you the way".

⇒╫ ╫⇐

After the forensic squad had done their bit, and the ambulance had taken away the body, Pendelbury said goodbye to the two women. They were now looking through old photographs, and commiserating. The phone started ringing as the detective left. So, the news was out. That did not take long, he thought. He found Hatton outside the front door smoking. He crushed it under his heel when he saw Pendelbury.

"Are we through, Sir?"

"Not yet. I have to make a last call. Stay here until I come back".

"Yes Sir".

Pendelbury made his way back to the porter's lodge. The porter was reading the local newspaper on a wide desk. He stood up when Pendelbury walked in.

"Last port of call, if you don't mind. I need to talk to", and he referred to his notes, "the acting Headmaster Brian Sawbridge".

"Yes Sir, right this way, Sir".

The porter led the way across the quad. It was now alive with activity. The boys were all going to the great hall for their evening meal, books under their arms, their faces covered with scarves to keep out the mist and cold, the scarves different colours to denote the houses. There was a strange silence. It wasn't the schooldays the detective remembered, with shouts and running and noise. Here, it was all controlled and ordered, hushed.

"Army school", muttered Pendelbury under his breath. "Poor blighters".

The porter led him across the quad to the other side and into an annex. Then they made their way up some stairs and to the first floor. Another 'house' was there, with a long dormitory with beds either side. All the boys were in the great hall having dinner. The porter then led the way through the long barn to a door at the end.

"I think you'll find Brian Sawbridge here. He knows you are coming".

"Thank you". Pendelbury was beginning to feel distinctly uncomfortable and could not wait to get into the Jaguar and away from this set-up. The cold, the hush, the stories of beatings, the death—he wanted to be by his gas fire and to have Maude and the kids close. He knocked on the door, and heard a sonorous 'Come in'. He opened the door was met by Brian Sawbridge.

Pendelbury did not know what to expect, but the man who offered his hand was quite a specimen.

A very flushed face covered with close-cropped crinkly fair hair; deep-set intense blue eyes, a body slightly bloated. How much was hereditary and how much was possibly the booze Pendelbury could not guess.

"Please sit down".

The room was quite spacious, with a gas fire lit at the end. A large chair was behind a desk, and Sawbridge offered the detective a blue armchair in front of the desk. Pendelbury sat down with care. He wondered if this armchair had been used for similar practices he had witnessed that afternoon.

"A drink?"

"Not while I am on duty".

"I understand. You don't mind if I do?"

"Not at all". Sawbridge poured himself a very liberal amount of whisky into a glass which was already on his desk. The room smelt sour, a combination of spirits and cigarettes.

"Smoke?"

"I have my own pipe".

"You don't mind if I light up then?"

"Please. Be my guest" said Pendelbury.

Sawbridge reached for his packet and took one out. Pendelbury noticed his hands were shaking and that there was a cigarette lit already in the heavy glass ash tray on the desk. He said nothing.

"So, a nasty business". Pendlebury let the silence hang in the air.

"Indeed" he said eventually.

"And the cause of death?"

"Too early to say. Until the forensic boys have done their bit, an autopsy, you know, all that. But it seemed he hit his head after some sort of struggle".

Pendlebury noticed the blue eyes dart here and there, never still.

"Bad business altogether", said Sawbridge, "and it could not have come at a worse time, I mean with the Head being away. Do you have any suspects, if you think there is foul play?"

Pendelbury decided to play a hunch.

"What do you know about a boy called Bates?"

Sawbridge immediately took a long drag on his cigarette. He turned his body and head away from the detective. Trembling in his hands. He then turned to the detective.

"Bates? Yes, a musician. One of mine, as it were".

"Yours?"

"Yes, I am second master but also second music master. Strange, but true. One of those anomalies of the school. Bates, you were saying? Well, he was all right but he went into the tunnel a few months ago, and has not come out".

"The tunnel?"

"Yes, that's what I call it, when a boy goes into the adolescent phase. The tunnel. Then he comes out and all is well. Actually he was, is, one of the best musicians we have in the school. I gave him the lead part in the Gilbert and Sullivan we put on this year. Showed my faith in him".

"Let me get this right. You give him the best part in the play, and then he goes into 'the tunnel' as you call it".

"Yes, that's right. Shame, damn shame. Why all the interest in this particular boy?"

"Well, he might be able to help us with our enquiries. Have you checked if Bates is in the school?"

"We wouldn't check up on a boy until the evening perhaps, or if he wasn't in his bed" said Sawbridge.

"Well, I suggest you do a check as soon as I leave". Pendelbury got up and looked around again. He noticed the photos on the desk.

"Your children?"

"Yes, my three kids".

"And this is you ? In uniform?"

"I was in Korea".

"That can't have been fun. A musician in Korea. Did you see action?"

Again the darting eyes, the quick inhale of smoke.

"We saw some pretty heavy stuff. Yes. Very heavy stuff". Sawbridge took a long swig at his whisky.

"Well, thank you. I suggest you make that check on all the boys in the school as soon as possible. Here is my number. I'd like to know just who is and isn't in the grounds. Who is missing. By tonight".

"Of course, detective". Sawbridge then took a picture off the wall. Here, have a look at this". It was the picture of the school, all 600 boys together.

"Is it recent? I mean, is Bates there?"

"It is recent. Last spring. And Bates, let me see, Bates..... here. Sawbridge picked out the boy.

Pendelbury looked at the boy's face among all the 600 other boys in their jacket and ties.

"Can I take this, just for the moment? It will be returned to you as soon as we can. It gives us a face to a name".

"Of course. Until this dreadful business is over".

Pendelbury shook the hand offered. The palm was strangely sweaty.

"I can find my own way out, thank you. I'm sure you have calls to make".

"I'll get on to the matter straight away. Goodnight detective".

"Goodnight".

Pendelbury shook the hand offered and left the room. He could not get out fast enough. Luckily his sense of direction led him out of the dormitory, and through the maze of stairs and annexes to the lodge. Hatton was waiting there.

"Let's get on our way, Hatton".

"Sir".

They both walked fast to the Jaguar. Hatton opened the door for the detective, who seemed to appreciate this gesture. By the time Hatton had got in the other side, Pendelbury had taken out his pipe and was lighting up whatever tobacco he had in the bowl. He opened the window to let some of the smoke out. They drove in silence for several minutes. Hatton kept quiet. Then the detective broke the silence.

"What were your schooldays like, Hatton?"

"Can't quite remember, Sir, that well".

"Did you get hit around a bit?"

"My father was pretty rough".

"At school?"

"Playground stuff, mostly. But I learnt to defend myself".

"Canings by staff".

"Weren't common in my day, Sir. More reports and parents evenings".

A long silence. Then Pendelbury muttered to himself:

"Poor bugger. Between the devil and the deep blue sea".

Then he picked up the radio and called in to the station: Victor Bravo on our way back. Over.

And by the time they had arrived a call had come through from the College. One boy was missing, yes. Julian Bates.

CHAPTER 5

ESCAPE

A week later Julian was on a train very early Sunday morning from Victoria to Dover. He had said his goodbyes to Simon and Hugo the night before, and slunk out in the drizzle at 5 to get the first tube from Deptford to the station. It had been a week, lying low, not going out, reading the newspapers. There was a small 5-line column in the *The Daily Telegraph* about a housemaster, Harold Darke, being found dead in suspicious circumstances. So; there it was. They would be out looking for him. He'd better be on his guard.

He had learnt as much as he could about Hugo's family and as many chords on the guitar as he could get his fingers around. The tips of his fingers had the beginnings of calluses on them.

His beard had grown in the week to be a fair attempt at camouflage, and Julian liked the moustache so much he decided he'd keep it. He had worn the freaky clothes every day in the flat, and he felt comfortable in them. He was no longer Julian Bates of the lower sixth, but guitar-playing, French and Italian speaking Hugo Romand off to Israel to work on a kibbutz. Hugo had organised everything in that week, the route, the contact details and some money. It was to be paid back when he could. A friend indeed.

There had been no obvious police presence in Victoria at 6 in the morning, although Hugo had warned him to be vigilant. They might be checking in Dover and on the alert. The sun was breaking through the clouds as he passed through Rochester. He seemed to remember Dickens had been born here, or lived here perhaps. He would check later. As the train went over the bridge he watched the little boats on the river at the moorings, so compact and safe. This was the best of England, and he was being forced to leave it. The alternative of years spent in prison was too awful to consider, but he felt as if he were leaving the very reason for being on this planet. This was who he was, and he was not allowed to be. The hedgerows in spring, the blossom, the wheat fields, cricket, the smell of cut grass. All this was over.

As for his own family, he had no idea how they were taking it, nor what was being said. He had disappeared, and that must have looked bad. Innocence stands its ground; the guilty escape.

The plan was for Julian to get off at Dover and walk to the large service station where lorry drivers stopped to fill up before crossing on the ferry. He had already stocked up with packets of Marlborough, and his French was good enough after a week of coaching from Hugo in the argot he would need to allow him to converse and make himself understood. His first test would be the station. There might be police there. Hugo had advised him to sit in the middle coaches and get off with everyone else. Best of all would be to try and make friends with someone on the train. Luck was on his side. Seated in the same carriage was an old lady with luggage. He would help her off the train and past the ticket barrier. The train slowed into the station, and yes, shit! there they were. Two tall, large bobbies either side of the barrier. Julian tried to convince himself that they could be there for anyone. It was Dover, there were lots of immigrants, it was a big port. But in his heart he knew they were there for him. Well, he would need to be a great actor or it was mail bags for life. He positioned himself in front of

the lady so he could help her down. There were not many people at
this hour, mostly foot passengers, day-trippers, cheap booze punters. One couple were obviously off for a dirty weekend, and they
had been snuggling up to each other the whole trip. Julian was
travelling light, but not so light as to attract suspicion. He had his
guitar in its case, and a small parachute-silk bag which could con-
tain enough for a week or a day. Julian tried to calm himself as the
train came to a halt. He repeated like a mantra: don't panic, don't
panic. He would be so polite to the old lady. He always got on with
old ladies anyway. He opened the door, and jumped down, then
turned to see if the lady needed help. That way he could keep his
back to the police. And yes, she needed help. If Julian had been
Greek he would have promised a whole bull to the Gods; he sent
up a silent prayer.

"Can I help you with your bags?" he asked.

"Oh, that is so kind, really. I don't know what I would have
done otherwise".

Julian took the two bags from her and then offered her his hand.

"Thank you so much, so kind of you" she was saying.

Once she was safely down on the platform Julian slung his bag
across his shoulders and took one of her bags in his free left hand.
The guitar was in the right.

"So kind of you, especially as you have all that to carry yourself" she said.

"No problem, really" Julian said. His heart was beating
faster now, as they came close to the barrier. He kept his
head turned to the old lady. Conversation, conversation,
come on Julian. Think of something.

"My son plays the guitar. It is a guitar you have there, isn't it?" she asked.

Julian thanked the Gods once more.

"Yes, it is. I'm not very good at it yet, but have been taking some lessons".

Twenty yards to the barrier. Think of something else. Talk, talk, you idiot.

"Is your son a professional?"

"No, not anything like that" she said.

Ten yards.

"Does he want to be?" Julian asked.

Five yards. Julian could see the policemen out of the corner of his eye. No eye-contact ever, advised Hugo. Walk slowly, no odd movements. They arrived at the barrier.

"I'll just find my ticket" he said.

"Oh yes, I'll get mine out too".

They must have seemed an odd couple, but not odd enough to be suspicious. Julian hoped his hand would not shake as he handed in his ticket. It shook, but was not noticeable. The old lady handed hers in too, and they passed through as if they were mother and son.

"Thank you so much", she said. "I really don't know what I would have done without you".

"No, thank you, you have no idea" replied Julian. "Do you need any more help?"

"Oh, I'll just get a taxi from here, I think. Thank you so much"

Julian watched her get into the taxi and wave. He would never forget her face. But he hoped she would forget his.

⚍ ⚎

That first ordeal over, Julian headed for the garage Hugo had suggested. It was by a big roundabout where the lorries turned either for the port or out of Dover to the motorway. He suddenly felt a sharp pang of hunger and saw the Dover Cafè to his right. He'd have a full English breakfast as his last meal in the UK. The paint on the woodwork outside the cafè was cracking slightly, probably due to the constant battering it got during the winter months. The run-down effect made it seem more homely. Julian could not see that much through the windows as they were steamed up, but he took a chance.

He walked in, and the little bell on the door tinkled. There were quite a few locals, it seemed, but no truckers. It was off the main route. No matter. No one turned round and studied the newcomer. The flow of people into Dover made him just one of many, and his clothes also did not attract attention.

The leather jacket hid the gaudy colours of the kaftan. He was just one passing through. Only the guitar might have caught the eye, but everyone there was minding their own business and had their heads down into their plates. Julian sat at a window table which looked out onto the road. It was bright now, and although windy, the rain had stopped. It was weather he liked, the sort of weather only a Brit could appreciate: the air freshened and cleaned by the rain, the wind, the smell of salt, the cries of the seagulls, and channel in front of them. Another unwanted sniffle in the nose came. Damn! Why do I have to lose all this? he said under his breath. Just then the young waitress came:

"Can I take your order?"

"An English breakfast, but without the fried bread and to-matoes, please". Julian had had enough of those things at school.

She noticed the guitar.

"Are you a musician, or something?"

"I play the guitar. Badly. I'm just learning, really".

"Oh, that's nice. My boyfriend, he's learning too" she said.

"Good luck to him".

"Yeah, he says it's really hard on the fingers at first".

"Yes, it is".

She smiled and walked off. Julian thought about that exchange. If someone asked about him later, what would she remember? The guitar, perhaps. His appearance? Tall, beard, leather jacket. Not a lot to go on. From hymns and cricket to paranoia about someone being able to give a description.

The waitress brought the food. It was a hundred times better than a usual College breakfast; and the hunger and the sense of urgency helped. He finished it down to the last baked bean, then paid and was out.

Now the second phase. He would need his ticket first. He walked along the sea front to a booking office which was offering last minutes deals. He went in, the warm food and the success of getting through the ticket barrier at the station had emboldened him. He was relaxing into his role.

The ticket for a foot passenger was £5 return. Next sailing 10.45. When was he coming back? Julian stumbled, then remembered Hugo's teachings: never a single trip. Return.

"In a week. Next Sunday" he replied confidently.

The clerk wrote in the date. It was early and he did not seem to care much who came or went.

Thank God for Sundays. Hugo was right. The clerk was probably hung-over and resentful that he had to do the Sunday shift. What did he care if Julian came back in 5 years' time?

Now the garage. This was going to be hard. It would mean his newly-acquired patois French would have to kick in. He checked his cigarettes. Five packets of Marlborough at the top of his bag for easy access. He walked slowly along the sea front, the wind in his hair and pushing the guitar case against him. An odd, lone figure if anyone had bothered to notice, but no one was out and about at this time. He started practicing his chat-up lines: *Bonjour, est-que l'un di vous va sur Paris?*

Outside the garage in a lay-by he noticed some lorries parked, with curtains drawn, the drivers obviously getting their obligatory kip before going off to Aberdeen or wherever. But some were up and about, chatting, smoking. Julian checked their number-plates. Again, Hugo's teaching: French ones are black on white with the two letters in the middle. Those two tell you which region it comes from. You do not need to know the exact region, but offering cigarettes to Polish drivers is a waste of time and tobacco.

He walked slowly to the group of three drivers who were beside their lorries and chatting. As he got closer he noticed two of the number-plates were French. He might be in luck. He got close, put his bag and guitar down, and took out a packet of cigarettes. Then he walked slowly to the group, and offered them one. They all took one, a good sign. Then Julian put one in his mouth and they offered him a light.

(Goodday. Is anyone going near Paris?)

The first drag seared his throat, but he managed to stifle a cough.

"*Ca va?*"

"*Oui, ca va*".

"*Est-ce que l'un de vous va sur Paris?*"

The drivers looked at each other.

"*Peut-etre*".

It was not going to be a walk-over. Julian supposed afterwards that these sort of proposals were a common thing, and could get them into a lot of trouble if they went wrong. Losing a licence, suspensions. It was a risk. He tried to be casual.

"*J'ai besoin d'aller aussi pres de Paris que possible, ou allors d'aller dans une ville qui a des trains pour la capital*"..

"*J' peux pas, je vais sur l' Allemagne. Et toi, Jean?*"

The other of the two French drivers looked Julian up and down.

"*Je vais jusqu'a Reims. Je peux vous deposer la-bas si vous voulez, mais pas plus loin*".

Julian tried not to show too much joy.

"Ah, super".

(How's it going? Yes, fine. Is anyone going near Paris? Perhaps. I need to go near to Paris or a town which has trains to the capital. I can't, I'm going to Germany. You, Jean? I'm going to Rheims. I can drop you off there if you want, but not any further. Ah, great.)

"Vous avez votre ticket?"

"Oui". Julian scrabbled a little too fast for his ticket. Slow, slow it down. He pulled out the ferry ticket.

"Pour la prochaine traversée?"

"Oui"..

"D'accord"..

Julian handed the rest of the packet to Jean. There was laughter between the men. They finished their cigarettes and Jean made a sign for Julian to climb into the cab. And it really was another thing up there, high up, commanding a view. It made him think of getting a licence himself one day. A wonderful sense of power, and when Jean turned the Renault engine on and swung the thing out onto the road, Julian could barely suppress a roar of simple delight. Then Jean pulled the cord above him to create a massive klaxon hoot as if they were cowboys herding on a ranch. He turned to Julian to see his reaction. He had a stupid boyish smile on his face.

"Ca va?"

"Shit! *Oui! ca va*".

The whole cabin shook with the noise, enough to break your ear-drums. If I ever get out of this hole, this is what I'll do, he thought. What a way to earn a living! The only trouble was talking. The noise of the engine was such that nothing less than a shout could be heard, and even then you had to repeat it. The port was close and they were soon in the queue. Julian did not know if there was the usual police activity. Jean did not seem to notice anything strange. He got his passport ready and Julian handed over his, but Jean noticed his hand was trembling slightly, and

(You got your ticket? Yes. For the next crossing? Yes. OK.)

his knee began to shake too.

Julian immediately put his hand on his knee, and held it there. The trembling stopped but he knew at that moment that Jean had understood something was not right. He was not the usual hippy strummer out for kicks. He looked at the passport.

"Etes-vous Francais?"

"Mon père l'etait. Ma mère est italienne".

"Et vous parlez anglais? Votre accent ne semble ni l'un ni l'autre!"

"J'habite longtemps en Angleterre".

"Avec un passeport francais".

"C'est juste".

Jean looked at his passenger hard. He must have decided that he was not dangerous, and perhaps needed a break.

"Ouvre ta guitare".

"Quoi?"

"Ouvre ta guitare. Tu m'as entendu. J'veux pas de drogues. S'il y a de la drogue, tu sors du camion".

"Il n'y a pas de drogues

(Are you French? My father was. My mother was Italian. And you speak English? Your accent does not seem one or the other. I spent a long time in England. With a French passport? That's right. Open your guitar. What? Open your guitar. You heard me. I don't want any drugs. If there are drugs you get out of the truck)

Julian took the case and opened it. The guitar looked innocent enough. Jean touched the cloth inside roughly, searching for bumps, lumps, something other than the lining. Then he shook the guitar. There was nothing there. He seemed satisfied, but uncertain. Things did not tie up.

"*OK, tu peux rester. Mais je te préviens, tu descends a Rheims*".

"*D'accord*".

Then it was their turn. The customs police asked for their documents. They opened them, looked at the photos.

"*Votre passager?*"

"*Mon cousin*".

Julian realised that was a large step. A passenger might be anyone; he was vouchsafing for his cousin. Julian would buy him a whole bloody boatload of cigarettes. And then they were through and away. Hugo's photo was good enough. The beard, moustache and clothes had done it.

They drove in silence for a bit. Then Julian said quietly:

"*Merci*".

Jean did not reply, but shrugged. He was waved into the hold of the ferry, and he manoeuvred into the space, set the handbrake firmly, turned off the engine and they both climbed down. Jean was still silent. They went up the stairs to where the *routiers* had their own special space. Julian said he needed to take some air, and left Jean to himself and his other driver mates.

(OK, you can stay. But I warn you, you have to get out at Rheims. OK. Your passenger? My cousin. Thanks).

He went up the stairs and found a shop and bought a carton of Marlborough. That would be to say thank you for the '*mon cousin*' episode. He then exchanged some of his money into French francs, enough to get him to Paris, a meal, and a very cheap hotel room. He loved the crisp beautifully-made French notes, the very quality of the paper made them a joy to touch. Then he walked to the back of the ferry. It was moving off slowly already. The sun was out now and the water was strangely blue with the white foam being stirred up by the propellers.

Other passengers were at the stern as well, but not one, thought Julian, had a heart so close to breaking point as his. The white cliffs were there, as they should be, but as they receded slowly into the distance they seemed to have a strange green moss on them. After 20 minutes they seemed hardly more than an inch high, and Julian was reminded of a picture he had seen once of an Irish couple setting off for America in a rowing boat, both faces strangely impassive, although you could read the despair and suffering they had gone through to reach that point—famine, hopelessness on one shore, a very uncertain promise of a future on the other. She wore a headscarf, her face still young and pretty; he had the burning eyes of someone who both loved and hated his home country. Julian looked into the wake; his life was unravelling behind him.

In the middle of the channel another ferry passed them going back to England. He could see their faces and some waved. Julian was gripped by an absurd desire to jump ship and swim to the other boat. He went to the prow to try and discern what he could see of the French shoreline. The day was clear, the sea calm, and France was bare and flat, and green. He could make out little white square shapes which turned into squat houses as the ferry got closer. Two little sailing boats were near the shore. It was the sort of scene an impressionist would have loved. Closer in Julian saw well-kept, orderly farmland either side of the port. And instead of the cliffs there were long sandy beaches, the sort of beach that was at Dunkirk, he imagined. Soldiers pinned down there, no hiding place, no shelter except for the lines of dark wooden breakwaters.

And quite discernable now on either side of the port were little spires of the Normandy churches, and the tall grain silos and factory buildings with white plumes of smoke rising high into the sky.

The ferry was almost into the port. Calais was also used as docks, and there were large, dull brown cranes on either side of the entrance. Gay little French flags could be seen here and there.

He liked the touch of national pride. This is us, look! Quite different already! He heard the announcement for passengers to return to the vehicles, and so he made his way down to the lower deck to find Jean. Jean was already in his cabin, staring ahead, bored, waiting to get off, probably not caring much if his passenger ever turned up. But he seemed more affable to Julian as he climbed in. A meal and a rest had helped. They both heard the shudder of the engines reversing and then the stillness as it moored.

"*Ca va?*".

"*Ca va. Tiens, c'est pour toi*".

Julian handed over the carton of Marlborough. Jean shrugged, and smiled.

"*Merci*".

"Non, merci a toi".

Nothing more was said about the crossing or passports. Jean swung the Renault onto the road, seemingly more relaxed and surer about what he was doing. He turned on the radio and got a mixture of news and weather reports interspersed with the ubiquitous accordion.

"Tu peux me passer une cigarette?"

"Sur".

Julian broke open the carton and took out a packet, opened it and offered it to Jean, who took one and lit up, drawing the smoke deep into his lungs. He was inclined to talk now.

"Alors, ou est.ce que tu vas?".

"Rhiems, Paris".

"Et puis?".

Julian thought about lying, and then decided not to. He had bullshitted this guy enough.

"Pres, je vais aller travailler dans un kibboutz en Israel".

"C'est quoi?"

"Un genre de ferme".

"Pourquoi?".

"Ca me semble une bonne idee".

"Alors, qu'est-ce qu'il y a avec le passeport e le main qui tremble?".

"C'est perso".

"C'est perso?".

"Oui".

(So, where are you going? Rheims, Paris. And then? Then I'm going to a kibbutz in Israel. What's that? A sort of farm. Why? It seems a good idea. So, what is it with the passport and your hand trembling? It's nothing. Nothing? Yes, nothing).

And the conversation ceased. The countryside outside Calais was marshy, full of dykes and ponds. From time to time there were indications of some historical even which had happened at this or that spot: The Field of the Cloth of Gold. Julian remembered some absurd incident of the English and French aristocracy trying to outdo each other by the quantity of jewellery and gold they had woven into their capes. Early Anglo-French relations, and better than blowing each others' balls off in a battlefield, he supposed. They had done that before.
After about an hour Julian saw indications for Rheims, and knew he would be on his own again.

Well, it had been a break, he had got through. Jean indicated the exit, and, as a last touch of generosity, took Julian into a suburb where he could get a bus to the station.

"J'peux pas aller plus lion, ca me fairait faire un trop grand detour e je perdrais trop de temps".

"Tu as été tres sympa".

"Bonne chance".

"Bonne chance". Julian threw the bag out first, then clambered down with the guitar.

"Au revoir".

"Au revoir", although Julian thought this was extremely

unlikely. He waved as Jean headed off once more, and got a wave back. He would remember Julian for about as long as he smoked the cigarettes, perhaps.

(I can't go any further, it will take me out of my way and I'll waste time. You have already been so kind. Good luck. Good luck. Good-bye. Good-bye).

CHAPTER 6

STAINS

Pendelbury drew up outside the coroner's office in Watford. He had been sent the report the day before, and wanted to go over one or two details, some anomalies of the case. He parked the Jaguar in the car park outside the office, put his pipe and tobacco in the right pocket of his jacket, picked up the report from the passenger seat, walked to the door and rang the bell. The coroner, Mark Triefus, came to the door. All very formal, jacket and tie, mid-forties, black hair smoothed back from his forehead. A dark complexion with very white teeth. The men had known each other for many years, and had dealt with many deaths: the gruesome car accidents with limbs missing, the domestic violence, the suicides.

"Good day to you, John".

"Good day to you too".

"Come on in. You know the way by now".

"I do".

They went into the front office. The report was on a folder on the zinc table.

"You have had a read, I presume?" asked Triefus

"I have".

Pendelbury started taking out the pipe and tobacco.

"Do you mind?" he said.

"Have I ever objected?

Pendelbury started to fill the bowl. The smell of fresh tobacco entered the air.

"How does it seem to you, this Harold Darke case?"

"Pretty straightforward, actually". Triefus opened the red folder. "A fall, probably pushed. Wound to the head with severe loss of blood. Injury to the second and third vertebrae. The fire knob was probably the murder weapon, as it were".

"Nothing else?" asked Pendelbury.

"The stains?"

"Yes, the stains" said Pendelbury.

Pendelbury had the pipe bowl full by now and searched for his matches. Triefus shrugged.

"It can happen, you know. Semen. Involuntary spasms in the death-throes".

"Semen, not urine. Under these circumstances?" There was incredulity in Pendelbury's voice.

Treifus hesitated, scratched his neck, turned his gaze to the window.

"Unlikely". But added quickly: "Although it can happen, you know?" he said.

"It can?"

"Oh yes",

Pendelbury struck a match and slowly brought the tobacco alight.

"Which circumstances?"

"Hanging, for example".

Pendelbury took the pipe out of his mouth.

"You have witnessed this personally?" asked Pendelbury.

"Not personally. But it is a known fact. Policemen working in Africa have actually witnessed it. They did a lot of hanging there, as you may know. After the riots, and all that Mau-Mau stuff. It's in the text books as well, if you care to look".

"Or? Nothing else?" Pendelbury was not going to let it go. Another puff.

"Or.......?"

Here Triefus looked at Pendelbury hard, then turned his gaze back to the window.

"Or the man was sexually aroused when he died" conceded Triefus.

"And what do you think?"

Triefus looked down at the report, then up again at Pendelbury's blue eyes.

"I don't know".

"But if you had to give evidence?" insisted Pendelbury. "And you will have to".

"If I was in the box, you mean, in front of twelve just men?"

"The same".

Triefus rubbed his chin; there was a sound of scratching on the bristle.

"I'd say….. he was sexually aroused at the time of death. Yes".

"Strange".

"Strange indeed" said Pendelbury.

Pendelbury drew on the pipe.

"A drink?"

"A small one".

Triefus opened the bottom right hand drawer, took out a bottle of Famous Grouse and two small glasses, and filled them.

"Your good health".

"And yours".

They drank. A calm pervaded the room.

"So, John, how does it seem to you?"

"The whisky? Just the same!".

They men laughed. Both of them had witnessed enough blood and guts in the past to warrant drinks.

Pendelbury puffed, Triefus drank some more. Tiefus broke the silence.

"Well, it is one or the other. He tripped, or was pushed, and fell, hitting his head, and…"

"Or…..?" suggested Pendelbury.

"Or he was sexually aroused, his assailant saw him, rebelled, and they fought. He then fell and hit his head. Have you caught anyone yet?"

"There is a young man we have our eyes on. But he seems to have slipped through our net. Surprising for one so young. He may have been helped, of course. Quite who we do not know yet".

Pendelbury dragged hard on his pipe. More smoke, another sip.

"Difficult thing to prove, I would have thought", said Treifus. "And pretty nasty stuff to come out for his family".

"Quite".

"Those schools attract some strange folk" he added.

"It seems they do indeed".

"Well, I'd better be getting on", Triefus added. "And the funeral?"

"Tomorrow. The body is at the Funeral Directors. Whites".

"They'll do a good job, I expect" said Triefus.

"They are as reliable as any".

The two men got up, finished their drinks and Pendelbury made for the door.

"Well, I suppose we'll meet again soon enough" said Pendelbury.

"Unfortunately under these circumstances" said Triefus.

"I'll be going to the funeral"

"Oh, why is that?" asked Triefus.

"Just a hunch. It is a murder enquiry, after all".

Pendelbury went to his car, the smell of the cracked leather seats coming to him as he opened the door. He put the report on the passenger's seat, started the engine and waved to the coroner as he drove out and away.

CHAPTER 7

FAMILY

The journey to the vicarage started in mist. By the time Pendelbury and Hatton had got past London and towards Guildford there was bright sunshine and the air was crisp. It put them both in a good mood. Pendelbury had brought with him a new tin of Sobranie mixture, and as he opened the new tin the aroma came to him mixed with the leather of the seats and the vague smell of petrol. Black Sobranie. It was a heavy smoke, the tobacco in shards which you had to finger and break into smaller pieces. Just the smell of the stuff and Pendelbury thought of Istanbul, of veiled women, of men with rifles on their shoulders and long moustaches, of donkeys carrying the harvested, dried weed to the market, the wide leaves one on top of the other and then folded. He picked out some of the tobacco, rubbed it in the fingers of his right hand and then started packing it into the pipe bowl. Then a bit more. It was a delicate balance between packing too much in too tightly and not having enough in the bowl for the tobacco to light up and keep on burning for a fair bit. The Sobranie mix was almost wet to the touch, so moist you thought it would never light up, and the aroma was so good you were tempted to eat it. Pendelbury felt for his matches

They were coming to countryside John Pendelbury knew well. Past Haslemere, along the narrow roads towards Midhurst. There were several pheasants dead along the side of the road. A lot of shooting went on around here. Pendelbury as a boy had been a beater on some of the shoots and there was a bit of pocket money and a brace of pheasants as reward. It was fun for a boy to be out with the guns and the dogs and the men. After the war he had gone off guns. The artillery had shown him the carnage they could inflict. He broke the silence.

"Good pub there. The Greyhound".

"How's that, Sir?"

"I said: a good pub that, The Greyhound". Pendelbury pointed out the window.

"How would you know Sir? Are you from around here, or something".

"I grew up near Midhurst. Father was a carpenter".

"So you know the area pretty well".

"Pretty well. Haven't been back for a while. There must be some changes. Lots of building, for sure".

They carried on for a few miles and the saw the turning to Heyshott. Down through some country lanes, over a small bridge, and then into the flat plain of the village under the downs. The vicarage was the first house on the left, a tall, impressive building with two gables. They drove up the gravel drive to the front door. Both men got out and Hatton rang the bell. They were met by the vicar, a small man, slight of build with a beak of a nose, bald and with horn-rimmed glasses.

Pendelbury introduced themselves: "Detective Pendelbury and Sergeant Hatton".
"Please come in. Through here into the sitting room".

They took off their coats and left them in the hall and came and sat down on the sofa. There was a baby grand piano on the off-white carpet and long bright curtains. Enough elegance to greet the parishioners who might come. The vicar's wife came and offered them something to drink.

"Tea would be fine for us both, I think. You, Hatton?"

"Fine for me Mrs………."

Shortly after she came back with the tea and sat close to her husband.

"You know why we are here?" asked Pendelbury.

Mrs Bates had a handkerchief in her sleeve pocket and brought it to her eyes. The vicar was of sterner stuff.

"What makes you think Julian did this thing?" the vicar asked.

"He was the only boy not back that evening. He was…..being punished, let us say….for something he had done. There was a struggle. There are fingerprints. He left the scene of the crime. We would just like him to help us with our enquiries". Mrs Bates sniffled once more into her handkerchief.

"Well, we will help you as much as we can", said the vicar.

"Do you know where he is?" asked Pendelbury bluntly.

"We have no idea".

"No phone call, nothing to anyone in the family?"

"Nothing that we know of," said the vicar.

Pendelbury sat and watched them. He believed them.

"And you would tell us if he does try to get in touch?"

"You have our word on it, Detective".

Pendelbury got out his little note-book and a pen from his jacket pocket.

"If Julian has done this thing" said Pendelbury, "and he does get in touch, then you must try and convince him that it is best that he gives himself up. For the moment we only want to put a few questions to him".

Both the parents nodded.

"But if he is not here", Pendelbury continued, "and he has not phoned, do you have any idea where he might be? A friend, a relation?".

The vicar and his wife looked at each other.

"His friends were at school, really", offered Mrs Bates.

"No one close?" asked Pendelbury.

Again the vicar and his wife looked at each other to confirm their statement.

"No friend from the past?" asked Pendelbury.

The vicar then turned to his wife.

"Do you have any idea? What about that friend from the sixth form, Steven, Simon…..

His wife looked uncomfortable.

"I really can't remember very well", she said. "He has left now, of course. I am not sure Julian even sees him. Or ever really.........if they were close friends, as it were.............." Her voice trailed off.

Pendelbury sat with his pen raised, waiting for the last name.

"Are you sure you can't remember it, Mrs Bates?"

"I really, Inspector, really, it was something like Simon Pro, Pra, I really..................."

"You really must tell them, dear" insisted the vicar. "If Julian is blameworthy then we must help the police. That is your Christian duty". In a very soft voice, the mother whispered:

"I think Simon's last name was Parker".

Pendelbury wrote the name down.

"Any idea where they lived, his family?"

"Kent, I believe" she said in a whisper, and added "The school will know, I'm sure".

"Kent. A Simon Parker". Pendelbury wrote this down in his notebook.

Mrs Bates nodded, then sniffed into her handkerchief.

"If it is alright by you, ... and if there is nothing else, I'd like to go now" she said.

"Of course". Both policemen stood up, as did the vicar.

After she had left the room, Pendelbury turned to Hatton.

"Have you checked the tyre pressures recently?" he asked Hatton.

"It was done at the station yesterday, Inspector".

"I think they need checking again" insisted Pendelbury. His voice was strangely hard.

Hatton looked at him. Pendelbury stared hard and added:

"Just the tyres, Hatton".

"Yes Sir".

The vicar and the inspector were left together. Spring sun was coming through the window. The vicar looked frail and tired as he sat alone. Then in a little voice, almost to himself:

"I find it so hard to believe all this".

"Had you been having problems with him?" asked Pendelbury.

"We'd had a report and a letter from a music master saying that he was behaving badly. I told them to act as they thought fit. They boy has to learn".

"May I see the letter?"

"Certainly". After a few minutes in his study, the vicar brought the letter and gave it to Pendelbury. He read it in growing disbelief.

"So you went along with this music master Sawbridge and his opinion?"

"The boy has to learn".

"Don't you think you might have been a bit harsh?" ventured Pendelbury.

"In my day, we were taught that if a head came over the wall, hammer it, hammer it hard" said the vicar.

"Well, they certainly did that". Pendelbury handed the letter back to the vicar.

"And talking of your day, Reverend, you were at the same school, I believe".

The vicar altered his position in the chair.

"That's correct".

"Was there ever an incident when you were beaten, and in public?"

The vicar stared at the inspector then looked down at the ground.

"Reverend?"

"I was punished for playing the organ" he said in a faint voice, surprised that the policeman had heard the story.

"Why exactly?"

"I was college organist and I played a variation of a popular tune. I was punished".

"In front of the whole school?"

"Yes". There was a long pause before Pendelbury spoke.

"I see. They beat you?".

"Yes".

Pendelbury did not want to hear any more, and the memory was obviously painful to this frail man. He did not want to inflict further distress. Pendelbury got up.

"I'll be going now". Pendelbury got up and the vicar rose as well, opening the door. Pendelbury took his hat and coat and walked to the front door and the waiting Jaguar in the drive.

"If Julian does try and get in touch, you will contact us, won't you?"

"Of course" said the vicar.

They shook hands outside the porch and The Reverend Bates watched the Inspector and Hatton get in the car and drive off.

"Any luck, Inspector?"

"Poor blighters. Both of them" was all he said for the remainder of the journey back.

CHAPTER 8

KIBBUTZ

Tel Aviv was another thing altogether. Whereas Paris was European, and they spoke a language he had studied, however badly and academically, and the buildings were these great blocks of monuments, and the people dressed in fashionable but normal clothes, this place, Israel, was quite, quite different. It hit you the moment you got into the airport. It was late evening when they touched down. Getting into France had been the great test; now passport control did not frighten him so much. On the card they gave him under 'reason for visit' he wrote: work on kibbutz. It dawned on him that possibly everyone else on the plane was Jewish and they were either returning to the homeland or about to start a new life there. *Next year in Jerusalem.* He could be a British Jew visiting Jerusalem for all they knew, a Zionist caught up in the struggle. Half the seats were taken up by what he thought were rabbis, but later found out were just Hassidic Jews. The hats, the beards, the glasses (why the steel rim glasses they all wore?), the long black coats, the puffy white faces, the strange aplomb of the convinced, the righteous. And they were going home. The plane wheeled round in the sky, they all started nodding and praying for their safe return, muttering under their breath. It was their show, their land. And he hoped their prayers secured their safe landing.

It was his first flight, and the wings wagging and the deep turns made him feel slightly sick.

In the airport itself the impact was of a country at war: men with machine guns and combat fatigues everywhere, with hard, closed, attentive dark faces. The airport was a rudimentary military set-up rather than a civilian one. There were women also dressed in army-fatigues, small, intense, dark and pretty, guns on their hips. It made Julian feel both frightened and protected. There were large family groups waiting to greet their relatives, no one formal, all with open shirts, garish colours. And then the groups of Hassidic Jews, their boys just miniature men, with their hanging, sideburn locks and the shaven heads and caps. Shouts of joy, names screamed: Eliiii……. !! Haiaa……!! and the language: guttural, harsh, barked. Julian made his way through the running children and the pushing and shoving to the exit.

The instructions from Hugo were to take a taxi to the bus station and then find the bus going near the kibbutz. He had changed his money at the airport and got in return a mixture of crumpled much-used paper money and the light base-metal coins. It gave the impression of being impermanent, new, a border country.

Outside it was already dark. There was a line of taxis waiting, many with drivers dressed in the long whitish robes and the head-gear. The air was warm and scented. Insects were humming, and street stalls were cooking kebabs and falafel. It was to become a staple food for Julian in the next months.

He walked to the front taxi and asked for the station. The driver got out, put his one bag and guitar in the boot and got back in. Julian took his place in the back and waited. And waited.

"Excuse me, why are we not moving?

"We wait.

"We wait for what?

"We wait other passengers". The driver looked into his mirror at Julian. He rubbed his two fingers together.

"Cheaper".

This was novel for Julian. But cheaper was acceptable and he was not in a rush. And soon the taxi was full, front and back seats, with another two women and two children and a single male in the front. And as they hurtled through the streets from time to time, the taxi would stop and let someone off, and another would get in. Fuel-efficient and economical. They got to the station and the driver got out and opened the boot.

"Ten".

Julian paid. It might have been a lot or nothing. He hadn't worked out the exchange rate or taxi fares. It was strangely liberating, after his culture where paying an extra sixpence, buying a platform ticket was something that had to be debated and anguished over.

The bus station was just an open depot of a series of fading, blue Scania buses with white tops. The engines stuck out like snouts. Julian went to the shack which served as the ticket office. Three men were talking, lounging there, feet up, eating sunflower seeds and spitting the kernel out onto the floor in front of them. Open shirts, hairy chests, sunburnt faces, amulets around their necks, once more the guttural shouts, the radio with the whining, bending women's voices singing Arab songs in quarter-tones. It would follow Julian wherever he went in this country.

"Kfar Menachem. Please".

Julian read the name from a piece of paper Hugo had given him. It was in Hebrew and English. One of the men reached up without a by-your-leave, took the paper, read it, scowled, said something to the man next to him, and handed it back.

"Number 7. Twenty". Julian handed over the money and took the ticket.

"There". The man indicated to his right. "There. 10 minutes. Number 7. Ask driver Kfar Menachem".

Julian nodded, and said thank you. His thank you was not acknowledged. They went back to the sunflower seeds. It was direct, at least, and fast. The common courtesies were dispensed with. Later Julian was to realise that it was their way of doing things. A country at war, urgent, determined to survive, and also you were a bird of passage and possibly not a Jew. It was the famous Sabra, the prickly-pear description of the Israelis. They were spiky on the outside, and then sweet on the inside, or so they said.

After an hour in the bus the bus driver stopped and turned, looked at Julian and shouted: Kfar Menachem. Julian had arrived. It was 10 in the evening and pitch black. He got off the bus with his one bag. The driver pointed in the direction he should go, down a dusty dirt road, and then the doors closed and the bus was off. There were no street-lights, so the stars were extraordinary. He had never seen this display, truly the firmament. And then the cicadas humming away incessantly. Julian picked up his one bag and guitar began a lonely walk along the road to the lights half a mile away. There were no signposts, just a few houses at the end of the road. That was it.

"Jesus!" he said aloud. Where was he going? Did he have an alternative? No.

His contact was Thin Benny. He thought back to the days in the flat with Hugo, not more than seven days ago, but seeming an eternity.

"Thin Benny? You must be joking. I can't just go into another country and go up to someone and ask for Thin Benny!"

"Trust me", Hugo had said. "This is what you must do. You go there and ask and they will tell you where he is living. Last time he was practically in a tree house, it was up a flight of stairs and close to this eucalyptus tree. Nice perfume in the morning when you got up. Made me feel like Tarzan".

Tarzan. Thin Benny? He laughed out loud, and he hadn't done that for a bit. He was on a journey all right, and the hot breath of the police seemed more distant. As he got closer he heard the roosters crowing. Didn't they go to sleep or something at night? Apparently not here. And he was to learn other things about Israel's natural life: the flies which bit and left a bleeding mark; of the baby tortoises which just waddled out of the scrub; of the humming birds and chameleons; and of the snakes and scorpions. A tad different from Deptford. Or boarding school.

The kibbutz was still awake. This was another thing Julian was to learn. They did not sleep much. Some of the kibbutzniks snoozed for an hour or so in a hammock in the early hours of the morning, but that was enough. When asked, they said their army training had upset all sleep rhythms. Sometimes they were forced to stay awake for 100 hours, only to sleep two, and then they were off again on a march. The training was considered to be one of the hardest ever, and the army was thought to be the toughest and best in the world. Every man was taught to kill with his bare hands and they were capable of eating anything, snakes, rats, you name it. Every young *sabra* had to undergo 18 months of hell, with possibly some fighting and killing thrown in. Tough, young men, not your bookish intellectual. And there was no doubt in their minds. Julian was never to meet any anti-war dissenters. It was kill and stay alive in this scrap of a country, or be killed and be wiped off the map forever. The Holocaust was still fresh in their minds, with survivors from the camps on the farm, as Julian was to find out. He was to see tattooed arms and stick insect bodies, frail and seeming never to recover.

By now he had reached some lights in a one-story house. It was obviously a private dwelling. He entered further into a compound. Some dogs started barking in the distance. They were still 'at war', but no one had shouted 'Halt' or taken a shot at him. He ventured further in. More lights, a bigger complex, and a sort of square. Some music was playing, the same whining sound of a woman in distress. Some young people were standing around a kiosk which was offering drinks. This was their open disco. Julian walked slowly to them. He was now observed. No guns were pulled out, but he was a stranger walking into their territory, their world. He did not feel threatened, but he realised he had better not make any fast moves. Then two men, smaller than himself, very muscular and wide came up to him.

"Shalom" said Julian.

"Shalom" they replied.

"Do you speak English?"

"We speak English". Their hard stares did not give anything away.

Julian put down his bag and guitar case and pulled out his piece of paper with the address and name written.

"A friend, Hugo, gave this to me. Hugo? He worked here once. I'm looking for Thin Benny".

They took the piece of paper and read it, gave it back.

"Hugo? French Hugo?"

"Yes, French Hugo".

"We remember him".

They conferred in Hebrew for moment.

"Why you want Thin Benny?" they asked.

Julian lapsed into almost childish English:

"Benny is Hugo's friend. I want to stay here for a bit, work here. Like Hugo. Worked" he added.

No free rides here, he thought. Better make it clear.

They moved away to confer, called another man, an elder who seemed to have some say in matters. More talking in Hebrew. The elder, bald, about sixty-five came up. In slow but correct English, as if he were translating, he said:

"Give me your passport" he said, all the time staring at Julian.

Julian searched for his old English one. He got out the dark-blue British passport with his name in blue ink on the front. If they accepted him, he was Julian again, a Brit. Enough of the play-acting. A relief. More conferring. A younger man with a crazy Afro haircut came up. He was tall and very thin. More studying, staring, as if he were in front of a tribe. No hands were held out. Then another nik came up, one they seemed to rate very highly. The passport was handed to him, and he studied it, looking at Julian from time to time, checking the photo. Words were exchanged, voices raised. He handed it back to the elder, there was more discussion and arguing in Hebrew, and he finally gave it back to Julian.

"This is Thin Benny". He pointed to the tall, thin, young man with an Afro.

"Hi".

"Hi". This time a hand was offered. "You a friend of Hugo?"

"Yes, I was staying with him a week ago". Benny looked at the case.

"You play guitar?"

"Yes, a bit", said Julian.

"Good. I play too".

Julian got a smile this time. Some women came to observe the stranger. Kids were running and shouting behind the houses, some on bikes. The elder, Schlomo, then spoke:

"You are a friend of Hugo, and I hope a friend of Israel. Are you a Jew?"

"No, I'm not. Is that a problem?" asked Julian.

"No, it is no problem. It is enough that you are a friend of Israel. You can stay with Benny for first few days".

Thin Benny shrugged. It did not seem to worry him.

"But you must work. Everyone here works every day. Hard. Every day. Do you understand?" asked Schlomo.

"I understand. I work. I'm strong. I can do anything".

"Good. We need strong arms and legs here on Kfar Menachem. And if we like you and you work hard, then perhaps you stay".

And he held out his hand. Julian shook it. He had passed the first test.

The tree house was really just a two-story house built close to a eucalyptus tree which had then grown to gigantic proportions over the 30 years that the kibbutz had been in existence. There were stairs outside the house taking you to the top floor, so it really did seem a tree house. A fun place. Julian followed Benny up the stairs. Benny did not seem to be too worried that he had a visitor, and after a few weeks Julian was to see why: there was a constant flux of new people passing through, volunteers from all over the world coming to have the 'kibbutz experience'. Some were Jewish. It suited the elders as they needed cheap labour for the fields during planting and harvest, and both were going on almost continually. There were two rooms and a kitchen area.

"Put your stuff in there".

Julian noticed he had an American accent. Later he was to discover that they all had American accents of some sort if they spoke English. It was the culture to imitate and eventually to escape to if they wanted. And many visitors were New York Jews coming to spend a year in Israel, or had been sent by their parents to offer moral support to the country. Two brothers from some state were draft dodgers from the Viet Nam war. Julian put his bag and guitar down and sat on the simple iron bed.

"You OK here?"

"Yeah, I'm fine".

"So…" and Benny went off to get two beers from the fridge. "How you know Hugo?"

"He's a friend…. of a friend, as it were. I was staying with him recently, in London. Very recently. Two days ago, to be exact".

Benny came back with two beers, and handed one to Julian.

"Hugo. He was something, man! We all remember him here. He was always after the women. Used to hang out by the showers to see them come out. Pissed them off no end. Then" (here Benny started chuckling) "then he got bugs, bugs in his hair, what they called?"

"Lice? Nits?" suggested Julian.

"Yeah, that sort of thing. So he shaved his hair off and that made him seem weird, 'cos here, if you have your head shaved you are a prisoner, you have been in jail. Everyone thought he was a convict of some sort! They avoided him for a bit. Then well, it grew back and he got back amongst them women".

"Sounds like Hugo".

"So, why you come here?"

He gave Julian one bottle and clinked them, saying *L'haim.*

Julian measured his words.

"I came here because Hugo said it was a place to see and an experience not to miss".

What were Hugo's words? Keep it vague. That would do. The reply seemed to satisfy Thin Benny. Julian studied his host a bit closer, now that there was more light. He was extremely thin, with dark skin and regular features. Small, thin moustache. The hair was done in a natural Afro cut. Possibly not much older than Julian.

"How come they call you Thin Benny?" Julian asked.

"Because there is another guy on the Kibbutz called Benny and he is small and fat, so when people want to know which one they are talking about, they began to say Thin Benny and Fat Benny".

Julian shrugged. Simple really.

"So, play me something on the guitar".

"I started only recently. I really don't play much" said Julian.

"Give it to me".

Julian handed over the case and Benny took it out, looked it up and down, and then played a few chords, tuning it slowly and carefully, and then launched into a solo, humming slightly as he followed the tune, then adding the Hebrew words. He was good. Julian felt the beer dissolving the tension and the fears of the last few days. He was in a tree house, with a beer and a guitar player and accepted and no one was asking questions. He was safe.

"Now you".

Shit! thought Julian. Well, he would have to show he could do something.

Julian chose an easy folk song. He took the guitar and started: Fare you well my dear I must be gone / And leave you for a while / If I roam away, I'll come back again / Though I roam ten thousand miles my dear / Though I roam ten thousand miles.

The calluses on his fingers hurt, and he slithered over the chords. But he sang.

Benny listened respectfully.

"Well, for someone who has just started, it isn't bad. You sing OK too".

When they finally went turned in to sleep, Julian was kept awake by the cocks crowing. I'll get used to that, he thought. And he did. After a week he didn't hear them at all.

≈+ +≈

The next day Julian woke early to bright light and a dawn chorus of squawking parrots. It took him some time before he realised where he was. He saw the branches and leaves of the eucalyptus tree outside swaying slightly. He got up and went into the next room to see Benny still fast asleep with his mouth open snoring faintly. Julian went back to bed. He felt strangely safe, protected, remote. He realised that he had been living like a wild animal, watchful, alert, always ready to flee, a bag packed, a lie to tell. The life of a criminal on the run. He turned on to his right side and tried to snooze until he heard Benny get up. It was about 6 when Benny stirred.

"Hey, man, how you doing? You sleep OK?"

"Yes, it was fine. What happens now?"

Benny scratched his chest and yawned.

"Well, we go for breakfast and then find some work for you to do".

"What sort of work?"

"Depends. Nothing too bad. It'll be picking oranges and lemons, or the hen-house or some shit like that".

Oranges and lemons …say the bells of St Clements. Could be a lot worse, thought Julian.

The dining hall was only a hundred yards away. Everything was pretty close and walkable. There were no cars, and as Julian was to find out shortly, there were only a few televisions in houses. There was one large communal television which was placed outside, close to the kiosk where they gave out drinks in the evenings. It was on the politics channel night and day. Perhaps there wasn't another channel. What happened in Parliament, the Knesset, was of vital importance for the survival of this young state. Golda Meir, looking and sounding more masculine than most of the ministers around her, gave her evening broadcast. A call to arms might come at any moment.

The dining hall was quite spacious, with long metal functional tables. The idea of community life was very strong: you ate together, worked together for the survival of Israel. Walking in with Benny no heads turned. He was just another bird of passage. He was just one of many volunteers who drifted in and out of the kibbutz life. Everyone was in work clothes, men and women in blue or brown shorts and open shirts. Some had a sweater on, as the mornings could be cold. And everyone worked, this was true. Men who looked as if they should be drawing their pensions were also in work clothes. And most of the faces were tanned, the skin peeling.

There was a small queue to get coffee or tea and something to eat. But the breakfast was strange…fresh white bread and rolls and then a boiled egg, a tomato, a cucumber, cheese. A gherkin. Julian took a roll and some cheese and a boiled egg and followed Benny to a table. As they sat down Benny grunted something in Hebrew to his fellow niks, and also what Julian took to be an explanation and introduction of this new arrival.

Heads nodded, and a curt 'shalom' was offered in his direction. Julian cracked open his egg and ate it with the fresh roll. So far so good. When they were finished, Benny got up and showed Julian the hatches for the washing up, and then they walked to the front of the canteen where the day's work was posted. It was all in Hebrew, these strange squiggles.

"Oranges" said Benny. "They have decided you are picking oranges today. You missed the first session. It starts early at about 4.30. I'll find out who is in charge".

And Benny then went round the canteen until he found a group of men who seemed to know what was going on. Benny came back.

"Stick in here until you see that guy leave, then follow him. His name is Pinchas. I'm out now. Gotta do some stuff with tractors. Oh, and they have put you in another room with 2 other guys. British. You OK with that?".

"I'm OK with that". Benny saw the disappointment on Julian's face.

"Look, I don't make the decisions around here, and besides, I have a girlfriend, and, you know, we need a bit of privacy from time to time".

"That's fine. I get it. Good for you".

"Anytime. We're friends. No one goes anywhere here. We'll hang out with our guitars, man".

Benny left and Julian sat down again watching the *nik* indicated. He was fairly short, tight, close-cropped hair with his head slightly on one side. Julian found out later that his nickname was 'ten to six' because of the way he held his head. He was also, and this was so hard for Julian to imagine, a war hero. He had been in the front lines in a previous conflict, and had proved himself to be courageous and deadly with a machine gun. 'Ten to six'. Who would have thought it? But then nearly every male in Israel had been through the army training, many had been in the war in '67, and they were on call as reserves all the time. When Pinchas got up, Julian followed him out of the canteen. He walked beside him for a bit, then introduced himself.

"I know who you are" was all he got from Pinchas. Some of the *niks* spoke very good English, and some were good farmers and soldiers. He was a good soldier. They walked on for a few minutes until they came to an open area with a few houses and a small square with a tiled base. A tractor was there pulling a long, wooden trailer which was hitched to the back. Some people were already on the truck waiting. Pinchas indicated with a nod of his head that Julian had to get on it. He started trying to climb up and a hand was held out. He grasped it and was pulled up.

"Thanks"

"No problem" one said. "Hi, I'm Michael Brewer".

"Hi. I'm Julian Bates".

The tractor roared into life and they jolted off to the orange groves.

The group was quite a crew. Young men and women aged between 18 and 40, most dressed in very shabby work clothes, shorts, crumpled shirts, and floppy hats. Some of them had peeling skin on their faces and sunburn on their arms and legs. They all looked strangely dumb, a sort of lassitude and resignation. It wasn't until Julian had done a few 4.30 starts that he realised they were exhausted by the work-rhythm.

The orange groves were a 15-minute drive along dusty, dirt roads. The groves themselves were vast, and the trees had been there for at least 30 years. Lemons and oranges, those 'busy orange trees', as Julian remembered in Herbert's line. 'Busy' because they produced flowers and fruit all the year round, although the early spring was the most productive time, it seemed. They jolted their way along the tracks, and Julian began to inspect his fellow travellers. Next to him, there was Mike. Long dark hair, an open smile with a toothy grin, no guile….he was about to go to Oxford and study History.

And Gillian, she was a social worker from the London taking

a year out. And Peter, Pie to his friends and family, was a fair-haired and rather red-faced, smallish imp of a young man. Then Daniel who was an English Jew doing his year in Israel bit. Blonde Caroline with a square jaw and heavy make-up, and a slightly older woman with blonde plaits who turned out to be a nurse. Further down there was a plumpish Scottish girl, Julie, and then a small dark girl, Anne, who kept herself to herself.

"And you?"

"And me?" Keep it vague, keep it vague, thought Julian.

"I am a friend of someone who worked here for a time. Hugo. You may know him. French".

They all shrugged. Before their time. Better that way. It seemed to satisfy them. Quizzing over. He was harmless and his reason to be there was convincing enough.

The orange picking was really quite simple. Three or four people to a bin, the bin being a large canvas sack tied to four poles. The group had to fill it by noon. There was a break for breakfast, and then the hard slog until mid-day when the sun was hot, and made the work tough. As they approached the groves the smell of blossom was in the air, and when they got close Julian could see the little white flowers in the trees. The new crop of oranges was ready and it was these they were going to harvest.

The tractor stopped and the volunteers jumped down. There were some bags on the floor of the tractor which Pinchas then distributed. You slung one over a shoulder and it hung down to your knees. The deal was then to climb up one of the pointed ladders already placed in the trees and fill the thing to the brim, then climb down and empty it. Repetitive, and quite tiring. But it was a chance to chat. The trees were not far apart and the group worked on two or three at a time. Julian was put with the blonde Caroline and Mike. And so that morning Julian found out about Wigan and hairdressing. Caroline's father was a gentleman's barber.

"He makes more money selling condoms than he does cutting hair". Her accent was flat, her laugh raucous. "That's 10 shillings. Anything for the weekend?".

The boys laughed.

"How old are you anyway? You look too young to be out on your own at night".

"Old enough" replied Julian.

"Old enough for what?" Her voice was insinuating.

"Old enough" said Julian.

Julian climbed down the ladder and emptied his bag. The oranges were dirty and unappealing. Before they got to the shops they had to be washed and polished. From an orange grove in Kfar Menachem to become Jaffa oranges in the UK. Julian picked one out of the pile, peeled it and ate it. Well, at least he'd stay healthy on this diet. Then up the ladder again. He looked at the other trees and their pickers. The whitish legs of the girl volunteers, the long, thin tanned legs of the men. Some of the volunteers had their sleeves rolled down to their wrists, and after the first morning Julian understood why: the orange trees (the lemons were worse) had spikes on them, sharp protruding thorns which grazed and tore as you picked. One girl had the scars of scratches up beyond her elbows and displayed them over breakfast to anyone who cared to look.

The work became repetitive: pick what you could see, down the ladder, empty into the bin, despair of ever filling it, move the ladder into an area where there seemed to be a lot of fruit, climb ladder and begin again. Somehow the bin got filled. When it came to mid-day and the sun was high in the sky, 'ten-to-six' started walking around the bins, picking hard himself, trying to fill the quota. Some bins were woefully empty, and then he called the whole group around that bin to pick for that one only.

It was not always the laziness of the volunteers. Some trees just did not have a lot of fruit on them. Julian later learnt that the kibbutz elders also called in outside help (often they were Arabs) and they left the trees broken and despoiled, with the branches torn, snapped, the leaves wrenched off. But then time, money and deadlines were involved. When the bins were adjudged finally full enough Pinchas called the group together.

"We go home now".

And so they all climbed up onto the wooden benches and, in a daze of physical tiredness, let 'ten-to-six' drive them back to the buildings. There they washed, changed and went for lunch. The work-day was over.

The routine was soothing for the first month. The 4.30am start, scrabbling for clothes in the dark, getting to one of the two loos, with everyone else standing around waiting, listening. The girls tried to put on make-up, and then slowly found it too much effort and did not bother. They all ended up looking like unfit farm hands, which they were. A coffee or tea before they set out, and then into the truck and a bumpy ride to the orange or lemon groves. Then back for breakfast at about 9, and the second shift till lunch at 12. It was simple and mind-numbing. And he got to know the two guys in the room better: Mike Brewer and Pie. Mikey was the son of some academic in Cambridge and Pie was the son of a fruit-farmer. Both there for 'the experience'. Nice kids. They did not tread on each others' toes, shared socks and shirts, and fitted in. Julian found he could not sleep in the afternoon, and lay awake reading or just pondering on the events which had got him there. Mike and Pie snored their afternoons away.

And the lull in the chase was restorative. Viewing it from there, his past life seemed so far away. The chapel, the bells, the sport, the classes, the prep, the ties, the scarves, the absurd competition between houses, and the beatings. What a madhouse! Much, much better was this simple life picking oranges and talking bullshit about the world and everything and nothing. Had it really happened? Would they ever let him forget it? What did Hugo say? *Les flics* are remarkably obstinate when it comes to murder. He had to remember that every day. He should never let his guard down.

⚔

After about a month the orange-picking routine changed. The volunteers were huddled around the list in the dining hall, trying to decipher who was doing what. Some were shouting out the job allocation.

"What did you get?"

"Where is the chicken house?"

"Irrigation?....what does that mean? Where do I have to go?"

"Slaughter block? What the hell is that meant to mean?"

Julian drew the long straw and got irrigation with Mikey. Others were not so fortunate, as he was to find out.

And he truly had lucked out. Irrigation. Word came back that the elders had mistaken his name for Richard, one of the other volunteers who was a farmer's son and knew all about tractors and had a licence. Instead, Richard had been put in the chicken huts among the squawking, hysterical feathers and the smell of dung. After the first day Julian was certainly not asking for a change of job as it turned out to be heaven. He got to rise an hour later, just at sunrise, so he had coffee with the *niks* and not with the volunteer group, and then they had use of a small jeep which he slowly

99

learned to drive, crashing the gears all the time, and nearly spilling his *nik* boss Barak and Mike into ditches several times. Barak did not seem to mind, and Mike just laughed. There was a strangely cavalier attitude to the machinery.........if it broke it got mended. After one particularly unpleasant gear-grinding moment, Barak just turned and said:

"Careful. We need car tomorrow".

The jeep took them to the irrigation sheds where the tractors and the irrigation pipes were stored. The system was this. Each farm had a water quota, and the crops needed irrigation, so the *niks* used a pump and long pipes to get the water from the River Jordan to the corn or cotton which might be a field or two away. The River Jordan was hardly as Julian had imagined. It was shallow, with brown water, and barely two metres across. You could jump across it. Julian could hardly believe it wasn't a mile wide with boats on it, yet this one little river irrigated the whole country, for Jews and Palestinians. The pump sucked up the shallow water and then sent it along the 3-metre long pipes which were connected one by one with simple, metal latches, and the water was directed to the part of the field which had been designated that day. They worked along, through the crops, one day here, the next day there. The water came to a powerful nozzle and sprayed an arc of water about 20 yards, automatically returning on itself and its path when it got to the end of its cycle. It clicked back to its starting position. Ingenious and simple. The petrol water-pump was on for two hours, their treasured ration, and the farm had their crop of corn. It grew at an amazing rate, and from tiny rather feeble insignificant plants, the corn was transformed by the water and constant sun into a dense crop of 2-metre high small trees. And once the corn was grown and cut and down, the ground was ploughed, cow dung was spread and the cotton went in. There was always work to do, and this irrigation was at the heart of it. Julian and Mike felt important. They were truly helping the farm survive and feeding mouths.

They started getting the hang of the job after a week. They had to load the pipes on to the long specially designed irrigation pipe-carrier, hitch it up to the tractor and then set off to the area under the guidance of Barach, take the pipes off the truck (they were not light) and then connect them to the right length. The most important part was to put a bung at the end of the last pipe in the line where it was connected to the nozzle, as this kept the precious water in the system. No bung, and the water just spilled out into a big puddle for half a day, and that made the niks very, very angry. Water was gold here.

The other volunteers were not so lucky. The chicken house was not so bad, they said. It meant cleaning, and putting drops into the eyes of the yellow chicks to prevent Newcastle disease. That was fun. The shit shovelling was OK when you got used to the smell which you did after about two hours in the sheds. The first impact at 5 in the morning could have you gagging. Caroline had thrown up the first day, but stuck with it. Some said it was also because she had been up drinking and smoking with the *niks* all night. But the stench could be smelt on the clothes by anyone sitting down close by. They soon got into the habit of stripping off and showering and changing before they came to lunch.

The cow shed was also fun, as the job was to clean the yards and to give straw and orange peel to the cows. The cows seemed not to mind their diet, and the milk tasted strangely of oranges. Often in the evenings the volunteers used to go down to the milking sheds and scoop up the frothy creamy milk from the large vats.

The shortest straw was the chicken slaughter house. Pie did a week of that, and came back to the dining room after the first morning looking shell-shocked. He sat down at the table with the other volunteers. His face looked pale and he did not eat much, sipping at his coffee. After a while, hearing the chatter of the other foreigners about their new jobs, he told them about his morning.

"Don't go there if you can help it".

"Why?" The other volunteers stopped talking and centred their attention on him.

"Just....don't go there if you can help it". He sipped a bit more. His eyes were unresponsive and he stared at the table.

"What goes on in there?"

"It's where they slaughter the chickens". He let out a strange bark of a laugh, more a cry than an expression of humour.

"Shit!"

"No way!"

"I'm not going there".

"Better shit-shovelling than that!"

Then he began telling them about what he had seen, and what now to avoid.

"You see your name on the list? Get it taken off. Better laying the tables, better anything than this".

"Why? What is so awful? Tell us"

Again the strange bark of a laugh.

"It is all kosher, for some reason or another. There is this Rabbi dressed in his robes and gear and you have to take out the chickens from these crates, and they are shitting themselves, and half of then have had their legs or wings broken by whoever has pushed them into the crates (they do it at night, I suppose) and you have to put you hand in and try and take one out. They fight like crazy".

He rolled up his sleeves and showed them the scratches and cuts he had on his arms.

"Ugh!"

"Not me!"

"Never!"

"What is it in Hebrew again?"

Pie continued his story:

"Then you have to get the bloody thing still and tie the legs together, and put the left wing under the right wing and hand it to the Rabbi who then slits its throat with this tiny knife and hangs it upside down by its legs with blood spurting out everywhere and throws it into a revolving bucket….."

He trailed off. He looked as if he was going to be sick, and took another sip of his coffee. No one said anything.

"He then hangs them on a sort of conveyor belt coming from the ceiling. Then another machine takes the feathers off. And all the time he's yelling: More chicken, more chicken! You do that for a few hours. I tell you, the stink, the shit, the feathers…….. Don't go there".

He drank more coffee……

"They hose the blood down at the end. And the Rabbi gives you hell if you get the wings wrong, or the legs are not tied or….. just don't go there if you can help it. I'm moving as soon as they can find me another job. And chicken is off my menu, I can tell you. Some of the birds run around without a head…….. just…………"

The break time was over, and the other volunteers dispersed to their own tasks, making sure they never went through what Pie had seen and done. Julian and Mike went back to their tractor and irrigation pipes in the open air and bright sun.

⇒╪ ╪⇐

There was another positive side to the job: Barak. He was in charge of irrigation most days. He was a strange *kibbutznik*. He had come from outside, married into the farm, and seemed remarkably content. He was also a music lover, opera, Lieder, oratorio. It was an odd thing to find on a communal farm.

He slept very little (they all just had a few hours in a chair, many of them not even bothering to go to bed) and his eyes were often bloodshot. In the evenings he used to invite some of the volunteers to his house, and there, after some food from the canteen, or some tea, perhaps a beer, he would put on a record of someone famous singing.

His house was pretty much the same size as anyone else's. It was just the furnishings which were different. Julian knew Barak was married and had children, but he hardly ever saw Barak's wife, and he had no idea who his children were. This was normal, as the children were brought up communally and lived in each other's families.

One evening Julian was invited around with several other volunteers. There was Elena and Mike and Pie. It was not their sort of thing, the classical music. Barak put on Brahms's 'German Requiem', and while Julian was transfixed it sent the rest of them into a deep slumber. Barak noticed that the ponderous opening had a sleep-inducing effect on his guests, and he quietly smiled at Julian in recognition that perhaps his music choice was not for everyone's taste. Besides, under that sun, and from 4 in the morning, it had been a long day. Barak got up and changed the track. It was a German singer Schwarzkopf singing the soprano solo: *Ye who now have sorrow.* Her voice came out of the machine, in this

104

most unlikely setting. The others asleep, in their kibbutz clothes, and the pure, honed blade of a voice soaring out into the night. *Ye who now have sorrow.* It was beautiful, but it was also his mother's voice. The silvery notes, rising, now falling, the line seemingly endless, the strings sustaining, all this cut through the reserves Julian had built up. His mother. How was she? Where was she? Was she alive, even? Suddenly he was in tears, large drops rolling down his cheeks. He tried to cover his eyes, and turned away from his host.

"Oh Jesus!"

He did not know if Barak had seen him. He surreptitiously wiped the tears away, and tuned in again to the wondrous sound, effortless, riding over the orchestra, so cleanly in the note, so right in its direction. The music finished in its falling cadences, and the voice lingered till the end, falling, falling into the final chords. Something had stirred in Julian. It was as if some strange illumination had taken place. He could hardly formulate it, but it was vaguely: I want to do that. What she had done, I want to spend my life doing. I want to sing. I want to be amongst these sounds. To speak it then would have seemed absurd. With mud on his feet, hoisting irrigation pipes most days, and here, at midnight, with the warm air blowing in through the doors, the smells of the vegetation pungent with the night's moisture, he made a wish to the powers that be: Please let me do this. Somehow.

When the baritone solo started: *Lord, Lord...that I be made sure..........* it was as if the composer was talking to him. Perhaps there would be a way, but for sure it was not on the kibbutz.

═╬ ╬═

The days went on like this: early start, jeep, irrigation, tractors, pipes, breakfast, more pipes, home. The occasional party. Trips to Jerusalem, through the Sinai desert, swimming with sharks and barracudas in the early morning in the Red Sea, trips to Eilat where he met up with some other travellers. Then back on Monday morning to the irrigation. His body was tanned and wiry from all the lifting. Mike and he took turns with the tractor and the pipes, loading, unloading, fitting, unhooking, moving on to another field, more corn, more cotton. He had been there almost 6 months now, and the elders had accepted him. As long as he worked, then there was a place for him, it seemed, and he was fit and good at his tasks, never complaining, never shirking. The work-ethic on the farm was strong, but then it was also survival: it was a new country which had been created from nothing mostly by displaced persons, war refugees, holocaust victims and sympathisers, and the nation had almost been swept into the sea once already by the '67 war. As long as Julian worked hard, they asked no questions, nor suggested he leave.

That Monday morning he was up with Mike in the fields. Mike, too, had been transformed from a rather refined intellectual type into a long-haired, pot-smoking muscular *nik*. He had a girl from New York, doing her OE, Miriam. He had learned to drive the jeep and tractor with quiet skill. He was still going back to Oxford in the autumn, but until then, he was where he was.

Both he and Julian had developed cracks in their feet from walking in the soft moist earth as they laid the pipes, and they had asked the farm cobbler to make them some shoes which would stand the mud and water. Julian liked this exchange. You worked for the farm, and in return they gave you shoes and some spending money. The supermarket/shop was another joy. You took what you wanted, or rather, needed; only alcohol and some goods considered luxuries were to be paid for, and even then they were cheap. Condoms were free. Beer was not.

That Monday it was Julian's turn to drive the tractor. The machine chugged out with the pipes on the trailer, and Mike sat on the engine beside Julian. It was another beautiful morning. There were storks in the fields on their migration, hunting for small snakes and frogs, almost oblivious of the tractor and the men on it. The smell of orange blossom everywhere. They stopped at the foot of a rise in the land. The field was a new area which they had not dealt with before. To the left was a deep ditch which ran along the side of this field, and they had been told that they had to lay the pipes along the left side and wait for Barak or another *nik* to come and connect up the nozzles and direct the jet of water. They always left that bit to the experts. Mike had lifted off the first four pipes, and laid them in a line. Julian put the tractor into gear and started going up the rise. But it was steeper than he had expected and there had been rain in the night. The earth was soft, and the wheels started skidding. Julian thought changing down in the gears would improve the traction. The machine had endless gears and two separate gear levers and it seemed made for all weather conditions. So he changed down, but in the moment he was changing gear the tractor started slipping down the rise; the trailer was pulling it back down the hill. Then the engine stalled. Julian panicked and tried to re-start it, but it was too late. The sheer weight of the full load of the pipes was pulling the trailer and the tractor down. Just before it fell Julian stood up and shouted out:

Mikey! Mikey!

But Mike had his back turned away from the scene. Julian's shout made him glance up to his right but it was too late. The pipes and the trailer fell on him, crushing him. The tractor itself was then jerked up into the air and crashed down into the 20-foot ditch.

⚔ ⚔

Julian was drifting in and out of consciousness in the two-bedroom clinic in the kibbutz. They had given him some drug of sorts which took away the pain and he was hooked up to a drip on one side. His head was bandaged and his right knee felt stiff and immobile. The second time he came round he saw some figures in the room, the Doctor, a nurse, and Thin Benny. He was sitting to his right. Julian found that he could hardly speak, his voice was so weak.

"What happened?"

Then, as he slowly recalled those last moments, he asked:

"Mikey?"

Their eyes dropped to the floor.

Later that day, when the anaesthetic was wearing off, he asked more, and they told him. Mickey had not made it. The pipes had crushed him and he died almost instantly. Julian had been thrown clear and the tractor must have bounced over him. It happens. He was very lucky.

Benny was there also as an interpreter for the Doctor and Nurse. The Doctor told him just what his injuries were and what they had done when he was under the anaesthetic. There was concussion, which was not serious. He had ruptured the ligaments in his right knee and that the knee would never heal on its own. He would probably limp for a long time. The other stuff, the gashes, the bruises, were minor. His right eye was safe, but was so swollen it might seem he had smashed it more than he really had. Again, his friend had not been so lucky. When they had left, Julian tried to get as much news as possible from Benny.

"The British police are coming out, and the ambassador from Tel Aviv was here today. They wanted your details, and so we had to look through your luggage and find something. And they found Hugo's passport. Man! what were you doing with his stuff? The elders were not happy. They were pretty mad, but because of the accident and all had happened to you, and you were a good worker, they sort of stood by you. Besides, this is their land, their territory.

The Jews are strange: they don't like anyone telling them what to do. But, man, what were you doing with Hugo's passport? You aren't French or anything, are you? And what about Hugo?

Julian croaked out a question:

"Who has the passports now?"

Benny shrugged. "I guess they are still with the elders. I don't know".

"Shit!"

Julian turned away and stared at the window. He could see the blue sky through the top panes. He thought hard, and then turned again to Benny.

"Benny, what day is it?"

"Wednesday".

So two days had gone. Two days for British police to be contacted, come out and deal with Mikey's death. And ask questions.

"Benny, I've got to get out of here" said Julian.

"Man, you aren't going anywhere like that".

"Benny, look, the whole passport thing is bad news. I can't tell you now, and possibly can't tell you ever. Do you understand what I am saying?"

There was a long silence.

"I am not a bad person" Julian continued, "but I did something in England and I can't go back. If the police find me then they'll take me back and my life will be......not good".

Benny sat motionless in his chair, smoking a cigarette.

"I don't know, man, what do you want me to do?"

"Help me?"

"How?" asked Benny.

"Get me out of here. Get the passports back. Get me to another place and a job. A job where I don't have to lift or walk much".

Thin Benny started chewing his thumb-nail.

"I'll have to talk to my Dad. He may know some guys from the past. I don't know anyone but *niks*. My whole life I lived here".

"Do what you can. Please".

Benny came and touched Julian's palm, imitating the American films he had seen.

"I'll do what I can".

An hour later Benny was back with his father. They drew up chairs and came close, whispering, but there was no need as there was no one else in the clinic. Benny's father was Russian, but spoke a simple English. He had been in the war and then fled to Israel in the late 40s. He had met his wife on the kibbutz.

"Benny tells me about you and police".

Julian nodded.

"We did not know"

"No one knew".

"We want help you. We do not think you are bad man".

"I am not".

"I made phone call to friend in Jerusalem. In hospital. You can work there. No pay, very little money. But you can work there".

"A hospital".

"Yes",

"Can I go there today?" asked Julian

"We think tomorrow is better". And then he started talking rapidly in Hebrew to his son. Benny then gave Julian the details. They would take him to the main road outside the farm and have a taxi waiting. The trip to Jerusalem was an hour. They would do this in the lunch break when the Doctor and Nurse would be out. No one got any blame that way.

"Tomorrow?" asked Julian.

"Tomorrow".

Julian held out his hand and Benny's father took it. He held it for a long time and Julian thanked him in Hebrew. And just as Benny's father was leaving Thin Benny pushed a small, taped packet under Julian's pillow. When they had gone, Julian opened it and found the two passports and some money.

CHAPTER 9

JERUSALEM HOSPITAL

B reakfast was usually quiet at E-Lyn. The night-shift nurses were leaving, and the new shift were taking over, having some coffee, catching up on news. They kept themselves to themselves, the foreigners at their tables, the Israelis at another. If you sat down with one of the nurses it was no big deal, she did not get up or anything, and you stumbled through in your Hebrew, and they in their English. Some were French-Jewish and so that was easier. There was also a group of Germans there doing social work rather than military service. They spoke excellent Hebrew, and seemed far more integrated in the hospital than other nationalities. Strange irony that. The kids didn't seem to mind or even know what had happened. Thirty years ago the same men might have been obeying orders and ordering them into cattle trucks rather than gently cleaning their arses and washing them. To the Jewish kids in the beds they were just bearded foreigners who were helping them and spoke Hebrew.

Julian got to understand the routine pretty fast: wards at 7.00am. Cleaning and then breakfast; then games and activities, perhaps a trip out for the more mobile; then lunch and after, some gym practice, physio, sometimes the over-heated pool. Dinner was all over by 7pm and the kids were in their beds and ready for the night. It was a simple, calm existence, just what he needed.

His head wound had almost healed. It would leave a scar over his right eye and he still walked with a limp as the tendons in his knee had been badly torn; he could slip on water on the floor and suddenly find himself on his back. He was told he'd either have to wear an elastic support for the rest of his life and build up the muscles, or have another operation done. Operating tables could wait, thought Julian. And an old man's pink knee support just was not conceivable. He'd risk the knee giving way for the moment. If he braced it and held the knee in place with the muscle it worked all right, even when lifting. He'd manage.

And he slowly got to know some of the staff. There was an American dentist Brad he saw most mornings. Brad often sat on his own at a table, and seemed glad to have a bit of company and to talk English. Julian took his typical hospital breakfast: tomato, cucumber, boiled egg, and came to the table:

"Do you mind? This seat taken?" asked Julian.

"No, please, come. Sit yourself down. So, what's cooking?" said Brad.

"You know, day to day".

Julian started cracking open the boiled egg, mixing it with the tomato and slicing the cucumber.

"You like it here?" asked Julian.

"It's OK".

"Yeah, it's OK".

Julian knew that Brad worked in two places, the hospital and his own private studio. And some days he looked so tired Julian was amazed he got through his shift. His hair was already going grey and he always wore glasses with steel rims. Today they were patched up with tape.

"What's with the glasses?" Julian asked.

"Oh, yeah. I fell asleep and must have rolled over and smashed them. Isn't that the pits? I've done that so often. I fall asleep on the phone these days. I wake up and hear my sister talking to me from America. It sucks the big one, doesn't it?".

"Guess it does". Julian smiled. It was enough encouragement for Brad to continue:

"I mean, I'm working like a dog. And my balls are scraping on the floor. I hear sparks come out the other day I tripped over them when I got up. Is that normal?"

Julian was laughing loudly. He was a good audience.

"Now you are the guy who had that accident right?"

"That's right" said Julian.

Brad looked him over once or twice.

"And that eye wound?" asked Brad.

"It's OK. Seems to have cleared up".

"Vision?" asked Brad.

"Fine".

"Well, that's good. Now, are you getting any? You know, pussy?"

"Pussy?" asked Julian.

"Pussy, yes, getting laid. You don't use that expression in Britain or wherever you come from?".

"Well, I suppose we do".

"You know, you gotta loosen up, you have. It's out there, go and get it".

Julian started in about his eye wound, his knee, being shaken up.

"Listen, get a date, will you listen to me? It'll make you forget all your troubles. A little pussy and you'll be"-and here he put his fake upper class British accent on: "you'll be as right as rain, won't he darling? Top notch, top hole, old man".

Julian was laughing again.

"You like that? Did it sound real to you?"

"You could do with some practice" said Julian.

"So could you, by the sounds of it. You know, you got to lighten up. Listen to me. I mean, the dames they don't like a long face. I know you had this goddamn accident and all that, but hey, forget it, have fun. You are alive".

He took a sip of his coffee.

"I always remember what my father said to me: Brad, he said, when your ocean cruiser goes down and you are in a lifeboat with fifteen other people, and there are ten foot waves towering over you, and it is dark and there is one pair of oars, and you are surrounded by sharks, smile! Look happy! Because: they may have eaten already!"

Brad collapsed into laughter. The nurses looked their way. He was wiping his eyes now with a tissue.

"OK, OK, seriously....." said Brad.

He looked at his watch." Damn. Gotta go".

"Now listen to me buster". Brad's face got intense and serious. "You have to get in there. You have a girlfriend, or what?"

"I like one of the nurses".

"Who is she?"

"She's on the other ward".

"That's OK. Nurses. Lots of contact, they like that. Describe her to me?"

"Well, she's got lots of blonde hair, and I think she speaks English well. I heard her the other day. She was with you in the corridor".

"Oh you mean Jitka? Is that who you mean?" asked Brad.

"I don't know what her name is" said Julian.

"Well, if it's her she may be taken. She's going out with one of the male nurses. But he's, well, he's two-timing her I think. Don't you say anything, but I think.....well, he's just in there for the fun, as it were. Anyway, it may be someone else. So, let's say it is this Jitka girl. Now, where are you going?" His voice had this upward lilt full of expectant insinuation.

"I hadn't invited her anywhere yet. I thought.....I thought of taking her to that guitar concert and then getting her back here saying I want to cook for her".

Brad looked at him down his nose

"Now that, if I may say so, is a mistake".

Julian was defensive: "I like cooking. I'm good at it. I do great sauces, and I like talking to people while I do it".

"Listen to me. You are going too fast. She'll think you only want one thing, which is of course, what you do want, but you mustn't let her know that. It'll be too fast. You'll frighten her. Women are like horses, they spook easily. And they are like kids as well, they want little surprises, gifts, trinkets, jewellery. You gotta keep them happy, surprised, little things. They are children, really. You gotta humour them. Believe me".

"I thought if that didn't work we could go to a Chinese?" said Julian.

"A Chinese ? Here? In Jerusalem?" Brad's voice shrieked with incredulity.

"They say there is one on the other side of the city".

"Well, it might be a front for an opium den, but that's OK. You go there, make her feel as if her every desire is your ultimate wish. Perhaps she likes crappy guitar music. You say: Darling, crappy guitar music is what I have always wanted to hear. She says: I would love to eat Chinese, and you say: Darling, Chinese is my idea of heaven. She says: I would love to go to that new place where they serve you piles of steaming sheep shit, and you say: sheep shit is what I am really into, dear".

Julian was helpless by now.

"I'm telling you. You listen to me. I gotta go. Listen to uncle Brad for once. Sheep shit? I love it".

And he was off, gathering his bags and papers, to the dentistry department.

=+ +=

Two days later Julian saw Brad once more in the canteen.

"How's it going, buster? How was it? Was my advice good? Hmmm?" He beamed through his glasses. "Was uncle Brad's advice on the spot. Hmmm?"

"I didn't go anywhere with anyone. I think you're right. She's with that Israeli nurse" said Julian.

"Well, don't take it too hard. Look at the mess I'm in! I don't want you to make the same mistakes. I mean.....look at this". Brad turned his gaze on the canteen and the view outside. The hospital looked out onto the drabbest area of Jerusalem, where it was all building sites and scrub-land. The canteen was small and cramped.

"I mean, I could've had a life, another life, not this one. My friends, I go back, they have these mansions, three floors, and they are buying their holiday home in Florida. I have my arse out. I tell you I'm taking it up the poop, the Hershey-highway".

Julian was laughing again.

"It isn't funny. And don't get any broad pregnant, I'm telling you. Or you really will be in the shit. I made that mistake, and look what happened to me! My ex-wife says I had a choice. I mean, your daughter is 1 year old and her mother says: I'm going back to Mummy. In Jerusalem? That's a choice? I mean, that isn't choice, that is blackmail. I followed her. I love my daughter. Who wouldn't? But, Jeez, women really have you by the balls, don't they?".

Julian did not know what to reply to this. He let it go, and shrugged. Pregnancies and babies seemed another world to him, and not one he wanted to join soon.

Brad continued: "So, first rule: don't get anyone pregnant! And that's what they all want. I'm telling you. A baby goes past and their nipples harden".

Julian laughed at this.

No, it's true. They do. Their nipples harden. I'm telling you, buster. You watch out, a pair of ovaries on legs, that what they are at that age, and whoever she is she'll have you married and back in Britain".

Julian suddenly became serious: "I can't go back there".

"Oh is that so? Why is that?"

"Stuff happened there. I can't go back" was all Julian ventured.

Brad knew he had to back off and not pry. So many people were in Israel for one crazy idea or another.

"Hey, did you hear about the loonies who go crazy here, the religious nutters? Read it in the paper the other day. They come here and they go crazy, and the psychiatric wings are divided into Old and New Testament, according to their particular religious character they are impersonating! Isn't

119

that something? I've come to see my father. Old or New Testament? Isn't that wacky?"

"That's quite something".

"So, as I said, no lots of little half-Brits running around the hospital. Or you'll be back in that fog and damp before you have time to say: *Shalom*! Look at me! I tell you. All I do is run from the Department to my studio and back. And I pay taxes on the studio, and taxes on the money here, and it all goes to the ex-wife. You know?"

He paused.

"So, what else? Another venue? Second date?"

"I thought about the beach at Ashkelon, and then a small hotel. What do you say?"

"Nice. You see each other in a costume, you both see what is on offer".

The New York lilt was there. "Nice food, nice bed. I like the idea. Have you asked her yet?"

"Who, the blonde? No".

"Don't leave it too long. Long enough but not too long; you have got to sound interested but not slavering".

He looked at his watch.

"I gotta go. My patients will be waiting for me. Tell me how it goes, buster".

Julian looked around the canteen. Nurse Shalva was there with the other male orderly. Four other nurses from the various wards were having their coffee break.

CHAPTER 10

TRAVEL

The next morning Julian got up at 6.00 am as he was on the early duty. It meant getting down into the wards with the nurses who were either just getting off their night shift or coming on the day shift. The kids were sleeping mostly. For the nurses, you were just one or another of the volunteers, and had no medical experience. Useful for helping lift the kids, wiping their arses, fetching water and carrying the food to the beds. Julian popped his head into the sister's space and asked:

"Can I help?" he asked.

"Not yet. They are all sleeping. Maya is up and about, but she can take care of herself".

Julian nodded, and left her to her magazine in Hebrew.

He looked down the ward and saw Maya, the emaciated but so pretty girl in her wheelchair, making her way to the ward. Such a delicate face, and then one day she revealed this amazingly sweet singing voice, like a little bird's: *Figaro, Figaro, Figaro,* she sang. And once she saw that Julian liked her singing, she sang that and other phrases every time they met. This little nightingale, destined probably to be dead from muscle-wasting in a few years. He couldn't think about that; didn't want to rather.

Julian went along to the canteen on the bottom floor. It was strictly kosher, as the hospital was run, as far as he could make out, by the ultra-religious Hassidic Jews. These families came on Saturdays, *Shabbat,* to help their offspring who God had decided, for some reason, to send into the world malformed and with diseases.

The men were and dressed in their crazy, impressive get-up: the full hats with the fur, the long dark beards and side-burn ringlets, and the pebble glasses. Too much reading when young, too much in-breeding, who knows, thought Julian. He was to see exactly the same fathers and sons, so pale and short-sighted, in East London many years later. Pebble glasses, hats and ringlets, and Volvo estates. He asked his Jewish friends about the Volvo estates, but got no satisfactory answer. Good for a lot of kids, was one answer; and they had a lot. The wives were always wearing road-kill wigs as well. Another thing he never understood.

The canteen offered strange things. An English breakfast with pork would have closed the place down in the time it would take to say shalom. Other food on offer was exotic and much better for him, he thought. Yoghurt stuff, called, as far as he could make out 'leben' and which he was never able to find again. It was a white nectar with a strange milky crust on top. Once tried, it was Julian's staple for breakfast. Then the boiled eggs and the cucumber and the dry bread in the season for dry bread. Julian did not question the dietary regime. It was free, it was tasty, and no one was asking questions. Yet.

He saw Brad, the American dentist, on the other side of the room next to the blonde.

"Hi Buster, what ya doin? What's cooking?"

Julian put his plate down and sat opposite them on the non-swivel plastic chairs.

"Do you two know each other? I thought you knew each other. No? Let me introduce you. Jitka, this is Julian. It is Julian, right?"

"Nice to meet you".

The blonde put her hand forward to be shaken. It was strangely formal in this so informal of countries.

"Hi".

"Yeah, Jitka here, she deals with the disabled kids here, does the therapy and that stuff. She speaks excellent English" added Brad.

"No, you are too kind".

"Sounds good to me", said Julian.
"I spent some time in England, no Britain, as you insist on calling it. But it was darkest Kent, near Hever castle. I came to know Lady Astor, after her marriage break-up, that is".
Julian was so impressed by her English, accented but so confident. Her eyes were dark blue with intensely dark irises, and her blonde hair was stylishly dishevelled. She wore bracelets and rings.

"My real name is Miroslavachenka, but the British had trouble with that. So I just shortened it to Jitka".

Julian laughed.

"They have trouble with anything that is not Joe or Jim, or Sue or Prue".

Jitka laughed an open wide laugh, showing her teeth. Her back teeth were discoloured and full of fillings.

"No, they were very kind to me, the British. Besides, it is my childhood name".

"More coffee?" Brad tilted his head on one side like a quizzical cockatoo, and put as much insinuation as he could into his voice. Julian stared back with eyes that told him to back off. Jitka did not pick up on it, or pretended not to.

"Yes, that'd be nice. Thank you" said Jitka.

"I'll have some too, thanks".

Brad poured with care.

"What do you make of the food here?" he asked.

"Where I come from, there was no choice. *Is* no choice. It is either this or if you are lucky, that, and you don't complain. You are grateful. Very grateful".

Jitka made a face which was a mixture of contempt for her country as well as a bit of contempt for this very young man in front of her. What could he know, what did anyone know of her country? Sacrificed by the Allies to Hitler, abandoned to its fate, taken over by the Russians, and suddenly that startling wonderful terrible moment of the Prague spring. Then.....everyone stopped singing, and the Russian tanks took over and once more there were two types of coffee. Some escaped in time. If you hadn't you were lucky if you got a three-room state-owned flat. And convinced yourself that this was the best of all possible worlds.

"It isn't an English breakfast" Julian said

"Do they really serve up that shit, the fried bread and tomatoes and stuff like that?" Brad asked.

Both Julian and Jitka laughed.

"Hey, don't knock it. When you have been out of some scaffolding from 7 to 9, and that cold wind is whistling around your...... and you get your break and I tell you, you eat everyone of those baked beans and even the fried bread goes down fast. Calories, but no cuisine, as my father used to say".

"I have to go now" said Jitka. Jitka got up and gathered her plate and cup with her.

"Goodbye. It was nice meeting you" she added.

She extended her hand and Julian took it, a firm business-like exchange. She then patted Brad on the shoulder.

"I'll be seeing you around".

"That's for sure", replied Brad.

Julian watched her go through the canteen and up the stairs to the wards.

"She was nice".

"Jitka? Yes, she's nice enough. A bit too Slavic for me, all that blonde hair and the communism shit".

"Is she with anyone at the moment?" asked Julian.

Brad raised a quizzical eyebrow.

"So you are thinking of getting in there?"

"I like her".

"So do all the other men here".

"Is she really with that male nurse?"

"I heard so. They sit together at lunch. He's nice enough. Heavy, black glasses, lots of hair. She may like that sort of thing, you know. No accounting for tastes, as far as women are concerned. I don't know how close they are or anything. Besides, I also heard he was getting married. She's just a bit on the side, although she may not know that".

He took a sip of his tea, ate another mouthful of his boiled egg in a dispirited way.

"You know these guys here: have fun with the nurses, but when it comes to marrying, they choose the girl their mother wants, 'cos the broad from abroad won't know how to cook the gefilter fish or the meat balls, or rub his neck as his mother does. And the Jewish ceremonies, she won't know what to do, and then the brood of little Schlomos, will they be all Jewish? Blondies going to Eastern Europe? No, no. Haia or Ester or whoever will make sure he marries the right one, so she can still have him by the balls and get him back at lunch for her chopped liver, just as only his Mummy makes it".

"You think?"

"Think? I know".

"So, I have a chance?" asked Julian.

"That I don't know. Listen. I've got to run. Tell me how it goes".

Brad got up, grabbed his over-spilling bag, and made off to the dentistry department. Julian finished off his coffee, took it to the rack of dirty plates and mugs and went up to the children's ward to see if he could be of help. Mostly it was just carrying stuff, or getting water, occasionally wiping bottoms for the bigger kids. Then some activities like swimming or just outings to and around Jerusalem. Nothing hard. Even the arse-wiping was no big deal, although some of the other volunteers hated it. And some of the female nurses did it badly.

He got to the ward:
    "Anything I can do?"

═╬═╬═

Lunch was much the same. Julian looked out for Jitka, and then he saw her sitting beside the Israeli male nurse in his green scrubs. He was very hairy with tufts of chest hair coming out of his jacket. Julian inwardly quailed at trying to beat off the competition. The nurses always went for the Israelis, it seemed. Julian kept on sneaking a glance at the two, to see just how close they were. It seemed not a lot was going on, or rather, a lot was going on. Jitka was silent as Eli spoke and shrugged. Then it was her turn. And she had a lot to say. She shoved the cutlery around on the plate, pushed the glass towards him, pressed the table hard with her hands and almost banged it with her fists. Eli remained impassive. Julian thought back to what Brad had told him. Perhaps it was the show-down at the OK corral.

He imagined the scene:

"I'm getting married".

"You are what! When? Why didn't you tell me? How long has this been going on........?"

Quite something to hear over the chopped liver. After a while she got up and took her things to the racks where the plates were washed and walked out. She didn't turn her head back, not glance.

Wow! thought Julian, and then he looked at Eli. He seemed not to be upset at all. Perhaps she really was just another foreign nurse who he had had some fun with, then went back to the waiting, adorable, submissive Ester who would marry him and give him lots of brats.

After a while Eli took out a cigarette, lit it and then took his dishes to the rack. Impassive. Strong in his country and his family and his job. She was just another Eastern European trying to make trouble. Eli took a long drag and exhaled. His family and friends would back him for sure. They'd already discussed her merits, her statistics, what they did and had done. The positions, when and where. He took another drag.

Foreigners were easy game. They should know the rules before they set foot in the place. The blondes were for fun; but the dark Esthers were for the family and the race. Any blondie who had other ideas was a fool. That was settled, then. He stubbed out his cigarette, got up and left his plates next to Jitka's. After a few days she would get over it. Or leave. What did he care? They never stayed for long anyway. They got homesick or their contracts ran out and they decided there were no job prospects here, and they left. A book, a record, a bit of a party, and they were forgotten before they had even reached the airport.

⇥╪⇤

The next morning Julian went to the canteen and looked for a spot to sit with his tray. Brad was again with Jitka. She didn't look that good, as if she hadn't slept much and had been crying.

Julian circled the table a bit.

"Do you mind?"

"No, no. I was just leaving actually. Jitka?" asked Brad.

Jitka shrugged. Julian sat down opposite them.

"How is it going?"

"Well, let me tell you, apart from my balls thing dragging on the floor and emitting sparks and my arms being nailed to the cross, I'm doing fine".

Julian started laughing into his coffee, almost spluttering. Jitka was distant, far away.

"What was that?" she asked.

"No, nothing. Brad was running through his routine of his persecution complex".

"Well, if you have one, it's the right place to be" Brad added.

Jitka smiled faintly.

"Listen, I have to go. I'm late. I'm always late. Why is that? Anyway, have a good one. Bye" and Brad walked off.

Julian and Jitka stared at the table. Julian stirred his coffee. There was a long silence, and Julian thought of walking off. It was embarrassing. His heart started to race and pound, and he was certain she could hear it from where she was sitting. Shit, ask her out. What does it take you? She can only say no. Thump, thump, thump. More silence. Sweat and heart-attack time.

Then together: "I just thought; I wondered..........."

They looked up at each other, smiled. She had lovely blue eyes, but with great hurt, and the whites were bloodshot.

"You first..." he said.

"No, please, you" said Jitka.

Thump thump.

"I wondered if you would like to go out some place?".

Jitka looked at him hard, as if she were assessing his bastard quotient.

"You have kind eyes; the kindest I have ever seen".

Julian waited for a reply.

"I mean, I know you think I am too young and all that, and you...."

Jitka put her hand to his mouth.

"Stop. Don't spoil it. Don't say silly things. I know you are young, very young. But I am not too old either. I am not, what do you say, an infant stealer? Jo?"

"Cradle-snatcher is perhaps the word you want?" Julian offered.

"Yes, cradle-snatcher. That is good. I'll remember that".

"How old are you?" he asked.

"Now is not the time" she said tersely.

Thump, thump, thump. Think of something, fast. Anything to keep her talking.

"I have always wanted to see Capernaum, you know, and the lake of Galilee, and follow the footsteps of Christ". (Oh, God she must think I'm another little Christer, some religious nut about to take orders after he tries to get over his doubts. A little Jesuit, some adolescent screwed-up Anglican).

"That would be really nice!" Jitka replied with enthusiasm.

She looked into Julian's eyes with warmth.

"I've always wanted to go there as well, but I didn't want to travel on my own. Eli never wanted to go".

The reference to Eli hurt Julian, a cut to the soul. She was with another man, they had been having sex only yesterday. In his arms, those arms. His hand, his fingers, his.................

Jitka saw the pain cross his face.

"It is over with Eli. He is getting married".

"I know".

"You know? Everyone knows! Except me. Funny, isn't it? The one person who should know is the last one who gets to know. Not just seeing. You say seeing, yes?"

Julian nodded.

"No, not just seeing!" She spat the word out like a date stone. "Not just seeing—but getting married". She wiped the tears from her eyes, looked for a handkerchief.

"I'm sorry. He means nothing to me now" she added.

Then brightly:

"Yes, let's go. This weekend. I have days off; do you?"

"I think I do".

"Then let's ask and go", she said brightly. She touched her open palm against his face.

"You are a kind boy. You won't hurt me. I don't think you even know how, or what I am talking about, do you?".

Julian shrugged. His heart rate had lowered to under the 200 beats per minute. Imminent seizure was past.

"Good, I'll ask for this weekend now. You do the same, yes? And tell me at the lunch break". And she was off, saying over her shoulder:

"Bye".

"Bye". Julian waved back at her.

⇥ ⇤

They met at the bus station in Jerusalem on Saturday morning. Jitka was dressed in jeans and a blue shirt, with a small necklace hanging outside. She had a simple nylon bag for her things; everyone travelled light in Israel. Julian had asked around in the hospital for cheap hotels near Capernaum, and Nurse Shalva told him of a place she knew close to the lake. It sounded perfect, and with the few shekels Julian earned at the hospital, it was affordable.
"How are you this morning?" he asked.

She lent forward to kiss him on the cheek. Julian was not used to such closeness so quickly.

"I'm fine". She smiled her wide toothy smile.

"So, let's go. Which bus?"

Julian had got there earlier to find out. The destination was written in Hebrew and English on the front. These buses looked as if they might break down at any time, but they never did, not once on the many trips Julian took. Some of the engine casing at the front had been removed to help cool the engine on the journey; the seats were hard with a tough linoleum surface. Built to last. You bought the ticket on the bus and it wasn't much. Travel was essential in this country, and the ethos was such that to become a bus driver was like being a top surgeon. On the city buses they would drive with one hand, negotiating the tight corners with ease, give change for a ticket with the other and still find time to talk to a passenger and argue about politics in a loud voice. It was scary the first time, but after that the insouciance, the sheer bravado and skill kept you calm.

They got on and found two seats half-way down up. Jitka sat in the one by the window. The air was so heavy, so humid. All the windows were open, and Jitka took out a small flat wicker fan to cool them both. Julian had never enjoyed such feminine attention before. She was so sure of herself, so prepared.

"If you travel on a bus in this country you need a fan. Here, I have one. I got it in the market yesterday".

And they talked about the Jerusalem markets, the stalls, the streets, the noise, the haggling, the smells, getting lost, the relief at finding a familiar sign, the wailing wall with the 'nutters' doing their thing, dressed in their long, black, gabardine coats, the hats, the rocking too and fro as they chanted their prayers, then the Dome of the Rock and Julian leaving his shoes and marvelling at the intricate fretwork and design, then the Chagall windows in a synagogue, and having to put the *kippah* hat on in the presence of God. After half an hour Jitka put her hand simply into Julian's and snuggled up to him. All this was new to Julian. It was intoxicating and so simple. Why had he not done this before? Circumstances.

Julian looked out onto the fields as they went past. Endless rows of sweet corn and then tobacco. The orange groves with trees that must have been 50 years old as well as the small recently-planted ones. The water pumps threw jets of water high into the air. The Jews had done a good job with their irrigation. From what seemed a small stream they had watered an entire country.

There were always people on the side of the road, some waiting to get on a bus, always some soldiers hitch-hiking either back home or to their base, their rifles slung across their shoulders in nonchalance. Then Arab vendors selling sweet corn, and falafel in pitta bread.

"What are you thinking?" A voice from his left shoulder.

"I thought you were asleep" he said.

"I was, sort of. What were you thinking?" she asked.

"I was thinking how lucky I was, you, me, this trip". She snuggled up closer.

"What time will we get there? About?"

"Well, another hour maybe; not dark anyway".

Jitka lifted herself from Julian's shoulder, licked her finger and wiped under her eyes, like a cat washing itself. Then she re-arranged her hair. He was seeing her at her worst. If they liked each other after that, well, there was some chance maybe.

They travelled in silence, looking out onto the orange groves, the people standing around at the side of the road waiting for a bus, Arabs in their long white or grey robes, their head-dress, their skin like brown dried parchment, and with two days' bristle. The women were in black, and always with some bags and children. The bus had slowly filled up as they went, and Julian and Jitka started observing their fellow passengers. There were mainly Arab families sitting in silence stoically enduring the journey. From time to time the bus stopped in the middle of nowhere, and there was a little group of people waiting. No sign of a bus stop, a shelter, nothing. No sign either of human habitation. They had come out of the desert. Julian looked around as far as he could see. Nothing. No house, tent, nothing. Where they came from was a mystery. The men barked out short commands, the women followed. Others got on, composed themselves for the journey.

There were also some Israelis, soldiers who just slumped into a seat, arms cradling a rifle, and went to sleep almost seconds later. The training was the hardest in the world, it was said. They did endurance tests, not sleeping for 100 hours; battle training with obstacle courses which included mines and live ammunition. It was a strange peace, these Arabs and these Israeli soldiers almost side by side. Julian could detect no actual threat in the air, but it may have been an uneasy truce.

The sun was going down, but it was still light. The slight damp made the scents stronger, and the smell of the orange blossom was pervasive, wonderful. It was a scent which was sweet, hopeful, one of growth and simplicity. The tobacco also hit their noses, dark, heavy, pungent. And the sudden sound of the sweep of the water jets. Then more desert.

It was around 7pm when they got to Capernaum. There was nothing much announced, just a battered, rusting sign in Hebrew and English. Julian slowly came to realise that for the Israelis, the Christian story was just one big myth, a mass delusion about the leader of a small religious sect (there were hundreds of them at the time) who may or may not have existed, and if he did, got on the wrong side of the law and died a rather nasty death. The Old Testament was fact, with their kings and wars and deeds. The other stuff tacked on was mass hysteria.

So, for an Israeli, Nazareth was a small town outside Jerusalem where you could get good dates, and Capernaum was a small fishing village with nothing special to see, a few houses, one or two hostels for the mad pilgrims, two shops which sold tacky artefacts and souvenirs to the unsuspecting deluded tourists, and a general groceries store. This was the biblical place Julian had read about in his much-battered bible at school. Capernaum. They got out with two Arabs who started off in the other direction and then strode off into the fields. The bus driver gunned the engine and was off into the dusk. The dust fell slowly around them. They walked down the slope towards the water's edge and the little church.

"It isn't what I expected" said Julian.

Jitka looked at him and registered his disappointment.

"You thought it would be different?"

"Yes, to tell the truth. I thought it would be more important. You know, the place where Christ walked, the sermons, the fishing, the miracles. Instead, I don't know...... it's just a few houses and, nothing, really. I wanted, I don't know, something more spiritual".

"Perhaps it is closer to what it was. It is more real than the churches and the silver and gold and the priests in their .... how do you say, the long dresses they wear?"

Julian stumbled. He hated this, the walking dictionary, and often he did not know, the word eluded him, and he thought he knew his own language.

"Um, cassocks? Robes?"

"If you don't know, how should I?" asked Jitka.

"Good point. Cassocks. I'd go for cassocks".

"So, with their cassocks and their hats....."

"Mitres" said Julian confidently.

"Mitres? This is a word, or did you make it up?".

"No, it is a word, THE word, actually. The right one, in this context. I think".

"So, the sexless men with their cassocks and mitres. Is this not better? I could imagine Christ here" said Jitka.

"You believe?" he asked.

"I don't know. I'm trying. That is also why I am here, perhaps. Religion was frowned on. You were meant to worship the state, if anything. Lenin, Stalin. Breznev. Tractor production. Not Jesus. He didn't seem to be around a lot when I was growing up".

"You must tell me about it".

"I will. But not now. Later" said Jitka.

"Later".

They walked down towards the little church placed so close to the water's edge. Julian tried the door. It was locked. Hardly a church, it was a sort of stone sanctuary, but befitting, simple, holy.

"For tomorrow, perhaps" she said.

"Tomorrow".

They walked closer to the water's edge. The small waves came up to the shore and retreated slightly. Jitka put her hand through Julian's. It was the perfect lover's scene, hand in hand, a walk on the side of the shore at the Lake of Galilee. There were trees right down to the shore, no beach. Jitka took away her hand and placed his around her waist. It felt like something definitive. He felt his manhood swell just as a result of that gesture. It was a promise, and Jitka knew it.

As they walked under one tree, she stopped, then exclaimed:

"But this is, how do you say? this is *granatove jablko*! Pomegranate! Here, up here. In her voice was a mixture of surprise and joy".

And she reached up and pulled at this red and brown, rather ugly fruit and wrenched it off the branch. The surrounding branches were spiky and scratched her arms slightly. Ah! But she had her prize.

"What is it?"

"You do not know? You know so little. In my country these are highly prized, they cost a great, great deal. Here, they are free. I like this. The Garden of Eden. God provides, and we are walking in the evening. Though not naked. And that is a pity".

She gave Julian a sly smile.

"We will eat it in our hotel room. Which is exactly where, Mr Guide?" Then she laughed a little to herself. She liked the idea.

"I am the Eastern European witch come to lead you out of the Garden of Eden, you say that, yes?"

"I think it was an apple. But what the hell! Let's find the hotel".

Julian put his arms around her. She turned and put her mouth to his, and they kissed long. Her lips gave way and became gooey, and she turned her mouth to the other side and then touched him quickly and lightly with her lips. Then they broke away.

"I think you have much to learn".

"I am a quick learner" said Julian.

"Come. We eat this at the hotel. I love this fruit. We'll come down to the lake after dinner and walk around at night. It will be so romantic" she said.

She turned once more and kissed him hard, felt his manhood tighten against his jeans.
Then took his hand and they walked with their small bags to find the hotel.

⚒ ⚒

The hotel was closer to the small group of houses further up the road. Very simple, small, clean, and rather dusty outside. They walked into the reception. A large middle-aged man in shorts looked up from his paper behind the desk. He had reading glasses on, and looked mildly irritated that anyone had disturbed his reading. A small electric fan was whirring fast.

"Shalom" he said.

"Shalom" said Julian. "Do you speak English?"

"Enough" said the hotel owner.

"We booked a room. A double room. The name is Romand".

He got up with a sigh. His white net vest hung loosely around him, and he had flip-flops on his feet.

"You rang before?"

"We rang, yes. From Jerusalem. A friend of Shalva's".

He turned the large crisp pages. Julian looked through at the same time.

"There, there it is".

Julian could decipher his name in Hebrew by now.
The hotel-keeper nodded. Stuck his large index finger on the name. Grunted.

"You stay one night, two?"

Julian did not dare to look at Jitka. "One night, maybe two" he said.

"Passports?"

He hardly looked up. He spared Julian and Jitka any blushes. Israel was at war, the young needed their time together, they were *goyim,* unmarried, who cared? So were all his customers. He looked through the two passports, the Czech one with its green embossed outer cover, and then the French more subdued one. The hotel-keeper laboriously copied out Jitka's name and passport number. The Czech name was not easy. Then Julian's. As he copied he spoke under his breath:

"Hugo Romand"

As he gave the passport back, he said to Julian:

"Merci".

Julian replied: "*Merci bien*"

He gave them a key on a large heavy weight with the room number.

They walked along the corridor in silence until they found the room. Julian put down his parachute silk bag and opened the door. It was simple, clean and with two beds close together. Clean white sheets turned down, a shower and toilet to the right, shutters which opened onto a small garden and some scrub land at the back of the hotel. Julian went and opened the shutters. A small irrigator was pushing water around the garden, the ubiquitous swish, swish. Julian then closed them again. Insects, mosquitoes, better avoid them.

"I sleep by the window, do you mind?" Jitka asked.

"No, not at all. Anywhere. Anywhere, as long as it is in this room, that is?"

Jitka smiled and shrugged her shoulders. Always humour, these English. It was fun most times, but not everything was a joke. Her country was not a joke. Jitka sat on the bed. Placed her bag at the side.

"Why do you have a French passport? You speak English. And your name is Julian, but it does not appear on the passport".

Here we go, thought Julian.

"Julian-Julienne-is my nick-name. They all call me Jules at home. It was a film, Jules et Jim, and my brother is called Jim. *Voilà!* Jules et Jim. Do you not have nicknames in your country?"

"We do, yes. But you seem, I don't know, not to be happy now I ask".

"My parents lived in England since I was so high. Since I was a nipper".

"Nipper?" she asked. "I do not understand".

"Young child".

"So you speak French"?

"Some. Badly. We spoke English at home. Most of us. We were 7 kids in all. Italian too".

Jitka smiled again. Perhaps he was telling the truth. She would try and trick him.

"*Come va?*"

"*Va bene, anzi, benissimo grazie. E Lei? E' piaciuto il viaggio, cara?*" he fired back.

Jitka laughed. He had convinced her. Families do grow up speaking several languages.

"Jules. Jules et Jim, is it?" she asked. Julian shrugged.

"Then I'll call you Jules" she said.

"My family docs".

"Jules, Jules. I like it". She nodded her head.

"Come here, Jules. I want to say your name, and taste you".

He went towards her.

"No first, turn the lock. Lock the door". Julian did as she said.

"Now come and kiss me".

Julian sat on the bed and went to her. She kissed him with strength, her tongue darting her and there on his. Then she broke off.

"I'm going to take a shower. Then I'll get in to bed; I want you to do the same. Then we will make love. But when I come out of the shower, you close your eyes".

"OK. But you can use a towel".

"Have you seen the size of the towels?" Julian looked.

"Small. Making economies. It is Israel. And they are at war", said Julian

"I'll be back". She kissed him lightly on the lips and went into the bathroom.

Julian lay back on the bed, his blood ringing in his ears. He could not think straight. He could not run now, nor wanted to, though the passport moment was tricky. He thought she had been convinced. He had convinced himself. Jules et Jim. Where had that come from? *Jules et Jim!* Some arty French film he had read of somewhere. He heard the water running, thought of her body, that slim, lithe skier's body. He got up to turn off the lights, leaving only the sidelight on. Nakedness had never been a big deal for him as he had grown up in a place where there was no privacy.

The shower stopped. He turned his head away so as not to embarrass her as she came in.

"It was good. Are you sleeping?" Her voice was mock indignant, shocked.

"Trying to, but the shower and your singing were making too much noise".

"English humour again. Why do you always joke?"

"Deflates the situation".

He turned and saw her wrapped in a small towel, water still coming off her shoulders. She walked to the other side of her bed and got under the sheet.

"Your turn. Get the dust off. And the sweat" she ordered.

Julian turned and stripped to his pants and went into the shower cubicle. The air was steamy. He undressed and got in the shower. His cock was half-swollen and looking more like something one saw in the nature programme under a baby elephant, dangly and out of control and with the animal having no idea what to do with it. He turned on the shower and concentrated on the water. Jitka obviously knew the ropes. He'd do his best. It was not going to be the sexual Olympics, though he had never worried about his size, or that it worked. It had never let him down so far. He looked down his body. It was tanned from the orange groves and the tractor work, almost skinny, nothing too muscular, but nothing out of place. It was God's handiwork, and he was happy with it.

He turned off the taps and dried himself. He took a deep breath and came out into the bedroom. Jitka had turned down the lighting even further by placing a magazine around the bedroom lamp. Julian looked at her under the sheet. She was very pretty. Her blonde hair was dishevelled on the pillow, she had kept her necklace around her neck giving her a sort of Christmas present look. Her eyes were dark and inviting.

"Come", she said simply.

"I'm coming".

Julian turned and let the towel slip off him, so she did not see the baby elephant's rubber hose. He sat on the bed and turned to her. She lifted the sheet and brought him to her.

"Come", she said again.

"I'm coming, he joked. Fast as I can".

"Not too fast. We have a lot to do. Then we go for a meal, and perhaps do it again, yes?

"Sounds a good programme to me".

Julian's voice had drifted into a low drone. Julian turned his face and body into hers. It was still cool and slightly damp from the shower. He put his arm around her waist and kissed her. Jitka's lips were at first set and hard, and then under his kissing became mushy and relaxed. She kissed him back hard, their mouths opening and their tongues touching. Jitka's did a little dance around his, flicking and moving away. Julian let his hand move down her body and put his hand over her pubic hair, then tentatively placed his fingers between her legs. She opened her legs to accommodate him, and he touched her with his fingers. She was wet inside, and he started exploring. He felt her heat, the slippery folds, and the animal need to have him inside her. Her hand came down on his, directing, orchestrating, pressing down on the back of his, now pulling his fingers higher till they were outside and touching her most sensitive spot. Then her hand became firmer, almost aggressively pushing and circling. Julian let her do what she wanted, she knew her own body. Then the rhythm became urgent, her back arched and she started breathing rapidly, saying incoherent things in Czech. At her climax she bit into his neck. Then lay back, her breast rising and falling as if she had run a marathon. There were little beads of sweat on her upper lip. Slowly her breathing calmed, and she turned and looked at him.

"You don't mind?"

"What?"

"That I, how do you say, by myself had a climax? Is that what you say in English, or is there some other word?"

"No, we say that. I am not an expert in these matters. Quite a novice, in fact. I suppose you could say...you.. came. Had an orgasm".

"Good, I will remember these words".

"You have never.....?" Jitka propped herself upon one elbow and looked into his eyes in enquiry.

"No, I mean, not quite the first time, but nearly".

Jitka laughed to herself. Her face showed triumph.

"Well, we have a lot to learn. Together".

She lay back and with her hand touched him, found the baby elephant's nozzle.

"We'll have to do something with this soon. Give me a few minutes. I need to get my breath back".

She rested her left hand on his cock, as if it were quite normal, the most normal place to put a hand. Julian waited for her to get her energy back. He had no idea of a woman's, this woman's power to regenerate herself. But it was just nice having a woman's hand on him, touching him, caressing him lightly, tickling him. Julian's blood was pumping in his ears.

"Now I am ready. Come to me".

As he moved on top of her she opened her thighs and with her right hand directed him into her. As he entered her, he heard her sigh in sheer delight. Then he felt her thighs encircle his back, as if she were riding a rather untamed yearling, and was not going to let him go easily. Julian started moving slowly and he felt her ankles directing his rhythm and thrusts, a little faster there, a little deeper there, whispering constantly:

"That's good, don't stop now, a little faster, yes, faster now".

She ground her pubic area into his until their hairs touched.

"Now! she said savagely. Do it now!" And then some Czech word grunted into his ear. Julian climaxed with her.

After what seemed an eternity Julian rolled off her. She was slight under him, his weight must have been crushing her, and he felt the relief of her body. He left his hand lying on her stomach which she found and held. After a couple of minutes' silence, when they could only hear the fan and the Arab music wailing from a distance, she spoke:

"Thank you".

"Thank you for what?"

"It was very nice. And we worked together the first time. That is not common, you know?"

Julian glowed with stupid male pride. It was as if all his problems and mental anguish had disappeared suddenly. His brain had been emptied of all the worries and insecurities that had plagued him in his life up until then. It was good; it was where he should be, doing what he should be doing. It was where he wanted to be from now on.

More silence, then she got up.

"I have to wash otherwise I'll be sleeping in a damp place".

"Patch".

"Patch. Whatever the word is".

She did not bother to hide herself as she went to the shower, and Julian watched the lithe body, the shapely legs, the small breasts and the tuft of blonde hair. As she closed the door, he felt both wonderful and angry, that this had not happened before, and many times. Why wait? If it could be this good and this simple! A silly smile settled on his lips.

Jitka came back from the shower, cool again and fresh, as if nothing had happened while sperm was still running out of the hose and drying and sticking to the hairs on his stomach.

"What are you smiling about? Hmm? All men are the same".

"I'll have to wash too soon".

"Stay with me now for a bit. Don't go away".

"Why would I do that? Where would I go?" Julian turned his head to her, not understanding.

"Men do that". Jitka's voice became hard now, despising, angry, contemptuous.

"They go away. They make love and then they go away, either physically or just they start doing their business accounts or thinking how much they spent on the food in order to get to this point, or they start planning, I don't know, their next"....Jitka searched for a word...."encounter".

And suddenly:

"What colour are my eyes?"

"I'm sorry".

"What colour are my eyes?"

She was serious now. Very, very serious.

"What colour are my eyes? Without looking, what colour are they?"

Without hesitation, Julian replied:
"They are blue, a deep, deep blue".

"Not that deep. More grey".

But the answer seemed to appease her.
"Stay with me now. Put your arm around me. Here, like that".
Julian turned into her snuggled up, his head on her shoulder.

"I'm starving".

"Stay a bit longer. Like this. Just a bit longer".

"What did you say in Czech? When, you know, you were a bit carried away?"

"Oh, I don't know. Something like, this crazy Englishman weighs two tons!"

Julian lifted his head.

"I hope you are joking. You are joking, aren't you?" he said.

Jitka laughed: "You'll never know".

Julian rested his head on her shoulder again.

"Well, get someone else lighter next time".

As he said it the thought of Eli went through his brain like a knife. He felt Jitka move away slightly; the memory had hurt her too.

"I'm sorry. I should not have said that. It was thoughtless of me". Her voice was deadpan.

"Yes".

"Let's get up now. Go and wash. I don't want to be sleeping in your...patch either! And I am starving too."

Julian got up and walked to the bathroom. Jitka did not turn but lay hunched staring out through the blinds to the garden outside.

⚒ ⚒

After the meal in the restaurant, grilled meat and salad, so simple, cheap and good, they wandered towards the shore.

"We'll see the church tomorrow morning. Do you mind?" asked Jitka.

Jitka had her hand in his. They were two lovers. Eyes in alleys watched the golden couple as they strolled to the water's edge. It was quite dark now and her hair shone out, making her the subject of conversation from the doorways. She noticed but did not care; Julian was oblivious. They came to the water's edge. The moon was just coming up and reflected on the water, the little waves jumping and inviting. Jitka released her hand and took off her shoes, leaning against Julian. She put her feet into the lake, walked a bit.

"It isn't that cold. I expected colder. Do you think he really walked here?"

"Who?"

"Who? Who? That is English humour again? Who? No, you people really make me laugh. Who?"

Julian smiled. He was glad for her mirth after the stupidity of his remark. She had regained her good humour.

"Who?" Her voice rose in a whoop of laughter. "Just the most famous man who ever lived and walked in this area and may have walked on water, this very same water, and was the most successful fisherman of his day. Here! This lake! Who?" She burst into laughter again.

"No, you make me laugh".

"I am glad I do".

She came up to him and kissed him tenderly, her body relaxed into his. Then she took his hand again and they walked along the shore. Pine trees came down to the water's edge, and the shore was covered in pine needles, so little grew there. It was so warm still, the breeze hardly cool, even by the lake. In the distance they could see the outline of the hills the other side. The constant chirp of the cicadas was there, like a background tape one had forgotten to turn off, could not turn off. Incessant, pushing, determined. As they walked Jitka looked further along the shore and stopped.

"Look, a boat!" She ran towards it. A rowing boat was there on the water's edge, with just a rope tying it to a tree. The oars were in place. A fisherman's boat, perhaps.

"Let's row out".

"What?"

"Let's row out".

"We can't. It isn't ours. It is stealing".

"Not if we give it back. Come, please". She came close and kissed his ear, licked his neck.

"Come".

"But Jitka, we can't. I mean, it isn't ours".

"But we borrow it, yes? That is the right word? Borrow? That is not stealing. We row out, we row back, who knows?"

"He may need it?" said Julian.

"Now?"

"Fishermen go out at night".

"In which case, we come back after half an hour. Please. Jules. Please".

She looked up at him with her big eyes. Julian shook his head, reasoned that it was not stealing if they borrowed it for half an hour. He sighed and gave in. He untied the rope, got to the prow and lifted it slightly so it slid into the water and sat bobbing slightly. He sighed again, but Jitka was ecstatic, and climbed in.

"Do you know how to row?"

"Of course I know how to row". His pride was hurt. "Everyone knows how to row, don't they?"

"I don't" said Jitka.

"Something you don't know! Amazing".

She sat at the stern, looking out at the moon as Julian rowed out into the lake. The wind was getting up slightly and the waves were choppy. Julian rowed steadily, not quite sure where he was going or what he was doing it for. But Jitka was happy, and so he was happy. Sort of.

Suddenly she stood up.

"Stop rowing".

Julian upped the oars and put them into the boat.

"Listen".

The waves lapped against the boat, but apart from that, there was nothing, no cars, planes, music. It was so peaceful and could have been two thousand years ago. Jitka sat down and started taking off her clothes.

"What exactly are you doing?" he asked.

"I'm going for a swim".

"Excuse me?"

"We are going for a swim. You do know how to swim. I have seen you in the pool with the kids".

"Here? Now? At night? In the Lake of Galilee?"

She now stood totally naked in the moonlight. The moon's rays reflected off her hair, off her pale skin.
"What about....? I don't know, sharks, animals............?" Then the absurdity of what he was saying hit him.

"OK, no sharks, but snakes, large fish which bite your balls off".

"Your problem, not mine", And with that she dived off perfectly into the water.

Julian sat stunned. One moment she was there, the next she was in the water. He heard her surface and swim to the side of the boat.

"It's freezing, but bearable. Come".

"What? In there? Who is going to look after the boat?"

"The boat is not going anywhere. Where is it going? Is it going to run off without us?"

She swam away again, into the night. He could see her pale body in the dark water. He had run out of arguments. He laughed to himself, muttering that he should not be doing this, that it was a mistake. But he took off his trousers and shirt, and rather less expertly, and with a worried look at the boat and how far it was to the shore, dived into the lake. And it was very cold, she was right about that. Julian struggled fast to the surface and looked around immediately for the boat. It was there, bobbing up and down, safe, had not gone anywhere. Jitka swam towards him and touched him, and yanked at his cock which had shrivelled to nothing in the cold water.

"Where has it all gone, Jules?"

"It's fucking freezing!"

"It's a lake, not a heated swimming pool".

She came close again and kissed him.

"I'm getting out of here", said Julian "before I lose whatever manhood I had, and before some horrible Galilean monster comes and bites me in the butt, or worse".

Jitka shrieked with laughter and swam away again. Julian swam to the boat and drew himself up. It was not easy to get back in, and he had a moment of panic that he would not make it. But he found if he propelled himself hard with his feet and hoisted himself up at the same time he could make it. Ungainly, but safe. He was back in the boat, although looking to the shore, he realised that he could swim it easily if he wanted. He was panting from the exertion and shivering slightly. He then looked around and saw Jitka coming back.

"Help me up. Jules, help me, yes? I can't do it by myself I think".

For a moment she had lost her composure and looked unsure of herself, scared even. Perhaps the cold, dark waters at night had unnerved her. Julian lent over the side and gave her his strong right hand while holding onto the seat with his other. At the first attempt he could not lift her.

"Try again, but kick hard with your legs, swim into the boat. You may be thin, but...."

She did as he said, and this time he hauled her up. Her skin was icy and she fell into his embrace. He saw a moment of fear in her eyes.

"OK?"

"Yes, OK. It was not easy, getting in the boat again".

"No".

"How did you do it on your own?"

"Practice. Tree climbing. I don't know".

Jitka straddled Julian on the boat, taking warmth from him, shivering in the breeze.

"Hold me tight. Keep me warm".

"No towels"

"No, no towels". She laughed.

"You will have to hug me warm". And so he did. He rubbed her back and held her tight, and they together restored their body heat. Julian felt himself getting hard again. The cold water had not dampened it totally. Jitka felt him under her, his warmth rising, knocking at her. She kissed him and opened her lips. Warmth in her mouth, and warmth down there in her body. She reached down and placed him inside her.

"Stay like that, please. Don't move".

They stayed motionless, looking up at the stars, the boat rocking under them, the breeze on their skin.

"Do you think it is wrong?" he asked.

"Wrong? What we are doing? You mean the boat? We'll bring it back".

"No, I mean, this, what we are doing now. You, me, the lake, love, sex, Jesus, all that".

"My mad Englishman, how can this be wrong? He gave us what he gave us, and we are using it, ...them. I think he would be happy for us. In his lake, on a boat. I think he would smile on us. And who is to say he never did anything himself, hmm? Stop talking now. Concentrate, or this won't happen".

And with that her right hand came down between them and she touched herself again, expertly. Julian felt her orgasm growing and followed her.

"Now. Now!" And she started talking in Czech, oblivious to anything but her pleasure and the night.

After, they disengaged slowly. It was as if something sacred had happened and they were aware of it. It was as if they had joined with nature and the cosmos and it had been benign and smiled on them. Jitka moved to the side of the boat and slid in to wash herself, not losing her grip, then hauling herself up safely this time and with no fear, putting her right leg over the side as if she were getting on a horse.

"Pretty athletic".

"I ride. Back home, we all ride. One of the things the Communists allow us to do".

Julian put his clothes back on, took the oars and began rowing back. Jitka dressed herself as he rowed. Finally they reached the shore. Julian got out and pulled the boat up the sand and shingle and tied it up again. He used a better knot than before. Night had been their accomplice. Jitka took his hand and looked at the scene.

"Borrowed?".

"Borrowed".

"Guilty?"

"No. Sort of. No, not guilty. Innocent. And happy".

They made their way back to the hotel, through the narrow streets and the sound of the half-tone music wailing through the night air. Jitka had her head on his shoulder and this time was unaware of the eyes that followed them every step they took.

When they got back to the hotel, the television was blaring out some 40s film in black and white. The owner was sleeping heavily in a chair behind reception. No one else seemed to be around. They walked back to their room hand in hand, calm and relaxed, without the sexual tension there was there before. In such a short time they had moved into a sense of couple: my side of the room, my bed, my lamp, I read until I fall asleep. Jitka turned on the side-lamp which gave just enough light. Julian opened the metal shutters and the scents of the garden came into the room, the damp earth and the heavy vegetation. Night smells. Jitka took off her clothes calmly, protected by the night and their intimacy. There was no shame now.

"Come and lie close to me".

Julian stripped and lay close, an arm across her. She took it and wrapped it around her, placing his hand between her breasts. Suddenly Julian felt her sadness envelop her.

"What are you thinking?" he asked.

"Of my father" she said.

"Why?"

"Because you remind me of him".

"I look like him?"

"No. Yes, in a way. But not the physical thing. You remind me of his....weakness".

Julian lay still.

"My grandmother said he was weak. And I suppose he was. But you have to live in a communist country to understand. They can crush anyone, you know?"

"I don't know".

"Yes, it is strange, this not knowing. It angers me, and yet why should you?"

"What do you know of England?" She stayed silent for a while.

"I suppose you are right. But you take so much for granted" she said.

"How much do you know of my country then?"

"I read about it, read you authors, the ones who are not banned. I read the history books" she said.

"OK: We have an amazing literature". But why should I know about your country? Why not Japan, or China, or I don't know, New Zealand? Why do you fire this at me, accuse me of being poor at geography and post-war politics? Why should I know so much about your country?"

Jitka lay still and then held him tighter to herself.

"I suppose you are right. Why should you? We are all so egocentric about our countries and culture and that we are so special" said Jitka.

"Everyone is and is not special, it seems to me" said Julian. "Thinking you are more special is dangerous and arrogant, no? Someone told me that China considered itself the centre of the world, the universe. The Swedish also think they are pretty special, and the Brits on a bad day, well, the war, the victories, the British bulldog stuff. Pathetic really, I suppose. It is a sort of self-defence perhaps. But tell me. Your father, you were saying"

The water from the sprays swished on through the night, and the cicadas grated out their incessant chirping.

"I loved him. He died last year".

"I'm sorry".

"That is why I came to Israel, I suppose, to escape. Everyone loved him. My friends loved him. But they did not know him. Not really. We used to go skiing together, father and daughter on the slopes, early in the morning, no one there, the snow untouched by anyone. He was such a good skier. I am too".

"I noticed the legs".

Jitka elbowed him gently, in mock disapproval. Julian tried to place his hand between her legs, but she pulled his hand back up.

"No, don't. I can't talk if you do that".

Julian removed his hand and placed it back between her breasts and snuggled up. Her voice came from afar, as if she were saying these things for the first time, saying them to the world, anyone could be listening or not.

"He drank".

"So do I".

"No, he drank till he was incapacitated. You say that, yes?" Julian nodded.

"He drank till he could not walk, till his glasses fell off, and he.............. I had to take him to bed. My mother would have nothing to do with him. This happened every two weeks, at weekends. We did not talk about it. No one knew".

"Why?"

"Why what?"

"Why did he drink?"

"I don't know" she said.

"People don't just drink like that, do they? I don't know any alcoholics, or drug users, really. Why did he get like that?"

A long silence followed.

"You know, I have never thought about it like that. Why? Perhaps because all his dreams of a new free country were destroyed. I suppose those who did not flee the Russians drank to forget. Perhaps they were not cowards at all. What were they going to do against the tanks? They were bought by Russian flats for their family and safe jobs. You know, I can't read 1984 anymore".

"Why?"

"Because it is all true. How Orwell knew so much I don't know. But he did. Poor, poor, poor Papa'. Drinking to forget a life that was not the one he chose, not the one he wanted".

And then he heard her crying silently, he heard her sobs and felt the tears streaming down her face. She finally let herself go, and she turned to Julian and wept into his chest, hiding her face from him. The crying finally stopped and she snuffled, turned and dried her eyes on the side of the sheet. Then she got up and went to the bathroom. When she came back she got in silently, found a position which suited her, nestling against his body, and fell asleep. Julian heard her breathing grow steadier and only then let himself follow her into that temporary oblivion.

When he woke next day he reached for Jitka and did not find her. From the shower came humming and the sound of water splashing. Julian lay back and thought about last night, the emotion, the release, the pent-up tears which finally were shed. He felt almost an intruder, someone who had triggered this memory and had then to watch and try to comfort as well as he could, a bystander at a car accident with no paramedics about. Sleep had seemed to be a great healer. She was singing in Czech, having a good time. And then he thought about the boat trip, the night and its benison, the love-making so natural and good and exciting, their bodies open to the elements. He felt twinges in his arm muscles from the exertion, but his mind felt clear.

Then suddenly she was out, drying her hair, all a whirl of energy and determination and white towels and shampoo and soap.

"Lazy bones. Get up!"

"Why? What is there to get up for?" He reached for the towel she had around her waist, and she avoided him.

"Ah, you think of one thing only. You had enough yesterday, no?"

"Yesterday was yesterday".

She laughed.

"Ah, the English humour again. You never stop".

"Come, sit down here now. Close to me".

Jitka came and sat on the side of the bed. She smelt so good, of soap, of newly-washed hair, of perfume.

"What is the plan today?"

"We have plans?" asked Julian in an anguished voice.

"Yes, we have plans, Mr Guide".

"I thought we could take a trip around the world lying in bed".

"What?". Jitka turned her eyes on to him, a full, concerned, incredulous gaze.

"Yes, you could say a syllable and I'd have to guess where it was and then tell you what there was to see there".

"For example?". Her voice was still not clear where this was leading.

"For example, I'd say: 'rife' and you'd have to guess Tenerife, and then I'd tell you everything I knew about Tenerife, which strangely is quite a bit, as I've been there".

Jitka looked at him as if the sun had done something to his brains.

"Then you'd say.....'tu', and I'd make a wild guess and say Timbuctu, which might be the right answer, if you felt it was the right answer and knew something about the African city, and then you could tell me anything and everything you know about the place, knowledge which would be extensive and wide-ranging as your family lived there as importers and exporters of ivory in the 1950s....... for example".

"That is.... a game? Is this more English humour? Or are you mad? Totally cracked, you say?".

"Yes, we do say 'cracked' my little European witch. We also say, and you can note this down in that little red vocabulary book you carry around with you: a nut, lost his marbles, three apples short of a picnic (though don't ask me why), a screw loose, barmy, flipped. There must be many more. Can't think of them off the top of my head".

Jitka stared hard in incredulity at her companion. Perhaps he was slightly unhinged. Or funny. Both. She laughed. Julian lent over and kissed her shoulder.

"It is just a way of keeping you here and not going outside. Let's stay in bed".

"No! I want to see things, places".

"What?".

"I don't know. The country. The sea. Places. Not a hotel room!".

Julian thought about it and realised she was not going to hang around. He shrugged his shoulders.

"OK. Sight-seeing it is. Mr Guide says first we see the little church which was locked, then we walk a bit to see the countryside around here, and then make it to the beach at Ashkelon, a swim in the Med, a hotel there and then back to Jerusalem. How does that sound?"

"It sounds lovely", and she reached down and touched his cock which grew stiff in her hand.

"Later" she said.

Later. Julian lay back. Always later. The deferred pleasure principal. He's rather fuck his brains out now. The deferral could be a lifetime, had been a lifetime. The child in him was screaming: I want mine now! The adult got up and found some underpants.

═⫛ ⫛═

They dressed and made it to the small area where breakfast was served. Fruit juices, bread, jam, butter, yoghurt, some cereals. There was hardly anyone else in the hotel, just a middle-aged couple with two children, Israelis. Another western couple, possibly French, and an Australian couple who talked loudly and almost obliviously, as if no one there might speak their language.

They took their breakfast and sat near the window. The

water-jet was still pumping around the garden. From afar there was a radio with a woman's voice singing the Eastern wail so appreciated by these countries. Julian couldn't make head or tail of it. It always seemed to his ears a long lament for the country, womankind, lost friendships, lost love, children. Jitka ate with undisguised appetite. He liked that, passion, appetite and rude health. And there were no strange silences, and eyes cast down studying the tablecloth, wondering what to say next. It was easy to be with her.

"So, we pack, wander around the place a bit, and then take a bus or hitch to Askelon".

"You want to hitch?"

"If there is no bus. Everyone hitches here. The army moves by hitching".

"I know, Jules, but I am not happy with the idea. We don't do it in my country. It is dangerous".

"But they all do it here. It is free. I think the idea is great" he said.

"Maybe for you, but I am not you. I am a woman, and attractive, if only for my blonde hair".

"OK, we'll use the bus when and where we can".

"Thank you". Jitka gave him a smile.

They went first to the little church by the water's edge. It was so unobtrusive, and simple, and did not shout its presence out to the world. They tentatively opened the large wooden door, open now, and were met by a priest in a black cassock. He was as surprised as they were, it seemed.

He spoke to them in Hebrew, and German.

"*Nicht Deutsch, aber Englisher*", was all Julian could muster. Jitka spoke more fluently, but it seemed the priest didn't have much of a grasp of anything but Hebrew and German and a bit of English.

"From England. Yes. You come to see Bible".

"Yes, to see where Jesus walked, lived".

"Is here. Please. Look".

And they walked around the little church, a mixture of Byzantine finery and New England simplicity. There was the Lord's prayer in several languages written on a wooden board. Morning light flooded into the knave. Julian felt it was just the right sort of edifice for pilgrims to Capernaum, not gaudy, showy, encrusted with gold, with badly painted figures of the saints. It prompted a deep peace, a sense of rightness. Jitka put her hand in his. They remained in the centre of the aisle, almost as if they were giving their marriage vows, this couple who had only met several days before. Could he live with this blonde witch? The past 48 hours had been good.

"What are you thinking?" she asked.

"About us. Here. In the church".

Jitka squeezed his hand, as if asking him to go on.

"I can't say. It would sound silly" Julian said.

"Say. You started".

"No" he said.

"You started. You must go on. It is not fair".

"I was thinking how happy I was with you, that's all" he said.

"And?"

"And...nothing. It is a good moment".

"Nothing more?" she asked.

"Nothing more".

"Oh". Jitka sounded disappointed. She had been hoping for more. Some declaration. It had not happened.

"You know I like you very much. You know that, Jules".

"I like you too, Jitka", he said.

He turned to her and their hands came up together as if they were taking a vow.

"It has been good these days".

"I agree".

Then suddenly she broke away and walked out of the church. The priest was outside smoking a cigarette, scowling at the sun hitting him hard on the porch.

"Finished, yes? You see what you wanted?"

"Yes, thank you". Jitka had walked to the water's edge, the little waves lapping, coming to the pine needles.

"Let's walk a bit. Thank the priest. Did you leave an offering?"

"No, I didn't. We don't have much, Jitka".

"You must leave him something".

Julian went back to the church and left a 10 shekel note in the box. The priest seemed happy and murmured something in Hebrew.

"It leaves us short".

"We'll hitch, then".

"OK. We'll hitch".

They walked along the water's edge; Jitka took his hand again. They came soon to a path which led up into the hills through the pine trees. They walked until they came to a clearing and could turn and see the lake and the hills the other side quite clearly. Several boats were together, fishing. Julian hoped the owner had not noticed, though the knot would have been different, and the oars were probably placed differently. The lake looked so calm, peaceful, right. And generations upon generations of fishermen had lived and died there. It seemed a good place to live, an occupation with dignity. They walked on a bit further and came across a cultivated area with three men harvesting water-melons. They were Arabs. They greeted these foreigners with warmth.

"*Salam maleykum*".

"*Salam maleykum*", Julian replied.

The oldest of the three, possibly the father, took a melon, smashed it on the ground so it split open and offered a piece to Jitka and then to Julian. They accepted and ate from the great chunks.

It was still cold from the morning dew, and was the best water-melon Julian had ever tasted.

"I don't know about you, but this is amazing".

The juice was running down her chin. The Arabs were also eating with them.

"It is wonderful. Thank you, thank you".

"You want more?" they asked.

The oldest of them went towards another melon to break it open, but Julian stopped him.

"No, we have had enough. Really".

"Take, take with you".

"We can't. We are travelling". Julian mimed the walking and gestured to the space around him.

"Ashkelon, the sea" he said. Then he mimed swimming.

"Ahh. Ashkélon. Yes, that way. Far, very far" one of the Arabs said.

"How far?"

"You have take bus" one said.

"We will take a bus" Julian replied.

"2 hour, maybe 3".

"We'll do it. Thank you".

"Thank you".

They walked down the path towards the hotel, through the whispering trees, the cicadas manic grating.

"That was kind of them".

"Yes, it was. If we had been Israelis I am not sure they would have been so kind".

"True. But still they were kind and helpful".

"Yes, agreed. It is the sort of thing I would love to do".

"What, harvest watermelons? You don't know how to grow anything".

"One can learn".

"And sit on the hills of Galilee and grow water-melons?" Jitka said.

"Nice view" Julian replied.

"You are, what is that word again, cracked in the head, Mr Jules".

"Probably".

Suddenly Jitka stopped and knelt down. She had seen something move.

"Look. It's a tortoise, a baby tortoise".

And true enough, this tiny tortoise was clawing its way through the undergrowth, quite intent on reaching some spot, and almost oblivious of these two terrestrial monsters high above him. Jitka picked it up.

"Look, how sweet!" And she stated talking to it in Czech, baby words, crooning to it, as if it were a child.

"Where were you going, baby? Hmm? Want something good to eat? I'll find you something".

Julian also looked at it close up, its strangely old man's wrinkled neck, the bobbing, sensitive, bald head. It did not know what to do, either withdraw completely until the danger was past, or struggle on. It decided to struggle, and its feet paddled on Jitka's hand, very determined to get where it had been going, or anywhere out of this strange terrain with no undergrowth or ferns.

"Let's keep it, Jules". Jitka turned to see his reaction.

"Where?"

"In my luggage, and then we can let it go in Jerusalem".

"Jitka, I am no biologist, but I really don't think baby tortoises are meant to travel to the sea, to be under the sun, not drink or eat, and then find themselves in another terrain which would be the scrub land outside the hospital. Not a great move for a tortoise, I would suggest".

Jitka kept it in her hand, feeling its little dark claws scratch on her palm. She looked again, saying nothing. The shell was so perfectly formed. She stroked the underbelly, and the tortoise retracted his head suddenly.

"That frightened him".

"Her" she said with authority.

"Her. How do you tell a tortoise's sex, please?"

"It's a her".

"OK. It's a her. Happy? Now, are you going to let it go, and can we get on with our trip to the sea?"

"Just one more moment, Jules".

Jitka held it to her, talking in Czech once more, putting her lips close to its head, almost kissing it. Then she knelt down and released it into the bushes. It began clawing its way to safety, any direction would do, just away from the pink flesh and no leaves where he had been. In a minute it had disappeared.

"No gratitude, I say. Near adoption on a sandy beach with ice-cream for food and it races off into the undergrowth".

"It was so sweet. I want one".

"Well, perhaps you could ask the hospital management to create a place for stray tortoises. Actually, the kids would have a great time, the ones that could actually hold them, pick them up".

Jitka looked at him to see if he was joking again.

"No, I'm not joking", Julian continued. "Occupational therapy for Nathan, and Esther would adore a tortoise. We could place the wheelchairs close to the animals and they could watch them, touch them, I don't know".

"You are joking again?"

"Strangely not this time. I think it a great idea. But not now. I don't think this little blighter would last the journey".

"You are right. Let's go", she said, and Jitka walked on ahead, down to the hotel and their bags".

⇥⊹ ⊹⇤

They took a bus to get to get to the main road, and then made the Israeli sign that they were hitchhiking, the finger pointed down, a sort of imperious: stop here now for me at this moment!

The second car did stop, and it was a huge Mercedes with a businessman type at the wheel. Never in the UK would someone like that stop to pick up hitchers, thought Julian. He ran up to the lowered car window and asked if he was going anywhere near Ashkelon. He was going close enough, he said, and could drop them where they could get another ride. Amazing. The second car.

They got in and let Jitka sit in the front. It was a subtle form of payment....she got the good seat and he got to talk to the blonde. Julian thanked him profusely, more than was necessary.

"No problem. Everyone hitches here" he said in American-accented English. "Besides my son is in the army and the government asks us to help the kids get back to their homes and families. They may get 24 hours off from training, so, the country-you know, we all help when we can".

The maize fields passed quickly. The unusual luxury was a gift. Jitka, sex, the sun, the sea and now free travel too and from these exotic places. Julian chatted away, interested in the man and his family, especially about his son and the stuff they put him through.

"That training. I mean, they teach him to kill with his bare hands, they have him running hikes in the sun with that kit on, he shoots like a WW 2 vet. Quite some boy. The girls too" He looked over to Jitka. "Yeah, I have two girls as well. But what they make the boys do, well, he went out skinny and came back built like a full-back. Frightened to get into a fight with him. So, tell me, why are you two here? Seeing the homeland? Just on vacation?"

"No, we are working in Jerusalem. Jitka is a nurse; I am an orderly. Before I worked on a kibbutz".

"You got a funny accent. You're not from Boston or any-where? I have a cousin in Boston".

"No, Britain. England. Jitka is from the Czech Republic".

"Oh! Sort of Service Overseas, or something?"

"Something like that".

"What are your names, if I may ask?"

"Julian and Jitka".

"Mine's Sammy. Not my real name actually, as it is Samuels, but everyone calls me Sammy. Started in High School. Better than Kike, or something, I suppose. Real name is David Samuels. Your names, they are not Hebrew names, are they?"

"No".

"Oh".

With that he fell silent. Turned on the radio. What seemed a gruff man's voice was heard. Sammy turned to look at Jitka. Then smiled at her smile. She did not seem anxious now, and was enjoying the seats and the smell of leather and the sun on her face and the pause from the dust.

The air-conditioning was another unusual boon. She turned her face to it, and the sweat dried quickly on her skin.

"Now, who do you think that is speaking ?" He nodded to the radio.

Julian and Jitka did not answer. They did not want to spoil his de-light in telling.

"I mean, is that a man's voice, or what?"

"It seems like a man to me", said Jitka.

Sammy thought it a great joke.

"That, my friends, is our Prime Minister! That is Golda Meir! That is the woman with the most....balls, excuse me, young lady, that we have in that country".

He turned up the volume.

"Listen to her, will you? Isn't that something? Doesn't matter what she says, they all listen to her. Even the Arabs quake in their shoes. They can't blow her away, she's like their mother! What a woman!"

Both Jitka and Julian laughed. He turned to see the reaction as the car sped on, laughing into their faces. Julian was not entirely happy at this division of labours. But the roads were fairly free at this hour, and traffic was just a few lorries loaded with water lemons and other produce in front. Several army trucks were going the other way, and some beat-up cars, windows wide-open with at least 5 Arab-looking men inside with their head-dresses flapping in the wind. Sammy's car was the newest on the road.

"Hitching, huh?" said Julian. Jitka smiled and turned.

"OK, Mr Guide. This time you may be right". They did not say any more in front of Sammy.

But as they sat and watched the country roll past, Julian thought this was the best. Shared rides, economy, trust, meeting people. It was how the world should be, but Golda Meir's husky voice read on, calling her people to constant vigilance, prepared to fight the necessary fight, uniting her family, leading them out of the wilderness.

The journey suddenly came to a halt. Sammy pulled over just before a crossroads. Dust surrounded them.

"Well, this is it. Sorry, but I have to turn off here and head up to close to the heights. Not much going on up there now, but you never know".

He held out his hand and shook Jitka's. She got out, and Julian lent over and shook Sammy's hand from the back. Thank you so much.

"My pleasure. Have a nice trip. Ashkelon is that way, straight ahead and down. You'll see the sea in about 5 minutes".

Then the cool machine sped off into the distance.

They walked over a little rise in the road, with the occasional melon-carrying truck speeding past them, and then saw the blue of the sea. The Mediterranean. The sun was high now and it sent little sparkles off the waves. It was so inviting sea you just wanted to jump from there straight in, a natural swimming pool in front of them, given by God.
"We have lucked out. It looks great!" he said.

Jitka put her hand in his and they walked the last mile down to the beach. They went through some one-storey houses with the white stucco paint peeling off the walls. It was like that everywhere.
The beach itself was not well-kept and there was hardly anyone there at this time of year. Only one restaurant was open and that was empty too.
They walked over the large echoing hall, past the many chairs and tables. There was a bar at the far end, and to the other a concrete floor just jutting out towards the sea. A construction still under construction. Her footsteps brought a sign of life to the place

and a youngish, dark-haired girl came to see what was going on. Julian was worried she would say they were closed, or something. They looked closed.

"Shalom".

"Shalom".

"Are you open?"

"Sure", She came closer.

"Can we eat here?"

"Why not?" Julian smiled. Why not indeed?

The girl looked as if she had just woken up, but was strangely welcoming.

"I'll bring you some falafel and bread". Julian was counting his money carefully now for the ride back that evening.

"Um, just two, thank you. And some water. Is that OK?"

"That's just fine".

The girl went away into the kitchen to prepare. Jitka and Julian held hands and then looked out onto the sea from the first floor. The beach had litter here and there, but was not off-putting, and the sea was so inviting, with the waves breaking and the sound of the surf reaching them.

"Perhaps we should have swum first, then had something to eat".

Jitka put her hand into his once more, and lent over to snuggle up to him.

"It has been two really nice days, Jules".

"Not over yet. We'll have fabulous swim, and then hitch back to the hospital. Might get another Merc. I had never ridden in a Merc before. You?"

"No, never. In my country only politicians and the army bosses get to ride in them. Prestige. You have no idea. It was so strange. We were taught German, but never used it; taught Russian but could never go there, and then when Brezhnev died, our great Russian leader whose country we were not allowed to visit, we as children had to sit and watch his funeral all the morning. All the schools closed, everyone at home watching Comrade Brezhnev being wheeled though the streets with the army and the guns and tanks and so on. It was so boring for children. Quite mad. A waste of time". And here she broke into Czech and it was quite obviously not complimentary.

"What was that?" he asked.

"You don't want to know. Untranslatable. Something to do with his reproductive equipment. Or not, rather. Having them, Whole. As it were". They both started laughing.

"Quite a translation. Quite a phrase".

They burst into fits of giggles again and were laughing when the girl brought the food.

It was a plate bursting with 5 pitta breads crammed full of good things, meat balls, salad, egg plant, eggs, cucumber, tomato. Julian was uneasy.

"We only ordered two" he said uneasily.

"Oh, I didn't hear you correctly. I thought you said 4 and then I added an extra. Please, just pay the same. No extra. Just pay for two". Julian paid the 4 shekels she asked and she left. They still had some money left. Jitka looked at Julian and the shrugged.

"She must like you".

"She may just be generous. It was a nice gesture. Maternal. Keep the boy's strength up. She may have brothers in the army".

They began eating, the food so simple but filling and good, costing practically the price of a small ice-cream back home. They finished it all, and sat back and watched the sea and the light glancing off the blue waves. Hardly anyone was around. There was an old man on the shore washing himself using soap, the suds floating around him. And one or two families with kids playing close to the water's edge, but otherwise, it was out-of-season and still early in the day. Hardly anyone around. And no one swimming.

"Almost our private beach, it would seem" said Jitka.

"Complaining?

"No. Not at all. Wonderful" she said.

They went and sat under one of the pine trees which grew on the scrub between the shore and the built-up area.
"Let's go for a swim now" she said. and Jitka was taking off her shorts and shirt, revealing a bright green and blue swimsuit. She looked so pretty but out of place, so foreign and pale in this land of dark-skinned beauties. "We can leave our stuff here, can't we?"

"I'll keep an eye on it all the time. Besides we are not going to be long, are we? You are not planning more passion in the surf?"

"No", she shouted as she ran to the sea. "No passion in the surf!"

Julian followed her, his kibbutz regulation shorts serving as trunks.

When they got to the water's edge, they ran into the warm water without hesitation, splashing themselves and each other. At first it was warm and inviting. But there were waves on this stretch of coast, and the undertow was immensely strong. It knocked them both of their feet, and Jitka was suddenly dragged out of his reach.

"What is this? Help me, Jules. Jules!" Her voice was almost a scream. Suddenly she was quite a distance and swimming hard to get back but making no progress.

Julian waded into the water, getting pulled off his balance every time the wave retreated. He reached her and started pulling her out. As he was holding her he was knocked down again and had to time it when he got up between the waves. He reached her again and dragged her close enough to the shore so she could stand up and get her balance. They both struggled out of the waves and the menacing current and rested exhausted and panting on the water's edge.

"That was a bit scary" said Julian. Jitka said nothing for a time.

"You OK? "he asked. She was breathing hard from the exertion and that dark look of fear had come into her eyes again.

"Does this normally happen in the sea?"

"Any sea, or this sea?"

"Any sea. I am from where I am, remember? No sea. No boats. No Czech navy". Her voice was hard and ridiculing.

"No, this is strange. I thought the Med was calm and pacific. Not so, it seems. It happens in Cornwall with the surf. But here, I had no idea".

"Thank you".

"For what?"

"For......... helping me".

"You would have done the same. Julian conceded this.

"Yes, that is true. So, this is why no one is swimming with their kids in the sea. A fucking death-trap. I mean, one moment you are frolicking in the surf, the next you are fighting for your life".

"Good that you can swim" said Jitka.

"Yes, it is rather, isn't it?" Was terrible at school, but now I quite like it. But not a water person. A goat is my star sign. Obstinate, stupid, a bit devilish".

Jitka came up close, her lips almost white with the cold and sudden fear, and kissed him.

"Thank you anyway".

They stayed at the water's edge, not daring to go in further, for several minutes, until their bodies warmed up. Then they walked hand in hand back to their clothes and sat drying off under the tree. Jitka laid out a small towel on the sand and lay on her front. Julian examined her more closely, the bony back, the slight build, the muscles in the calves from skiing, so different to the girls he had known before. He lay back on his ex-kibbutz towel close to her, their bodies touching and let himself relax into sleep.

"You snore, you know?"

Julian came round slowly, as if after a deep anaesthetic. The voice was not familiar, the warm breeze on his flesh was not familiar. He squinted at the sun, and then turned to the voice.

"Jitka?"

"Where were you? Dreaming of some nice little British lady who brings you your slippers and pipe and the dog in front of the fire and the roast in the oven, hmm? And sensible sex every Saturday once a month when the children are in bed".

"Do you women ever let up? And actually, yes, her name's Mary and she works for the Women's Institute".

Jitka moved back a little.

"She exists?"

"Only in your imagination".

"Anyway, you snore".

"Perhaps I do. On my back. Roll me over in the night otherwise.

Jitka came and lay close in his arms. They listened to the waves on the shore. The palm tree overhead kept them in the shade.

"How long here, Mr Guide?" she asked.

"As long as you want. The only problem is that we have to both be at work tomorrow morning, so either we go back this evening, or we get up early tomorrow and make a dash for it to be there at 7am. I am not sure about the buses and when they start. We could find out". Julian stroked her arm.

"What do you want to do?" he asked. Jitka did not reply immediately.

"We had better go back tonight", she said. "Do we have enough for a bus?"

"We have, I think, enough for some of the bus, but not all".

"So?"

"So, we hitch a bit and use the bus in emergency. How about that?" he suggested.

"Sounds sensible. I want a BMW this time. An open-top BMW so my hair can dry in the wind and I can get the sun on my face".

"Ah ha! The tastes of a rich man's wife without the rich man. You'll have to get out there and flaunt your wares before your tits hit your knees". Jitka moved away slightly from his embrace.

"That wasn't a very nice thing to say. And my breasts are not heavy and won't hit my knees. Ever".

"It was a joke".

"Not a very funny one, if I may say so". Suddenly a veil came between them.

"Jitka, I was joking".

"Don't joke like that. About my body. Ever".

"Why?"

"Because it is not nice" said Jitka.

"OK".

"No, Jules". She put a finger to his lips to stop him talking.

"It is not that. It is...you know....." A long pause came before she began speaking.....

"When I was young I was not beautiful at all. I may not be beautiful even now, but I am better. Don't say anything. No, when I was young I had these terrible glasses, these communist glasses, all black frames and heavy plastic, and I was the joke of the school. Everyone made fun of me. I was so ugly. I was the 'ugly duckling', yes, you say that? In the playground it was torture as I could not play the games, and the boys teased me, and the other girls avoided me".

"Kids can be monsters, can't they?"

"Some. Most".

"And..............."

"And then at fifteen I got contact lenses, and have never looked back. I was transformed. I suppose you could say it was not a very happy childhood. But now, I have my eyes, no glasses, my body, my skiing, and a job. Not such a bad result".

"And me" said Julian.

"Smitten?" asked Jitka.

"Totally smitten".

"Come, let's go".

The sun was going down now, and they had to pack fast. Julian never liked travelling in the dark, and he did not know what the buses were like on a Sunday. They walked back to the crossroads which was 10 minutes hard walking uphill. The sun was blood red. There were not many cars on the road at this time and the lorries carrying produce had got to wherever they had to go. They both stood on the road pointing their fingers down. Nothing. One after the other, there was no kind Sammy to stop.

""Damn! Jitka saw the apprehension on Julian's face.

"Let's try and find a bus at the station".

"What's the matter with them? We'll give it another ten minutes, and then we'll admit defeat. I'm sorry".

"It is not your fault. We just should not have spent it all on the hotel and the food. And the tip at the church. Simple Maths".

"But it was a fun time".

"Yes".

And then, as they were distracted, a small white American-style pick-up van stopped a little ahead. They were not sure if it had stopped for them. They picked up their bags and ran towards it. There were three men in the front seat. They were not wearing their head-dress, but were Arabs, not Israelis.

"Where you go?"

"Jerusalem".

"Get in, we go that way".

Julian looked at Jitka for her approval. She shrugged her shoulders, but whispered: "Don't ever leave me, Jules. Alone".

"I won't".

The first Arab on the passenger seat side got out and made room for one person. The other beside the driver did not move. There was a moment, a stalemate, where Julian and Jitka expected them both to get out. But they were not moving.

"Get in". The driver was insistent, urging.

Julian was caught between gratitude that they were being given a lift, and Jitka's insistence that they were not parted.

"I'll be in the back with the other guy. What do you say?"

Night was falling fast and they either took this van or ....

"OK. In the front. But don't leave me".

She sat in the space provided by the other Arab and put her bag on her lap. The men in the front said nothing. Before Julian hopped into the back of the truck he went round to the driver and said:

"Jerusalem?" Julian asked

Yes, Jerusalem", and he indicated ahead with an offhand gesture.

Julian climbed onto the back and seated himself on the metal seats on the right. He put the towel from his bag under him to cushion the blow. The van took off into the failing light. No one said anything for a bit. Then the man opposite him asked suddenly:

"Your wife?" And indicated Jitka with a finger. They could be seen through the back window, although not be heard. Jitka was sitting staring ahead, tense, determined.

"Not quite my wife. Close friends".

"Not wife?" Julian became offended and exasperated.

"We are very good friends. Engaged. To be married". Julian was reluctant to say these things. They were not true. He hated lying. Besides he might offend Jitka: "Why did you tell them we were getting married....it is not remotely true..... how dare you?....do you think you are so important to me.....I have a boyfriend in the Czech Republic.....who do you think you are?..etc, etc...."

"Not married", repeated the other Arab.

"But engaged to be married".

Julian started looking harder at the guy. He was dark-skinned and his face had the signs of pockmarks, of very bad acne in childhood. He was about 35, and had heavy jowls. He did not smile much, unlike the driver. He stopped questioning suddenly and stared into the distance. The truck went on through the dusk. Julian had no idea if they were headed in the right direction. He had no map. No compass. He could not read the stars. He watched Jitka as she sat tense and aware like a wild animal in the front seat. Then the truck came to a stop at a petrol station. The driver and the men got out and the driver started filling the tank. The other two said something to each other and went into the shop. Julian got down from the truck and talked to Jitka.

"I am not sure. It seems OK. What do you think?"

She was sitting straight. She shrugged her shoulders.

"I just don't know if we can trust them. Jerusalem can't be far off. Shall we stop here and say we'll take a bus, or what?"

"We go on a bit more until we see a sign-post and then if we are close we stop and get out. I don't even know where we are. Do you?" Julian looked down and shuffled the earth with his shoes.

"No, I don't".

"Well, we continue a bit more until we see a sign, OK?"

"OK".

The other two men came out of the petrol station shop. They had bottles of beer with them, and gave one to Jitka and one to Julian. Julian accepted, while Jitka refused. In the back, the Arab flicked off the beer top on the metal border of the seat, and showed Julian how to do it. At the second go, Julian managed and thanked the Arab for the trick. He was all smiles now, and Julian drank from the bottle. His vigilance was lowered slightly. What could go wrong? They were close to Jerusalem, these guys did not seem violent. Perhaps he was just being too hard on them.

Then the truck took a turning off the road to another side-road. Julian registered alarm. He started talking to the man in the back, but he shrugged and pointed to the driver. He could see Jitka's face looking first to the driver and then to his. The white truck sped on through the undergrowth, the tobacco leaves, the maize. Julian asked again, shouting into the wind:

"Where are we going?" The man just indicated with his head and arm: ahead, ahead.

They finally came to a clearing. Julian was thinking if he could tackle these men physically. The pick-up truck came to a halt. Julian jumped down and left the beer bottle in the back.

"Where is this?"

The three Arabs were close together, and the driver who spoke better English, said in a casual voice.

"This is Mount Carmel. We thought you like see Mount Carmel".

"Why do we want to see Mount Carmel? It is dark!" Julian was torn between the seeming desire of these men to help them, show them their country, offer them a beer and a lift, and the incongruity of it at dark. Jitka came to his side and held his arm.

"What is going on?"

"I am not sure. They say this is Mount Carmel and we should see it. Historic site, and all that".

"I am not certain, Jules" she said.

"Nor am I".

Julian looked around them. He could see pockets of light under them, little villages with lights, so far away. Otherwise, around them there was almost dark. No large city was in sight. Julian walked towards the driver, and summoning as large a voice as he could, asked:

"Where is Jerusalem? We need to go to Jerusalem".

The driver spoke something to the others, and then came forward with a smile and took him by the arm, leading him to the side of the hill, pointing out something in the distance. Julian walked with him, but turned to see Jitka standing with her bag, isolated, her blonde hair clear in the darkness.

Julian did not see the blow, or the man's arm lifted, but heard her shout:

"Jules, look out!" Then it was all black and he crumpled.

When you get hit by someone or something, just before you lose consciousness, you know in a split-second what has happened. You feel the bottle on your skull, the fist on your jaw. You might actually look into the eyes of the person who has hit you just before your legs buckle. You have the mixed emotions of incredulity (why is he doing this to me?) and anger at your own stupidity (of course, that's what it was all about). All this happens in the nano-seconds of clarity before it all goes black and you fall in an ungainly heap on the ground.

══╪ ╪══

It was totally dark by the time Julian regained consciousness. He was lying face down, his mouth full of dirt. He spat it out. Ants were crawling over his face and he brushed them off. He slowly moved into a sitting position. His head hurt badly, and touching the back of his skull he felt a gash and blood. He started talking to himself, making sure he had not lost the power of speech: I'm all right, I'm all right. He tried to gather his wits, and shook his head to try and focus on what had happened. Survival usually means thinking of oneself. It was only after a few minutes, sitting in this position that he remembered Jitka. He hardly knew her. What had happened to her?

"Shit! Don't panic, don't panic", he said to himself. "She's all right. Pray God they didn't kill her. Abduct her. Hurt her".

Julian slowly, ever so slowly got to his feet. His head was throbbing badly, and warm blood was running down his back. He would think of that later. He was alive. His brain was not damaged.

He looked around from the hill and could see the lights of those small villages in the distance. So calm, and all this had happened. He called out in a croak.

"Jitka!"

Nothing. He tried again.

"Jitka" Nothing. The worst scenario was they had raped her, killed her and buried her. Best was...there was no best. Least bad was rape. And no beating up, bones broken. Julian tried to see any sign of movement, of clothing. He walked around the hilltop, with its sparse vegetation, the spiky plants, the rocks. He stumbled and fell twice, scratching his hands and arms further.

"Jitkaaaaa!"

He walked to the other side of the clearing, where there were rocks and some trees. Nothing. But if they had left her here, they might have tried to hide her. Julian walked to the rocks and looked around. Nothing. Then he looked over the cliff and saw her. Her bright clothes and her blonde hair stood out in the darkness. Her body was crumpled and her fall had been stopped by a tree half-way down. Julian started the descent. It was not steep, but the rocks and shale slipped under his feet. He could not risk another fall. He looked again. There was no movement.

"Shit!" she might be dead. "Please God she is not dead".

Julian slithered a bit more, hanging on to trees and shrubs as he made his way down to her body. He finally got there and crouched beside her. She looked dead. Her face was pale and scratched and her clothes were in shreds from the fall. Her dress was around her waist and her pants had been torn off. She was scratched every-where. Her shirt was torn and only one button remained. Julian bent close and whispered her name. He tried to pull the dress down to cover her. He was crying slightly now, the shock of what had happened to him and the sight of her had unleashed the emotions he had tried to control.

"Jitka", he sobbed. He touched her now. Her body was still warm. She might be alive.

He did not know what vein to press in her neck, but any movement would mean a heartbeat.

He held her hand in his and tried to press as hard as he could on where he thought her pulse should be.

"Come on, come on", he said. Then he felt it. There was something. Her heart was beating. Just. Thank God, thank God!

And he moved closer to her, cradling her, trying to warm her, talking to her. Jitka then moved slightly, coughed. Her eyes and face were swollen and bruised by the fall. They may have hit her as well, he thought. She murmured something in Czech. She was not going to think in English for a time. He held her in his arms like a mother would hold a child. She was like a rag doll, her limbs boneless and heavy. He rocked back and forth, thinking what he was going to do now. They were half-way up a hill. The best bet was to slither down. They couldn't stay here, that was certain. Then he thought they might come back to make sure they had destroyed the evidence. But if they hadn't killed them by then, he thought it unlikely. But it sent a shiver over his body.

"Now, think, think Julian".

He started talking his way through the situation: She is alive, but hurt. Possibly badly. You are alive with all limbs working but with one mighty gash in your head. Can you get her down off this mountain? Possibly. Is there anyone else around? No. Where is the nearest habitation? Down in the valley. Can you get there? On my own, yes. With her? Well, you can't leave her, can you? Can you? So... can you lift her? You'll have to.

Julian took a deep breath and put his hand under Jitka's knees and placed her rag-doll arm around his neck.

"Listen" he said out loud, "you have got to try and help me in this one, Jitka. I know you can't hear me but you have got to try. OK? Now, I'm going to lift and carry you down this hill and then we are going to get to a house and clean you up. Good idea? Good idea. Glad you thought so".

So Julian lifted, and they started their slithering, sliding, falling descent on the stones and scrub and bushes and rocks until they made it to the bottom. Julian had ripped his trousers and shirt and a lot of his flesh. But they had made it. Jitka was still unconscious. And heavy. Julian was panting for breath and the gash on his head was pumping more blood on to his back. He felt the warm, sticky flow descend. That was the least of his worries, he thought. As long as I don't faint now. He thought it was unlikely.

He looked around and saw a light in a one-story house about 500 yards away. He could make that; they could make that. Then he thought of how he might get Jitka to help him. He took off his shirt and tied one of the sleeves to her left wrist, and the other to her right arm. It was an improvised sling which would help. Then he put the sling and her arm over his neck and lifted her from under her knees. Like this, he could do it. His legs were strong from all the sport he had done. Thank the weirdos for that, he thought.

He started walking along a dirt track, sand and earth, which was uneven but dry. He could do this. After 100 yards he had to stop. The muscles in his arm were quivering with the effort. He rested, going down on one knee and resting Jitka on his thigh. She was still out to the world. Concussion at the least. But she was warm and breathing. There was life. OK. Another 100 yards. Julian lifted once more and walked slightly faster this time. His legs would carry him, but his arm muscles were giving out. Another 100 yards, and he stopped again. He was breathing heavily, panting. We can do it. We can do it.

Another hundred. Julian was seriously labouring, his breathing was a raucous pant, and he knew he did not have much left in him now. The last 100 yards were a stumble before he dropped to one knee again. But dogs had started barking. He was close. He saw a white house with a vine above it, and a concrete seat built into the wall. He would get there.

"OK, last bit. We can do this". And with that he made his last burst to deposit Jitka on a concrete tiled slab outside the first house. Their movements, the noise had caused concern. A light came on. A face appeared out of a door at the side. A harsh enquiry in Arabic was shouted out.

"*Salam, salam malaykum*"! Julian shouted out.

A brown face outlined by the white shawl came from behind a wall. The man observed the situation. He called gutturally to his wife. Children also poked their faces from around the wall and were told to disappear, which they did. His wife came soon and summed up the situation. Then the husband and his wife came and helped Julian take Jitka into the house. They took her through the kitchen space into the main bedroom and lay her down on the bed. The man's wife now took charge and shooed them out of the room, covering Jitka's body as best she could from the eyes of the men. The door closed and the woman took over.

The husband led Julian outside to a wooden chair.

"Please. Sit". Julian collapsed into the chair.

Faces of children came around the door to watch in wide-eyed amazement. The father came back with a collarless shirt and some reddish tincture and a sponge and bowl of water. He began cleaning the scratches, sponging down the blood with tenderness. He did not speak. The father could imagine what had happened. At the best, a fall, and that would demand kindness and commiseration from anyone. The girl badly wounded; the man at the extremes of his strength. He bathed the wounds and let them dry, taking thorns out where he could. He murmured in Arabic as he took the larger thorns out and laid them on the wooden table, like bullets. The gash at the head took more time, and he came back to it three times, sponging off the dried blood and then cleaning it up. He made tutting noises. The warm water stung but the blood had stopped running. It was the worst wound, but it was not serious.

He then took the bottle and covered the gashes with the red tincture, which Julian assumed was an antiseptic. It made the gashes look worse than they were. He motioned Julian to let that dry, and then he gave him the collarless white shirt. Julian put it on with difficulty, the arm-muscles still quivering. It stained the shirt slightly, making the wounds look worse than they were. The father then went indoors and came out with some mint tea which Julian thanked him for and sipped slowly. He sat down with Julian. The children watched from afar at the corner of the house, ready to scamper off into the safety of the other side of the house.

"Thank you"

Julian inclined his head in a bow.

"*Parlez-vous francais?*"

"*Un peu*".. I prefer English." What happened?"

"We fell off the mountain, or rather, the girl, Jitka, she was pushed. Some men took us up there in a car and then one hit me on the head with...... a beer bottle, I suppose".

The father nodded as he took in the information

"Why were you there at that time?"

"We were hitchhiking". The man did not understand at first. Julian made the sign.

"Yes, I understand". A silence fell between them.

"I thank you again for your kindness".

"It is nothing".

"I must see the girl".

"I will ask my wife how she is".

The father stood up and went indoors. A short while after he came back.

"She is better; and awake. But very weak. She says she will see you".

The room had been transformed. Candles flickered on a side-table. The shutters had been drawn. Jitka lay in the centre on the bed, her hair brushed and laid out as a child's after it has had a bath.

Her clothes had been changed and she wore a simple cotton top with a little red braid on the collar. Her necklaces and bangles were gone. Julian came close but did not know what to do. He was being watched by the couple. Jitka moved her eyes slowly to take him into focus. They saw him but the gaze was far away, the gaze of a person has who has been close to death and comes round from the abyss. Her look was not angry or kindly, just a cool stare at the person in front of her. Julian came closer and kissed her on the forehead, then sat down and took her hand. Her grip was weak.

"Jitka. It's me, Julian".

"I remember who you are". Her voice was faint and from afar.

"How do you feel?" There was a silence, and then she said in a whisper:

"I think I have broken ribs. It is painful to breathe or talk".

"Anything else?" Jitka then turned her eyes on him, the full gaze. She held his eyes for what seemed to Julian to be several minutes and then replied:

"No, there is nothing else".

"They didn't....."

"I said: there is nothing else". And with that she let his hand go and turned her face, to indicate the conversation was over. Julian pressed her hand, got up and went to the door and walked out with the couple.

The wife then spoke in Arabic which her husband translated:

"She is so tired and hurt here (she indicted her chest). But she will live. We should call a doctor".

"Yes, a doctor. What is the time now?"

"It is 11"

Julian sat down in the chair outside and tried to think. The hospital, the shift, money.....
He began: "I have no money on me. I can get money from the hospital where I work. E-Lyn?"

They had not heard of it. It was exclusively for Jews.

"I can get money from them and come back. Today. Tomorrow. Can I leave her with you, and you call the doctor and I pay the doctor when I come?"

The couple nodded talked briefly together and then agreed.

"I think you should sleep now and rise early in the morning for your journey.

You can sleep here, we have a bed". And he went and unfolded a white thin mattress which he laid on the ground on the veranda.

"It is all we have".

"It is more than enough. Thank you again".

"You will take the bus tomorrow?"

"Yes".

"You will need money. You have none?"

Julian searched in his pockets and found they had taken that as well.

"No, I have nothing".

"Take this. It will be enough for the bus". And the husband gave him a crumpled 10 shekel note.

"Thank you. I will leave early".

"I may be up".

With that Julian bid them goodnight, slumped onto the mattress on the veranda, and lay back with his arm under his head. The cicadas were grinding away. Seconds later he was in a deep sleep.

⇥ ⇤

He got in to the hospital at 8am. No one had really missed him, and he went up to the volunteers' rooms to see who was about. Andy, the Northerner, was still in his bunk asleep.

"Andy, it's me. Julian". Andy opened his eyes slowly.

"Andy, could you cover for me today. I'll return the favour tomorrow".

""Yeah, sure. What's up?

"Nothing. I just have some things to do, people to deal with. It's L-ward, you know, the pretty one from Morocco. The one you like".

"OK. What time is it?"

"Eight. But you have time. Thanks. Have to get on".
Julian sighed with relief. That side was covered. Now the money. How much did he need?

Enough. Who could he hit? Who would say yes?

He went down to the canteen and looked around. Brad was looking at an old copy of The New York Times. He had the broken pair of glasses strung around his neck and was peering through his reading glasses. Brad looked up and smiled at Julian.

"What's up buster?"

"Hi!" Julian sat down hastily, warily, looking around him to see if people were looking.

"You look dreadful, if you don't mind me saying. What happened with Jitka? Didn't it work out?"

"Yes, no....Listen Brad, I can't tell you now, but things went wrong and she is not well and she is the other side of the country and needs medical help and............please, this is between you me and the gatepost, no one must hear of this, OK?...."

"OK, buster, anything you say".

"So, I need money for the medical care and the trip. Can you help?"

Brad did not hesitate.

"Sure, how much do you want? I don't have much on me, but I'll give you what I have".

"I need, I need...what've you got?"

Brad took out his wallet and looked inside.

"I can let you have 400 shekels. That is all I've got right now, otherwise it leaves me short". Julian took the money without counting.

"That'll do. I'll pay it back before the week's out".

"No rush, buddy. Take it easy. I mean, is she ill? And what happened to you? Is that a gash you have on your head. Let me see that. Julian turned his head slightly and Brad stood up to get a better view.

"Looks nasty. But clean. Who did that to you?"

"I don't know. Or rather, I do, but there is nothing I can do about it now. They didn't kill me, us. But I have to get her out of there and back here where she can get good medical attention".

"OK". Brad left off examining the wound and sat down. "You want something to eat?"

Julian thought about it. Something to eat. A drink. He suddenly realised how faint he was.

"Yes, something. It would be fine".

"Here, let me get you some stuff. You look all done in. You sure you are all right?"

"Yes, I'm fine".

Brad got up and went to the counter and took a yoghurt and some fruit and a coffee with milk and sugar.

"I didn't know how you took it so I put a bit of both in, sugar and milk".

"You did just fine". Julian ate with total concentration, not looking up, like a wild animal. He then drank the coffee and looked up. Brad was studying him closely.

"If you don't mind me saying, you really don't seem to be in the best of health. You could do with a rest".

"I'm all right, believe me. It is Jitka who needs the help".

"OK, no more prying. But you need to get that gash seen to when you are back. You hear me, buddy?"

"Yeah, I hear you. I've got to go now. Thanks".

And Julian got to his feet and walked out the canteen door to the front of the hospital.

It took him a little over 2 hours before he had arrived back to the cluster of white one-story houses at the bottom of Mount Carmel. The taxi left him there, and Julian made his way through the jungle of the buildings. There were no house numbers, no indications, just left past the eucalyptus tree, right at the corner. When he came to the house there were three people outside, the husband and wife and another man. They watched Julian as he came towards them. He walked up the three wooden steps and shook hands with the couple. The other man was introduced as the doctor. He had the Arab robes and a lined hard brown face and the head-dress. At his feet there was a worn brown leather bag.

"Salam".

"Salam Maleykum".

"You can speak English or French if you like if you do not know Arabic".

"I would prefer English".

"Please excuse my many mistakes. Let us sit down".

"Jitka? The girl?"

"Is sleeping. I have given her something to make her sleep".

"Can I see her?"

"Not now. She has taken the sleeping medicine".

They sat at the table with 4 simple chairs. The wife went to prepare some mint tea, and put a bottle of chilled water and glasses on the table. The husband poured and they all drank slowly.

"Thank you for coming. Thank you for finding him".

The Doctor made the gesture of touching his head, meaning no thanks were in order.
Julian trembled before he asked the question.

"How is she?"

"She is alive. Concussion. I do not know how bad. She will have to have tests when she returns. There is bruising outside, two broken (he searched for the word, and indi-cated)...... ribs, which will mend on their own, and...... and...(his voice dropped slightly, and in almost a murmur) .....some bleeding inside".

Julian did not say anything, nor enquire what, where or why. The Doctor then looked at him steadily. A silence came on them, each with their own thoughts.

"Can she travel?"

"Perhaps. It is up to her".

"How much do I owe you?"

"I will take 100 shekels. Can you pay that?"

"Yes, I can pay that". Julian took out the several notes that Brad had given him, and peeled off the amount.

"Thank you so much".

The Doctor took the money from across the table and placed in an internal pocket inside his robe.

They got up. He extended his hand and picked up his bag.

"She will be a bit...vague for a few days. Do not press her. She will probably not want you to touch her. You understand me? She may not want to be touched for some time. You will have to be patient".

"I understand".

The husband led the Doctor to the street, who then quickly moved though the children playing and the hens, and at the corner turned without looking back.

"He is a good man. Abdullah al Suleiti. He cares for us all. Takes so little from us. A good man". They sat down again.

"I must see Jitka".

"I will talk to my wife".

He went indoors and he could hear their voices, the indistinct growl and the firm female voice coming back in return. The husband came out.

"She says you see her in 5 minutes. She try and prepare and wake her. Not well yet. The pills make her sleep". He mimed a person sleeping. They sat down together again, and sipped the mint tea. Julian took out another 100 shekel note and offered it to the man. He refused.

"When anyone is in pain, our houses are open. One hopes you will do same to me or my family one day. *Inshallah*".

"*Inshallah*. Thank you. I'll probably call a taxi and travel back today with Jitka. If she is well enough".

His wife came out to the doorstep.

"You can come now".

They both got up and Julian went cautiously into the room. He needed a bit of time for his eyes to get accustomed to the dim light. On the chest of drawers some candles burned.

Jitka was in the centre of the double bed, her hair spread around her, her face thin and pale. Some scratches were very evident on her face and arms, red weals made even stronger by the paleness of her skin. They all stood watching her. The woman went to the chair by her side and said her name. Jitka opened her eyes slowly. They recognised him but expressed no joy or surprise. She stared. Julian came and sat on the chair; the husband and wife withdrew. He took her hand. She did not respond, and then gently released it.

"How do you feel? "Jitka looked at him with eyes that no longer saw the world as he saw it. Her eyes were of someone who had seen a war crime and the image was burnt into the retina. Her voice when it came was a whisper.

"I am OK. Nofà is so kind to me. Thank her for me please".

Her voice trailed away.

"The Doctor gave you something to sleep, so that is why you are feeling as you are".

"He was kind too. The Doctor".

"Abdullah".

"Yes, Abdullah".

"He says you can return to the hospital if you feel up to it", said Julian.

"Perhaps a bit later" she whispered.

"We'll take a taxi".

"Money? Too much, isn't it?"

"Brad lent it to me".

"Nice man, Brad".

Her eyes drifted off towards the wall. He took her hand again, and she let him take it.

"Jules". He lent close. Her face was looking the other way, but he heard her.

"It was no joke this time. No more joking". And then, as her voice trembled and broke:

"I told you not to leave me. You did not protect me". And

the tears flowed down her face, she did not sob, just endless tears that flowed down her cheeks, she did not try to stop them or hide them or wipe them away. They just flowed as if there had been some terrible leak deep in her soul and nothing was going to stop them for the rest of her life. She turned her head away from him.

Julian stood up and left her crying. He could not bear her grief. He walked to the doorway, his own tears welling up. He waited until the emotion left him and then went out to meet the couple.

"She says she can travel. Later". The husband made a little bow of his head, as if to say: Let God be praised. The wife went back to look after her patient.

Four hours later they called a taxi and helped Jitka into the back seat where he stayed with her, his arm around her shoulders. She did not seem to mind either way. She stared into the distance hardly speaking and her bony shoulders resting on Julian's chest. She never fell asleep or closed her eyes for the whole journey. At the hospital, after paying the driver, Julian turned. Jitka picked up her nylon bag.

"Nothing happened, OK?" she said.

"I don't understand".

"Nothing happened. We went to Capernaum. We had a nice time. Nothing else happened".

"OK. Nothing happened. Julian went to kiss her but she turned her face. Then without a word she walked off into the revolving doors and to her quarters. Julian picked up his bag and went to the canteen".

The next morning Julian was in the ward at 7 doing his shift. At 9 he went to the canteen, hoping to find Jitka. She was not there. He asked around. She is taking some days off, was the answer he got. So it was for several days. Julian was subdued, but did not open up to anyone about the real cause of his injury. Or anything that had happened to her. He owed her that, at least. Then at the end of the week she was in the canteen, talking with Shuli, one of the Israeli nurses. He looked her way, trying to catch her attention, but she avoided his glances.

"Shit!" He took his coffee and breakfast and sat near Brad.

"Hi there, buster. What's cooking?"

"I'm fine". Julian reached inside his orderly's green shirt and pulled out some money.

"Here. What I owe you".

"You sure?" asked Brad.

"Yeah, I'm sure. Please. Take it. Thank you" said Julian.

"Your head?" asked Brad.

"Better. Healed".

"Your heart?"

"Broken. Sort of." said Julian.

"What happened at that weekend? Or shouldn't I ask?"

"Don't ask. And you don't want to know".

"Oh, OK. Not the right moment?"

"No, not the right moment". They sat in silence. Julian knew he had to leave now. He could not stay and work in the hospital with Jitka there.

"I may have to go".

"Go? You mean leave? Here? Why?"

"Just I may have to leave. Can't stay here. If she is staying, I can't. Simple as that".

"That is a bit, what's the word, impetuous, if I may say so?"

"Brad, things are not that easy".

"Well, it isn't easy for any of us, that's for sure. Just look at the kids we are treating!"

One look and he took in the kids outside in their wheelchairs, heads propped up with steel supports, bodies bent into distorted shapes. Julian was humbled and ashamed.

"Agreed. But...I can't stay here".

"So what you gonna do, buster?"

"I think I'll have to phone a friend of mine back in the UK".

"Mr Fixit?"

"Yes, that sort of thing. He knows people around the world, knows what to do in a tricky situation".

"Nice friend. Well, tell me what you decide before you do go, all right?" said Brad.

"Right". Brad looked at his watch.

"Always late. Why is that? See you around, buddy". And he gathered his briefcase and plates and took off.

CHAPTER 11

ON THE TRAIL

At 4.30 in the afternoon in the quiet country town of Tonbridge Wells, Detective John Pendelbury and Sergeant Hatton walked up to the doorstep of Mrs Parker's house, No 54 Judd Street. The path was well-kept, with neat borders and yellow and dark red primroses. A well-trimmed hedge on either side fenced in the garden and kept a certain privacy from the neighbours. Hatton knocked. They heard step to the door, and then a tall, willowy woman of about fifty opened the inner and outer doors. She stood at the threshold, quizzically eyeing the two men in their brown mackintoshes.

"Can I help you?" she asked.

"Yes, Ma,am, we hope you can. It is Mrs Parker isn't it. 54, Judd Street?"

"Yes. That's right".

Already uncertainty and some panic were entering her voice. Both men had their police ID papers ready and showed them.

"Police?" Her hand went instinctively to her throat, covering her front, hoping to ward off any bad news.

"What is the matter?" Mrs Parker did not know what to call

these policemen, sergeant, constable, detective. Pendelbury stepped forward.

"I am Detective John Pendelbury, and this is Sergeant Hatton. We are sorry to bother you, and there is no cause for alarm". Mrs Parker let out a sigh of relief.

"But we do need to ask you some questions" continued Pendelbury.

"Questions? Whatever for? Have I done something wrong?"

"No, nothing wrong".

"My boys?"

"No, not your boys exactly".

"Well, we can't stop all day here talking on the doorstep. Please come in".

She led the two men into the living room. It was dominated by a grand piano. Chairs were placed around this instrument. A tasteful bowl of flowers was on the lid, which was covered by a red cloth tapestry, slightly African in design. The chairs and settee was of a light blue and well kept. Cushions were placed at each end.

"Please do sit down". She gestured vaguely, and the two men sat on the settee, rather ill at ease and on the edge.

"Tea, coffee?"

"Some tea for me would be just fine", said Pendelbury.

"And for me, if that is not too much of a bother".

"No, no bother at all". Mrs Parker went into the kitchen and started the preparations. Pendelbury looked around, taking it all in, his notebook at hand.

"Sugar, milk", she called from the kitchen.

"Both for me. And for me" said Hatton.

There were a few sounds of teaspoons and cups, and then she was there with a tray which she put on the small table in front of them.

"Please help yourselves".

The men put sugar and milk into their cups, stirred, and sat back a little. Mrs Parker sipped her tea and put the cup down on a small side-table to her left.

"Gentlemen?"

"Yes, well, Mrs Parker, you may have heard from your son, or read in the papers, of a strange death at the school where your son went".

"Simon was there until a year ago, that is correct. About the death, I know nothing at all. He tells me very little, and I don't read the papers that much these days. My late husband did, you know, The Telegraph. But I don't seem to find the interest anymore".

"Your husband died recently".

"Yes, not so long ago. A sudden heart attack".

A chill in the conversation settled.

"I'm most sorry. If this is not convenient...." said Pendelbury.

"No, no, please. Let us continue".

"You were saying...." said Pendelbury.

"Yes, well, we are investigating the sudden death of a teacher at the school, and also we would like to find a young man who could help us with our enquiries".

"Which teacher was it?"

"Harold Darke".

"I didn't know him. Just by name. Another house, you understand".

"The boy?"

"Julian Bates".

Mrs Prentis moved her body backwards slightly and her face had a quizzical expression.

"Julian? But he would never hurt anyone".

"That is what they all say, strangely".

"Do you think Julian harmed the man? Deliberately".

"We can't say Mrs Parker, at this stage".

"I see".

"So, you do know him".

"Yes. He came once or twice, listened to music with Simon, upstairs, modern stuff I really didn't like much, to tell the truth".

"Your son Simon is in the house".

"No, he's in London. Shall I call him now? asked Mrs Parker.

"No, I'd rather we.........."

"No, really no problem Inspector".

"Please we'd rather call on the off chance..." said Pendelbury.

"Well, you'll never catch him, he's out all the time, so I'll ring him now, in front of you".

"Really, Mrs Parker, there is no need, perhaps an address".

"Well, the address won't help at all. In the depths of Deptford. Nasty place actually, but the flat is amazingly cheap. Condemned housing, he tells me. Shares it with three others, so really, it costs nothing at all".

And before they could stop her she was on the phone. There was no reply. She put the phone down and took her seat again.

"No reply".

She looked for her tea. Sipped. A long silence ensued. Then Pendelbury asked if he could smoke.

"Yes, I don't myself, but my husband did. Far too much, I always thought. And but I'm not sure I can help you any further, and I am certain my son can't".

"Yes. I'm sure".

He turned towards Sergeant Hatton.

"You do smoke, Sergeant, if I am not mistaken".

"I do".

"Here's something for you. Filters". Pendelbury went to his right hand jacket pocket and fished out a packet of filtered Players Senior Service.

"Inspector, that's extremely kind. I'll be off outside, then" said Hatton.

"Check the tyres while you are out there, will you please?"

"But I checked the tyres only the other day".

"It's been a long drive, Hatton".

"Oh, yes, I see what you mean".

Hatton left the house by the front door. Seconds later he was leaning on the car and lighting up with obvious relish. He walked around the car for good measure, kicking the tyres as he did his inspection. Both Mrs Parker and Pendlebury watched in silence. Pendelbury pulled out his pipe and tobacoo pouch.

"You don't mind?"

"No, really. As I said, my husband smoked. I rather like it. The aroma is still on his jackets. A, well, a masculine smell".

She went a fetched an ash tray. Pendelbury began filling his pipe.

"And Simon is not considered a suspect in any of this?" she asked.

"No, not at all. It is just we are asking people who know, or knew this young man who now has escaped our net, as it were".

"You have no idea where he is?"

"Unfortunately, no. Seems to have vanished into thin air, as they say. For the moment".

Pendelbury struck a match and started lighting the pipe, the dark brown strings of loose tobacco crackled and flared up. Mrs Prentis sipped her tea again. Put her cup down slowly on the saucer.

"May I ask, then, just why you are here? I am not sure how I can help you".

Pendelbury put the spent match down on the side of the saucer, and puffed twice to make sure it was alight.

"Well, it is just a bit of a routine, really. I was at Bates's family home, and I was told that Julian was quite close to your son, and that he was his 'best friend' as it were. Perhaps someone to go to in a time of crisis. And this certainly is a time of crisis for young Mr Bates".

"I see".

"Nothing more, just routine". He sent a haze of smoke up to the ceiling.

"You wouldn't have that address for your son, would you, by any chance?"

"An address? Well, not exactly. It is in South London. Somewhere. I am not sure", Her voice trailed off. Her hand went to her pearls and throat.

"I see".

"No letters which you have had to send on?"

"No, no post really. No".

"That phone number, perhaps?"

Here Sarah Parker looked trapped. She sought a way out with her eyes, stared at the corner of the room, outside the garden, the pictures on the piano.

"Mrs Parker?"

"I may just have a number, um, somewhere...."

"Perhaps the one you used a few minutes ago?"

"Ah, yes. Silly me. One gets so distracted".

"Do you think I could have it? Just routine. I may not even have to talk to your son. It may all be over by tomorrow. We'll be chatting to Julian on his own by lunchtime".

There was a pause. Later she thought she could have refused. But then more suspicion would be thrown on her son. She stood up and went to the table by the phone and searching in a worn brown telephone book for names.

"I have it here. It may be the right one. They change them day and night. This is the last one we had. I'll write it down, Inspector".

"That would be most kind".

Mrs Parker wrote the London number on a small piece of paper, and handed it to Pendelbury. She felt as if she were handing over state secrets to an enemy power.

"You do promise that Simon is not involved in any way".

"I cannot say for sure at this moment".

Pendelbury puffed a little longer at his pipe. Mrs Prentis sat down once more.

"Did Simon have any friends of any sort, international perhaps, people who might allow Julian Bates to go abroad?" Mrs Parker did not hesitate to go through a few names, anything to deflect police attention from her son.

"Well, there is David Cleave, but they hardly see each other now. New school, moved away. Then there is a newish friend, they went on holiday together around Europe, as one does. Student train ticket. Remarkably cheap, really".

"And this friend's name?"

"Hugo, I think".

"Hugo....?" Pendelbury's voice trailed off.

"Hugo".

"Does this Hugo have a last name?" asked Pendelbury.

"Not that I know of".

"Is he English, with a name like that?"

"I hadn't thought. Simon said he spoke several languages, French and Italian, and had lived abroad. He may be French, I suppose". Mrs. Parker's eyes stared at the floor as she said this. Deflect the attention, anything away from her first born. Pendelbury puffed one more time.

"Hugo. French. I see".

"Or Italian. French. Or Italian. I think". Pendelbury left the conversation hanging.

He made movements to go. He stood up, and Mrs Parker stood with him.

"Let me take you to the door?"

They stood the hall door now, and Mrs Parker went for his coat and hat. He put them on slowly, with care, so as not to knock over any vase or ornamental things. He had made that mistake before. He held out his hand.

"Thank you so much. I am so sorry to intrude".

"Inspector". Mrs Parker shook his hand, but not with the warmth of before.

Pendelbury walked out to the car and Hatton who was on his third Senior Service.

"Hop in, Hatton. Back to the force".

As he got in he turned to the house and noticed Mrs Parker watching them from the window with the net curtain pulled slightly back. Their eyes met. She did not avert her gaze.

"Got what you wanted, Sir?"

"I think we might be on the trail". And with that he fell into silence and puffed at his pipe for the entire journey back to the station.

After a decent time Mrs Parker went to the phone and rang her son's number. Again there was no reply. At 8 that evening she did manage to contact him, and explained what had happened. Simon was strangely tense and evasive. And an enquiry by Pendelbury to the French Embassy had revealed that a certain Hugo Romand, of French nationality, resident in London, had reported a passport stolen and applied for a new one a month ago. And yes, they did have his current address.

CHAPTER 12

HOT FUZZ

Hugo was smoking in a cigarette in his underpants when he heard the doorbell ring. It was Saturday, 8am, and he had spent the evening and most of the night chatting up and finally pulling a bird from North London. There had been sex, and then the drive back in the beaten-up old Porsche. The image was everything. The Porsche, the glitzy clothes....it usually worked. It had last night.

He got up and went to the intercom. It might be for his sister down below. The postman, a delivery guy, someone. Still, shit! It was early.

"Yeah!"

"Inspector Pendelbury. Good morning. Could I speak to Hugo Romand?"

Hugo did not reply for 30 seconds. He held the phone at arm's length, as if by keeping it at a distance it would go away.

"Hello. Mr Romand?"

He brought the phone back to his ear.

"Yes".

"Inspector Pendelbury here".

"Yes". Hugo tried to be as non-committal as possible.

"I wonder if we could have a word with you".

"About?"

"About a passport which you reported lost or stolen to the French Embassy".

Hugo did not know what to do. He had confirmed his name, so he couldn't pretend he wasn't. He could refuse to open the door, but they would be back, and it would look highly suspicious.

"Mr Romand?"

"Yeah?"

"Can we come up?"

"We?"

"Myself and Sergeant Hatton".

"Yeah. Come for a coffee. I'll put the kettle on".

Hugo buzzed the intercom and he heard the door open. He had about a minute before they would be at the door. He scrambled for a pair of shorts, then went through his story. They were here for the passport. It had been stolen. On the tube. Why was he carrying it? Force of habit. ID in France. Which tube? Northern Line. Why that line? Think? Involve no one else. Northern Line. Coming, going, where. Involve no one else. The Heath. Hampstead Heath. Saturday. Kensington House. Art...... Museum.

Then he heard the knock at the door. He lit another cigarette, hoping his hands did not shake and went to the door, opened it and stared at the men outside. One in a brown Mac, the other in usual policeman clothes.

"Yeah?"

"Inspector Pendelbury and Sergeant Hatton".

Hugo did not reply. He took another drag on his cigarette.

"We'd like to ask you a few questions. May we come in?".

Hugo looked them over once more. The alternative was to close the door in their faces. Then there would be further shit probably. Better minor stuff now than major stuff later. He shrugged and gave them space. They came in.

"Coffee? Tea?"

"Not while we are on duty?"

"Saturday?" said Hugo with incredulity.

"The law never sleeps" replied Pendelbury.

"So. You don't mind if I do?"

"Not at all" replied Pendelbury.

Hugo went to the kitchen and they followed. He turned on the gas and lit the ring, then put water in the kettle. Another drag on the fag. He kept his back half-turned to the men. They watched his every move. A heavy silence fell on the room. Hugo kept quiet, thinking about what he could say, what might be dodgy. He told himself in his head: keep it simple. Stick to the story. Nothing extra. The whistle on the kettle boiled and he took turned off the gas, picked up a cup, spooned some coffee into a mug and then sat at the kitchen table. He made a sign for them to sit down. They both drew up the metal kitchen chairs, scraping them on the floor.

"How can I help you gentlemen?"

Pendelbury noticed the accent, certainly not English.

"We wondered if you would like to accompany us to the local station to answer some questions".

"About?"

Pendelbury tried to size up this young man. His eyes were bleary from a night out, possibly there was some alcohol still inside him. But he was obviously being cautious and playing for time.

"As we said, about a passport you reported lost or stolen".

"It happens".

"It happens, of course".

The two policemen sat immobile. Hugo looked at them, then at his coffee. He lit another Gaulloise.

"Questions?" he asked.

"Questions" replied Pendelbury.

"And why not here?"

"We like to take notes. In a more formal setting".

Hugo shrugged. Better not antagonise, be sweetness and light.

"Sure. Let me get some clothes on. Wash. Something. Would you like to wait outside?"

"We'll be fine here" said Pendelbury.

"Then you won't mind if I......."

"Not at all".

The policemen sat unmoving as Hugo go up and walked to his bedroom. He gathered some clothes with him—nothing too fancy, the cowboy boots and the sequins might give the wrong idea—and walked to the bathroom. The policemen sat and watched his movements. Hugo took his time, closed the door, brushing he teeth, shaving, showering. Time to make sure of his story. No hesitations. Keep it simple. And calm. Let them ask you a thousand times the same question, you can out-bluff them, have more patience. His hand shook ever so slightly as he shaved. He took a long time over shaving. A nick and a bit of blood would not look good. Besides, it was unsightly. Bits of toilet paper stuck to your face. He showered slowly too, the whoosh of the water heater and the hot water were reassuring. He could do this.

"Mais, oui, mon brave. Certainement". He finally came out dressed and showered and ready.

"Shall we go, gentlemen?" asked Hugo.

The policemen got up in silence and walked out the door. Hugo locked it behind them and they began their descent of the two floors to the car. Hugo sat in the back with Pendelbury.

"So, I am going to be interrogated?"

"Mr Romand, that is hardly the word I would use. It reminds me of the war and Nazis and torture".

"It is the word we use in French".

"Let us say we are going to ask you some questions".

223

"And then let me go? Hugo asked.

"And then decide what to do with you" replied Pendelbury.

"Then I would like an interpreter".

There was silence in the car.

"An interpreter?" asked Pendelbury.

"*Oui*. I am French. And Italian. I don't want to say yes or no to something I do not understand".

The two policemen did not say anything at first.
Then Pendelbury spoke:

"Make contact with the station and get them to provide an interpreter Hatton".

"Yes, Sir".

Pendelbury turned to Hugo.

"Which language would you prefer?"

Hugo thought about it for a moment, and then said:

"Mandarin Chinese? Just joking. French".

Hatton relayed the request to the police station.

The room the station used for questioning suspects was pretty bleak. There were signs of much use, the borders of the solid wooden table with its vinyl top were scuffed and stained. It had not been cleaned recently and the smell of cigarette smoke lingered in the air. An empty ash-tray was in the middle. The window had bars on it and had not been opened, it seemed, for several months. To Hugo it was an unpleasant reminder of institutions and just where he might end up. But that was only a remote chance in his mind. Pendelbury was joined by another man rather then the sergeant. The heavies, thought Hugo. His heart raced ever so slightly. Hugo was left there for a few minutes on his own. Then Hatton came in to inform him that the interpreter was on her way. Hugo took out a cigarette and lit up, adding to the stale air. He was considering his options when Pendelbury and another detective came in followed by a woman of about forty-five. Diminutive, slight, crinkly, black hair tied back in a bun.

Pendelbury introduced her: "This is Mrs Sylvie LeBlanc".

Hugo stood up and took her hand. Sylvie was at first totally professional. She had done this several times. Saturday was a good day for her as the children were back at home with their father. This call at 9 am was an easy one to take. And the money helped.

"Bonjour". She held out her hand, shook his professionally.

"Enchanté", replied Hugo. He looked her over before they sat down. English husband, two kids, disillusioned with England, faintly despising her husband, the weather and food terrible, the people cold and remote, and secretly could not wait to find an excuse to leave this job and her teaching and return back to her beloved country. All this would help. She must also have been very pretty once. Her face had hardened into a lined mask.

They sat down on either side of the table. It was a practiced procedure for the policemen and Sylvie.

Hugo and Pendelbury sized each other up like boxers before round 1 began.

"So, Hugo, this passport. Declared missing to the French Embassy on the....." Here Pendelbury checked his notes, ..."on Friday the 24th January at ten in the morning".

Sylvie turned to Hugo and translated quickly and efficiently. Their eyes met and Hugo's charm slowly began seeping into her.

"*Oui*".

"Yes" said Sylvie.

"And when did you notice you had lost it?"

Sylvie translated.

"When I found I no longer had it on my person".

"And when was that?" asked Pendelbury.

"When I got home".

"That evening?"

"That evening" replied Hugo.

"The 23rd".

"The 23rd".

Sylvie was in her role, no emotion, just translating. Hugo took another drag on the Gaulloise. Round 1 to Hugo. No hurt to either party, but Hugo was quick on his feet and had landed a blow to the face to show he was there.

"And why do you carry your passport around on you?" asked Pendelbury.

"It is our habit" said Hugo.

"Your habit?" asked Pendelbury, slightly uncertain.

"*Oui*, our habit. We carry identity with us at all times. It helps society protect itself. In France you carry la Carte d' Indentitè. It helps the citizen. It helps the society. It helps......" here Hugo paused"...... the police.

A faint smile came to Sylvie's lips as she translated. The pride of France and their system was in evidence. The *'pour aider la Lège'* made her heart glow.

Round 2 definitely to Hugo. Hard blow to the body, one or two stinging jabs to the face. And he was still dancing and fresh. Pendelbury looked at his notes, picked up his pipe, and started filling it. He made them all wait until the bowl was full.

"Do you drive, Hugo?"

"Yes, of course" said Hugo.

"What make of car?"

"A Porsche".

"You must make a lot of money to run such a car".

Hugo shrugged. "I bought it second hand. I am single. The women like it".

Sylvie translated, not letting any emotion into her voice.

"How did you travel that day when you said your passport was stolen?"

"By the tube" said Hugo.

"Where?"

"To North London".

Pendelbury let a silence linger in the room. He put the pipe to his mouth but did not light it.

"You have this Porsche but do not use it?"

Sylvie turned her head quickly to Hugo for a reply. Hugo stared out impassively, then shrugged:

"I use public transport when I can. It saves money, helps the traffic. And, of course"—and here Hugo shrugged and looked with feigned amazement as two men of the world could even consider such a question—"why take the car when one is travelling alone?"

Sylvie nearly smiled at this last comment but kept her professional pose. Round 3 to Hugo. Nearly a clinch, but avoided body blows, and landed a heavy jab to the face.

"So, if I have got this right, you chose to travel to North London by tube, where you presume to have lost or had your passport stolen".

"That is correct".

"And why did you go to North London that day?"

"The Heaf?" said Hugo.

"I'm sorry?" said Pendelbury.

"The Heaf".

Both Hugo and Sylvie said the 'th' with an 'f', so the policemen were perplexed.

"The Heaf?"

"The Hampstead Heaf".

"Ah!" Pendelbury turned to his colleague. This time it was their chance to show generous understanding for their incapacity to pronounce English, as well as the choice of place.

"Hampstead Heath", enunciated Pendelbury.

"Ah. My mistake" conceded Hugo.

"And did you meet anyone there?"

"No".

"No one saw you?" asked Pendelbury.

"No. I tried not to be seen".

Both policemen sat up and leant in when they heard this information so readily given.

"You tried not to be seen?"

"That is correct".

"And why would you go to Hampstead Heath not to be seen?".

A clinch, heavy blows to the ribs, damage being done. Both policemen were triumphant.

"Because I am a bird-watcher".

"*Quoi?*" Sylvie did not really believe her ears, and had to get Hugo to repeat it.

"Because he is a bird watcher". She almost burst out laughing at the absurdity of the statement.

Hugo continued:

"*Oui, vraiment.* I go there to watch the jays and the hawks and the....".. Hugo paused. Sylvie was translating word for word.......... "to watch the green pileated woodpeckers".

At this Sylvie laughed out loud. *"Quoi* ! I do not know this word! The.....".at this she shrugged and gave up.

"Desolèe" she said, "but I am not an expert in ornithology".

Hugo took another drag on his Gaulloise, and lent back, blowing the smoke to the ceiling. The two inspectors looked hard at Sylvie, and then at each other. They were being played with.

"So, you went bird watching on Hampstead Heath on the 23rd of January, no one saw you, and you make the journey there and back by the underground, and it was on this trip that you lost your passport. Is that correct?"

"Yes. Correct" Round 4 to Hugo.

Pendelbury tried another tack.

"Ever heard of the name Julian Bates?" He watched for the tell-tale signs of body language.

The hesitation, the eyes looking off to the right, the legs crossing, the arms folding. Hugo displayed none any of these. He just shrugged.

"Is that a yes or a no?" Hugo looked at Sylvie. Lying was not hard at this point. He had made it a way of life to lie to his girlfriend or the police.

"No".

Pendelbury struck a match and started to light his pipe but kept his eyes all the time on Hugo.

"You know"....puff..... "a false declaration can lead to a

prison sentence, or quite simply..." puff "......" we can send you back to France".

Sylvie translated fast with slight anguish for her fellow countryman. Hugo froze slightly. He did not know if this was true, and he did not want it to happen. Quite likely they could evoke some law from the 18th century, or alter another to suit their purposes. Round 5 to Pendelbury.

"And if this passport is eventually found, and they do have a strange habit of turning up eventually, then you can be charged with aiding and abetting a suspected criminal, a young man wanted for questioning about murder. The judge might not be so lenient. Or the French police".

Hugo remained still, like a cornered animal, trying not to give away anything.

"Do you want Mrs LeBlanc to translate?"

"I understood" said Hugo.

"And the prison sentence could be anything up to 5 to 6 years. Am I not right Inspector?"

Pendelbury turned to the other Detective.

"Correct". Round 6 to Pendelbury. Two body blows and a direct hit to the jaw.

"Anything else you want to add, Hugo?" asked Pendelbury.

Hugo said nothing.

"Anything, Inspector?"

"No, not from me".

Then Hugo spoke for the first time directly to the policemen:

"Can I go?" he asked. Pendelbury puffed for a time, and then replied:

"If you are prepared to sign a statement that what you have said is a true account of the facts, then yes, we'll let you go. But don't plan any trips abroad, Hugo".

To this he did not reply. The fighting was over for the moment. Equal points. Both with damage to the face and body.

"Well, that seems to be all. Thank you so much, Mrs LeBlanc, for coming today".

"I'll need to stay for the translation".

"Will that be necessary?" Hugo looked at Sylvie:

"Yes, that will be necessary".

And so while the statement was being typed out, Hugo and Sylvie chatted away, occasionally breaking into cackles of laughter which could be heard outside the room. When the statement was brought in, Sylvie read through it and translated as she went, making faces at the legal phrases which seemed absurd to her in French, but she knew the jargon. It was her job. Hugo signed, gave it to the waiting policewoman, and then he and Sylvie walked out of the room together, talking and ignoring the rest of the station. At the entrance they shook hands again and kissed on the cheeks. Pendelbury stood watching at a distance. Then he turned to Hatton:

"Language and culture thicker than the law?" said Pendelbury.

"Seems so, Sir".

"He was lying of course".

"Certain, Sir?"

"Certain. We'll keep a check on him, though I fear the bird has flown the net and has migrated".

"Sir?" asked Hatton.

"Ever heard of a green pileated woodpecker, Hatton?"

"No Sir".

"Nor have I. But Mr Hugo Romand, who drives a Porsche, has".

And with that he walked back into the station and talked to the other Inspector.

CHAPTER 13

PHONE CALL. JERUSALEM.

A few days later Julian went to the public telephone outside the hospital with a pocket of change. The lines were never good, but they worked. Most times it sounded as if the other person was on Mars, but through the static and the crackling you could have a conversation.

"Hugo, it's me" said Julian.

"Who me?" asked Hugo.

"Julian me. *Possiamo parlare due minuti?*"

There was a pause. Hugo did not recognize the voice at first, then he replied quietly:

"Non qui. Non adesso. Le cose sono cambiate. Chiamami a *questo numero frà cinque minuti"* And he gave Julian a public phone number for a booth at the end of the street.

Julian rang 5 minutes later.

"Hi. What was that about?"

"As I said, *les flics* are being very attentive, my friend. Nothing Hugo can't manage, but surprisingly thorough. They were around here. They found the story of the missing passport very interesting".

"How did that happen?" asked Julian.

"Not sure. Some of them are not stupid. Far from it. Quick even. Anyway, nothing I can't handle. But don't phone me for more than ten seconds at home here. And never with your name or in English. *Capisci?*"

"*Capisco*".

"So, whats up?" Hugo took a long drag on his cigarette.

"I need another escape route".

"*Amico*, it seems you can't get one right, can you?"

"This time it was not my fault".

"Everyone says that".

"Believe me, this time it was different". Hugo sighed.

"OK", he said "But this time it is the last. And when Hugo says the last, it means the last".

"Understood" said Julian. The line crackled, hissed.

Then Hugo came on the line again:

"There is one solution. It is not nice, but it works most times I'm told. You can disappear, but you might disappear for ever if you don't play your cards right".

"What are you saying?"

"The Legion".

"What Legion?"

"The Foreign Legion" said Hugo.

"Does that still exist?"

"*Mai oui, mon vieux*. Truly".

"It was not what I had in mind". said Julian.

"What did you have in mind exactly?"

"I don't know"

"So, get to Tangiers"

"Tangiers?" asked Julian.

"Tangiers. And don't go anywhere near Gibraltar. Too many English. Too many police".

"OK. Then?"

"Then you look for the Caffè des Anglais on the main road near the port. Ask for Pierre".

"Pierre".

"They'll know why you are there. And don't answer too many questions. This way you don't exist for a few years, or for ever. And don't call me for a long time. *Capisci*? Now piss off!"

Julian heard the phone click and go dead. He put the receiver down and walked slowly back to the hospital.

CHAPTER 14

FOREIGN LEGION

The journey from Israel to Tangiers was long and hard. Julian decided that a ferry and trains were the safest, and so it was a ferry from Haifa to Brindisi, and then a long trek by train from Brindisi to Rome and then on up the central part of Italy to Florence, and then a change at Genova and along the coast, past the border at Ventimiglia (hardy any passport checks, especially at night), then through France, Marseille, Montpellier to Spain and finally Algeciras. From there he could get a ferry to Tangiers. On the way he met people with amazing life stories. He listened as two women talked the entire evening about one of them deciding to break up with her husband and return to her village just outside Aix-en-Provence. As she got off the train in Monpellier her friend embraced her fervently, and then returned to her seat and sat silently for the rest of the journey, staring ahead with tears coming down her face.

The Caffe' des Anglais in Tangiers was on the main street which ran adjacent to the coast-line and harbour. It was typical: white metal tables and chairs, nothing to set it apart from other places. Julian was amazed at the camels and donkeys and Bedouins walking calmly past the cars. The desert was also in the city.

He went and sat at one of the tables and waited for someone to come and serve him. A young Arab boy eventually appeared and Julian asked in French for some water and some cold lemon tea. His presence did not seem to attract attention. It was a tourist town, and there were many foreigners who had made it their home. Writers, homosexuals, smugglers. He drank the tea and the water and slowly tried to take the measure of the place. It was small, and he felt it strangely lawless. Bright sunlight with all the shops having awnings. Date trees lined the streets. Arab boys with shaved heads roamed here and there. One or two beggars sat in doorways. It was both Arab and international, just the right place for the Legion, Julian thought.

He finished his tea, left his bag in full view, and went to the bar inside. A tanned, muscular man of about thirty-five was behind the bar washing glasses. The tap was running. There was one other customer in the corner, a man reading a newspaper in Arabic and a white concoction for a drink in front of him. He was smoking with a holder. His braces held his trousers and his noticeable paunch in place.

"I am looking for Pierre" said Julian to the barman.

The barman looked up, and then went back to his glasses. Julian tried again.

"I said I am looking for Pierre"

"I don't know any Pierre" said the barman.

"I was told that in this bar someone might know where he is and how I can contact him"

The barman stopped his job but kept the water running. He dried his hands on a towel and then turned to Julian.

"Who wants to know?"

"I do".

Julian was scrutinised once more. He had passed the test.

"Tomorrow at six in the evening. Here. Sit where you can be seen, at the table near the tree". He indicated with his head. "No luggage, but some identification"

And with that he went back to his glasses and the washing up. It had taken all of a minute.

So it was that simple, or at least so far. Julian now needed a hotel and some rest. He went back inside the bar and asked for somewhere *'assez modeste'*. The barman dried his hands and walked outside with Julian. He pointed to a corner building about 400 yards ahead.

"It is sufficient"

"Thank you" said Julian.

And it was. Julian checked in and then walked along the sea front. He did not know what he was doing except once more he was on the run, more evading, lying, avoiding. The Foreign Legion was his last hope. He had no idea what it was for, amazed even that it still existed. What was its purpose? Who financed it? He remembered books from schooldays, of Beau Geste, of forts being attacked by black men in robes, or defending a country which looked more desert than human habitation. He remembered stories of white ladies being kidnapped and these intrepid soldiers of fortune saving them from the fate of being sold into slavery and a harem. It still existed? The only other thing he knew was that they all spoke French and they had to change their name into a French *nom de guerre*. They truly did disappear and were reborn as another.

At 6 he sat at the spot, waiting. Nothing. No one approached him. He waited 15 minutes. Still nothing. He was about to get up and leave when from behind him a man in his forties sat at his table. No invitation, no handshake, no name. He had dark glasses on, and the sort of tanned skin of a ski instructor. He was lean with a lined, almost scarred face, although the lines were just hard living, Julian thought.

"You were looking for me?"

"You are Pierre?"

"That is what the call me" said Pierre.

"A friend told me I might find you here" said Julian.

"Your friend was correct".

Julian was conscious of an intense scrutiny. The silence

continued. Julian felt he was being x-rayed, judged, his whole existence being weighed in the balance. Julian stared back.

"Come with me. You have a passport?"

"Yes".

Julian followed and they walked to a green Peugot parked on the other side of the road, and he now realised that he had been under observation for all that time.

"Get in the back".

He did. Pierre got in the other side. A driver and a minder in case he tried to jump. They drove out of the town for a bit. The white, peeling buildings gave way to sporadic constructions along the roadside. The journey must have lasted about 20 minutes. They stopped outside a nondescript, brown, single-story house. The dust settled slowly.

"Get out".

Julian got out. He looked at the driver more closely, and saw the same parchment skin, the same close-cropped hair. Almost identical. The clothes too, the light beige, almost army shirt and shorts revealing dark skin and muscle and dark, wiry hair.

These men were fit, thought Julian. The dark glasses and the physique were a type of uniform. They walked into the hall then a room to the left. There was a table and two chairs.

"Sit" said Pierre. Julian sat.

"Passport".

Julian took Hugo's passport out of his pocket. Both men took off their sunglasses and Julian noticed their eyes were dark brown and had deeply etched crows' feet. They were supremely confident and exuded a subtle menace. Pierre took the French passport and read it through in silence, paying a great deal of attention to it, far more than a custom's officer might do. Then he handed it to his partner. More silence. Julian heard a lorry go past, some roosters in the distance. The partner handed the passport back to Pierre with a nod of the head.

"Why are you here?"

"I thought it was obvious" said Julian.

"Why are you here?" repeated Pierre. A long pause. Julian shrugged.

"I want to join the Legion"

"Why?"

"I need a new life" said Julian.

"Why?"

"Things".

Pierre got up and walked around the room. Then from behind Julian he suddenly whispered in Julian's right ear:

"You speak French like shit. How is that?"

"I lived in England" Julian turned his head.

"You do not forget a language". Then Pierre came from the other side.

"Tell me about this Hugo Romand. Fast. Tell me about your childhood, your brothers and sisters, your holidays in France, where? Tell me everything!"

He was shouting at this point. Julian started stumbling through the rehearsed lines of his family, although he could not remember much about Hugo's French and Italian connections. He stammered, stopped, repeated himself, finally came to a halt.

"Don't lie to me you little shit!" Then quite unexpectedly Pierre smashed Julian in the face with the back of his hand. It was like being hit very hard with a squash racket. The blow threw Julian off the chair and onto the ground. Blood came gushing from his nose, and tears to his eyes.

"Fuck! What was that for?"

Pierre came a crouched down close to Julian, almost paternally, and then spoke in amazingly good English:

"You know, when people are under stress and they are hurt and then they swear, they do so in their own language, their mother tongue. It comes out unbidden. They don't put the little cap on it, the seal breaks off. You are not French. Who are you?"

Pierre then grabbed Julian by the hair and pulled his neck back and shouted:

"Tell me who you are?" He then let Julian go.

"Get up" said Pierre. "Get up. Sit".

Julian clambered back onto the chair. Blood was pouring onto his shirt. He tried to stop it with his hand. The other man gave him a handkerchief, And Julian blocked as much as he could.

"So, you are not French?". Julian shook his head.

"You are................?"

"British".

"This passport is not yours?"

"No"

"Stolen?"

Julian hesitated. Then nodded.

"So your friend Hugo gave it to you because you needed to escape"

Julian did not reply.

"Nice friend. And your friend told you about us". Julian nodded again.

"Show me your hands". Julian placed his right hand on the table. Pierre took it, felt the palm, turned it over.

"The other"

Julian changed the handkerchief into the other and placed his bloody left hand on the table. The same scrutiny. Then Pierre let it go, shoved it away. He had seen enough.

"Why are you here?" he asked again.

"I need to hide. For a long time."

"So what is new? They all do here".

"I can't go back to Britain" said Julian.

"Murder? Drugs? Sex?"

"Two out of three" This answer seemed to please Pierre and the partner. They laughed.

"Not bad for a novice".

"*Ecoutez*. Hugo, whatever your name is. I do not want you. You will not fit. You are not hard enough for us. I have men who if I hit them they try to kill me, they'll bite my ear off, try to break my neck and balls. They do not succeed because I am stronger. But they try. You just lay there in your blood.....and tears. They are animals, *mon vieux*. Well-trained animals after I have finished with them. But animals. They have killed and will kill again and think nothing of it. They would murder their own grandmothers if the Legion told them to. Probably have done already. And for a few francs. This is not for you, believe me".

"I can't go back". Julian croaked out the reply.

"But yes you can. I don't know what you have done and I don't care. But go back. Avoid *les flics*. Change your name and identity. You did it before. It has got you this far. Go back".

He picked up the passport from the floor, wiped some blood off and handed it back gently to Julian.

"*Ecoutez-moi*. It is the best way. Go back. We do not want you here. Jean will give you a lift. I have some work to do".

He held out a hand and Julian reluctantly took it. Pierre's hand was like leather inside. Then he turned and was out into the hall and another room. Jean indicated with his head that they were to get into the car. He had not said a word. Inside the car, Julian in the passenger seat, he offered a cigarette. And they drove back in the dusk. The blood had almost stopped now and Julian tried to return to return the handkerchief. Jean shrugged and pushed it away. True, who wants a bloody handkerchief? Julian kept it until he got back near the hotel and then dropped it off in a bin. He washed his face in a jet of water coming from a broken water-pipe, then he climbed the stairs to the 4th floor and his room. He closed the door behind him, locked it carefully, and lay on the bed. When he awoke it was quite dark and he had no idea where he was. Then the hotel ceiling and the fan and the sounds of the traffic came to him. Damn! What now? Not even the Legion wants you. And later Pierre's words came to him: Go back.

Julian watched the fan circle round. He might have to. Where was there left to go?

PART TWO

CHAPTER 15

WORLD'S END

A month later Julian was existing in a three-storey red brick semi-detached house, courtesy of the Royal Borough of Kensington and Chelsea. But grand and royal it wasn't. A friend of Simon's was an architect, and they had 'liberated' a short-life house in an area which was going to be redeveloped, and therefore the council had moved everyone out and left some properties empty. It was a squatter's haven. An apprentice architect Sven knew about the proposed council project and had entertained ideas of some brilliant architectural solution which would then get published in a magazine. A room had become available as one of his architect friends had backed out. Did Julian want a place to stay? He did.

The estate was set apart, off a main arterial road which came past the embankment and snaked up to the North of London. Lorries thundered past only two-hundred yards from the house, and the foundations juddered. It was a five-minute walk to the bus stop, a number 14 bus to Sloane Square, and then from there to anywhere.

Julian met Sven at the property on Saturday morning. On the phone he had sounded very laid-back about the whole thing.

"The LEB is still on, as is the water. The top room could be yours if you want it".

"What's the LEB?"

"London Electricity Board. If they cut that off, then we are screwed. But so far it is on, so we can keep warm. 14, Lot's Road. Meet me there at 11. Knock loudly as there is no bell or anything. Or shout".

The bus stopped the World's End pub. The name was apt, as Julian was about to leave The King's Road and the trendy shops and enter another reality. A short walk on a bright winter's morning, with his A-Z in hand, and he found himself in an estate which had deliberately been put on hold. Most of the houses were boarded up with heavy brown wooden panels over the windows. Some had large letters in red paint on the paths leading up to the front door: LEB off.

It was the death knell, Julian was to find out, as trying to get the electricity put on again when you had no legal rights was almost impossible. A sign like that meant the house was dead, the local council had intervened, and you had better look elsewhere. 14, Lot's Road. Julian walked through the series of streets, the area getting more and more depressing as he continued. There was one corner shop, which sold anything and everything and looked as if it had not changed since the war. Some second-hand furniture shops, an off-licence, and then house after house boarded up. The overall impression was of dark, satanic mills. No flowers, no gardens, no colour. Lowry London. A power station in dark brown brick loomed to his left. It was a strange comfort that the energy supply was so close. But apart from that, his spirits sank.

Number 14 was in the middle of a row. The houses either side were boarded up. Scraggly weeds and plants were trying to survive in the abandoned little plots of earth either side of the front door. He knocked. He knocked again. He shouted:

"Hello! Sven!"

A window opened from the first floor and a head of blonde curls looked out.

"Hi. I'll be down".

Sven was in his twenties, recently graduated from Cambridge. He opened the door in quite respectable clothes, and it was part of his double life. The jacket and tie—and then the squat and the bare floorboards and very basic furniture. The rooms could have been nice except that no one thought beyond next week as the council might come in and try and evict them. But the loo worked. The electricity was free. The rooms were large and enough for everyone. Sven had 4 six-inch nails in his hand and a hammer.

"Just putting a coat rack up". And with that he turned and slammed the nails into the wall behind the door. Whack, whack. "shit!"

He turned as the last nail had gone in.

"Somewhere to hang your hat!"

The house was so cold Julian decided not to hang his hat or coat or anything at that moment.

"Come on through and have some tea".

They went up on flight of stairs to the landing and then main rooms. An entire room had been re-designed simply by knocking half a wall down, and this hole, the width of two people, had been made to facilitate easy access. It was open-plan all right. Julian warmed to the idea. 6-inch nails for coat hangers, open-plan kitchen by knocking down a partition wall, free electricity. He wanted to stay.

"So you're a friend of Simon's."

"Yes, that's right".

Sven did not offer any reply. Julian thought he should add something.

"He said there was a room going".

"True. Another guy, John, dropped out. He's an architect too from the same practice I am in. We had this idea of redesigning a squat. But he couldn't stand the cold. It gets quite cold, as you can see. The windows don't close that well, some panes are missing. But we do have the LEB on, so just get yourself a heater and keep it on".

Which is just what Julian planned to do.

"Here, come and see the room while the kettle boils".

The squat had a kitchen area which had a sink and a gas cooker. After the college, and the kibbutz, this was luxury indeed. Sven took Julian up another flight of stairs, past a bathroom with a large enamel bath and sink to the top floor which looked on to the power station one side and a line of identical semi-detached houses the other. Bleak indeed. The room was just dark wooden floorboards with nothing else except a single mattress in a corner where the previous occupant had slept whenever he was around.

"Pretty basic" said Sven

"It'll do" said Julian.

"OK. Let's have that tea. And I'll tell you about how all this works. Or doesn't".

They went down the two flights of stairs to the kitchen. Wooden chairs, simple table.

"All the furniture comes from the street. People just throw out stuff and we take it in. Sofas, beds, mattresses, chairs. Even that carpet. Well, actually, that carpet we got from a house down the street. A break-in job".

Sven laughed to himself, and then poured the hot water into two cups with tea bags.

"Sugar? We don't have milk. Well, we do sometimes, but not today. One of us usually tries to remember to buy some".

"Just sugar is fine".

"Good".

"Now, if you decide to come...." said Sven.

"No, no I'm coming".

"Well, if John comes back you'll have to go, but I don't think he will be....But as I was saying, the set-up is this. We stay here for as long as the council let us. They then take out a court order; we go to the court, pay the fine and stay here for a bit longer, and then move on".

"How long can this be?"

"We've been here a few months now. The squat over the road lasted 3 years. But they are getting close to the demolition deadline now, when they start the re-development, so"—Sven shrugged—"it could be anything from a few weeks to a few months. And we can move to another house if we need to".

Julian chuckled. "Pretty mad".

"Yep, well, it is hard times for us all. What do you do?"

"Um, nothing at the moment. I..." Julian began a sentence, and then stopped. Better less than more. "I've been abroad for a time".

"Oh, where?" asked Sven.

"Here and there". Sven did not seem to be that intrigued about the where or when.

"Well, what else? Downstairs we have a potter, Tilly. She used to live across the road, but had to move on and came here. She got the phone connected".

"You have a phone?"

"Yes.. Crazy, isn't it? We have all the mod-cons here. Heating, lighting, phone......furniture to be found outside". Julian began to warm to the place.

"I'd really like to stay".

"OK. As I say, if John comes back, you have to leave, but otherwise, consider yourself at home".

"Can I move in today?"

"Don't see why not. I'll have to get a key cut. Stay here for a bit".

And with that Sven put his tweed jacket on with his tie and walked out to the end of the road.

He could have been any young man about town with his pad in

the King's Road. Which he was, in a way. It was just a pad shared with others and the Borough of Kensington and Chelsea.

Julian wandered around a bit more. In the corner of the living room behind the door was a piano. He played a few notes.

Terribly cracked and out of tune, but it was a piano. He smiled. A room, a piano, a bath and a loo. He could live here for a time. Until the council kicked them out. Sven came back with a bright copper key on a plastic key ring.

"£2 squire". Julian looked for the money.

"So, make yourself at home".

And he handed the key over. And John did not come back and left all his things, such as they were. So Julian made himself at home.

The first thing he did was to go to the local shop and buy an electric fire. It had two bars, and sent out enough heat to warm one person if they were fully dressed and stood close. But over the months it was to save him. He left it on night and day, especially at night as the temperature often went under freezing, the whole house was engulfed in a polar grip where you woke to the taps frozen, ice in the bath. The two-bar heater shining out at night close to him was a comfort, a beacon of survival. Without it, in the top room, he might not have been able to get through the nights alive.

He used the mattress John had left, and went to find blankets and bed-clothes from the corner shop. The whole area gave Julian the idea of a war zone, of a station near the front where supplies were available, but you might have to leave at any time and at short notice. With the key and the bedclothes he had spent less than £8. That was economy. So he had a place to stay, at practically no cost, and in the capital. The police seemed to have given up looking for him.

Now all he needed income, a job of sorts.

It was 12 noon. It was a bright, clean day, those days you get at the beginning of September. He walked towards The King's Road and then towards the centre of the city. There were strange clothes shops and bistros and pubs and very modern furniture shops. He felt at home. An odd sensation, this idea of home.

'No other place underwrites my existence' he once found in a poem about the writer's return to his own country. He now knew what it meant. It meant not feeling a second-class citizen and having to put up with snide abuse. People not wrinkling their brows in feigned concentration as you supposedly mangled their language. It meant not having to be apologetic for your very existence on the planet. It meant being able to talk and explain and hold an opinion and be counted and not dismissed as some rather backward child.

He reached Sloane Square, a walk of 20 minutes. The trees were shedding their leaves. But the size of the buildings, the lack of bustle, the quiet, the proportion pleased Julian. He decided he would even accept the climate—it was what he knew. No more complaining. Honour they father and thy mother that thy days may be long in the land the Lord thy God giveth thee. Well, the Lord had given him Britain, and he felt it was his. He almost let out a little cry of joy! God, it was good to be back. Julian sent up a silent prayer. The police did not know he was here, nor his family, nor even Hugo. Just that phone call to Simon. Better that way.

He took the tube to the centre and got off at Embankment. Where now? He walked up through the square, loitered outside the National Gallery, and then made his way up the road, St Martin's Lane, past the church and then he was outside the open doors of the Coliseum. He hesitated, and then walked in. A silver-haired man in a green jacket, the uniform of the house, greeted him kindly.

"Can I help you?"

"I am just looking, thank you". Julian picked up a programme and flicked through that season's operas and ballets. Desperation made him brave.

"I don't suppose there is any job going here, sort of like yours? I don't mean singing. Like you in a green jacket".

The man looked him over once hard, and then picked up the phone. Julian seriously thought he was phoning security to have him thrown out, and started to back away, but the man gestured for him to stay. He talked in whispers for a moment a then put the phone down.

"There is a post of cloakroom attendant starting tonight at 6.30. Does it interest you?"

Julian stammered out a "Yes".

The silver-haired man was kindly:

"Just turn up at about 5.30 and get a jacket. Bring your own black trousers and white shirt and they'll tell you what to do up there".

Julian mumbled some thanks and turned and left. He walked up and the road, past the music shops, past the pubs, past the ironmongers, past the bookshops, the restaurants, and then came down again. He could not believe his luck! A house, albeit a squat which could disappear over night, and a job, which he had no idea how much it paid, but was in music. All in one day!

God was good. He walked around for a bit more, went into the Gallery and sat looking at the central painting, Caravaggio's Road to Emmaus. He sat for well over half an hour. No painting student would have concentrated harder. People walked past, and he did not notice them. He communed with the picture. The still life of food so expertly done on the right, the broken bread, the meal started and interrupted, the hands almost coming out of the canvas, almost knocking you to the ground in their surprise, the close-cropped heads of the fishermen disciples, the clothes, the strangely composed and un-suffering face of Christ.

I have been where he walked, thought Julian, and as for the Christ portrait, he looks too well-fed for my liking, but the picture is quite something. The sheer power of the moment, the realisation by the disciples that it was the risen Christ—no one had done it better, or rather, nothing that Julian had seen. He made a vow to try and come and see a new painting every day he was working. It did his soul good.

≕╀╀≔

The job turned out to be a strange mix of boredom and stress. The position had arisen because the management had forbidden them to take tips for leaving hats and coats and bags, and so the previous young men had walked off in a huff to work elsewhere in the theatre front of house staff. And they were distinctly unhelpful and cool towards the two new interlopers. He found himself working with another colleague, Ben, who was moonlighting, trying to set up a music agency while doing this and other part-time jobs. And it was Ben who saw the potential of the job.

"OK, it pays nothing. Rubbish. But we'll find a way around them not allowing us to take tips".

And so he placed a white saucer very prominently on the wooden surface while the blue plastic 'gift to support the theatre' collection box was discretely removed. The theatre-goers dutifully placed their small change in the white saucer. Ben placed half in the collection box, and everyone seemed to be happy. From £15 a week, he had £30 a week. No rent, no bills apart from transport and food. And even the food he could find cheaply. Most of the shows finished at about 10.15, and he got back to World's End from the frantic handing out of hats and coats at about 11.30. Outside the turning into the short-life housing estate was a greengrocer, and he left the day's rubbish and fruit and veg to be thrown out just by the corner of his shop. Julian rooted through like an alchie or a bagperson. Mushy avocados, decaying cabbage, wilting lettuce, all these he put in a plastic bag he had with him at all times, and took them home. More often than not, someone was up, and he shared what he had found with whoever was awake. The others all had families to go to when in need, and jobs. Their desperation was not his. But they accepted his windfalls for the communal larder.

An added bonus of the job was that the green jacket with the emblem of the theatre permitted him to walk back-stage and wander around the theatre whenever he liked, it seemed. If he looked confident enough he could watch performances from the wings, as long as he did not get in anyone's way. He could even use the practice rooms if he wanted. And it was there that Julian started very shyly to try and sing. He could not make any sound like the voices he was listening to each night, but he persevered. Some notes were good. They were weak, but there was resonance. His middle notes vibrated all through his body and it was a good feeling, like eating something nice. But the sound got thin at the top, and there were strange breaks where he seemed to change gear. He would start from the bottom on a scale and then at about Eb his voice would crack and the F above was wobbly. Then his voice gathered strength, only for the same thing to happen at the upper Eb. What was going on? Who knew? He needed a teacher, that was certain.

But watching the singers was a joy. Once the punters were seated and all the hats and coats in place and easy to get to, then he was free. Most of the other staff just chatted away, and others read. But Julian casually went back-stage to the opposite side of the stage manager's box and watched night after night. Getting back stage was not so strange as the canteen was situated at the back of the auditorium, providing easy access for the stage-hands and singers and chorus.

One more green jacket who was in no one's way did not create suspicion. And so there began Julian's musical education.

He could never imagine himself there on stage, either as a soloist or even in the chorus, but being so close he became entranced. It was a sort of drug with no harmful side-effects. And it was the Mozart nights were the ones he enjoyed most. Some Wagner operas rolled over him, but 'Meistersinger' he adored. Strauss left him cool although he enjoyed 'Arabella' and, of course, 'Rosenkavalier'. The operetta he rather snobbishly ignored. But it was Mozart nights he lived for, and 'Don Giovanni' in particular.

The drug began with the first chords, with the bass strangely held on over the end of the strings and woodwind. It was unsettling from the start. Then the strange syncopated tune on the violins, another hush, as if opening the door to something other-worldly which sent shivers down his spine, then the ghost's music, the music from the underworld, chromatic, rising, insistent, before settling into something more obvious and immediately comprehensible. He began to anticipate the special moments: the chords depicting the sword fight, then the music imitating the dying and the life blood of the Commendatore seeping away. Julian watched with wonder as the singers got through their parts, coming off sometimes sweaty, sometimes angry that a note had not gone well, often casually, as if it were just a breeze. There were so many moments that Julian did not know which part he preferred:

Elvira's sobs as she realises she loves Don Giovanni and decides to try and save him, or Don Ottavio's arias sung with light precision. Single lines got into his head and he found himself humming them for days: 'From this place I will not stir until some certainty I reach'.

He watched until the final scene and then hastily made his way back stage though the corridors and into the front of house. The other staff were getting ready for the assault on hats and coats and opening of the main doors. No one asked where he had been. The plate was in place, Ben was behind the counter ready to pick up the bags and hand over the coats and then off into the night. They had it to a fine art most nights, knowing exactly the position of the numbers and not getting in each other's way. The spectators were softened up by the music and some small change, a bit of silver, was easy to part with. One placed 10p, and then the others felt obliged.

Every night Ben did the trick, half for the theatre, half for them. It mounted up. It meant the pittance became a wage. No rent, no bills, hardly any food bills, and everyone was happy as the benevolent fund always had their share. Julian thought the benevolence should stretch his way as well.

After a few months, this rhythm of life became slightly boring. He almost forgot he was on the run. Tube, theatre, music, back. Get up late, listen to the radio. Chat to someone in the squat.

Then: tube, theatre. He hadn't made any contact with his family, did not know how they were, or if they were still on the planet. Then one evening as he was walking through Trafalgar Square to Embankment station he stopped and phoned his sister. He was sure enough time had elapsed by now for any tapping to be unlikely. Her number was one of the few he always had by heart. She worked in higher education, and was making her way up the ladder.

Her simple 'hello' could have been for any of her friends and colleagues.

"It's me. Jooly".

"Jooly?"

"Yep. Can we talk?"

"Jooly. There was a long pause. "Oh, my God! Where are you?"

"Can we talk? You know...?" he asked.

"I think so. I think so. Better make it brief. Are you all right?"

"Did they come round?"

"Who? Oh, yes, they did. Months ago. A chap called John Pendelbury. Nice enough. I told them nothing because there was nothing to tell. And they have not been back since. Jooly, where are you? Or shouldn't I ask?"

"Here" he said.

"Here?" she asked.

"Uh, huh".

"Here meaning?.."

"Close. I'd better make it short. Listen: Mum and Dad?"

"OK. Sort of. I can hear traffic".

"Yes, traffic. Listen, I......it's just good to hear you".

"Are you sure you are all right?"

"I'm all right. Just. Just". Julian stifled a sob. A word of kindness and a voice from the past and he was breaking up.

"Look, it's not as you think, you know. All that business".

"I know. I can imagine. They'd like to see you, you know. Jooly?"

"I've got to go now. I'll be in touch. Bye".

And he put down the phone. Tears began pouring down his face. The darkness of the night was a blessing, and by the time he was in the tube and under the harsh, florescent lights the moment of emotion had passed.

CHAPTER 16

MUSIC

I t was a South African pianist Greg who got Julian to audition
for a music school. Greg was also working front of house and
played for Julian once or twice during the shows they did not find
interesting. The operettas, after the third time, hung heavy and
known, and so they sneaked off to the back practice rooms and
went through some songs.

Julian had heard a Brahms song on the radio: *Wie bist du Meine
Koenigin* sung by Hans Hotter, and after that one hearing Julian
began humming and singing it to himself all day. He hardly knew
any German, but the very words seem to be filled with special
meaning, the descending line had a sensuousness which made his
body melt, and Hotter's voice was so masculine, so easy, so assured.
He did not know what all the words meant, but he imitated the
Germanic sounds, the umlauts, the guttural 'ch'. It posed no tech-
nical difficulties for Julian at that time, and so he had all of one
song to his repertoire. The pianist, Greg, a slight man with a goa-
tee beard and glasses, had studied in South Africa and now was in
the UK for his Overseas Experience, doing evenings at the opera
house, teaching privately, trying to get a job at one of the Colleges.
He was a kind man, and gave himself no airs or graces, although
with his proficiency on the keyboard he was truly slumming it by
helping Julian put together a song and an aria.

After several sessions Greg turned away from the keyboard.

"You could try to get in to one of the Colleges this September".

"What, you mean, study singing?"

"If that is what you want to do".

Julian was not sure what he wanted to do.

"But they won't take me".

"You don't know that. No harm in trying. What is there to lose? Ring them, ask for an audition, ask them what you have to sing, then turn up".

"It can't be that simple".

"Might be".

It was. Julian got the numbers of the major London Colleges from the phone book, and rang round in the morning. Some were not interested, but one just said simply that he had to come next week, 18th September, a Monday, at 3 o'clock, and to bring two contrasting pieces. Julian put the phone down in the booth near the World's End pub. His hands were shaking slightly. What the hell was he going to sing them? He only knew one piece.

He walked around in a daze. Next Monday. Today was Wednesday. Five days to learn another piece.

He was early at work and prayed that Greg would turn up. As they were changing into their white shirts and green jackets, Julian approached Greg and started talking in a whisper.

"Can we do some singing in the first interval?"

"Yeah, sure mate. What's up? You look worried".

Julian kept his voice down. To outside observers they might have been cocaine dealers fixing a price.

"I've gotta sing. Next week. Audition".

"So. We'll meet back stage. Room 1. OK?" Greg smiled in a kind, reassuring way. Nice man.

Julian got to the practice room as soon as the curtain went up for the second Act. It was *The Tales of Hoffmann,* an opera he usually watched as he found it absorbing and highly intelligent. Hoffmann and his shadow, the three women, facets of his desire who come to a bad end, and the evil genius who pursues him in several guises through his life. And his faithful servant always at his side, with art finally winning out. But tonight Julian had other things on his mind.

He put the music of the Brahms song on the piano and waited for Greg. He plinked out the vocal line and tried to sing it. He did some vocal exercises which he thought might help. He had no idea if they did. He tried half a scale on 'la'. Then another on 'mi'. He had no idea what he was really doing and there was no one around to guide him.

He paced up and down in the airless room. On the walls there were life-size photos of famous singers, looking stunning in their costumes and their demeanour. Luxon in 'Don Carlos' looking magnificent, every inch a soldier. He could not imagine himself ever getting to the level where he would be dressed by someone else and sing to 2000 people. One short song seemed hard enough. And to learn an entire opera, often in another language, and re-member it, and sing it so it got over the orchestra and to the audi-ence, and not crack up or mess the entries or trip over your feet, or come in with the others at the right time. He had only one piddly song.

He started panicking. Greg came at that moment.

"So what's the deal?"

"I have to sing at 3 in the afternoon on Monday, two pieces. I only have one!"

"So you learn another".

"In 5 days?" He felt his throat get tighter already.

"In 5 days. There are cases of singers who learnt entire operas in 3 days. They say Caruso learnt 'Elisir' in 4 days; Domingo says he learnt 'Ballo' over a weekend". Julian did not find this very helpful.

"Maybe. I am not them. What do I do? Bunk off. Not turn up. Ring and say I am ill. What?"

"You learn another piece, a contrasting piece, as they say".

"In 5 days?"

"A doddle", said Greg.

"What?"

"You sing something in English which is short and you read it from the music".

Julian nodded at this wise advice.

"And what do I sing?"

"'*Music For A While*' by Purcell".

"Easy?", asked Julian

"Relatively".

"You have the music already?"

"Yeah".

"High?" Julian asked.

"No".

"Short?

"Sort of" said Greg.

"We'll go for it. But can we sing this other one now?"

"Of course".

And so they did. Judged by a professional's standards, Julian's attempt was pitiful. He knew nothing about breath-support, there was no legato line, his German was mangled, and his sense of style was just a poor imitation of Hotter's. Quite often he was slightly out of tune. But the basic voice was good and easy on the ear and the range was excellent, as Julian had no problem going up or down. It was not a 'short' voice, as he was to hear later in singing jargon.

The next evening they met as agreed. Greg was remarkably kind and indulgent to this young man who hardly knew how to read music and did not even have two songs ready to sing. In hindsight Julian decided that Greg was bored by the evening on the stage (the 20th Hoffmann that season) and it was a chance for him to play the piano, his instrument. He was also perhaps a nice man who was just trying to help.

"Here it is".

Julian looked at it. Three pages, all central, nothing hard. Lots of repeats of words. A bit of squiggly stuff in the middle which meant he had to sing fast. Crescendo and diminuendo marks. Not long. He could do it.

"It was written for incidental music for the play 'Oedipus'.

It's beautiful, you'll find. There is something called an ostinato bass, or a ground bass, which goes on all the time through the piece, unchanging, and Purcell weaves this harmony and melody around it. Very clever and very moving. I'll play it through".

The bass notes on the rehearsal piano did not sound great, a rather dull un-vibrant plink-plunk of a sound, but the lines rose and fell, and the crescendo and the legato already spun a spell around Julian.

Greg sang very softly through the piece, and Julian watched and listened. *Music shall all your cares beguile, Wond'ring how your pains were eased.* Then the passage where the snakes drop from her head, and the words *drop, drop* felt like they really were easing the pain, and with every word the cares of the afflicted Oedipus fell away: *All, all, shall all your cares beguile.* Greg finished the song in a hush of a minor chord.

"Well, what do you think?"

"It's.............. beautiful". Julian could not wait to sing it. Something in his soul had moved, had been touched. How could anyone write such amazing stuff?

"It looks easy, but be careful", said Greg.

And then Greg began again, and Julian very falteringly tried to sing the words and notes together. He stumbled at the hurdles of the fast, embellished passages, and the notes made into naturals were out of tune. When he sank into his lower register the voice dropped and he was flat, and he could not understand the rhythm at one point. But when he got to the high line of *eternal* his voice rang out. He gained confidence. Then the return to the main theme, *piano*, hushed, the music and words deepened by what had gone before. The final crescendo and piano ending left Julian stunned. He wanted to sing it again, and again.

"Not bad for a piece, ay?"

Julian smiled weakly at this man he hardly knew.

> "Thank you for showing me. I'll learn it for tomorrow. Not by heart, but I'll know it".

> "I'll leave you to look through. I'll get back to *Hoffmann*".

Julian sat down at the piano and tried to make his way around the notes. The very few lessons he'd had as a kid only taught him to identify the notes through memonics: Every Good Boy Deserves Fun, E G B D F, and so on. But it was a start. He found the opening note F, and began counting. Someone had left an old pencil on the desk in the corner and he wrote in the beats in the bar: Music, that was 3 plus a bit more, one, as the whole thing was in 8. He put his head out of the practice room from time to time to hear the music and recognise where they had got to, and then went back to his labour. The show finished at 10.30, so he knew he could cut it fine and get back behind the hats and coats desk at 10.25.

By the end of the evening the music was covered with numbers up to 8, like a child learning to write the alphabet. But Julian felt he had made progress, had somehow conquered the task, deciphered the code. And the next day Julian was at the honky-tonk piano in the squat plinking out the notes quietly as the others either tried to sleep, or made their pots or went off to their architecture practice.

The audition was on Monday. 4 days left. A slow-burning panic was setting in. Julian became a bore in the squat, with Sven finally telling him to shut up and put a sock in it! after he had gone over one phrase a thousand times: '*Till the snakes drop, drop drop*'.

> "Why can't they fucking well drop off the first time?"

> "Sorry. Sorry" and Julian closed the piano lid. What now?

He wandered to the local library close to the squat, a small neat building off Kings Road, tucked in amongst the office buildings and the shops.

He went to the music section—woefully little there: scores of the operas and operettas in English, a lot of piano music, some collections of the musicals. That was it. Nothing on being scared shitless by an audition and what to do about it. Section: Panic. Subsection: faeces More a medical condition. Julian leafed through the scores aimlessly. He could ask. He picked out a kind-looking girl on the help desk.

"Do you have anything on auditions, by any chance? Please?"

"Auditions, you say? What sort of auditions?" she asked.

"Auditions, as in music, theatre, technique".

"I'll just have a look", and she looked through the list of books they had in stock.

"I have one here" she said. 'An Actor Prepares' by Stanislavsky. Translated, from the Russian. Is that any use?"

"Um, translated or not, I don't think it will help in my case. Might do. I need something more specifically on music" said Julian.

"Music, music…….. let me see………" She looked through her catalogue again.

"There is this one: it has the title: 'The Art of Auditioning' by Anthony Legge. Is that what you're looking for?"

"I don't know. It sounds promising", said Julian.

"And there is this one: 'The Empty Space' by Peter Brooke, all about acting. Do you want to try those two? It's all we've got" she asked.

Julian opened his hands and nodded his head.

"Anything at this point".

The librarian wrote down the sections and book numbers and handed the piece of paper to Julian.

"Good luck".

Julian smiled, thanked her and walked off to the indicated sections. The first book by Legge was bound in a hard green cover. It was small, the sort of thing you could stuff into a pocket and read on the tube.

He'd take it out and do just that. The other was a much-thumbed paperback with a picture of a group of actors dressed in shades of white. Julian chose the Legge book first. He flicked through the first sections: 'The right approach' and 'Should I bring my own accompanist' and then found: 'What happens on the day'. This he read carefully, about how performers wake up with a feeling of apprehension and nerves. And then a series of sensible pointers about having a schedule leading up to the time of the audition, not being rushed, and using breathing and relaxation exercises. Other bits about dress and presentation and CV and the state of the music you are going to ask the pianist to play. Useful, but nothing under: leg trembling, mouth dry, total frontal lobotomy break down and urge to flee.

In the Brooke essays he came across a long section of how various actors dealt with fear, ending with how even the top names and the really creative ones reach a sense of terror on the first night.

Well, that was a help of sorts. They were all shitting themselves out there, and the best were among them. Great. Not really much help other than the feeling he was not alone. But he did sit and read both books at leisure, slowly, with Legge indicating the best arias for an audition in each voice type, a short summary, and some ideas of what to do and what to avoid. Excellent, but at another level. Julian decided to take it out anyway.

He found a comfy chair in a corner close to the children's section where there was no noise and started reading Peter Brooke. It was inspirational, about opera on improvised stages in Hamburg just after the war, of 'Crime and Punishment' in a garret, The Berliner Ensemble, Stanislavsky, Craig and Shakespeare in a North London church, the shared experience of actor and public, then the need for distance and detachment. Brooke's knowledge and experience were far-reaching, and so many phrases cascaded out like a string of broken pearls. It did not help Julian much with the immediate problem of his terror, but it did make him feel in very good company. He'd take this one out too.

When he got back to the squat he found Sven cooking some mackerel by hanging them over the smoking fire. It was camp-fire stuff, but after a few weeks in the place, perfectly normal.

"Hi".

"Hi".

"Want some fish?"

Julian surveyed the string, the rudimentary pulley-system, the fish grilling and the juices dropping off onto the wooden floor.

"Looks interesting. I'll watch you first".

Julian sat in one of the chairs near the fire. It had its stuffing coming out at all sides, the horse hair, black bristles like a weather-lined Scot with a bushy beard.

"Sven?"

"Hmm".

"Do you know much about nerves?"

"As in disease? Didn't study biology at school".

"No, I mean, when you get nervous. What do you do?" Julian asked.

"When I get nervous? You mean, legs trembling panic sort of thing?"

"Yes".

"Can't say I do" said Sven.

"But have you? Ever?" insisted Julian.

"Perhaps before a presentation of a big project we've spent months on and the deal is worth several hundred thousand pounds".

"Yes, that's it. What do you do?"

"Hadn't given it much thought, really", said Sven.

"Could you think now? When did it go well, and when did it go badly, and why?"

Sven turned to see how the fish were doing.

"Look, are you sure you don't want one of these? They are far too much for me".

"Yes, I'll eat one and give myself food poisoning if it makes you happy, but please, tell me!"

"Why, what's up?" asked Sven.

"I just....have to do something shortly, and it is making me feel a bit queasy".

"More than the fish?" asked Sven

"More than the fish".

"Quite some risk, then".

Sven went back to his pulley system, the mackerel being toasted slowly on both sides, the hot juices hitting the exposed wooden floorboards. Minutes went past.

"Sven? Are you still there?"

"Yeah, I was thinking". The candles flickered around the room. Julian did not want to push him, but was not leaving or eating without an answer. Finally Sven turned away from the fish and came out with:

"It is sort of like this. When I don't really know what is going on, and the project has been bundled together by a group of us and we have a few all-nighters, and not one of us really believes in the stuff we are trying to get built, then I get a knee-trembler".

"Tricky", said Julian.

"Very tricky". Sven continued:

"But if it is a project I know well, believe in, know we have done a good job, then there is a bit of positive adrenalin and I can pitch it well, and we usually get the contract. I have a sort of, I don't know, an inner security".

There was a long pause.

"Does that answer your question?"

"Yes, it does in a way. Thank you" said Julian.

"Fish?"

"Of course. But if I'm hoiking my guts out tomorrow I'll come and put a fresh one in your bed".

They unhooked the mackerel and found some plates, and with their burnt and slightly raw fish in front of them, ate their meal. And all the way through, they chatted about who was doing what, who was going out with whom, how long this squat would last, what they would have to do it the LEB was cut off, where they could move, the thought came to Julian that if he was super well-prepared, and knew his music inside out and knew he could sing it and was confident he could sing it, then the mind-shredding nerves might go away, just not appear, be banished always. 'Inner security'. It was a good phrase. He'd use it. Understand it. Make it his own. But he had another problem. Even if they accepted him into the school, he'd need another identity, and a British one this time.

CHAPTER 17

RETURN HOME

A new identity. Hugo was out of the question, as was Simon, and he did not know anyone in the underworld who could provide him with a new passport. He could possibly find an old one.

In the end he had only one option: he'd have to return home and steal his dead Uncle's. Uncle Michael had died in the war in a submarine and Julian had seen his mother keep her twin brother's papers and belongings in the bottom drawer of the desk in her room. Among his personal effects was a passport. Michael Orton was not a bad name. He liked it already. He would get the photo changed, that was not too difficult. It should be enough. It would have to be enough.

He decided to go under cover of darkness, start the journey in London with the commuters and get there around 6. They'd be having their dinner then, and it would give him enough time to get back to catch the last train. He had to take a bus from the station for Midhurst and was not worried now by the police. He was certain they had lost track of him, and besides his appearance had changed so much that it would have been a miracle if they had caught him. He had read somewhere that if a man shaved his hair very short and then grew a moustache, not even his own mother would recognise him. So gone were the curly dark locks and the hippy guitar player. He now gave the appearance of the Ist World

War poet Wilfred Owen, his light brown moustache flowing over his upper lip, and the shorn hair give the air of a conscript off to the trenches. Not even his own mother, they said. Well, he might find out tonight.

The bus was almost empty at that hour and going to Midhurst was not something one did during the week unless one had business there and there were few who had that. He was almost alone, being driven through the night back to his family. He could not go in. He would have to watch from outside the windows, if anything. It was now dark and he could hardly see the countryside.

The houses, with their window frames painted in their bright yellow, stood out. The lights on the pub, and then darkness. One or two houses with their lights on. Then darkness again. He made out trees either side, places where had had walked and worked as a young man. The farm buildings at the top of the rise, and then down into the dip, Cocking hill, and the short run through the village to the approach to Midhurst. He got up and rang the bell. It was his stop. No one else was getting off. He waited for the bus to depart before turning into the lane. The driver did not seem to pay any attention. He was on his way back to the depot. One more, one less.

The walk to the vicarage was not far, over the small bridge with the stream running by, up a slight rise to the common and then the house itself standing stark and alone with its gables and outhouses. There were lights on. Julian's breathing was not steady, his heart was racing. What now? He hadn't thought that far. There would be the dog, he expected, who might bark.

He would go round the side and try and look through a kitchen window.

He walked on the grass, not on the gravel path so as not to make any noise. No one was around, no cars, so his walk along the drive, though exposed, was not noticed by anyone. He walked to the left of the house, though the brick arch and into the yard. The windows were closed but the lights in the kitchen were on. Julian's height allowed him to just about see through the bottom window. The scene was like something out of a 18th century painting, the mother baking, the daughter doing her homework. He saw his mother sifting flour and then vigorously kneading in a light brown bowl. His sister had grown and was now a young woman, her hair done in a fashionable way with ringlets down the side of her face. His father was not around, probably out in the church or visiting. Best thing. For that Julian was grateful. He stood and watched, trying to imagine what they were talking about. He was standing on tiptoe, and from time to time had to relax back into his heels. The second time he looked, he saw his mother standing near the sink, her back to him. She looked so forlorn, so sad. Her whole body seemed to have shrunk slightly and she looked thinner. He longed to just walk in and hug her, something he had never done even before the whole mess. He let himself down onto his feet and let out a deep sigh. Then decided to have one more look, but as he did so, and to get a better view, he stood right on the tips of his toes, and lost his balance slightly and nudged the dustbin. The lid rolled off with a clatter.

"Shit, shit!"

He stood still in the darkness. They must have heard something. He heard the back door open and his mother's voice. She had called the dog.

Duffy stood at the entrance, sniffing the air. The dog let out a deep growl and bark but did not move. His mother pushed him slightly and urged him on:

"Go on, go see, go see who is there".

Her voice was uncertain. Then the dog set off at a pace, out towards the field at the back. His mother stood at the door, with her clothes gathered at the neck, protecting herself against the evening chill. She waited for the dog to come back, and she called his name twice.

"Duffo! Duffo!"

Julian stayed absolutely still where he was. The darkness hid him. He waited until the commotion had subsided, then he heard the panting and the feet of the dog coming back. It stopped at the pantry door as it saw him. He did not bark but instead stood wagging his tail.

Julian crouched down, said nothing. Then the dog came slowly to him, hesitantly, almost embarrassed, making a little whining sound of joy. They had been good friends, walked miles, chased rabbits, shot some pheasants together. The whining got louder.

"Who is there?" His mother sounded nervous.

"Hello? Hello?" she shouted into the night.

Julian touched the dog's coat, stroked his head, crouched down. Then he held him close and hugged him, a gesture the dog backed out of after a while. He made a shhh-ing sound, but the dog bounced back in joy and did circles around himself, put his front paws down as if to incite Julian to play as they had before.

"Duffo?", called his mother. "Is anyone there?"

Julian would have to reveal himself now. He stood up and walked slowly into the halo of the back door light. His mother could see him now. She did not recognise him at first and drew back in fear.

"It's me. Mum. It's Jooly".

"Jooly". His mother did not know what to do, torn by her mother's love for her son and the terrible crime he had committed.

"Jooly", she repeated.

Julian came towards her. She looked hard at her son, then turned away to hide her tears. He went up to her and touched her arm. She did not move away. He put his arms around her and heard her sobbing. She broke out of his embrace, turned into the house and hid her face with her hand, wiping away the tears.

"Can I come in?"

She did not reply for a time, the tears streaming down her face. Then with a nod she turned and walked along the corridor into the house. He followed quietly, the dog behind them

"Mum?" His sister shouted out. "Was anyone there?"

"It's nothing. Nobody", his mother tried to reassure her daughter. She put a finger to her lips and indicated the sitting room off to the right of the house. She let Julian and in with the dog and then closed the door.

"We'll have to talk in whispers".

"Dad?" Julian asked.

"Out. Parish".

"Back?"

"Soon" she said. A long pause followed. Then:

"Why are you here? Where have you been? They said Israel, then they lost track of you.

"Someone said Jerusalem".

"Most of that is true" he answered.

"The police have been round here, but we knew nothing".

"Better that way". Another long silence came between them.

"It isn't as you think" Julian said.

"I am not sure what to think".

"It was an accident".

"Tell them then!" She raised her voice. Julian shook his head.

"I can't. Not yet. Not yet. I can't go to prison for life, Mum!" At this his voice broke.

"I'm just a young man, I have not lived, they can't lock me up for that. It was an accident".

His mother did not reply.

"Look, I need something from you". His mother looked up at him, her gaze stern and unwavering.

"We have no money, you know that".

"No, not money. I need Uncle Michael's passport".

She shook her head.

"Mum". Then quieter, an entreaty, imploring: "Mum. It is my only chance. I can begin a new life".

His mother bowed her head and tears dropped on to her hands.

"Don't you have some friends who have been helping you? I heard there was someone".

"They can't help anymore" he said.

Silence. Julian could not know what was in her head. Perhaps the idea that this document, one of the few she had of her brother, might strangely give life to her son, he might live on, through this photo, give her only son new life on this earth. She got up and went to the door, opened it and listened.

"Wait for me here". He heard go up the stairs. Julian waited, listening for a car's tyres on the gravel, or his sister in the kitchen. The clock ticked loudly. The dog lay at his feet, happy, calm, re-laxed. His young master was at home.

Eventually his mother came down. She had the blue passport with the name in ink on the front, and some money in her hand.

"Go now. Go. Dad will be coming back soon. He can't find you here".

Julian took the money and opened the passport. Michael's fresh clean gaze looked out at him, the hair dark, cut short, about to go into the navy. Julian closed it again.

"Thank you".

He kissed his mother once on the cheek, and let her go. He opened the door and listened. Nothing. He walked to the back door and opened the latch as quietly as he could. He turned to look once more at his mother, the dog at her side, she holding onto his collar. And then Julian was out into the night.

CHAPTER 18

FIRST STEPS

So Monday the 18th eventually came. Julian woke feeling nervous, as if there were some impending gloom about to descend on him, and then he remembered why. He lay back on the mattress staring into space. What was he doing? Trying to learn to sing. Was it what he wanted to do? Yes. If he failed did it matter? Well, it was only feedback. One decision was not the end of the world. He could try again.

Did he know his music? Yes, to the point of boredom. He had learnt to imitate Hans Hotter's German; the Purcell was deeply embedded in his mind. Two contrasting pieces. Well, they were that all right.

Nothing which stretched him too far, but both showing he was musical, could sing in another language competently. And as for nerves, well, he would have to deal with them when he came to it. His preparation was in place.

What to wear? Greg had advised him along the lines of: nothing too showy, but respectable, a jacket, a clean shirt and dark trousers. It had meant a trip to the local charity shop. He had found a light-blue, drip-dry shirt, size 17, at 10 shillings and a dark jacket with rather wide lapels (it was The King's Road) going for £1.50. Some black trousers he had already and had got them cleaned. They were hanging up against a wall (more 6 inch nails hammered into the brickwork). Rudimentary, but efficient.

He got up and went to the bathroom to stare at his face. Close-cropped hair, moustache, almost Wilfred Owen staring back at him. Even his own mother hardly recognised him. Hadn't recognised him. And now he was Michael Orton, aka Jooly. He could hide behind that disguise he thought for ever. How many friends at school had nick-names which were totally different to their real names? A lot. He tried it out: Hi, my name's Michael Orton but all my friends call me Jooly. Hello, my name's Michael, but I prefer Jooly. It's a family name. You have a similar thing too? Wow! What a coincidence! He could live with that, would have to live with that, and make Uncle Michael's life come back again in some form.

The change of passport photo was pretty easy. He had another taken of himself, and steamed the glue off the inside of the original one. It came away without much difficulty. He had then waited for the paper to dry and then smeared a bit of Bostik paper glue on the under side and pressed it down hard in the space. A customs official would have spotted it perhaps, but no one else. It looked authentic.

They might not even ask to see it. No one carried passports or ID as they did abroad. Hi! My name's Michael Orton. I'm here to sing at 3pm. And so it was.

The music school was strangely located, between the Thames and Fleet Street. It had a fairly impressive Victorian entrance and looked like a music school once inside, but outside you vied with enormous rolls of paper being delivered to the printing presses close by. Immense lorries arrived at 10 in the morning to have their loads lifted by crane and into the constantly rolling presses. The clink and clank of the presses were everywhere and even in the practice rooms you could hear the shouts of the drivers and the crane operators as they manoevered the rolls inside. The High Courts were also close, and you would sometimes see barristers in full wigs and gowns outside. Walking towards the tube and The Thames you were at the edge of the City of London, and secretaries and young bankers stood outside smoking. The place died suddenly at 7, and it was like walking around a mausoleum, your shoes echoing off the walls. No cars, a taxi here and there, one or two pubs with strange licensing laws, a golf club with no clubs in sight, and just an excuse for a drinking hole. Journalists hopped in and out between shifts-and during.

The lady at the reception in the school was friendly and plump. She didn't ask for any identification, passport, absolutely nothing. It was as Julian had predicted. The pianist was a certain Mr Cyril Gell. He was quite a character. Chain smoking, his fingers tarnished a dark yellow by the nicotine, all of 6 stone and just about avoiding the classification of a dwarf, he looked as if intensive care were more his environment rather than piano playing. He dressed as if he had chosen badly from cast-offs at a charity shop, and with his little sandy tea-strainer of a moustache and thin face, he resembled more a field mouse than a top accompanist. Julian was even doubtful that this man could actually get his hands around the notes, let alone play them with any vigour. He was wrong. Mr Gell led him into the practice room, a rather down-at-heel wooden structure which had obviously seen better days and had heard thousands of aspiring singers. There was a small window in the door so people could see just who was playing and singing, and that was that. No pictures of composers, concert halls, opera houses. Stark, functional, over-used. The field mouse sat at the piano, took the music and placed it on stand. He already looked more in command.

"Which one do you want to star with?" asked Mr Gell.

"Either, really" said Julian.

"Go where I can see you"

Julian placed himself in the curve of the baby grand.

"We'll try the Purcell first".

"OK".

"The panel will like something in English, and, well, it is Purcell—and this one in particular".

Julian began re-evaluating this little pixie of a man in front of him. He seemed to know what he was talking about. But could he actually play the notes? Then the field mouse put his hands to the keys and magic took place. His touch, the phrasing, the delicacy, the understanding, all in a matter of a few bars.

Julian felt as if he were buoyed up by this cushion of sound, this miraculous, ethereal combination of notes, dipping, slightly pausing, moving on, getting louder, then falling back. And his voice responded: he sang as if he had always sung it like that: confident, assured, poetic, and extremely musical. They came to the end, and the field mouse was no longer; instead a man of massive talent and experience sat unassuming at the piano stool. Julian waited for him to say something. Nothing came.

"Was it all right?" asked Julian.

The mouse thought a bit and then said:

"I am not a teacher, and you are in front of an audition. There are things I could say but I won't. It is more important you sing it as you have always sung it. For the moment. Now, the other one?"

Julian handed him the Brahms.

"I don't know this". Julian was surprised.

"Oh? I thought it was famous" said Julian.

"No, never seen or heard of it. But I am sure it will be lovely".

And with that he read, at first sight, the Brahms, the lines flowing, the ritardando coming at exactly the right place, the bass notes clear yet legato, and never drowning the right hand or the singer's voice, the piano taking on the singer's vocal line as if they were one instrument. And all this when he had never laid eyes on the music before. Julian realised he had walked into a place where outstanding talent did not display itself in a gaudy show.

"Um, that was a nice song. As I said, never heard it before. Very nice, and you sing it well. It suits you. Careful to sustain the top, you take it away too much, but again, sing it as you have always sung it. Now, when are you on? Pretty much now, but they are always late. Here, take the music and I'll see you in the audition room".

Gell handed the music back to Julian and was off with his shuffling walk (his trousers came over his shoes and dragged in the floor) to play for the next person.

Julian walked out into the hallway and saw other candidates waiting. There were a lot of young girls, dressed to kill and with a lot of make-up. Julian felt as if he were at a rather upper-class dance and no one had told him to dress smart. Still, it did not matter. He sat down on a bench and tried to concentrate on the matter ahead. He read through the music again, forcing himself to focus. It also meant he did not have to make eye contact with these very self-assured young people. Some seemed to know each other already, and were chatting away, talking about who was where and with who, and who was in the panel and their teachers and their pieces and where they were singing.

Julian waited. His anxiety started kicking in, so he thought back to Peter Brooke, and how even the most famous were shitting themselves, and then reminding himself that he knew his music very well indeed, and he would have an amazing pianist as an accompanist and the music was divine. It sort of helped. He tried deep breathing, and that helped. He thought of nice things, he thought of his childhood and the bike rides and the apples just falling on the road and eating them half smashed and the juice coming down his chin. He thought of his dog and the times they had gone shooting together, he thought of the countryside and the walks, he thought of what Hugo would say to deflate it all, he thought of........... "Michael Orton!" A lady's imperious voice sounded in the corridor.

At first he did not reply, but then at the second calling he came round from his reverie and stood up.

Better not let that happen again.

"Me. It's me" he said.

"You don't seem too sure".

"Me. No one else. Just me" he said.

She led him into the audition room which was really just a much larger practice room with a long desk and three men sitting behind it. They seemed more business men than anything else. Suits, ties, they could have been on the board in one of the companies only half a mile away. Later he found out that the Director of the School was at the centre, and either side were singing teachers. The piano was on the right of the room and the field mouse took his place there with the music, propping it up on the wooden stand. Julian watched him do this, trying not to have to face the panel. But after the music was well and truly placed there was nowhere to hide anymore. Julian turned.

"What have you brought to sing for us today?"

It was the middle one, dark hair, heavy glasses.

"A song by Brahms, and then one by Purcell".

They all nodded, and the middle one who had spoken leaned over to the one on his left. What he said was inaudible to Julian.

"And which one do you want to start with?"

"I'll sing the Brahms" Julian said.

They then settled down for the experience, moving slightly in their seats. The one on the left whispered quite loudly to the other two: "Never heard of it. Have you ?" The others smiled. Well, that was a good start, thought Julian.

He turned to the field mouse and he started playing. The slow cascade of notes in the right hand, the tune swelling up in the left. It sort of gave Julian a cushion. But his mouth was dry and his heart was beating far too loud, hammering in his chest. Could they hear it also?

His throat also tightened. Here, it is coming, the entry, here, now, don't miss it. Julian joined the music just in time, like a moving staircase. And he wobbled a bit as he got on. The voice was breathy and uncertain. Not a good start, but as he sang, he got more confident, and by the time he came to the second verse he was actually enjoying it. His voice rang out, round, good German, stylish, musical, Hotter-like. He hung on the suspended note and then let it drop. The song itself was a winner, but he knew the style and how to achieve it. The range had not stretched him vocally, he was well within his limits of a comfort zone. Brahms had written for a soirée, not an opera gala.

Silence. None of them spoke. It can't have been that bad. Then they looked down at their notes, and up again. Conferred in whispers. The one on the right in the lighter suit then said:

"Have you ever heard the record by Hans Hotter?" His accent was strange: German, guttural, European. Julian did not know what to say. If he said yes, then it would seem he was just copying it.

If he said no, he was lying, and then what? he said to himself.

"I have heard the record several times". All three men laughed. Nice to hear laughter.

"You sound like him. Which is both good and bad. And you are under the note slightly too, which is definitely bad!" The men all laughed again.

"Where do you come from?" This from the man on the left. Here it comes, he thought.

"Exactly who are you? British? You sound British but with some strange accent in it".

"I lived until recently in Israel. I was working there. Before, Britain" said Julian.

"One of yours, perhaps Walter", said the middle one.

"Perhaps, perhaps. We'll see. Musical education?" he asked.

"Pretty basic. Not much" Julian replied. Better be honest, thought Julian. They'll know anyway.

"So, and the next song, the Purcell?"

Julian felt more relaxed now, and he turned with a smile. The field mouse did not do smiles, it seemed, but his moustache twitched into something resembling a smile. His head went to the keys, then up at the music, then to they keys again. The bass line sounded out, measured, lilting, dipping, coming back, all within a bar of 8 crotchets. Quite a feat. Julian was so enraptured that he nearly forgot to come in.

Music, he sang, *music for a while, shall all thy cares beguile*..................
The words were beautiful in themselves, and were so well set, the
magic of the piece worked on the room. The three in front of him
seemed lost in thought. They stared ahead, seemingly in a trance.
Julian sang to the back wall, to himself, for the composer. He sang:
drop, drop, and it was as if peace itself came dropping. *'and the whip,
and the whip from out her hands'*. Then the refrain, the first line, this
time quieter, as if the singer was truly sending Oedipus to sleep.
Julian came to the last cadence and let it sing itself. He held the
last note still. It left a hush in the room. Something had happened.
There silence continued until it became slightly embarrassing.
Then the one in the middle of the panel spoke:

"There is potential there. What would you say, Walter? Do
you want him?"

They all looked at the teacher with the strange accent.

"I am not sure. You look like a Chemistry teacher. Not a
singer. What would you do if I said I didn't want to take
you?"

"I'm sorry?" replied Julian.

"What would you do? I say: No, I don't have the time or
space, what would you do?"

"Now, right now?" asked Julian.

"Yes, right now, 5 minutes after now". Everyone in the room
turned to him with surprise.

"Well, I'd go out of the room.....is that what you want?" asked
Julian. The man was nodding his head in assent....... "I'd go
out of the room, and down the stairs and into the nearest pub"..... there was laughter at this................ "and I'd sit
down and have a drink, and I'd think: well, he isn't the only

teacher in the world, and I'd phone another college and say I wanted another chance".

"And so I take you!" he said with some sort of triumph. The others chuckled slightly at the man's unorthodox methods. Julian turned to the Mr Gell and gathered his music. The field mouse was smiling as much as his emaciated cheeks and his moustache would let him. Julian walked out of the room to the secretary sitting outside.

"They took me" he said in awe.

"Glad to hear it. Fill this in, full name and so on, and address. We'll be in touch later in the week". And so it was.

CHAPTER 19

PROGRESS

And so began this part of his musical journey. He was too scared to get up in public at first. He knew nothing, but he was happy with that. He sometimes asked himself why they actually took him, and there was a rumour: his teacher, Walter Gruner, had had a bust up with a pupil from Korea who had then complained. He had no power in the College, was not Head of any Department, and although he had had some successful students who went on to become household names, recently no one rated him much. He did the Lieder class, and that was about it. Young sopranos with light voices did well with him, and he also had an eye for the ladies. There were stories of mistresses, ex-students. So why Walter Gruner really took him he never really found out. It may have been he just needed pupils, and a young man was something of a rarity amongst the 200 sopranos auditioning.

The first lesson was really just technique. The room was in the music school, a rather airless bare room.

The windows were double glazed as the school was in a residential area and Julian supposed the locals might not take to hearing endless vocal exercises or trumpet scales night and day. There was a baby grand, a piano stool, two chairs, and music stand which had seen better days as well-and not much else, just a faded portrait of a print of Mozart was on the wall in a very simple flat frame.

Walter had a series of breathing exercises on a rolled 'r' which took the voice up and down, and then an exercise to centre the voice very nasally. 'Rigamaza' was the word, going up and down on a four note theme. Gruner drew a little diagram to show where the sound should end up. Julian followed as best he could: up and down. Gruner made a strange face to indicate it should be more nasal.

"The nose is a good place to find for a young singer. I also have nose for talent. I am not sure of yours yet" he said.

Then he had to sing a song. Julian offered the Brahms again. Walter took it and read it. Then in his German-Jewish accent:

"I do not really know this one well. Never sung it myself. I have heard Hotter, of course. I do not know if Fisher-Diskau has recorded it. I like it. It is a good song. Very Brahms, very slushy. Good, let's do it".

And so Gruner sat at the piano, took out his reading glasses, and read through the piece. There were wrong notes, but the feel and sweep of the song was there. So Julian sang and felt himself transported on wings of inspiration. He sang without inhibition, half imitating Hotter, half just singing for the joy of it. It went very well. Certainly he had Gruner there supporting him, indicating where to slow up slightly, where to move it on, to pick up the original tempo, to take the voice off the note, the decrescendo. Gruner played to the end. Julian could tell he was satisfied.

"Yes, I liked that very much. You sing it well (High praise indeed, thought Julian). What next?"

"I only have these two songs ready. The other one I sang at the audition".

"You have nothing else?" asked Gruner in surprise.

"Nothing".

"Where have you been?" Gruner asked.

Julian stammered, looked away, was lost.

"I was in Israel".

"But are you Jewish?" Gruner asked hopefully..

"No, I'm not".

"But what were you doing there? I don't understand. You had family there?"

A lie at this point was the easiest.

"Yes, I had family there. I worked. In a kibbutz. Then in Jerusalem".

"Ah, I see. Sort of voluntary work after University".

"Yes, sort of". The explanation satisfied Gruner.

"And while you were there you started to want to sing?" Gruner asked.

"Yes, something like that. Yes".

"So, you know absolutely nothing, really. I mean, if I say: Learn 'Star of Eve' you do not know what I am talking about?"

"No" At this there was a long pause.

"The Count's aria for example? asked Gruner.

"No" replied Julian.

"I see".

The pause this time was very long. It seemed Gruner was evaluating the task ahead. Musical background practically zero. Voice green and very raw. No repertoire. It was going to be uphill. And he was no spring chicken. Julian watched the struggle in the old man's head.

It seemed it was going to be either the Korean he hated and was so aggressive to him, or this young novice. He'd take the novice.

"All right. Next week you bring and sing 'Linden Lee' by Vaughan Williams". Julian made a face.

"Why?"

"Why? Because it is simple and a folk tune—a good one at that—and the words won't get in the way, and it is a good start. Is that enough?"

"Enough" said Julian.

So Julian picked up his music and left, walking down the stairs to the cafeteria area where students mingled and drank coffee and criticized and picked holes in others and talked of concerts and boyfriends and girlfriends and where rooms were advertised and the smell of Bolognese sauce permeated the whole school. Julian did not stay long. A coffee was a luxury, but he bought one and sat and observed. The prim sopranos so sure of themselves, the weighty basses, the tenors parading in front of each other, some foreign students, Asian. Some Americans with big hair-dos and flashy clothes. One or two young conductors drifted about as if they were learning how to strut and be admired from afar. Julian felt strangely at home here. No one bothered him, no one cared about him.

He was just another face, an aspiring nobody who would get nowhere. He was not a threat. He dressed like a loser, and not enough sound had come out of the room, certainly not operatic sound, which might set the alarm bells ringing that there was someone to be watched. He was under everyone's radar for the moment, and he unconsciously chose to stay that way. No questions, no past. Don't complain, don't explain. He would try and be invisible.

⇒+ +⇐

The next session with Gruner a week later was the same sort of pattern: vocal exercises, 'rigamza', breathing, then the song he had prepared. 'Linden Lea' was a folksy tune, an imitation true folk tune by Vaughan Williams to words by William Barnes. It came easily and naturally to Julian, nothing too high, nothing too low. But Gruner became quickly bored by this. He moved on very fast to Lieder.

First, because Julian had heard a recording by the reigning prince of Lieder, Fischer-Diskau, they sang songs by Wolf, those strange, tortured, original chromatic versions of words my Moerike. Julian savoured them as a food connoisseur might appreciate some rare caviar. He found it so intelligent, and realised it would only be for a rarified audience. But he had acquired a second-hand record player from the local corner shop, a throw-out from a house clearance, and on this he played all the records he could get from the library. His classical musical education had begun.

Gruner was constantly amazed at his ignorance and ordered him to get recordings of the great names, most of whom Julian had never heard mentioned:

"Listen to Furtwaengler.I sat in on some rehearsals once. The orchestra never missed an entry......you know about his beat and baton technique, don't you?" Julian shook his head.

"And then listen, you have a record player, *ja?*, *gut*, then listen to the baritone voice. Yes, Diskau, he is very clever, and he had to change his technique to sing opera, you hear that, no?

Well, you will. Diskau is good, but listen also to the Italians and the Americans, the Americans, by God! Listen to Warren, *mein Gott*! Warren! and then Merrill, him above all. You can learn everything you need to know from Merrill. Then there is a new young man coming up: Milnes, Milos, something. He is good, very good indeed. And Hotter of course, everyone has to listen to Hotter. But Hotter is hard to follow vocally. He is not your voice type. And Wagner, Wotan, well, that is a dream for most".

And so he listened. He found a record of Leonard Warren in the local library, Warren who died on stage. Warren whose soaring dark menacing black caressing sound was silenced for ever after his big aria in *La Forza del Destino*. This sound was truly a revelation: something so wide, so dark, so easy, soaring up to the heights, staying there as it it were the natural place for the voice, the dangerously exposed and expressive Verdi lines seeming just a matter of play for him. Others strained and struggled; he just opened his mouth, it seemed, and it was there. Julian played over and over again the duet from *Simon Boccanegra*, the duet when Simon is reunited with his daughter. Julian sang along as a teenager would sing along to a pop tune. '*Ah, se la speme, o ciel clemente,or sorridi all'alma mia*'.

No one heard him in the squat as they were either all out or stoned or just didn't care. He hardly saw Sven now, who was working night and day at the architect's office.

Then came the American singer Robert Merrill, and Julian had total admiration: here was a beautiful voice, slightly less volume, a lighter sound, but again, a technique as solid as a rock, diction perfect, and style impeccable, with gut and feeling in abundance, something which he could aspire to as he felt Warren was beyond him. Warren was a 6 gold medal Olympic runner. The others were in the category of 'also rans'. Honourable silver medalists. Milnes was the only other young contender, and already he had the same wide sound, the same solid technique was in place.

And they also studied Wagner: Star of Eve from *Tannhauser*, a baritone's party piece, requiring amazing half-voice and sense of line, with a chromatic ending difficult to keep in tune. Then out came the books of Schubert Lieder: more revelation. *Erlkoenig*, the song Schubert wrote at 18, and Goethe never acknowledged. Gruner's theory was that he knew the music would become more famous than the poem. Which it did.

"Listen to the Russian, what is his name....?"

Julian offered a vague guess, the only Russian he had ever heard of in music: Chaliapin.

"No, no! Not him". Julian's ignorance irked him often. "The other one!" Julian remained silent.

"Klemp, no, Ki.....Kipnis" Gruner shouted out in triumph. "Yes, listen to Kipnis. Or rather don't, as you'll never sing again".

Julian got a record out from the library and listened, and Gruner was right. Julian wandered around for a week stunned at this man's vast voice geared down to singing the most beautiful *mezza voce* he had ever heard. He wanted to give up. And not for the first time. He was not sure where he was going and he didn't really care. He would never sing anywhere this well, the sort of quality he heard on the records, in front of a public. This was already clear. But he wanted to continue. There was nothing else. He had found himself in a sort of no man's land working evenings at the theatre, and studying during the day. He could just about survive hand to mouth from tips and the monthly pay-packet and also afford the part-time fees. For the moment he was not going to think about it. He was getting an education.

CHAPTER 20

FRENCH KISS

Then it happened. It started in the most unlikely way. Gruner had told him to get as much experience as he could. At the local town hall they put on operas, and with orchestra. Julian wandered in one Saturday morning to find a group of people waiting to sing. It was not intimidating at all, really quite friendly. It was a sort of amateur set-up, and no one was making out it was anything other than it was. Gone were the sexy slinky sopranos and the self-regarding pretty tenors. They were all housewives and plumbers wanting to sing at weekends. Julian liked the lack of pretention. And it also made him relaxed. He had never been so relaxed. He had chosen an aria he knew quite well, Bartolo's aria from *The Marriage of Figaro*, what they call a '*buffo*' aria, and he could rattle through the patter stuff in English rather than Italian……..that would come later.

On the left of him, seated, were two or three women talking together and two men who were about 40.

He was later to find out he was the interloper, as they were determined to get the lead parts as they did the year before. They did not expect a young student that morning and eyed him up suspiciously.

A lady came out to check their names. She looked at Julian over her bi-focals.

"What are you doing here?" she asked.

"I came for the audition. I read it in the paper. And 'Opera' magazine".

"Are you on our list?" she asked.

"Well, I am here. I am now, I would think".

There was silence, and then the lady scribbled his name at the bottom of the page and flounced off back into the hall. Outside they could here the voices, the silences, but it was not frightening at all. Julian felt peaceful, confident. It would be fun. Now that was something for the book: an audition that was fun.

He sat at a respectful distance from the men and the ladies, and flicked through the music. It was the Schirmer /Edward Dent translation version. They called in one of the ladies and he was left sitting fairly close to the dark-haired one. She was amazingly pretty for someone to be in the Town Hall, he thought. He found her incongruous. She looked nervous and ill-at-ease in the surroundings.

"Aren't you frightened at all?" she asked.

Julian looked over to her and saw her face for the first time. Shit! she was pretty.

"Um, frightened. No, not really. I have auditioned before, but here, no. It is sort of laid back and family and fun, no?" The woman was not convinced.

"Do you sing professionally?"

"No, good Lord no. I'd like to. I'm a student, and my teacher sent me out to get as much experience as I could as I don't know anything, or so he says! And he is right on this one. I know nothing".

"Well, you know more than me. I'm terrified" and she put her hands in his. The spontaneous gesture was so simple and natural. Julian clasped them and tried to make them warm.

"I really shouldn't be here".

"Why?" asked Julian.

"I don't know how to sing. I just want to".

"Here seems a good place" he said.

"I have nothing to sing".

"Sing a spiritual. Sing a nursery rhyme".

"I just don't know. Perhaps I should go". She withdrew her hands.

"No, just go in there and sing".

"I can't while you are out here. You go first".

Julian shrugged, then agreed.

"I really shouldn't be here", she said again.

"Michael Orton". The secretary's voice came from the half-open door.

"That's me. Or sort of". She looked at him in bewilderment.

"Can't explain. Too long".

And he went into the audition room.

It did not take long. He was brimming with confidence and sang Bartolo's aria with the verve and patter that it needed. He could feel the good vibrations from the panel. It was one of the first occasions he was to remember when he actually enjoyed the experience of auditioning. But he was too young to analyse and understand the implications.

"We'll be in touch. Thank you. Good of you to come along".

He walked out the swing doors of the hall and saw her sitting alone, twisting her hands together, looking frightened, like a wild animal trapped and seeking an escape route.

"Bye. I do hope it goes well".

"Oh bye". She hardly looked up. The dentist's chair was about to come. Her hands were grasping her music and her knuckles were white.

≕ ≕

There then started a period of uninterrupted bliss. And he was again too young to realise it. Or that bliss can end badly. His days were full and settled. The squat was ticking along. No one from the council was asking them to leave. It was spring, so the house was almost warm. He kept his one-bar heater on through the night as it could still be freezing. The other squatters were pursuing their lives.

Sven would stumble in from an all-nighter at the drawing board, with an hour's sleep in order to go an present the project to some company, his blonde Nordic hair all askew, his face flushed from alcohol. If his clients had known just how he was living they would have thrown him and his project out there and then. But the tie and suit (sort of), and the convincing air made them think he was an up-and-coming genius from Cambridge. They don't let anyone in, do they? Tilly was doing her pots and planning a trip to Japan where they had this thousand-year-old tradition. She had her basic potter's wheel downstairs run by electricity (courtesy of

The Royal Borough of Kensington and Chelsea), and the whole house rumbled along to the steady turn of the wheel.

A new arrival was Graham, a New Zealander, who just turned up one day saying he had met someone from somewhere, the ex-girfriend of a friend who had come to the house for a party, and he had come all this way from NZ, and could he stay? He added wisely that he had nowhere else to go.

Rolfe and Tilly looked at Julian. There was a room going. He was NZ, so the class barriers were down.

He looked sensible. They all nodded. They showed him the room. It was just bare wooden boards, but spacious. He liked it.

"How can I get bedding and stuff?"

"There's the shop down the road. Sells most things".

And they were suddenly all off to their various tasks, and Graham was left with a rucksack in hand, a room with bare floorboards and a vague indication of a place which sold most things. It was camping indoors, he realised.

"And the bills? he asked Julian" before he started playing the piano.

"Bills?" replied Julian.

"You know, electricity bills and so forth?" Julian looked at him blankly to try and remind himself about bills.

"Well, we pay the phone bill, as Tilly needs a phone for her work".

"And the electricity and gas, do you call it?" asked Graham.

"Oh that! Well, it's free for the moment".

"Free?"

"Yep, free. But they may cut us off at any moment and we pay up, and in which case we'll have to move on. I suppose". The thought filled Julian with dread.

Graham liked the idea very much indeed.

"Yipee! I've lucked out here. And look…" and suddenly Graham was spilling out his needs and plans.

"I need a job, something, anything. I'm a geologist, but over here for OE".

"OE?" Julian enquired.

"Yep, OE, you know, overseas experience. A year in the old country and then travelling around, and back to NZ".

"Well, the squat will last as long as it lasts. Which might be to-morrow. As for jobs, well, there are all these little workshops by the shop on the corner. Ask there, I should"

"Hey, thanks" said Graham.

"Welcome. Now please can I get on with this Italian *Aria Antica*?".

"Yea, sure, sure. Go ahead. Sorry to interrupt". And he went off to create a camp site in the room, his mattress in the corner. Later Julian observed that he really had turned it into a camp site, with candles by the side of the bed, his books neatly stacked in the other corner, his rucksack stowed away and his clothes in orderly piles on top of a towel. He must have thought he had won first prize: free everything, and in London. And within a day he was one of the family.

So the days flowed on. The trees along the pavements were in blossom, cherry and apple. People's gardens were springing into life. It was a delight to walk along The King's Road to the station and from there a few stops to the Music school. And the name thing was of no consequence.

It's my stage name. Julian, Jooles to you. So he was Jooles. One woman had changed her name from Haddock to something else because she did not want to laughed at when she sang Elgar's *Sea Pictures*. No one cared, really. The atmosphere was one of a strange camaraderie, of thinking anyone could become famous, the person sitting next to you might be: I knew her when…….. And……he was just this little fuzzy-haired punk when he first started.

But Julian was drunk on the songs. He could not get enough of them. The *Aria Antica* class was like entering the Renaissance through its music. Artificial mostly, courtly love, exquisitely ordered with immense demands on the singer to keep the line going, and just drop the consonants on the ends of the words.

An old Italian lady ran the class. Marika Durante was her name. She had been there for years but never lost her Italian accent or modified her temperament. She was volatile, passionate. For her, singing was a matter of life and death. Rumour had it that she had come to England because she had fallen in love with an English conductor but he was married and refused to leave his wife. So they continued to see each other and she never left the UK. She did some solo work and she taught Italian song, which in practice meant she bullied, tormented, raged at the incompetence, poor technique and language skills of students in her class. Julian waited for a few months before he found the courage to get up and sing.

He had chosen 'Amarilli, *mia bella*', a love song by Caccini. His pronunciation was rubbish, all wet 'ts' and no idea of single and double consonants. She also tore into his technique, something most teachers avoided so as not to give offence to other voice teachers.

'Where is the *appoggio*?' she would shout at him. 'Where? Where is the strength in your voice?

The metal? The power? *Dimmi* ! You are tall, strong, but your voice is weak. Where is the passion?

It is a love song! Show us'. Julian tried again.

'*Beh, un poco meglio.* And the top notes? They must shine. *Brillare e con squillo*'.

She had not done with him.

'You do not know the *passaggio*. I am not your voice teacher. Ask him or her. *Appoggio e passaggio*. If you do not learn these you go nowhere. And you are too old already'.

'I am only twenty-six' said Julian. Marika Durante shrugged.

(appoggio: breath support; Well, a bit better. Passaggio: navigating the voice to the upper register).

'You sing like an old man. Like a sheep. Baa-baa. *Appoggio*. The breath. The power. It is the engine. Your engine is old. Weak'.

She jabbed her fingers into Julian's side below the ribs. 'There, at the back'. She jabbed again at his back muscles either side.

'There. Build the sound. The foundation. *Sparisci*'. Which seemed to mean that Julian had to get down off the small platform. She had done with him. He was on a journey alright and though offended, felt she was imparting secrets, gold treasure, the hidden knowledge of a select tribe. He vowed to learn another song and return to face the refiner's fire.

Saturday mornings were his opera days. The group met in Hammersmith and there was this strange mixture of ex-professional singers, housewives, students who were never going to do much in the music world and hopeful amateurs who had stuck around along enough to corner the best parts. Men were always in short supply, and he found himself first singing Aeneas in *Dido and Aeneas*, and then *The Tales of Hoffmann*. In the *Dido* people had kept themselves to themselves, and Julian was reticent about talking about his private life. He was a student. That was that. But the costume they put him in was revealing, and the days on the kibbutz had given him a good body with tanned thighs. He did not know it, but the women quietly appreciated that. He sang the part with vocal ease, and the acoustic in the barn-like auditorium was kind to his rather weak sound. But the critic from the local paper liked him enough to mention him. 'and there was a well-sung

Aeneas from Michael Orton'. Julian was so surprised. And glad for his uncle Michael.

The other opera *The Tales of Hoffmann* he knew something about, as he had watched it so often in the theatre. It was to be sung in English (everything was sung in English). In those days Julian did not do any background reading, he just got the score from the local library and began to learn it in the honky-tonk piano in the squat. There was one aria for him, starting low and going up high, Dapertutto's aria. A bit of recitative and one or two exchanges between the soprano and himself, and that was it. He sang in the chorus for the rest of the time. But the second Saturday he was there, tired and only just out of bed, they were asked to pair up for the first big chorus. He stood at the back, as always because of his height, and the small petite dark-haired lady came and stood by him. He was surprised and grateful.

The director asked them to take their partners. Julian very tentatively put his arms around her and she leant back into them as if they had always known each other. Julian did not move away. After the music had stopped and they had sung the chorus the director said out loud: You all looked very ill at ease except one couple, Julian and Eva. All heads turned. They had been spotted before they had even realized themselves what might be happening. They broke away, Eva saying something about being so tired from the night before. But they had been seen. And Julian took it as a promise. He could not wait for the next Saturday morning, or the chorus bits. They were an established couple, and she just fell into his arms as if they had always known each other.

And they talked. They talked of their pasts, of a brother dead of cancer, of a divorce on her parents' side, of music (of which they both knew so little), of America, as she was half-American, of the countryside which they both loved, of books they adored, often the same titles. They talked through the breaks, they talked after the rehearsal was over. But they both had secrets. She was engaged to be married. Julian was on the run.

After the last performance they were not going to see each other again, and so at the post-performance party he talked to her even though her fiancée was close (the blindness of love, to think no one is watching!) and she said her number was in the phone book. He phoned the next day. Julian knew nothing about affairs, about marriages, about the 'rules', the etiquette of how to conduct such things. He was nearly in love. He phoned, she was there, they agreed to meet, and a coffee led to another meeting after the rehearsal. This time Julian took her to the squat. He did not care what she thought although he was strangely proud of the rambling Victorian shell of a house.

"This is a squat!" she shrieked with laughter as they went through the front door. Julian had become so oblivious to the squalor, the make-do nature of the place that it struck him as almost offensive. To his mind they were urban warriors, were making use of the abandoned properties of the rich and the laziness of the council. So what if the stairs did not have a carpet; it was the Swedish look.

So what if there was no hot water; you boiled it on the cooker. There was heating. What more could a man want? Eva was intrigued and a little shocked. This was how he lived?

"I'll make you breakfast. It's early enough".

And so as he cooked they talked more. About his plans: being a singer somehow, about her plans, being a mother somehow. And after eating the breakfast, they kissed again.

"Bed and breakfast?" he asked. They both laughed raucously.

Then: "I must be going back", she murmured.

He took her in his arms, strangely bold for one so naturally timid. She let him lead her to the bedroom, hand in hand. Later, Julian had supposed that she had decided to make love some time before. To him, it seemed spontaneous. But the primitive conditions must have shocked her. The one mattress on the floor, the slightly grimy sheets, the woollen blankets, the bare floorboards. But she followed him.

As they lay down together naked, he asked:

"Are you OK with this? It doesn't need to happen?"

"No, I want it to" she said. And so he moved over and entered her. He was too young and inexperienced to realise that she was holding herself in reserve. Her body did not want him yet.

After, they lay back. She had not come.

"I'm too nervous" she said quietly.

"Next time" Julian said.

"Next time. I must be getting back".

She dressed quickly and left Julian in his squatter's bed on the floor, a stupid beatific smile on his face.

CHAPTER 21

HEAVEN

And so it continued: he took time off the Music school, Tuesday mornings, and Eva took time off from her part-time job and steady man. The love-making got better, they came together. It just felt right. They wrote long letters, lovers' letters, full of the idiocies of those in love, how they couldn't wait for 'Bed and Breakfast' on Tuesdays. It was a time of bliss in Julian's life, although he did not know it. He was in love. And his life fell into a full and rich pattern: music school in the mornings and afternoons, then a race to the opera house to take bags, and after the trip of a few stops to the squat where he would usually find someone up, Tilly at her pots, Sven smoking and drawing and arguing about architecture with someone who had decided to pass by. Graham was working with a Vietnam draft dodger at the local yard, removals or any sort. And Julian brought back what he could find left out at the greengrocer's, or a bag of chips. They all had a sense of foreboding that the Council was about to chuck them out, but for the moment there was no court order, no summons.

His relationship with his teacher had deepened. They were now on first name terms He tried not to miss the Lieder class. They were usually Tuesday afternoons, and there was a strange intimacy of those attending, as if they were a band of brothers, a secret sect dedicated to the purity of true music. Nothing like that was ever said, but there was a core of faithful followers. The 'real' singers, the ones with bigger voices, went to the opera course, as that was where the future was outside the school. Julian did not want a commercial future. He just wanted to sing and let the music enter him. Love affairs with composer after composer.

Often Walter talked too long, as expounded on the roots of German romanticism. The singers champed at the bit, wanting to show him and everyone else how wonderful they were. But now and then Walter added snippets of information about each song, how it fitted the musician's character. And this was invaluable. It was as if he had just come from Austria after chatting with Johann Brahms about his latest symphony, or Bruno Walter about his tempi in *Fidelio*. And in a way, he had. There seemed to be a close connection, a generation or so before the very composers had been alive. The class, although they did not know it, or appreciate it, were talking with history.

Terms went past dedicated to new composers: Brahms and Wolf captured Julian's attention.

The wide, long singing lines of Brahms suited Julian and he listened to Hotter and Diskau, how they approached each song. Compare and contrast. Then try and reproduce, with your own interpretation. It was perhaps the best form of apprenticeship.

The master of all, Schubert, did not have his time shared with any other composer. Week after week was spent on the cycles, with no one really risking *Winterreise*. The girls did not have much to do as Walter insisted they were for men, and that was that. Any girl getting up to try and sing them, and the Americans always tried once, were sent back to their seats. And so Julian, sitting, listening, waiting, slowly got to know the great songs: *Erlkoenig*, which no one attempted, too frightened of Walter's scorn, or demands—but learning that Goethe never replied to Schubert's letter enclosing the composition. This young man of 18 had written a masterpiece, and Goethe, usually so polite, answering every attempt to set to music his famous poetry, this time never wrote back. He may have known that the music was equal to the words and that his poetry would be almost eclipsed by this unknown composer. And so it was.

Julian listened to Diskau, but then discovered Kipnis. The Russian, with his gravelly vowels and Wagnerian weight of voice captured the drama, the reassuring father's voice, the snaky, smooth insinuating sound of the Erlkoenig and the gasping, terrified voice of the young boy.

The pianist struggled with the repeated notes, and the sound of the horses' hooves and the wind. It was a magnificent piece of work. All the students quaked. Some tried it out, the recently arrived ones.

Walter was generous. He listened, and then tried to indicate what should be happening, sometimes taking the piano, sometimes singing himself. The wiser ones sat in their seats and only imbibed.

But Julian did try sometimes: he got up to sing *Der Wanderer,* the brooding, dark *geist* of Europe, the one who wanders and never finds peace. It was close to Julian's heart. The repeated triplets in the right hand, beginning so quietly and undermined by the dark upward bass line, then clashing with dissonance, a crescendo through the introduction, falling away to a muted minor chord. All *sturm und drang,* all the angst, all the displaced persons, all the wars and survivors seemed to be portrayed in those few bars. *'Und immer fragt der Suefzer, wo?'* The anguished cry of the poet and composer: And always asking with a sigh, where, where can I go? The vocal line soared to express the word: *Seufzer.* Julian sang it with goose pimples on his arm. He had no idea if it communicated itself to the audience.

In a way, he was singing it for himself, lost in the chords, the words, the emotion. The audience might not have been there for all he cared. Then the central section: *'Wo bist do, wo bist du, mein geliebtes Land?'* Here a change of mood, a cry, quickening the pace, Schubert following the words so cleverly, writing *'geschwind'* as a tempo marking, the hoped-for land, where? Where was this home, so green with hope, where my roses bloom, where my friends walk, where my deathbed waits for me, where my language is spoken. This land, where are you? Then Julian relaxed into the final repeat of the second section, finishing with the terrifying words: *'Dort, wo du nicht bist, dort ist sein Gluck'*. There, where you are not, is your happiness.

After Julian had sung the piece it was as if he had been away somewhere. Instead of the usual polite clapping, there was a strange silence. Then some perfunctory clapping started later. Walter was odd, almost moved. He took out a bright red handkerchief from his top pocket and removed his glasses and wiped his face, then put his glasses on again.

"Yes, very good, but there are some things", and he asked the pianist to move, and then played the song through, talking to the pianist at the same time:

"Yes, you started well here, but make sure the left hand is heard right from the beginning, there is a little accent there, no, you see it? Good. Now, steady in the pace but go through, move it to the *sforzando* chord, then die away. The whole song is there. Introduce it for the singer. Now, you, here, the *geschwind*, it must really go, nothing can hold you back from the first bar, you see your homeland, your forgotten friends............ he broke off before he got to 'deathbed'.

"*Ja*, try it again. Don't listen to Kipnis, you will never sing it again. And don't be too English".

Everyone laughed. Being too English was a crime in the Lieder class.

They performed it again, this time stopping, correcting, altering tempi, the weight on certain words, the stillness of some of the passages. It was line-by-line, note by note, intensive coaching, and Julian was never to forget it.

⇒+ +⇐

The Christmas holidays were coming. He phoned his elder sister one evening on the way back from work. It was a public phone box in Trafalgar Square as usual. It was late for her, but he knew she would probably be up marking exam papers until 11.30. It was 10.15, an early finish after a two short operas: Cav and Pag, as they were known, from the Italian *verismo* period. He dialled the number as the buses went by.

"Jooly? Jooly! Where are you?" Julian let the question hang in the air, and she realised he could not answer.

"Are you close?" she asked.

"Close enough".

Gill heard the noise of traffic in the distance, the shuddering of the bus engines.

"Sounds like British engineering".

"Might be". A silence followed.

"Jooly, Dad's ill". Julian stared out at the traffic in Trafalgar square.

"How ill?"

"I don't think he'll make it. He's in hospital. London, a care home for vicars, or something. Mum was there today. Between you and me she doesn't think he'll come out".

"Where exactly?"

"Baker Street, London. 154, or something. I can go and get the exact address if you want".

"It doesn't matter. I'll find it". Gill heard only traffic for a time.

"Jooly, are you still there?"

"I'm here. I just have to go now". She heard the emotion in his voice.

"Jooly, are you all right?"

"I'm all right. I have to go now. Say hi! to Mum, will you?", and he put the phone down. Baker Street. He'd have to go. And soon.

CHAPTER 22

WARD

The hospital was not easy to find. It was part of a large Victorian building and now was a private care home for the families of the clergy who either needed operations quickly or were on their last legs.

It reminded Julian of school, the wards, the beds, the quiet, the trolleys. If asked he would say he was family, and could prove it. A cousin, mother's side. Orton. That should do it.

He went up to reception. The nurses were dressed in a distinctly old-fashioned manner.

"Can I help you?"

"Yes, I have come to see The Reverend Bates".

"Relation?"

"Yes, nephew".

The nurse checked her files.

"Ward 6, room 8".

She did not ask for identification. And there was no tremor of uncertainty in his voice. A relation? For once, he did not have to lie. Julian chose to walk up the wide sweeping steps, his heart beating with the exertion and the emotion. Would his father recognise him? What would he say? He could hardly throw the dinner plates at him, if all his sister had said was true. He got to the sixth floor and started walking up and down the corridor, checking the room numbers. Odd numbers this side. He changed to the other.

"Can I help you?"

He jumped. He had not heard the ward nurse coming.

"I am looking for Reverend Bates".

"Family?"

"Yes".

"In you go". She opened the door and said in a louder voice:

"You have a visitor, Reverend".

The nurse allowed Julian to walk in and then closed the door.

The light was not bright. The blinds were half closed and his father did not focus at first. The bed was at the other end of the room, closer to the window. Over his father's head was an angle-poise light. At the side of the bed was a small set of drawers with some books. The Bible in its dark cover; some other reading. His father's notes on paper, with its squiggly, blue writing. The man Julian knew as the hell and brimstone preacher had gone. Instead, there was this frail body with a fragile head, a beak of a nose and cheeks which were falling in on themselves. He was not wearing his glasses and did not recognise his visitor.

A chair was close to the bed and Julian went and sat down. His father turned his bird-like head to scrutinise his visitor. He felt for his glasses in the bed and put them on. Even then he did not

understand who was in front of him. The years had changed them
both. Julian had kept his close cropped hair and a long dark moustache. His physique was that of a grown man. Julian sat, the tears
coming to his eyes.

Finally, his father spoke in a manner he used for visitors, polite,
inquiring, but was his voice now weak, not the booming sound
Julian had known.

"I'm sorry, my eyes have gone. I am not sure I know you.....".

"It's me. Dad. It's Julian".

"Julian". There was hardly any emotion in his voice. It was
almost a whisper.

"My son Julian?"

"Me".

The silence was long. A bumble-bee had come into the room somehow and was trying hard to escape the netting, buzzing and then
climbing, flying free again, and then buzzing against the window.
His father had kept bees and was always kind to them, trying to let
them escape and fly free whenever he could.

"There is a bee caught. Could you let it out?"

Julian went to the curtain and drew it back. The room looked out
onto a block of buildings, grey in the failing light. He opened the
top window with the old-style fittings from before the war. The bee
got caught again, but then smelt the fresh air and flew out.

"It's out".

Julian came back to the chair.

"Do you remember when we used to make honey?"

His father's eyes blinked and he turned his head to stare into the distance.

"I remember".

"I got stung once, badly. Near the eye, do you remember?"

"I remember".

"But you got stung all over the place. Arms, legs, face".

"Not often. The smoke does not always work. And they need to know you".

They both thought back to the bee hives in the rectory, the anti-quated bellows with its smoking cardboard to try and stun the bees into retreat and calm. The orchard, the paddock, the garden.

"I liked the extraction machine. It was yellow and you had to whirl it around to get the honey out" said Julian.

"I remember. It was yellow. You are right".

"Those were good times".

His father turned his eyes on him. His glasses had fallen off and his eyes were of a limpid blue. Julian had never seen them so blue. But they were not really focusing and his gaze was not in this world. He was already looking beyond. Julian felt he could not hold back any longer:

"That whole business. We fell together, you know".

His father's blue eyes held his gaze.

"He was trying to hurt me. He."...Julian's voice faltered....."he was touching himself. He hit me across the face. We fell. He hit his head".

His father turned his head away. Julian could not see if the information had made any impact or not.

"Do you believe me?"

"I believe you". His father sighed.

"What are you going to do now?" His voice was weaker, almost a whisper.

"I have no idea".

"If you give yourself up.....?"

"I will go to prison, most likely". His father nodded.

"It may be best. You know, in the long run". Julian shook his head.

"I can't go there. Not yet".

His father nodded. The light had fallen and inside the room it was almost dark. Suddenly the nurse came in and switched on all the lights. Both men looked startled.

"Quite in the dark here. How are you feeling, Reverend?"

"Better. Much better now".

"Had a nice visit from your family?"

"Yes, very nice, thank you".

"He'll be tired now, so I think you should be off".

"I was just going". Julian got up and lent over and kissed his father on the cheek, and grasped his hand. He felt the grip returned. His eyes filled with tears, and he made his exit out the door and along the corridor as fast as he could. He knew he would never see his father alive again.

CHAPTER 23

GLORY

Singing lessons with Walter proceeded. Schumann's Dichterliebe, more Schubert, more Wolf. Instead of having lessons at the College Julian went to Walter's house. The piano room was a large ground floor flat with a bay window. Julian met other students, some in careers, some just starting. Portraits of his most successful students were on the walls and on the shelves. They were household names in the music business. One morning Julian turned up at eleven, his usual time, and before they began the vocal exercises Julian asked if he could study a piece he had heard by pure chance on Radio 3 a week ago. He was uncertain how to pronounce it: *Lieder eines............* Gruner interrupted him.

> "*Lieder eines fahrenden Gesellen!* You want to study that! I was thinking the same thing. But, *mein Gott,* it is hard. You are attempting to climb Everest, you know that?"

> "I heard it on the radio".

> "Who was singing?"

> "Diskau".

> "The Furtwaengler version?" asked Gruner.

> "I don't know. Maybe".

"Well, we try. Do you have the music?"

"Not yet. I can get it out of the library" suggested Julian.

"I have it here. You cannot borrow my copy, but we can read through".

Walter sat down at the piano and opened his battered copy of the Mahler song cycle. There were notes in the margin in German and English. It looked as if it had been printed before the war. That war. He was Jewish. He had escaped. He let slip one day in a pique of anger that he had no one left, they had all been sent to the death camps. Julian, at 22, found this hard to comprehend and empathize with. It was just stuff he saw on the TV. But today Walter was in a good mood. The music inspired him and he though Julian might be ready. '*Wein mein Schatz Hochzeit macht*'. The introduction, jerky, slightly neurotic, gave way to a dirge for his beloved's marriage to someone else. Then the moderato country scene: bird song: 'How beautiful is the world' only to relapse into the dirge as he remembers his pain.

"*Ja*. It is good It suits you. We'll do it again. But you say you don't know the Furtwaengler recording?"

"No" said Julian.

"It is excellent, really. Get it. Diskau, well, there are some things, but he is such a musician. And he was young at the time. Furwaengler does some crazy things, tempi, well, you shouldn't really, but ......it works".

And so they studied the four songs in detail. The dusk came down. It was quite dark when they had finished the song cycle.

"Go and speak to the programme organizer, the bureaucrat, the one with glasses in the music school. I will talk as well. I'll say you are ready. They may want to do the cycle for the orchestra as it is repertoire, and the players need to know it before they get booked in the outside world. *Ja*, go tomorrow".

And that is how Julian came to be singing the whole cycle with an orchestra one evening in June. He had it by heart, although there were some entries which scared him. He listened over and over to the Diskau version. He was nervous, but not exceptionally. The rehearsals had gone well and he was rested. Amazingly, his sister was in the audience. That was kind of her. Michael Orton was on the programme. And no London copper on his day off was going to be at a concert sung in German. Punishment of this sort was well beyond the call of duty.

Julian was dressed in tails and shirt and tie. The tails, trousers, and cummerbund he had found in a charity shop. The fit might not be perfect but the price was all of five pounds. Julian had it cleaned and it looked the real thing. He was slowly learning about appearances. The conductor was a singer himself and was very supportive, following Julian's line. This was no carbon copy of a recording.

The orchestra began with their jokey, neurotic introduction. Julian started singing, slightly breathy, but not out of place for the music. He gained confidence. The delicate ending, with the placing of the B flat on '*Abends*' was worthy of Diskau himself. The second song about the morning jaunt in the country, which although went high in the voice, was strangely the easiest. Julian listened to the strings under him, the woodwind mimicking his vocal line. The final '*nimmer, nimmer*' in half voice he accomplished well. The third piece was the most demanding: it needed full voice, half voice, top notes, drama, amazing musicianship, his full range. Singing out loudly now and hearing his voice resound around the hall was inspirational. The final song was the poet trudging his way through the snow to his possible death. *Alles, alles! Lieb und Leid und Welt und Traum.* It was over. He had got through. No mistakes. It was musical and competent. He thanked the conductor, took a bow and was out into the practice room which served as the green room. Walter came to find him. He was speaking half in German and half in English.

"*Ja*, definitely. *Ja, wunderbar.* It was good. Well done. Yes, really very good. I am impressed". He shook Julian's hand.

High praise indeed from the maestro. His sister came to see him as well. They chatted amicably for a few minutes, then Walter had to be off. They would talk another day, he said. Gill stayed on.

"Jooly, what are you going to do?" she asked.

"I don't know. No plan B. Did you enjoy it?

"I did, although it wasn't my cup of tea, as you know. Your teacher really liked it. I heard him in the breaks, commenting". Julian smiled.

"You can't carry on like this" she added.

"Why not? No one knows my real name except you. Singers can have stage names, *nom de plumes*, or whatever they are called. Mine is Michael Orton, which is not a million miles away from our family".

"Whatever you say, Jooly".

She came close and kissed him.

"Take care. You look OK. Thin, but OK. You must eat properly, you know".

"I eat. Not always, but I eat".

323

She hugged him. "I will tell Mum you are OK. She is worried".

"I have no choice. You know that".

His sister looked once more at him and then walked out of the music school. Julian went to the green room and got out of his shirt and tails into his usual street clothes. He looked at himself in the mirror and thought back to Barak and that evening on the kibbutz. Somehow he had ended up here, five years later, singing difficult music in another language. Twists and turns on an un-likely journey.

CHAPTER 24

SURPRISE VISIT

Five years later the trail had gone cold and the murder enquiry was filed under 'unsolved'.

On a whim, Pendelbury decided to pay a surprise visit to the school and try and see Mrs Miller. He remembered she seemed to know a great deal about the history of the place and her mouth did not have a lock on it. He thought he might get another lead from her. The porter phoned her house to find if she was in and whether she would see the inspector. She would. The porter showed him to her house which was outside the grounds, about a five minute walk. It was drizzling slightly, and Pendelbury was grateful for the wide-brimmed hat; it kept most of the water out. As he got to the door, he saw her waiting for him.

"Andrew is out, so you've just got me. Never know where the man gets to. Either sport or art or some talk somewhere". She took a long drag on her cigarette.

"Come in, won't you. Take your hat and coat off. I'll be in the sitting room. Tea?"

"That would be nice".

She busied herself in the kitchen and Pendelbury went through to the sitting room and waited. The room was arty, with paintings finished and unfinished everywhere. Pictures of their children. Boys. One in the army. Good looking kids.

Mrs Miller came back with a tray and two cups. "Milk, sugar?"

"One sugar, a bit of milk, please".

She added both and gave him the cup and saucer and sat down opposite him.

"Do you paint?" asked Pendelbury.

"Andrew's stuff. Another of his fads. House full of canvasses and easels and paint. The smell of paint. Can't get it out of my nostrils". A silence followed.

"So, how can I help you?" she asked.

"I have come just to follow up matters. As you know, there has been no trace after the Israel sighting. Our main suspect, Julian Bates, has slipped through the net".

"Yes, well, he seems to be tricky customer, that one" she said.

"Have there been any changes since I was here?"

"Changes?"

"People coming, leaving, anything different?"

"Now that you mention it there has been a bit of a scandal".

Pendelbury sat up slightly and moved in his chair. A fish was moving the float around.

"Brian Sawbridge left suddenly" said Anne Miller.

"Why so sudden?"

Mrs Miller took another drag on her cigarette.

"Some scandal about a boy on a boat. A choir tour. The parents complained".

Pendlebury was not quite sure what she was saying.

"I am a bit lost". Pendelbury checked his notes.

"Sawbridge was married, was he not, with 3 children?" he asked.

"Yes, I know. All a bit strange, if you ask me. But they grow up in these places and don't know anything different. Not that it excuses them. And the boy wasn't the first, it seems" she said.

"So, Brian Sawbridge...............?"

"Look I'm not going to be a witness for you, or for anyone, if that's what you think. I'm not going to dish the dirt in public, as it were".

"There is no need. But can we get this straight? Sawbridge left because a boy complained that he had been"...... Pendelbury searched for a word...... "molested on a choir trip on a boat. Is that correct?"

Anne Miller crossed her legs and took another pull on her cigarette.

"Yes, that's the long and short of it. You could put it like that. Yes".

Pendelbury sat back in his chair, took a sip of tea, and let the information settle.

"As I say" Anne Miller continued, "I'm not going to stand up in any courtroom and say what I have said here. Forget it, Inspector. We have a College to keep going, and that's that".

"I do understand". Pendelbury took another sip. A long silence followed.

"Well, if there isn't anything else?" asked Anne Miller

"No, you have been so helpful". Pendelbury went to take his hat and coat. Anne Miller accompanied him to the door.

"I don't expect you'll be around this way again".

Pendelbury turned to speak:

"Mrs Miller, we do try and solve our murder cases in Britain. But you have been most helpful".

"Yes, well, remember that the College has to keep going. We all have livelihoods here, Inspector. And that Bates boy, well, who would have expected it?"

"Who indeed?" said Pendelbury. "Thank you so much for seeing me".

Pendelbury went off into the night and he heard the door close behind him. He reached for his pipe and took some matches and smoked as he walked to the car. The information made things better and worse. The water he was fishing in had suddenly got very murky. A sexually predatory closet homosexual housemaster, married with three children, writing letters to the boy's family and provoking enough ill-will against the boy to get him beaten.

For his attitude. It seemed almost perverse sexual jealousy. He shook his head as he got into the police Jaguar. Julian Bates did not seem quite the cold-bloodied murderer he had ten minutes earlier. The radio crackled into life, calling another car. Pendelbury drove back deep in thought.

CHAPTER 25

SQUAT PARTY

There was a party at the squat. Julian had invited some friends from the music school, and Graham and Sven had invited girlfriends. Tilly said she would drop in if she was in the house. It was Sunday, so the theatre was closed. No evening duty. The large open space from the living room on the first floor to the kitchen was being used. They had expanded the space just by knocking down the dividing door from the kitchen and now had a trendy open-space living room. The ceiling above immediately started to sag, but as everyone know it was short life housing, and was to be demolished, no one paid much attention. Julian felt the floorboards creak underneath him and he moved the mattress closer to the wall. He did not want to be crashing though during the night.

He went to the local market to get some things. The market was one of the last traditional markets in London, set in a Fulham street. There was everything that one expected from London stalls. Live eels, pie and mash, mash and peas, mountains of fruit (nothing exotic) all bundled into your shopping bag. Stuff off the back of a lorry, nudge nudge, wink, wink, and the wives crowded around. Beer palaces with the doors open and men and booze swilling out. Cars weaving their way through. Some black people, but not many, and no sense of racial problems.

Julian bought pigs' knuckles (how did you cook them?) and

other slightly crazy foods......Jamaican things: lady's fingers, sweet potato, strange breads. His girlfriend Eva could not be there. She was with her steady boyfriend. Julian tried to put this out of his mind. It was good what they had, and how could he offer her anything other than a soggy mattress in a squat?. Who would take that? What was on offer? Not much, he concluded.

And so the guests slowly came, slowly. A pianist Julian used sometimes, with her boyfriend from Cambridge. They looked a handsome couple, though he had a rapacious look, a sort of pirate without the cutlass or the black patch. Then some of Walter's pupils, most of them younger than Julian. There was the Indian girl, Patricia, with her soaring, pure voice. She dressed in saris when she sang in concerts, and looked like a bird of paradise. Her boyfriend was a pianist, so they were a good couple for each other. Then an Australian nurse who had helped Walter in the past when he was ill. Others who came because there was a party. Some dancers, actors. The place was filling up. People bought bottles of disgusting wine, and Julian had bought whatever he could afford from the local wine store at the end of the road. It was one of the first discount stores............ and also a friend worked there. There was a sort of squat camaraderie, where if you could help, you would. No one had any money and they got through somehow. If you ate where Tilly worked as a waitress the bill somehow got lost and you paid only for the water.

The party was going well. Graham chose Latin-American music, food came, drink came. Sven had bought some stewing steak and the pot had been on the go for 8 hours. The meat was still tough when it came out.

"Horsemeat, if you ask me. That's what they sold me. God, that's tough!"

Plates of congealing stew were left around the squat.

Neighbours from across the road shouted out from the window and Julian asked them to come over. They did. Julian saw a couple arguing in the street over fliers for a concert. A guy with wavy hair was putting leaflets through letter boxes and a weird-looking punk with blonde spiky hair, snaggle teeth and an earring was telling him what a shit band he was in. Julian shouted down to them and invited them up to join the party. There was heavy dance music on now. They looked up, settled their differences, and came up the squat stairs, joined the party. The wavy-haired guy could certainly dance.

People sat on the bare floorboards, smoking, the dope went round, the drinking got heavier. The talk was the usual music college talk: slagging off the teachers, saying how wonderful others were. Julian found himself sitting near another student he had seen but never talked to. She was Spanish, Nazneen, and was there to study to be a stage manager. They got chatting. She said her mother earned her living in the UK by telling fortunes. Her father had died.

"Tell mine", Julian asked.

"I don't know how".

"You must have seen your mother".

"I do not have the gift".

"Try".

Reluctantly Nazneen took his hand and looked at the palm. She was at first perplexed then excited.

"You had a hard childhood, very unsettled". She did not look at him for confirmation.

Then she looked harder: "You could have been a minister or something". At this she was excited. Then her face changed expression.

"There has been something terrible in your life, and....................." She dropped his hand as if it were something dangerous, contaminating.

"Go on".

"I can't".

"Why?" asked Julian.

"I can't see anything more".

"But there is more?"

"Maybe. But I don't know, as I said. I don't have the gift, as my mother does".

"Nothing else?" Julian insisted.

Nazneen looked away and refused to say more. Julian shrugged, thanked her, and walked off to find a drink. It was like the witches on the heath in *Macbeth*. Did he believe in it? What did she see? What he had done? He knew that. Was there more to come? He joined a group of singers who were still criticizing the school the music director, the conductor, the everything. It was a hobby. And then: who was wonderful, who was crap, and who was going out with who. But the palm reading had unnerved Julian. Was what she saw, if she had seen anything, all in the past? Should he believe it? She said she had no gifts, not like her mother. But the whole evening he thought about the encounter. Later he tried to find her, but she had left. And at the music school he only saw her once again in a corridor and then she was gone, and quite obviously was avoiding him. Strange behaviour, thought Julian, but he put it out of his thoughts. She said she had no gifts anyway.

CHAPTER 26

WANDERERS NACHTLIED

Christmas went. His sister invited him for lunch in Thames Ditton but he did not go. He did not want to spoil that day for her. His habit, living like a wolf, knowing he could be caught any moment, never left him. Julian sat with the window half open, the cold air coming in, the squat so empty, the street quiet and still. He let the dusk come, transfixed at the window, staring out at the grimy road and the down-at-heel houses with the boards up everywhere. Soot, cinders, decay. Hardly inspiring. He had no idea where his life was going and the course at the music school was ending. After that, nothing. He went to bed slightly drunk, sleeping on his mattress in the corner a few inches from the sag in the ceiling. At 1am in the morning, happy with the wine inside him, he laughed out loud. The squat was liberating in that respect. No one cared much who was there, what they did or who with. Graham had found himself a wild young French girl who came with a dog from the Battersea dog's home. She was pretty but mad. Her parents came for her one day and took her back to France, leaving the dog. It became known as squat dog, and the poor animal had to scavenge for itself. Tilly was off to Japan finally and was saying goodbye to everyone. She was leaving the phone on and they were going to have to pay the bills, as everyone used it, ok? They all nodded. How they were going to pay was in the future. Julian lay back and thought how the house functioned. They all had jobs. There was food. They were generous. Money was tight but no one went hungry. Things were shared. Julian smiled at the supposed eco-warriors in their commune who really were there, not because they were making a political statement, but just because it was a safe, cheap haven in the storms of their lives.

At six in the morning the phone rang.

"Shit! Who could that be? For sure a wrong number".

Julian walked down the stairs naked. He did not sleep with anything on. Sometimes he would meet others on the stairs and just wander past. He picked up the phone in the living room.

"Yes".

"Julian? It's Walter".

"Walter".

"Yes. Can you come round?"

"What now? It is really necessary?"

"Yes, I had a small heart attack".

Julian was still dizzy with sleep. And very reluctant.

"Is there no one else?"

"It is a Saturday".

"I mean, can't you call an ambulance?"

"It is not that serious. Besides they have my papers elsewhere".

Julian was so torn. It was 6 in the morning. It was cold and raining. It was Saturday. Julian debated a bit more, then gave in:

"OK, I'll come. Give me 30 minutes".

He got on the tube and took the Northern line to Finchley Road. The wind whipped up the stray papers in the tube entrance. Julian turned up his collar on his ex-army coat and walked down the curved streets to Walter's house. He did not know what to expect, Walter in his bed, unable to walk?

He knocked on the door, and it was Walter himself who opened. He did not look too bad.

Julian thought he would find him gasping for breath, but he seemed quite normal. A bit pale perhaps, but otherwise his usual grumpy, cantankerous self.

"Come in".

"How are you?"

"I had a little attack at 5 this morning, but am OK now. I need some breakfast. Can you help me prepare breakfast?"

"Sure. What do you want?"

"There is some orange juice in the fridge, and a boiled egg would be nice, with toast".

Julian took off his coat, and set about making this breakfast. He would eat something himself too. So Walter sat in the kitchen and Julian found the things he needed. The fridge was well-stocked. He thought of his own kitchen in the squat. Quite a difference. Nothing at all times. Perhaps a bottle of rancid milk. And some sour wine.

"I have phoned my doctor over the road. He refuses to answer. I know he is there. He just is lazy. It's Shabbat, so he won't get out of bed".

Julian smiled at this explanation and the easy venom the Jews had for each other. There were a lot of Jews in the area, they had made good and moved from the East End. Now they were all doctors or psychologists—or musicians. So they sat there, Walter eating a bit of toast, a bit of egg. He seemed OK. After, they sat in the large living room with the garden out the back.

Walter flicked through the channels on his TV. It was the latest model and the idea of a remote control for Julian was science fiction. Walter played with it like a child, pointing it at the wall, the ceiling and still the machine worked. He was in his dressing gown, and Julian did not know just how long he was meant to stay there. Didn't Walter know he had a life elsewhere?

Walter listened to some morning TV news programme, quite happy to stay in silence and oblivious to Julian's discomfort.

"Walter, um, how long do you think I should stay here, I mean, if you are feeling all right?"

"Stay a bit longer, *ja*? Until they all get up. They are lazy. It is a holiday. They are lying in. That doctor knows I am ill, but he does not answer".

Julian sighed. He was stuck with his teacher for the rest of the day. Eva might come round, and not find him and that would be that for another ten days or so. He stared at the long grass through the large bay window. He realized he loved this woman but could not do anything about it. She would not leave her boyfriend for a penniless musician who lived in a squat! Worse, a wanted man, a man on the run, something she knew nothing about, and would never:

"Oh, by the way, I want to marry you, but there is something I have to tell you. The police are after me. Murder, actually, since you ask. Not quite what you think, and I know it sounds bad, but if you can live with it, I'm sure it'll all sort itself out in the wash".

But he loved her. Yes, she was pretty, but it was more than that. They laughed at the same things, they had read the same books. It was simple. They did not have to try together. There was a sort of cosmic peace between them, of halves coming together. Perhaps the usual crap those in love said about their relationship. So special, nothing like ours, stars and moon. He had read of it in books, heard others say it. But it was a heady wine. Once drunk, it made you thirst for it again. Nothing less came near. It was truly the ambrosia of the Gods. The thoughts made Julian edgy. He got up and said he would make a cup of tea. He looked at Walter and realized he had dropped the remote control. He was not watching the programme and was breathing heavily.

"Walter. Walter!"

He came round and looked at Julian as if he were a stranger.

"I am not feeling very well. Could you call the ambulance?"

"OK. Ambulance". Julian walked fast to the phone.

"But I must be taken to the Royal Free" he shouted. "They have all my papers there. The Royal Free, tell them".

Julian dialed 999 for the first time in his life.

"Which service please?"

"Ambulance, please".

"What seems to be the matter?"

"A heart attack, I think".

"Name and address?"

Walter was shouting from the other room. "The Royal Free, tell them. Where my papers are".

"He wants to be taken to the Royal Free".

"We can't say where he will be taken".

"The Royal Free". Walter was shouting even louder. The receptionist could hear him.

"You must tell him" she said "that we can't send an ambulance unless he agrees to go where we take him". Julian told him.

"Then I don't want it. Tell them I don't want it".

"He says he doesn't want the ambulance unless it goes to the Royal Free".

"I'm afraid I can't accept your request, Sir. Are you next of kin?"

"No, I'm a friend, a student".

"Well, I suggest you convince Mr.......".

"Gruner" Julian said.

"You convince Mr Gruner that he has to go where we take him if he wants an ambulance".

"I'll refer that back to him. Thank you".

Julian put the phone down. "Walter, you have to go to where they take you".

"They are all incompetent! I tell you Hitler could have invaded on a Saturday and no one would have stopped him. I tell you!" White flecks of spittle settled on his face. He tried to wipe them off.

"Walter, I don't know what to say".

"Go and ring the doorbell of that last doctor over the road".

Julian did not know what to do, but asked for the address. He put the door on the latch and went across the road and rang. No one answered. He came back.

"There is no one there".

"There is, I tell you. He knows. He knows I am unwell. He is just lazy. Shabbat! Shabbat! What an excuse".

"Walter, calm down, please".

Walter's face had gone strangely grey, and his breathing was heavy, but otherwise he seemed in control. Yet Julian knew something was badly wrong this time.

"Can you do something for me?" Walter asked.

"What now?" Julian's voice was tetchy. No ambulance, no doctor.

"Could you go and call on Mimi? She is my niece. She lives close. Her address is on the table there".

Julian knew that his niece from Australia had tried to live with him, but they had fallen out and she had moved to a flat close by. Julian thought this was a good idea. At least there would be family around, someone else. He took the address and an A-Z and traipsed the streets until he got to the address. He buzzed the bell. It was flat 5, and 8 in the morning. No answer. He buzzed again.

"Mimi?"

"Yes". Her voice was drugged with sleep.

"It's Julian".

"Yes".

"Walter is not well. He had had a heart attack. He wants you there".

There was a long silence.

"I'll come as soon as I can".

"OK".

Julian walked back to the flat through the cold, empty streets, muttering to himself like a wino late at night. Why do I get myself into these situations? I am not family. Where are his family?

Shit! Fucking ambulance. I mean, just take the bastard to the Royal Free if they have his papers. Probably protocol. But it might be the closest anyway.

The cold bit into him. It was also drizzling. He got back to the flat. Walter had moved to the chair as it seemed to give him help in breathing.

"Was she there?" His face looked washed out and he was anxious.

"She's coming. She said she was coming".

"Those ambulance men, they should come and take me to the Royal Free.

"They said they could only take you………….."

"I know what they said! No one works in this country. In Austria it is different".

Julian kept silent. Walter's breathing now was raucous and he moved in the chair to find another position.

"Do you want some tea?"

"No, I do not want some tea".

Julian sat down and waited. The television was on and the programmes flickered across the screen. They both waited for Miriam to come. Finally they heard her footsteps on the pavement. She walked in and took in the situation, but seeing her gave Walter no pleasure.

But she was family, and she took over. Julian was grateful.

"How are you, Walter ?"

"The ambulance men won't come. I told them to come and take me to the Royal Free but they refused". Miriam took Julian into the corridor.

"He's bad this time. Call again" she said

Julian sighed and dialled.

"Hi! It's the friend again for the heart attack in Finchley Road".

"You do know we can't take him to just any hospital" the receptionist said.

"I know that, but he is bad. Please".

"I repeat........"

"I know, but he is bad, he'll go anywhere now".

The receptionist stated calmly: "I mean, and I hope you follow me, it is quite likely they will take him there, as it is the closest. But they will have to see what the problem is and then decide. Are you happy with that?"

"Yes, yes". And here Julian's voiced broke in anguish.

"Please come fast. He really is not good".

The anguish in his voice seemed to tip the scales. The receptionist changed her tone of voice.

"Ambulance on its way. 78, Finchley Gardens".

Julian he put down the phone. He went back into the sitting room. Miriam was with him, talking to him as if he were a rather disobedient child. But Julian could see now that he was gasping for breath. He had no idea what to do, and nor had Miriam. He tried to open Walter's mouth more, as if doing that more air might go through. He looked at the stained teeth from smoking. Walter was losing consciousness. Then he heard the steps of the ambulance men. The door was open. Julian ran to meet them and showed them to the sitting room. They saw what to do. They threw him down on the floor on his back, checked his breathing passages, got out the oxygen, pumped his heart.

"What's his name?"

"Gruner. Walter Gruner".

"Mr Gruber! Mr Gruber!"

"Gruner" muttered Julian. A final indignity. Not even his right bloody name! But they are doing their best.

"Mr Gruber! Can you hear me? Mr Gruber?"

But Walter was gone. Gone somewhere to his beloved Lieder and Hotter and Kipnis and Schubert and Wolf. He lay inert on the floor, his dressing gown and pyjamas in disarray. The men unfolded their trolley and placed him on it, then wheeled him out.

"Can I come?" Julian asked.

"Are you next of kin?"

"No".

"I am", said Miriam.

"Then you can come. Sorry, Sir. Regulations".

Julian watched them wheel Walter out. He was in tears. He watched them load the body onto the ambulance, then walked into the flat, found some keys and closed the door. He walked to the main road and hailed a taxi. The Royal Free, please. When they got there he found that Mr Walter Gruner had been dead on arrival.

CHAPTER 27

CONFESSION

Julian walked out of the Royal Free in a daze. He had somehow got as far as Kilburn, and there in front of him was a large
church with the lights blazing. Some function was going on. Julian
read the board outside, the gold letters on the blue background.
St Mary's, Kilburn. Priest in charge: Patrick O' Malley. What was
left for him now? He went to the porch and heard music coming from inside, an organ and some voices. He turned the heavy
oval-shaped handle and the door came open. The space inside
seemed immense. There was a vaulted ceiling, and naves left and
right and an altar far at the end with people standing and singing
at the front. The priest was by the altar and doing something with
his back turned to his congregation. An altar boy in white was
there, with some incense. Large candles were lit either side of the
altar. At 6 pm Julian supposed it was evensong. He had no idea of
the Catholic rituals, but felt drawn to the music and the warmth
inside. He sat down at the back of the church and steadied his
breathing, wiping away tears.

The congregation sat down, then stood up. There was singing.
The voice of the priest was microphoned, and boomed throughout
the church. It had a strong Irish lilt to it. Julian moved nearer to get
a better view. No one had seen him so far. He was an odd figure to
have at an evening service. There were mostly women, dressed very

sombrely. One or two children stood between them, mother and grandmother, Julian supposed. As he watched the goings-on he noticed the brown confessional box at the left hand side. He had never been in one, and had no idea how it all worked. Some films had scenes with a man or woman confessing. It couldn't be that hard. You told the lot, got it off your chest, said three Hail Mary's and walked out as blithe as a little kid. But he feared what he had to say would place a heavy burden on whoever heard him.

The service was coming to an end. Loud organ music signalled that it was all over, and the congregation started putting their things together and walking down the aisle. Julian tried to be inconspicuous but it was no good. He felt stared at but looked ahead. The priest was removing things from the altar, the chalice, the wafers. Julian moved closer. Father O 'Malley had not noticed him yet. He was tall, with corn-coloured hair, and very blue eyes. He had a reddish complexion and held himself very straight, almost military in bearing. He started moving off into the vestry, and Julian followed him.

"Excuse me?"

The priest turned his full gaze on this man.

"Yes?"

"I wondered if I could have a word?" asked Julian.

"Come into the vestry, will you, while I disrobe" said Father O'Malley.

Julian followed him. The vestry was dark, with all wooded panels. The altar boy had taken off his white robe and was making for the door.

"Good evening, Father" said the boy.

"Good evening. And I'll be seeing you tomorrow at mass".

"That's right, Father".

Julian noticed the Father this and Father that. He was not certain he could bring himself to call this man he hadn't seen by 5 minutes ago his Father. He'd call him Mr O'Malley for starters.

"Now what can I do for you?"

"I wondered if I could have a word?" Julian asked.

"Got some girl pregnant?" asked the priest.

"No!" This forced a smile.

"Getting married?"

"No".

"You want some money?" O'Malley asked.

"No!"

"So, you have me stumped. I can't for the life of me think what else you might be wanting from me".

Julian took a deep breath. "I'd like to confess".

Patrick O'Malley stopped de-robing.

"And why would you want to do that?"

"Why does anyone?"

"Good question" said O'Malley.

"I should tell you I'm not one of yours?" said Julian.

"Batting for the opposition, is it?"

"Anglican. We don't confess".

"And a poorer church it is for it. Well, if it is urgent, like?"

"You don't seem too keen".

"I wouldn't be wanting to steal parishioners, or the other team's thunder, as it were".

The priest stopped taking off the garments.

"Would it be a small thing, or perhaps something longer" the priest asked.

"I don't know how long they go on for. I have a lot to tell. A lifetime".

"Well, I just need to make a phone call to my housekeeper". The priest went to a phone in the vestry and explained he would be delayed. Julian could hear the woman's voice on the other end, reproaching him, urging him not to be too long.

"Now we are free. She worries about me. It's all quite un-necessary, but it makes her feel important. Please come this way".

He led the way to the dark brown confessional boxes, and opened the small door and drew back the curtain.

"There isn't much room for one like yourself, but do what you can. I'll be just next door".

Julian heard the priest get into the booth. He sat down and drew the curtain. It was nicely dark, almost cosy. He slowly got his bearings, and saw the grill at the centre and through it the face of the priest.

"How do I start?" Julian asked.

"Well, many begin by saying: bless me Father, for I have sinned".

"Sounds a good start to me. Bless me Father for I have sinned".

"And what might be troubling you, my son?"

"Tonight a man I was close to died in front of me. Heart attack. But that is not why I am here".

"Were you sexual partners, my child?"

"Good heavens, no! I don't mean that. He was 75 or so. He was a pain in the arse (excuse my French) music teacher and I happened to be with him at the time".

"I see. Well, God have mercy on his soul".

Julian went on to tell the priest about the tractor accident, about the rape.

"But you were not directly responsible, my son. These were terrible things, but not your fault. One was an accident, and you were lucky to save your own life, and the other was the action of bad men. Do you know how the young woman is now?"

"No, we lost touch. After the incident she did not want to see me again, and so I left".

A long silence ensued. The church was still lit, and there were some candles flickering near a Saint.

Then, in a small voice, Julian said: "There is something else".

"There is more?"

"Yes, there is more". Julian thought he heard a sigh from the priest and felt almost apologetic that he had to lay this information on the priest. Then perhaps he had heard almost everything already in his lifetime. Perhaps priests go and confess to other priests and take the weight off their shoulders.

"Many years ago I killed a man".

Now the silence was dense. It was as if thick, dark matter had entered the confessional boxes.

Julian heard Patrick O'Malley shift in his seat, and clear his throat.

"How did it happen, my son?"

"It was self-defence, and an accident, although it did not look like it", and Julian recounted the story of the housemaster's fall and death.

"I have been running ever since. I have changed my name and identity, learnt other languages, lived in another country, but it seems as if I am under some sort of curse. Wherever I go, some terrible thing happens. I almost bring bad luck on people".

Julian paused, and then asked quietly:

"What should I do?"

"My son, only God can tell you what to do. I am sworn to silence. But I am sure that if you ask God for help He will send it; and if you have truly asked for pardon, He has already given it. But on this earth, while we are in this earthly body, I suggest you face your past and ask for the pardon of your fellow men. Perhaps that was not the answer you were hoping for?"

"Perhaps it is the only answer I could expect", said Julian

Neither of them spoke for a long time.

"Is that all?"

"Yes, that is all. What happens now? Do I say a prayer, or something?" asked Julian.

"I don't think a Hail Mary in this case would be enough. You wouldn't be knowing the words anyway. You are familiar with the Lord's prayer?"

"That one, yes".

Then be that your guide. And Julian heard him speak in Latin: *In nomine del padre, del figlio, e dello spirito santo.*

They came out of the boxes, both dazed. Julian was surprised to see tears in the priest's eyes.

"Where will you go now?"

"I have a debt to pay" said Julian. "There is someone who has followed me in several countries. I think I can find him this evening".

"Good luck. And pray. I am sure He will listen and guide".

Julian offered his hand and the old priest shook it. He could not bear to look him in the eyes; he he'd had enough of tears for one day. He walked down the aisle and out into the cold night air. It was 8 o'clock. Just enough time to get to Watford.

CHAPTER 28

GIVING HIMSELF UP

Running for a lifetime was no option. The train ride was about an hour. He thought through the consequences: it would mean prison for a long time, and probably in amongst lifers. Manslaughter, homicide, whatever they called it. A murderer. He might be shown some respect, and then again he might be knifed on the first day. Some grim celestial justice. An eye for an eye, a man for a man. Darke's family would be pleased. Whatever the varnish of 2000 years of Christianity had done, it had not eradicated this primal urge for revenge. It may have to be done through the courts and with juries and bewigged judges, but the end result was always in sight: revenge on the culprit. If he shows a bit of remorse, then it might go slightly in his favour, a few years less. Then good behaviour, and perhaps he is out by the time he is wearing a truss and all his hopes have faded. A reformed character after a rush of blood to the head, a bit too much alcohol, or just being in the wrong place at the wrong time.

There must be hardened criminals though, those who saw crime as a way of life, a strange game of the perfect robbery, planning theft as one would a marketing strategy. Possibly highly intelligent, but on the other side. And Julian thought of the famous barrister who quipped he owed his living to these people; without

them the whole paraphernalia of the law-Laura Norder-the pris-
ons, the judges, the lawyers would be out of a job.

Well, he was about to find out. And the idea of giving himself
up, the release from the constant escape, the watchfulness, looking over one's shoulder, the pretence, the acting out a part—all
this would be over. He was almost grateful.

He did not know if Pendelbury was still alive, or if he lived in the
district but he would try him first. The train pulled in to Broxbourne
and Julian got out. The doors slammed hard. He was glad to be out
of the stuffy compartment. Outside the station was a phone box.
Julian felt in his pockets for change. A local call, needing only pen-
nies. There was a time when you could tap in numbers from a phone
box and not pay, but that was in his childhood. Hardly the moment.

He pulled open the door, and a smell of urine hit him. Why
couldn't they go and piss elsewhere?

There were enough bushes, for God's sake. Some battered and
thumbed local directories were on the right of the phone. There
can't be many Pendelburys in the area. There might not be one.

Instead there were two, and J.D. Pendelbury was listed first.
Julian felt his heart pounding inside him.

The line came to him: It's now or never. It might not be him,
but he would find out, at least.

Julian pressed the coins into the box and dialled. One shil-
ling, two shillings. The phone rang. It was late, 9.30. He imagined
the policeman sitting in front of the TV, his wife knitting in another chair beside him, the fire on, a dog perhaps, pictures of
the children on the wall. Warm, decent, honest, solid, unswerving.
Probably retired. A pipe-smoker. Heavy worn brown leather shoes.

Suddenly there was a woman's voice on the end of the line.
Uncertain, surprised.

"Hello?"

"Hello". His heart was beating even faster.

"Is a Detective Pendelbury there, or have I got the wrong number?" asked Julian.

"No, John is here. Who shall I say is calling?"

Julian paused. What should he say? Now or never.

"Say it's Julian Bates. He will remember". And then as an afterthought:

"Say it is 'the school case'".

He heard Pendelbury's wife put down the receiver and then the long pause. He heard some talking in the background. Then steps. Thump, thump. His breast was heaving.

"Hello?" said Pendelbury.

"Hello. I don't know if you remember me? I am the person you have been looking for about the....death in the school. You were involved in the case, I think".

"I was indeed". Julian heard the accent, southern, broad, and firm. Great interest.

Then a long silence.

"How can I help you?" asked Pendelbury. Not unkind, not censorious, almost caring.

"I am here. Close. Very close. And I want to give myself up".

Pendelbury started to say something but Julian cut him off.

"Only to you. I want you there. You can bring others, but I want you there" said Julian.

"I see. I am retired actually. And it is late. Another long pause. "But I can see what I can do. Are you armed?"

"Armed?" Julian was amazed. But he supposed it was a sensible precaution. More assumptions he had to discard.

"No, I don't have a gun".

"And you are on your own?" Pendelbury asked.

"Yes, on my own".

"Where do you want to meet?"

Julian had imagined the scene. There was only one place.

"I'll meet you outside the school at the front gates of the school in half an hour".

There was another pause.

"I think I should tell you I will be with others, Julian". (The first name was almost paternal). "There will be police cars" he continued. "I can't do this on my own".

"That's OK. I didn't imagine you would be alone".

"Half an hour it is then?"

"Yes".

Julian held the receiver up until he heard the click. Well, that was done then.

His heart stopped the violent thump, thump. He let out a deep sigh. The relief, the relief. And now the consequences.

He pushed open the door and looked around for a taxi. He got in.

"Where to, Sir?"

Julian thought for a moment. Outside the school at this hour was a bit strange. Something near?

"Could you take me to the pub near the school?"

"The Blue Ball?"

"I don't remember that well".

"Must be The Blue Ball" said the taxi driver.

The journey was only 10 minutes. Julian was closed up in his silence and thoughts. Thank God the driver was not chatty. Julian vaguely remembered the road. But it was night and the country lanes were not lit. There was just darkness and the occasional passing car. Then as they neared Julian felt a sickness, a lurch in his stomach. There it was, the imposing buildings, the dome of the chapel, the iron railings, the rugger pitches. Another life in another time.

The taxi stopped outside the pub, and Julian got out and paid. He thought of going in and taking a drink before the ordeal. But it was better to face these things sober, he thought. Like death, a firing squad, or something. The last minutes of freedom tasted to the full. He walked to the front of the drive, with the school motto in Latin and the heavy iron gates. It was incredibly windy. Only now did he notice. The trees were crashing together in the small coppice. A wild night. Julian stood firm and listened to the gusts. The wind penetrated through his jacket and made him shiver.

Was it Charles the First, facing his execution, who asked for an extra shirt as he felt the cold and did not want people to think he was shivering from fear? Well, he was shivering from both. No alcohol, no cigarettes to help him. He looked at his watch.

Come on, come on! He stamped his feet, walked a few paces. Did people behave like this in front of a firing squad. Get it over with! The courage of people. Or did they crumple and have to be held up. He suddenly remembered Arthur Koestler and his waiting in a cell and saving his last cigarette for the moment when they came for him. It changed his life. Nothing was the same again.

The arrogant, heartless idealism of a political faith crumbled inside him when he heard the piteous screaming and pleading of another prisoner being taken to be shot.

"Come on!"

He searched the road for headlights. Not much was moving either way. A taxi, a white Ford, nothing. Julian turned and looked down the long drive to the teaching block. Those little, cold cells where information was crammed into young heads. What a waste of life! The ties, the houses, the sporting triumphs, the chapel. To think his father half-bankrupted himself to put his son through this!

Just then he saw car headlamps reflected on the gates, and he turned. There were two police cars, their blue lights flashing. Julian tried to shade his eyes from the glare. He couldn't see the individual figures. There were several policemen, and a man in a long raincoat. Then two men came towards him. He wondered if anyone had a gun trained on him. He doubted it. This was England, after all.

The glare was broken by the two figures. The one in the raincoat must be Pendelbury, he thought.

"Julian Bates?" A voice, loud, strong, into the wind.

"Yes".

The man who had shouted was Pendelbury. His hair was white and dishevelled in the wind. Beside him was a younger man in standard but bulky police clothes. Body armour in case he suddenly tried to kill again, and whipped out a knife. They came forward slowly, never taking their eyes off his face and hands.

When they finally got close, Julian could now see Pendelbury's face, the man who had travelled so far attempting his capture. The nose had a kink, a boxer's nose. His eyes were a bright blue in reddish cheeks. His face was heavily wrinkled, and there was a deep line in his left cheek. Possibly from mirth, possibly from exhaustion.

They looked at each other, the captor and his prey.

"Hello Julian".

"Hello, Mr Pendelbury".

"I did a lot of travelling on your behalf".

There was a hint of a smile on both their lips.

"I hope you enjoyed the trips" said Julian.

"I found Israel a bit hot and dusty, to tell the truth. France was nice, the restaurants and café's. There was a sighting in Morocco. Then we lost you".

"If you wouldn't mind Sir", the other officer broke in. "Got to get on".

And in a flat voice the officer spoke his practiced speech: "I am arresting you for the murder of Harold Darke. Anything you say may be taken down in evidence and used against you......"

Julian looked again at Pendelbury's face. Certainly not an unkind face. Perhaps as unlikely a police officer as he was a murderer.

"I had imagined you ....meaner", said Julian.

"And I always thought your would be younger. And shorter somehow".

Julian shrugged.

The police officer spoke:

"Put out your hands, please Sir".

Julian did not understand at first, then he felt the cold metal and heard the snap of the handcuffs on his wrists.

"Where are you taking me?"

"To the station".

They led him to a police car, and opened the back door. There was not a lot of space for his legs.

Pendelbury got in the other side. Two police officers got in the front.

"I am sure you are doing the right thing" said Pendelbury.

"It is your job to say that".

"It is my job but also my opinion. And I am retired now".

"But you came out tonight just for me" said Julian.

"I came to complete this story. It has a certain…… symmetry".

"It did not escape me. Do we………. transgressors" – Julian could not bring himself to use the word 'criminal' – "do we really feel the urge to come back to the scene of the crime?"

"Yes, it does happen. Possibly more than we know, of course".

Then there was a heavy silence.

"What will happen to me?"

"That I can't say. For the moment custody, judge, bail or not". But, here": Pendelbury took out a card from his wallet and placed it in Julian's hands.

"The name on the card is a lawyer" said Pendelbury. "She is the best I know. You might be needing her. Unless you have someone else in mind?"

"I hadn't got that far. It has all been rather sudden". More silence.

"Out of interest, what made you give yourself up?" asked Pendelbury

"I was fed up with running. And someone died today. It sort of shakes it all up".

"It's been a big day for you, I see. A death, and then this".

"Yes. Death and then this". The warmth of the police car and the sense of completion made him relax. Julian closed his eyes and almost fell asleep. The rest of the journey was spent in silence.

CHAPTER 29

BARS

H is lawyer, Helen Lousada, was not what he had expected. After their first meeting, Julian asked around and found out that she had never lost a case. At the same time, word had it that she only took on cases she was certain of winning. Her wealth was also mentioned: a house here, another there, trips constantly abroad. Prosecution was her choice; only occasionally did she accept defence cases. Even judges were afraid of her, it was said. They quaked in their shoes as she did not suffer fools gladly, and would humiliate anyone who did not know their penal code, or stumbled over an interpretation.

When she walked in Julian thought they had got the wrong person: small, squat, not ugly but certainly not beautiful, she was someone who would go unobserved until she was in the court-room. There was an air about her of certainty, of someone who knew her worth, whose fame went before her. She sat down opposite Julian and placed her briefcase on the table. He observed her: the jewellery was expensive, and her clothes were exclusive: Italian design bought on trips to Milan. Unobtrusive elegance.

They were left alone.

"You called me last night", she said.

"I thought I was allowed to make a call to a lawyer" said Julian.

"I understand John gave you my name" said Helen Lousada.

"John?" asked Julian.

"John Pendelbury. The detective" she replied.

"Ah, yes. Detective Pendelbury. I have led him quite a chase". A long silence followed.

"I must tell you that I don't normally defend people" said Helen Lousada.

"Then why are you thinking of defending me?" asked Julian.

"John, perhaps. He told me of your case".

"I would have thought he'd have done everything to get me behind bars".

Helen Lousada laughed. "It was his job and his duty. He is tenacious but also very fair. He doesn't like to see a miscarriage of justice. And besides, you are behind bars" she said.

Julian smiled. He felt an enormous sense of relief, as if he could unburden himself. His lawyer would do the rest now.

She continued: "I make one demand though. You must not lie to me. If I find you are lying I leave the case".

"Do people in here lie to you all the time?"

"Most of the time. You get to see through it after a while. Some are very good, though".

"I'll try not to lie", said Julian

"Good".

"May I ask a question?"

Helen moved back away from Julian "I might not answer if it is personal".

."Where do you come from? A name like that. Lousada?"

"Portuguese Jewish. My father's side".

"Just asking. Thank you".

Then they got down to the details and the plea. After several hours Helen Lousada decided to take on the case. They would plead not guilty, being self-defence leading to accidental death and involuntary manslaughter.

"Will we win?" asked Julian

"I think, to be realistic, it is more a case of how long you stay in jail".

"And if we lose?"

"Probably life with chance of parole. They will try and prove murder. It might be 30 years, with early release for good behaviour".

Julian slumped in his seat.

"I can't win in either case. And I am innocent!"

"You say by your own admission that you pushed him, there was a struggle, you both fell, and he is dead".

"It was not quite like that. As you know".

"That is how it seems to me and will do to the jury".

"It was different. It was self-defence". Julian was almost shouting now.

"You pushed him" she said, raising her voice. Julian was wondering if she was on his side or theirs.

"Yes, because he hit me on the face…..and….."

"And what?" she asked.

Julian looked away and in a whisper said: "He was touching himself, he was getting thrill out of it".

Helen Lousada sat back. "Well, we can't prove this".

"It's my word. On oath" Julian said.

"Well, I'm sorry to tell you this, but out there it does not stand for much".

But she paused, stared out of the grimy police station window onto a block of flats, then turned.

"If I can prove this, will you stand up in court in front of his family? Because they will be there, and most everyone else, and they will be wanting revenge and to see justice done. Will you stand up and swear this is what happened?".

"Why not? It was!" he shouted. He was mystified that it could be any other way.

"Good". She now seemed satisfied. 'I think I need to look at the coroner's report again. We may have something".

Helen picked up her bag and walked to the door. She turned once to look at her client. He was staring at the table with a fixed gaze. Prison either way. It was not going to be fun. Julian turned.

"I have no money to pay you" he said quietly, now afraid.

"That is no problem. We can apply for legal aid".

"Another question: if not the money, and a chance of losing, why are you doing this for me?" said Julian.

"Returning a favour, you could say. And the pleasure of possibly winning. I like winning. Competitive nature".

"And what will happen to me now?"

"You will appear before a judge and then be remanded in custody, unless you can afford bail".

Julian shook his head and smiled.

"Again, unlikely to be given as you have had a history of evasions" she said.

"Being on the run is very tiring".

Helen smiled at him. "You know what they also say, people in your position?"

"No idea".

"That they are almost glad it is over".

Julian smiled and nodded. 'True' he said.

Helen Lousada turned and knocked on the door to be let out. Julian watched her go.

If only it were that easy just to walk out, he thought.

CHAPTER 30

AT HER MAJESTY'S PLEASURE

Life inside was another adaptation, although this time Julian's experiences in a boarding school and on the kibbutz had helped. Nothing could be quite as bad as boarding school. In prison, Julian realised he had to find out quickly who was running the place. He had to learn the unwritten hierarchies on every floor, every wing and even on the landings. It was certainly no holiday camp as some papers used to blazon on their front pages. There was a feral, animal smell all over the building, and stabbings, slashings and killings could happen at any minute.

Suicide was also on the cards, at birthdays and Christmas. Christmas was especially bad the other inmates said. Julian vowed he would never go down that route. Suicide was not an option. He had a goal, and family on the outside. They might never clear him, but they could hear his side of the story at least. Manslaughter maybe, but he felt almost a righteous sense of acting bravely and under fire. But he doubted the jury would see it like that.

After a few months inside, he was seen as a rather studious non-threat. He avoided the internal politics, kept away from trouble and drugs, worked-out a lot in the gym, but always with a friend at his side rather than be left on his own. On your own, anything could happen, and just for the fun on it, one gym-rat holding you down, and the other pumping his iron. You just had to be careful at every step. And there were the nihilists, who tried to fill his head with despair, trying to brainwash him into giving up all hope, and self-improvement was just a waste of time. He was going to be inside for most of his life anyway? So, take this weed, snort this coke, pop this pill and blow your brains out. Better, blow someone else's brains out. Many a time Julian had been tempted.

But there was the escape of books in the library. Julian immersed himself in DH Lawrence, then tried to understand Freud and Jung. Theology passed him by. He had been hurt by too many in the church, and he did not trust them. Besides, he was Cain, his brother's murderer, although the circumstances were different.

Occasionally he had a visitor. The visiting times were brief, and he did not expect anyone other than his sister and his mother. His father had died while he was inside and he had been allowed compassionate leave to attend the funeral. He was not sure what he felt. At the time, he was just numb. His elder sister stuck more by him than his mother.

One visitor did surprise him. It was Eva. He found her sitting the other side of a table, sweet, pretty, older, more lined. She was nervous that she had come as getting away had meant telling a lot of lies at home and work. But she had come.

"How did you find out?"

"I went back to the squat".

"Who told you?".

"Sven. He is still there, trying to claim squatter's rights and have the house. They are doing it all up, you know? The whole area".

"I didn't. Say hi! to him if you see him, will you?".

Eva wrinkled her nose as if that was not going to happen. Even getting here was a miracle.

"I can't stay long". She looked out-of-place amongst the other families.

There was a long silence. She leant forward and touched his hand. Touching like that was just permitted, but Julian was wary and removed his.

"You shouldn't have come here" he said.

"I wanted to".

"You are still with him?" Julian asked.

"Yes".

Julian grunted. "Wise choice. Look where I ended up!"

"Oh, Jooly". Tears came to her eyes. "Why did all this happen? Why did you......?"

"That'll come out in the trial. I can't talk now".

"I have a present for you".

Julian smiled. "I love presents".

She took out a book wrapped in bright paper. "You can guess what it is".

"I hope not a self-improvement book. I have read enough of those".

"No. I haven't even read it myself, but a friend was talking about it at a dinner party and it seems the next best thing.

I doubt if you can get it here. It has only been published recently in America".

"All good things come from America". Julian tried to joke. "Title?".

"The Denial of Death. By a man called Ernest Becker".

"Great title! Really. Could have been written for me".

"Jooly, don't. It may help".

Julian grunted and conceded. "Thank you. We can kiss later, when you leave. If you want to, that is".
Eva sat in silence. When Julian looked up he saw there were tears in her eyes.

"I can't stay any longer. Already I'll have to tell some...... porky pies".

Julian smiled at this phrase, so incongruous on her lips.

"I'll read it. For you. Come back and see me".

They got up and she planted a kiss on his cheek. Chaste, a final goodbye.

"I don't know if I can come again. I'm getting married".

Julian's head sank; then he looked up.
"When?" he asked.

"Soon".

"Well, that's that then"

Eva got up and leant over and in a whisper said: "I loved you, Jooly. And I always will. But don't ever come and find me. Please".

He watched her small, bony figure walk out the door.

But the book was an inspiration. It became his secular Bible. He carried it like Newton carried the Bible under his arm. The binding came apart, and was stuck together with glue and sellotape. He underlined it, and re-underlined it. Whole passages he had by heart. The only flare up of violence was when another prisoner got hold of it and threw it at the wall, and Julian turned on him and held him in a neck lock that threatened to take the life from him. After that, he was considered a bit weird but also not one to be trifled with. Others stayed clear. Besides, he had murdered before, hadn't he? Could do it again. The book gave him a basic introduction to human psychology, but also an overview and then the extraordinary comparison of the genius of a secular mind and the genius of a religious mind: Freud and Kierkegaard, and both coming to rather pitiful ends. Other analysts appeared: Rank, Adler, Erikson and his stages of man. Julian was overwhelmed by the ideas. And then there were passages which were sheer poetry, and he repeated them as if they were mantras:

> *This, after all is said and done, is the only problem of real life, the only worthwhile preoccupation of man: What is one's true talent, his secret gift, the authentic vocation? In what way is one truly unique, and how can he express this uniqueness, give it form, dedicate it to something beyond himself? How can this person take his private inner being, the great mystery that he feels at the heart of himself, his emotions, his yearnings and use them to live more distinctively, to enrich both himself and mankind with the peculiar quality of his talent?*

How could he indeed? What was the peculiar quality of his talent?

Running from the law, perhaps? Another passage gave him hope. It was about Kierkegaard's concept of a 'knight of faith'.

> *This figure is the man who lives in faith who has given over the meaning of life to his Creator, and who lives centred on the energies of his Maker. He accepts whatever happens in this visible dimension without complaint, lives his life as a duty, faces death without a qualm. No pettiness is so petty that it threatens his meanings; no task is too frightening to be beyond his courage. He is fully in the world on its terms and wholly beyond the world in his trust in the invisible dimension.*

These noble words Julian copied and stuck on his wall above his bed and read when the days were bleak and seemed unending.

CHAPTER 31

TRIAL

There were several other cases going on in the Old Bailey when Julian's case was being heard. Since it related to events quite long in the past, it was fairly low-key and unsensational, although the verdict was eagerly awaited by the school and Darke's family. The prosecution was going for murder, the defence for self-defence leading to unpremeditated manslaughter. A conviction of murder could get Julian 30 years; self-defence leading to unpremeditated manslaughter carried a far lighter sentence and was at the discretion of the judge.

Julian was led to the side where the witnesses sat. Up in the gallery he noticed some of the masters from school and Darke's family, his son and daughters. They had come to see justice done. All of them had aged, and Julian looked briefly for Mrs Darke, but she was not there. She was to be called as a witness.

The trial was set to start at 9.30, and it was already 9.35. Helen Lousada was in her place as defence counsel. She had a rather old but neat wool wig on, as did the prosecution counsel. He was a broad man, with a wide, tanned face, giving the idea of good living. He exuded confidence and practice; a safe pair of hands. Julian turned his attention to the courtroom, the new wooden panels, the Latin and English words inscribed.

Suddenly there was a loud knock on the door and a man in a

black don-like robe opened it for the judge to walk in. Everyone rose to their feet. The judge was really quite nattily dressed, in a purple and black gown, and he had his wool wig on as well. His chair was ornate, with green and black inlay. In front of him were the papers and files. Once he had sat down, everyone followed suit.

Then there was a hush as the jury were ushered in. A strange crew they were, thought Julian. How they had been picked he had no idea. First at random, he supposed, from the electoral register, and then vetted. They came in with their belongings (why could they not leave them in a locked room?), and several had rucksacks and bags with them. Nearly all were white, except one black man who looked Jamaican in origin, and an Asian woman. One rather peroxide blonde caught his eye.

The case started. It all seemed very matter-of-fact: the instances, the time, the forensic evidence, the admission of guilt. It looked as if it was going to be clear-cut. Julian had admitted he was there; the police officers had given their evidence which Helen Lousada could not shake. The fingerprints were clear, the photos of the body and the blood. It was not going to take long, it seemed. The court adjourned early. The judge seemed to want to be off, and his excuse was that the jury 'needed to get used to being juries'. Julian guessed he had a golf game to go to.

The next day the court heard a series of character witnesses from masters and friends, all testifying to Darke's exemplary behaviour. And then there was Mrs Darke herself. She wept into her handkerchief as she told the court of finding her husband in a pool of blood in the sitting room. More than once the judge asked her to speak up.

"He was one of the kindest, most decent men who ever... he never ever......." She broke down again into tears. The prosecutor suggested kindly she drink some water and compose herself. The mood of the room and especially the jury seemed to turn against Julian. He had killed this decent, kind master who was so well-respected and admired. Julian sat in silence. He was to face the full anger of the prosecution in the afternoon. Lunch was a dismal, silent, lonely affair.

In the afternoon, Julian took the stand. It was placed to the side, not close to the judge, and there was a small microphone. With one hand on the bible he was asked to raise his hand and swear to tell the truth. He swore he would. The prosecution set in on him.

"You admit killing Harold Darke?" the prosecutor asked. Julian had been told to keep it simple.

"We were involved in a fall. He hit his head. I did not kill him".

"Why were you in his private house? And alone?" asked the prosecutor.

"He asked me to come" said Julian.

"Why had he asked you to come?"

"He wanted to beat me" said Julian.

"Beat you? Just like that?" the prosecutor asked with incredulity.

"Yes" said Julian.

"Why was this?"

"For my attitude" said Julian.

"Your attitude? Had you done anything else wrong?" the prosecutor asked.

"Not that I can record".

The prosecutor then repeated Julian's words, as if they were full of some arcane meaning, or that the jury should savour them to realise just who they were dealing with.

"Was this common behaviour in the school, that masters just suddenly decided to beat a boy?"

"It was quite common, yes. Even boys beat other boys for their behaviour" said Julian.

"Boys beat other boys, you say? How extraordinary? Just like that?"

The prosecutor looked to the jury to see their reaction, as if to show how unreliable this witness could be.

"I mean, the senior boys, that is" added Julian.

"Senior boys decide to beat younger boys, just like that?"

"Yes. It happened".

"Often?" asked the prosecutor.

"Quite often".

"I see. And Harold Darke decided on a whim to beat you? Is this what you are saying?"

Julian shrugged. Then added: "I remember him saying that he liked to have beaten all the Heads of his House, so they knew what was what".

The prosecutor did not like the way it was turning.

Julian then tried to add: "It may have............."

The judge came down on him hard:

"You will only reply to the counsel's questions, and not add your own or anything that is not relevant".

"I consider that it is relevant".

"It is my job to decide that". The judge's tone was cold and ruthless. "Please proceed".

The prosecution counsel bowed slightly to the judge. He was on his side.

"So, you come to Mr Darke's house and you are about to be beaten. What happens next?"

"He was waiting for me and had re-arranged the room so the chair was in the centre. He asked me to take my jacket off and kneel down on the chair". There was a strange silence in the court as the details unfurled.

"I did as I was told. I took off my jacket and put it on the chair".

"And then? The prosecutor asked.

"Then I knelt down. And waited".

"For what?"

"The first stroke".

"And...........?"

There was a strange intense silence in the courtroom, as if some dark, satanic ritual was being narrated belonging to a medieval sect.

"It did not come. So I glanced up to my side and saw his reflection in the mirror".

"Come come, how could you see his reflection?" said the prosecutor.

"I suppose he had taken the cane out of the wardrobe and the door had come ajar. It had a mirror. I could see him" said Julian.

"And...........?"

Julian turned to the judge. "Do I have to say this?"

"If it is relevant". The judge's stare was icy, cold, hard eyes.

"The man's wife and children are here, Sir".

"You will reply to the prosecutor's question" said the judge.

"I saw him.....touching himself" said Julian.""

There was a gasp in the courtroom. "Silence, silence!" The judge rapped with his gavel.
The judge turned his attention to Julian.

"I didn't quite hear that. Could you repeat what you said?" asked the judge.

Julian cleared his throat. "I saw him rubbing himself with his hand on the outer side of his trousers".

"And why do you think he was doing that?" asked the judge. He had taken over completely.

"Because.....because I think he was gaining sexual satisfaction from beating me. I think.........."

The prosecutor tried to take over. "Me Lud, I really think this is supposition on the part of the accused.........."

The judge raised his hand. Then continued himself: "Then what happened?"

"I got up, and tried to stop him. I realised he was some sort of pervert".

"Me Lud, supposition, denigration, bias, speculation......I must object......"

Again the judge raised his hand: "Go on Mr Bates".

"And then he brought the cane down on my face telling me to kneel down, and I raised my hand to stop the blow, but he hit me, and there was a mark on my face for a time, and I lost whatever control I had and pushed him away from me. He tripped, grabbed at me and we fell. He hit his head on the brass …..bit, the knob, on the side of the fire".

"The fender", suggested the judge.

"Yes, the fender. When I got up, he was dead".

The court had gone totally quiet. Julian bowed his head, then lifted it and stared at the judge. The judge held his stare for several seconds, and then looked away.

"The court is adjourned until tomorrow, 9.30am".

He rapped once hard with his gavel and walked quickly out of the room. Julian was led away by two policemen. A small murmur began in the courtroom.

―⧾ ⧾―

The next day it was Helen Lousada to call her witnesses. Only two were on her list, but she called John Pendelbury first. He walked in with a slow step. A brown suit, tie and waistcoat. He was sworn in. His white hair was dishevelled, and his china-blue eyes seemed even bluer with the shirt he had chosen. He sat down, bowing his head slightly to the judge who nodded his acknowledgement. Helen Lousada got up to her feet. She asked about his profession, his length of service. The facts were impressive.

"Was there anything unusual about the deceased?" she asked.

"It was obvious there had been a struggle", he replied calmly.

"Anything else?"

"I noticed a stain in the deceased's trousers".

"Did you check this with the coroner's report".

"I did. I went in person".

"And what did the coroner say?" she asked.

"That it could have been the result of the struggle. But it was not urine".

"It was not urine?" Helen Lousada asked slowly and clearly.

"No. It was semen".

Here Helen Lousada referred to the paper that was in front of the judge. The judge picked it up and read it.

"As you can read me Lud, the coroner's report confirms the witness's statement. There were traces of semen". The judge remained impassive.

"Continue" he said.

"Have you seen anything like this before in your career?" asked Helen Lousada.

"Urine yes. Semen no. But I did ask the coroner. He replied that in his knowledge, this only happened in a hanging or....in sexual arousal".

"Hanging or a sexual arousal? And in your opinion......?" asked Helen Lousada.

"MeLud, this is just opinion........." The prosecution tried angrily to interrupt.

"Go on, Detective.........." said the judge.

"In my opinion, it is clear that hanging was not involved. I am inclined to believe the accused, and that the master was sexually aroused".

"Thank you. Your witness".

There was a loud murmur again in court. The judge rapped his gavel and warned that if this continued he would remove the public. The prosecutor then tried to undermine Pendelbury's statements, the time of death, the likelihood that the stain was old, it had nothing to do with the murder. He insisted on saying 'murder' so the jury could not forget why they were there. But the mood had changed from the lynch-mob of the day before after Mrs Darke's statement. What might have happened had been revealed. When John Pendelbury got down from the stand the whole case seemed to have swung in Julian's favour. At the end of the day the jury were sent away to deliver a verdict.

Helen Lousada came to see him in the break.

"We might make it". She seemed tired but assured.

"Thanks to you".

"The jury can be a strange beast".

"How do you think they will decide?"

"I have a good feeling about this one, but they may go for a reduced sentence".

Julian hung his head.

"It is not so bad in there. It is terrible, of course. You have to watch your every step. But I can survive. The shame, though. And after.............."

"After is a long way ahead. We have to win this one first".

CHAPTER 32

VERDICT

The next day they were all in court, Darke's family, Julian's mother and sister, friends from the music college and from the squat. Graham was there with Sven, both looking as if they had just got up after a night of revelling, bleary-eyed and obviously hung over. There was even some press interest, the story of the murder case and the public school boy and the unsavoury details. It might make a good story on the inside pages. Hardly front-page stuff, but good for a column.

The jury filed in again, their bags as usual with them. Julian felt his legs shake and his stomach go empty. His right leg started shaking involuntarily, and he had to put his hand on it to stop the movement. The door opened and in came the judge, as impassive and authoritative as ever. He sat and looked at the jury.

"Have you reached a verdict?" The jury foreman stood up.

"We have".

"And what is it?" he asked.

The head juryman had a slip of paper in his hand. His accent was south London, flat, matter-of-fact.

"We find the defendant not guilty of murder". A gasp and some cries went around the courtroom. The judge rapped with his gavel.

"Silence in court. I really will not have this. I have warned you before".

The judge looked slowly around the court, his court.

"And do you find the defendant guilty of any crime?" he asked.

"We consider it was a case of accidental death as a result of self-defence". There were even more murmurs and suppressed cries and the sound of sobbing. The judge waited for the noise to calm down.

"Please sit down" he said to the juryman.

He then started looking through his book of sentencing laws. Calmly he flicked through some pages, stopping here and there, making notes. Finally, he said:

"Julian Bates, please stand up". Julian did as he was told.

"You have heard the verdict of the jury. At this point the crown has no case against you. It is clear to my mind that you were defending yourself in extremely trying circumstances and that although you were involved in Harold Darke's death, you were not the direct cause of it, nor was it pre-meditated. It was an extremely unfortunate accident and you acted in self-defence. Therefore, from this moment, and considering the length of time already spent in confinement, you are a free man".

Julian looked at Helen Lousada and mouthed 'Thank you'. It did not need a lip-reader to understand. Loud voices were now heard from the visitor's gallery. The judge rapped hard again on his gavel and the court all stood up as he walked out, his robes flowing behind him. After a few minutes Julian was allowed to join his lawyer and family.

"What happens now?" he asked.

"You walk out a free man" Helen Lousada said.

"To what?"

"To what you want to do. And be".

"After so long in jail I am not sure" he said.

"There may be press outside. Do you want me to issue a statement later ?" asked Helen Lousada.

"I would appreciate that. So....you have never lost a case! Quite a record. I can only thank you" said Julian.

"I choose my cases, as I am sure they have told you by now. This one intrigued me. And John was superb. I must thank him".

"So must I".

Julian's friends came up to him, his family. His mother embraced him after so many years. His sister was crying. Graham and Sven were patting him on the back. As they walked out, a reporter and a cameraman were there.

"What do you feel now, Mr Bates?"

"Relief. It is over at last".

⚊⧢ ⧣⚊

An hour later, before they faced the cameras and journalists,

Julian gave a short written statement to Helen Lousada. He asked her if after she had give her own statement outlining the trial and verdict, she would read what Julian had written.

She quickly read it and turned to him.

"You want me to read it out loud after I read mine?" she asked. "I am not entirely sure about this. Sure?"

Julian nodded "Sure. I don't trust myself not to break down, or something".

Later, outside the court, in front of the press cameras and onlookers, Helen Lousada read out her short summary of the trial and its outcome. She then took out a piece of paper from her pocket.

"I have been given this note by Mr Bates. It reads as follows". There was a slight hush.

"Julian Bates wishes to thank the judge and jury for their kindness, competence and patience. He would like to thank the police. He would also like to thank his lawyer". She looked up and smiled.

"That is me". There was laughter from both family and crowd.

"He would also like to suggest that many boarding schools in the UK are often very unpleasant institutions, harbouring staff who are disturbed and who inflict damage on their pupils. And, just as important, they may produce citizens who, subsequently, in their professional lives, can prove extremely dangerous to society as a whole. Emotional damage in these places is the norm, not the exception.

Safeguards must be put in place. There will be outrage, but I believe most of them, even the illustrious, should be banned outright. It might heal divisions in our society".

Then Helen Lousada turned to Julian and said:

> "This one needs saying by you". Julian took the piece of paper and then looked up at the assembled crowd in front of him.
>
> "I would also like to encourage young people not to give up on their dreams until good sense or exhaustion make you realise that you might have to. And there is no shame in that. If you cannot win Wimbledon that does not mean you give up playing tennis". There was more laughter.
>
> "What are going to do now?" someone shouted from the crowd.
>
> "I hadn't thought that far ahead. Begin where I left off, I suppose: he said. "I would like to keep on studying. Keep on singing. Talent, like water, finds its own level. There is so much music out there and I have still so much to learn".

Then he walked on past with the small group and down the streets to the first pub. It was still fairly early in the morning, and hardly anyone was there. They sat around a large dark wooden table. A silence ensued.

> "What will you do now?" asked Sven.
>
> "I have no idea. I am still a bit stunned to tell the truth. I did not expect to win. I thought I was going to have to spend the next few years in prison".

His mother was looking at him, with tears in her eyes.

> "I told you it was not as you thought Mum".

She just lent across and touched his wrist. His sister had reverted to her 'take charge' mode and was ordering drinks and generally getting the group back into shape. The chatter was about the judge, the jury, his lawyer (who had not come to celebrate, she was busy), and Pendelbury.

"Odd he should give evidence that was so favourable to you" said Sven.

"He is a nice man, it seems. Followed me half way around the world. I gave him the slip I don't know how many times. But at least he did some travelling".

They laughed.

"But he is what I would call a very decent man. Fair. I must thank him".

"He was doing his duty", said Graham.

His sister came with the drinks.

"There is duty and duty" said Julian. "He behaved above the call of duty, if I can put it like that. And he would have done everything to send me down if he though there was murder, I believe".

They took their drinks. "To Joolian! To Jooly!"

Their glasses clinked.

"And now?" shouted Sven.

"I have no idea. No idea. But I'd better take my own advice and carry on playing tennis, as it were. There are music schools and I'm sure there are many good teachers out there. I wonder if Marika Durante is still teaching. If so, here I come".

THE END. 2025

ACKNOWLEDGEMENTS

Above all to Simon Prentis, who very kindly nudged me to publish. Also to Guy Pringle for encouragement, and to Sandie, my best reader.

The author is grateful to profilebooks for permission to quote two short passages from Ernest Becker's 'The Denial of Death'.

AUTHOR BIO

CV Jonathan Barry was born in England. He won a choral award to Selwyn College, Cambridge. He read English. He studied voice at the Guildhall School of Music and Drama in London, and later went to Italy. He began singing professionally in Naples, first with Antonio Florio and then Roberto de Simone. He won a place in the San Carlo Opera House in 1986 and sang there for 20 years. He also began his own opera company Vox Lirika, and his group performed both in Italy and the UK. Resident once more in the UK from 2008, he performed in concerts and in several roles for Guildford Opera. He lives in West Sussex.

Printed in Dunstable, United Kingdom

63667792R00221